Holt's Lady
-1-

Roman's Lust
-2-

Emerald Eyes Duo Compilation

F.L. MOON

TABLE OF CONTENTS

Holt's Lady

-1-

Emerald Eyes Duo Compilation

F.L. MOON

For my loving family, parents and for those who dare to dream.

<u>F.L. Moon.</u>

Prologue

Three brothers always liked to play cops and robbers, they chased each other and wrestled when they were caught. Roman, a twelve-year-old, the oldest of the brothers was always the tallest, strongest, and fastest. When he would catch his brothers, he would lock them in the shed; and say that they needed to stay in there until they were allowed outside for the day, as it was their makeshift prison. Holt, the eight-year-old; was fierce and always played hard, he didn't like to give up easy when he was caught by his big brother. Holt always managed to find a way out of the shed and snuck away without his older brother noticing. He was good at picking locks, he was stealthy, moving in silence.

"Got you." Roman yelled, as he caught the smallest of the brothers, four-year-old Finn. Finn was always kicking and screaming, and this alerted their mother who came out and told the boys not to play so rough.

"Roman Mason you better not be playing too hard, or I will make sure you're cleaning the porch with a toothbrush after dinner."

"Ok fine." Roman sneered, as he let his smaller brother go. Finn was quick to throw a small punch into Roman's crotch and laughed as he got away with it, or so he thought.

"Finn Mason, I saw what you just did, you better get inside and clean yourself up before dinner."

"Ok, coming." Finn called back, as he ran towards the house. As he was approaching his mother, Finn flashed his cheeky grin at her before she ruffled his hair.

"Love you mum." Finn looked over to Roman, who rolled his eyes as he was cleaning himself off.

"Little sucker." Roman grunted, as he knew Finn could get away with murder.

Roman made his way to the shed and opened the door, he was about to call out to Holt but as he looked around, he couldn't find him. He looked in all the hiding spots and even under the parked cars that his father was working on as a mechanic, but still, he couldn't find him.

Roman decided to go inside, just as he walked through the door, Holt was already sitting at the dining room table ready for dinner.

"How did you get out?" Roman asked.

"Stealth Op." Holt replied, as he was having a drink of water.

The boy's father sat down, and when everyone was seated, Holt started to talk to his father about the medals he had hanging on the wall.

"Dad, I want to get medals just like them some day."

Holt's father just looked at his son, he thought he should tread carefully, not to shatter his son's dreams.

"Son, there is something that you need to know about those medals, they come at a great cost and it's not one that I would want to pay again. I want you to think about that and really make sure you understand everything before ever joining the army, sacrifices are made, and some are-"

Holt's mother cleared her throat as she looked at her husband, she didn't want the explanation to get too disturbing for the young boys. So, Holt's father took a breath and thought of the right words to say.

"Some are life changing and things will never be the same. Just remember son it's not like what you see in the movies or your comic books, real life is very different."

Holt scooped up a big spoonful of mash potato eating it with delight.

"Is there mash potato when you join the army dad?" Holt's father grinned, as he ate the steak his wife cooked for him.

"Well, it's nowhere near as good as your mothers, you should do yourself a favour and stay away from the army food and eat at our table instead."

Holt grabbed a corn cob and nibbled at it; kernels flew out of his mouth while he spoke.

"I like all food; I will be taller and faster than Roman." Holt grinned at his older brother and kicked him under the table.

"Whatever you say, General." Roman told him, as he kicked his brother back.

"You, wait and see." Holt retorted, as he slurped his last bit of mash off his spoon.

"I will be like a superhero." Holt smiled, as he picked up his plate put it into the sink and made his way to his room.

Chapter 1

As Lady sat in her car, she checked her teeth in the rear-view mirror, scanning for any breakfast that might have been caught in them. She smoothed her hand over her hair, which was tied back into a long brunette ponytail. Her blue eyes, and dark, thick, hair, were something she always liked about herself as many people with dark hair had brown eyes. When she looked at her hair it reminded her of her mother and the way she used to play with it. After Lady's mother passed away unexpectedly and suddenly, Lady swore, she would never cut her hair again and let it grow as it was her mother's favourite. She straightened her collar of her work blouse and straightened her shoulders before reaching for the paperwork out of her bag.

"One more glance and then on with the day." Lady said, as she ruffled the sheets.

Client information: Holt Mason, forty-five years old, retired from Army Services and amputee of both legs from the knee, PTSD, Anxiety, Major Depression, suicidal behaviour, and anger issues.

Lady frowned as she looked it over one more time, and wondered why she was sent to this man of all the people she had ever cared for. In her time as a personal carer, she'd never had someone so dark. Despite thinking about the difficult clients, she has had in her five years; she knew that her studies and work experience would be tested. Even though she was on her way to start her last year of her psychology degree, she wanted to open her own counselling and psychology practice for young adults.

"Doctor, Lady Myne." Lady told herself, as she thought about the studies to come. She couldn't wait for it to all be over and finally start living the way she wanted.

She put the paperwork away and finished the puzzle she always carried. It was a two-by-two block with six sides and different colours on each square, it was a small obsession she had but never really admitted that to herself. Lady was able to do it with one hand, she always had to do something while she was reading as it helped her focus on the task.

She enjoyed puzzles, and it was a way for her to distract her mind from her own problems and misfortunes in her life. In a somewhat therapeutic way, solving a puzzle was a way she could solve a problem and then feel satisfied when it was done. It was a way to compensate for many problems and things in her life she couldn't solve and failed at trying in the process.

As she got out of her car, she saw the house was clean and very big on the end of the court where Holt lived. It had cars everywhere as he was a mechanic who worked from home. As she looked in the reflection of the window, she straightened her clothes once more and locked her car. Lady was short and full figured, she always thought she had a very curvy body, perfect for childbearing. She was naturally maternal and loved being a mother. She grew more patient since having her son and a thicker skin was a welcoming addition.

It was in Lady's nature to always put others before herself. She always thought she was never good at anything else, so caring for others made her feel like she had purpose.

As she walked up to the house, she could hear music playing. There was a younger man sweeping and cleaning up, he then turned away and sat in one of the cars and started the engine. She guessed that this was an apprentice of some kind helping her client. Moving the cars may have had been a problem for the amputee she was here for. She went to the front door and knocked three times.

As the automatic door opened, she looked at the man in front of her in the tall wheelchair. His arms were covered in grease and his hands were black. A grumpy rockstar, was the first idea that popped into her head when she saw him. Without knowing his age, she would have guessed he was at least in his late forties. His upper torso was evidence of strength from supporting his body, his hair was black and tied back, he had a long, overgrown beard that covered his face.

As her gaze met his, she smiled and held out her hand introducing herself.

"Hello, I'm Lady, you must be Holt Mason."

The man was stoic and expressionless as he looked at Lady, he quickly glanced at her feet and then her face. Considering his army expertise background, he took everything in, calculated and sized her up without her even realizing. He went to hold out his hand but paused, as he realised it was filthy, before he could pull it back Lady took it and shook it anyway. He spoke softly, his eyes didn't blink, and his voice was deep and dark.

"I haven't had time to clean up, but your welcome to eat and drink whatever you like."

Holt simply left the meeting at that; he turned his chair to go back to the garage and continue his work. As he pushed himself out the back, glass sliding door, Lady noticed that the glass was covered in muck, grease and even dirt. Lady was hopeful that Holt was happy with her, and she hoped she could please him so that she could have work here until she was done for the year. As she put her bag down on the small dining room table, she searched with her eyes for things that needed doing. She rolled up her sleeves, and started to search the kitchen for cleaning cloths, glass spray and detergent, she frowned as she was a little taken back by the simple meeting, she started thinking too much.

When she saw the client's medication box sitting on the kitchen counter, she could feel her OCD, kicking in, as there were pills and open boxes everywhere. She always carried a spare desk tidy drawer in her car, as it came in useful for her clients. The agency she worked for would reimburse her for things that she supplied, because it would make her life and the life of her clients easier.

As it approached midday, Lady could hear the back door sliding opened and Holt pushed himself inside. He made his way to the sink to take a quick break. Holt reached for the cup he always used, but it wasn't by the sink where he always left it. He looked around and noticed that the kitchen was spotless, and the dishwasher was on. He could hear music playing in the bathroom and noticed that it was a well-known one from the eighties. The washing machine was running and his catastrophe box that held all his medications was replaced by a small drawer style box with large numbers on it. He opened one of the drawers and it was divided into sections for morning, midday, and night. As he stared into the sections, he realised how many pills he was taking each day, and this angered him as it was these tiny things that kept him on this earth.

He pushed the drawer closed and opened the cabinet under the sink to get a new cup. He filled it with water and heard footsteps making their way down the hall. Lady was singing as she carried a laundry basket on her hip, she also rotated a tiny puzzle in her hand and made her way to the kitchen table where she would lay out the clothes and fold them.

Holt kept his face forwards as he looked in the reflection of his kitchen window and without turning his head, he could see Lady and everything she was doing. He went to fill his cup one more time before drinking it slowly and reaching for his phone, he checked it and Lady at the same time. Holt was always aware of his surroundings, but he wasn't really bothered by Lady, if anything he yawned as he felt suddenly tired. He thought it was because he was up late working on the cars, but that wasn't it, he never slept much and always had to take pills to rest.

Lady hummed and finished her puzzle as she put it on the table solved and continued folding the clothes.

To break the ice, Lady decided she should try to make conversation while she worked.

"I noticed that you have an electric drum set in the back room, must be awesome playing the drums, I always wanted to learn but never did." She smiled as she looked up at him hoping he would engage in conversation.

Holt turned slowly and he looked into her eyes as she spoke. She felt a little uncomfortable as he looked right through her head, or at least that's what it felt like to Lady. Holt put his phone down and drank deeply from the cup, filling it one more time. He reached for the pill box as he started to talk.

"I haven't played for a very long time, too much work at the moment."

Lady kept going with her chores before she replied, trying to keep the conversation going.

"Fair enough, working is good keeps the body and mind busy don't you think?"

As she smiled, it wavered while she watched him take his hand full of pills in one swallow. He emptied the cup and placed it back in the sink. Holt started to make his way back over to the back door moving past Lady. She needed to know if there was anything else that she could do to help him, as she wanted to make a good impression. So, she smiled again and asked him.

"Is there anything else I can do to help you Holt? Anything at all that you haven't had time for?"

He paused at the back door and slid it open, before he looked at Lady the phone started ringing in the workshop and he had a million things go through his head that he wanted to say like, get my legs back, let me die, and even make me happy, but grimly he didn't really say anything except for, "My life!" grimly, he smirked, and it faded just a quickly, as he closed the door behind him.

Lady was unbothered by his comment and just kept going with her work. After finally folding all the clothing, she made her way to put them in Holt's room. Her hours passed very quickly, and it was nearly time to pick up her son from school. She went out the back door and noticed that there was a huge swimming pool. It was clean but seemed like it was unused. The cover was half on and most likely for maintenance only. She walked up the back path into the back door of the garage and noticed that Holt was elbows deep in an engine held by a hoist above him. She didn't want to startle him as she spoke out to him softly.

"Everything is done for today, I will be back on Wednesday morning, you have a lovely home, Holt."

"Thank you." Holt replied, in a flat tone, as he didn't turn his face from his work.

Lady walked through the garage and made her way out. When she reached her car and climbed in, she noticed that Holt was still working away in the distance and seemed vexed by something, as he threw his tool at the wall and moved out from under the car. Lady thought she did quite well for her first day while she reported everything in her notebook before leaving. As she drove, she was smiling while turning her small puzzle with one hand, she turned up her music and thought about the day on her way to her son's school.

As she pulled up to the parking lot, it was buzzing with cars, students, and parents. She saw her little boy running out of the gates with something he made. Looking closer it was a project, stuck together with masking tape, pieces were flying off in the wind. He smiled and giggled with his friends as he made his way to his mother's car. The back door flung open; Bobby jumped in and kissed his mother on the cheek. He had a huge smile on his face and was always so happy. Lady turned to him and saw his sweater was inside out and back to front. Lady laughed as he was so adorable.

"I made an ocean mummy." He said as he held up the project so that his mother could see. Lady smiled as she looked at her son's creation; a three eyed fish and a fluffy crab with one leg, covered in blue cellophane, it all dangled from a string in a cereal box.

"Wow Bobby that's beautiful sweetheart, I will put that in the kitchen." Lady replied, as she readied herself for the drive home.

"Yay!" Bobby clapped his hands and started talking about his day as she drove home.

Pulling into the drive, Mark and Matthew, her neighbours, were outside tending to their garden and playing with their two small, adopted children. They waved at Lady and made their way over to her. Happily, in a same sex marriage, Mark and Matthew loved Lady and Bobby. They always thought of them as family. Even when they were all younger, they grew up in the same small neighbourhood and never parted ways. They all went to same middle schools and high schools. Lady's mother knew both Mark and Matthew since they were born. As the two young boys turned into men, they developed a bond with each other which everybody took as a brotherly bond, but as the years moved on, they developed a much, much deeper connection and have never parted with each other.

Chapter 2

Mark and Matthew had many things in common, even though they were opposites, one was a sports fan, the other a geek and chess player. This is why they were the perfect example of a high school story, where the jock made fun of the geek in the presence of onlookers and the schoolgirls, but behind the scenes he needed him to tutor with homework and studies.

Lady's mother was a mother to all of them and even the two men were heart broken when she passed away. Lady and her family accepted the two boys, who are now men, into their lives and loved them both for who they were, rather than what society expected them to be. Bobby called out the car window as his mother pulled into the drive.

"Look, I made an ocean." The little boy squealed with delight, as he held it up and showed the two men.

Mark was bouncing Martha a small eight-month-old baby girl on his hip, and beside him was his son, 3-year-old Maddison. Maddison loved Bobby, they grew up together and have always been in each other's company. Mark reached out and took the ocean in his hand.

"I want one just like it, come on let's see if we have any boxes inside." Mark smiled as he spoke.

Lady's son hopped out of the car and all the children followed Mark inside. They would keep busy while Lady had a chance to unpack and get things ready for the evening. Matthew made his way over to Lady; he was chomping at the bit and super excited to know how her day went with the new client.

"So, how was your day love? tell me everything." Matt asked, looking at her with his big blue eyes and blonde hair.

Lady placed her son's bag over her shoulder and Matt took Lady's bag, her coat, and her notebook, along with her lunch bag, drink bottle and snack wrappers that were on the seat. Lady scrunched up her nose, as the afternoon sun was in her eyes. She knew exactly what he was asking but she wouldn't get into any details just yet.

"Well, there isn't much to tell, he didn't really speak much, and I guess work is work." Lady replied casually.

Matthew followed Lady inside and helped her dump everything in Lady's front door entry. He whizzed past her and walked into the kitchen, opening her fridge, and grabbing a big bottle of wine. Lady had to laugh as it was way too early for her to drink, she hadn't even had dinner yet.

"Matt, how am I supposed to cook if you're going to get me drunk at this time of the day."

Matt laughed as he opened her dishwasher and took out two small glasses. "Well, I'm getting drunk, you are not, besides I already cooked you a lasagne for dinner it's just finishing in the oven at home." Matt winked at her while he poured.

Lady sighed and threw her arms around Matt; she kissed him on the cheek and thanked him for his help. Matt just laughed as he explained himself.

"I was bored, Mark was boring me to death with his chess show today, so I had to do something, you know Mark, always proper and stiff lipped, god I love that miserable man, so grumpy all the time what a spunk." Matt took a big drink and almost downed half the glass.

Lady laughed so hard, she spat her drink out in the sink and they both giggled like two schoolgirls who were in a gossip session. Lady wiped her face and drank again before she thanked Matt once more.

"I love you two and my mother loved you both, I'm so grateful you always help me, I would be lost without you both, I can't thank you enough."

Matt waved his hand at Lady before emptying his glass and refilling it.

"Nothing to thank, we are family." He said as he clinked his glass with Lady's, and they took another sip. Matt sighed as he looked at the photograph of Lady's mother on the wall.

"I adored your mother, and I miss her so much She was the most beautiful woman, her hair was like red fire and her eyes were so green, they could look straight through me even as a small child. I could talk to her about anything, and she always listened. I love her so very much Lady, I'm so sad she is gone. I can't live without you and your boy next door to me, you're my sister as far as I'm concerned and that's how it is."

Lady was so touched by his words that a tear fell from her cheek, Matt wrapped Lady in his arms and held her tight.

"I love you girly." Matt squeezed her tightly.

"I love you too Matt, never leave me please?" Lady asked, while she was in his arms.

Matt shook his head as he kissed her forehead as he answered, "Never ever." Matt released her and downed the rest of his glass; then he took Lady's hand, "Come on Lady, let's check the food and Mr. Grizzle guts next door.

***

Holt examined his work before sending the owner a message that the car was done. He grunted because he had two more left that he had to finish. It was a long day and he needed to make sure he chased up people for money and do the books, but he hated that part of the work. He missed the shop he used to have and the freedom of moving about with legs. His past partner Emily organised the administrations part of the work, but they weren't meant to be, as things took a turn for the worst. Holt had no patience for women or relationships because he hardly had time for his own problems. He hated himself enough to keep his mind completely occupied. Emily had moved on since then, and he was happy that she did. He always believed she deserved better, a bad combination of psychotic outbursts, pain killer addiction and suicidal behaviour was something that Emily didn't need in her life. Holt made the decision for both of them, a blessing in the end as Emily had two children and was happily married in another state.

The clock ticked over to well past midnight, and he was done for the day. As Holt locked up the garage, he decided he needed to clean himself up and eat some food. He was tired and his stomach was growling, he could smell the sweat and grease dripping from his hair. The warmer weather was well under way, he was never a fan of the season though. He loved the cold, he always toyed with the idea of moving to a colder climate, but everything that he needed to stay sane was close by, so he let that idea sit on the shelf for a very long time.

As he made his way inside, he slid the back door closed and pushed along into the kitchen. It was clean and spotless. He made his way to the bathroom where he stripped everything off and lifted himself out of the chair onto the bathing chair, he turned on the tap leaving grease on everything he touched. As he looked at his clock in the bathroom it was two am in the morning. Grunting to himself he took hold of the soap along with a big rough brush, the black muck slid down his body and into the drain. Holt remained seated in the shower until the water ran cold, he was done with being in the damn chair, so reluctantly he turned off the tap. He enjoyed the cool water, he always used to love the water.

Holt sat on the floor in his room and dried off, he was too tired to push himself around so, wrapping a towel around his waist he pulled his body slowly into the kitchen. As he opened the fridge, he enjoyed the light and the cool air. With the door open, he took hold of food and started eating premade meals like a fresh salads, cold roasted chicken, and fresh bread. He took the alarm off the fridge door years ago, as he was sick of it beeping when he left the door open. With everything he needed right in reach, he saw no point in making dishes and sitting at a table. He grinned as he was sliding a beer out of the shelf, he popped it open with his rough hands and closed his eyes as he drank deeply. He moaned in pleasure as the cold beer went down to his stomach.

Blissful peace and quiet, he thought as he sat there eating and drinking. Finally filling himself he closed the fridge and made his way to his bed. He lifted himself on the mattress and threw his sheet over himself. He didn't have to wake up early, as it was only paperwork to do tomorrow. He reached into the bedside drawer and popped out two sleeping pills, after swallowing them, he rolled over thinking about his life. As the minutes passed his eyes and body grew weak and heavy. Momentarily right before he was about to go into the darkness, one face he saw in his mind was that of Lady.

Holt woke up in the morning, feeling groggy from the sedatives. He reached for his chair and pulled himself in. Holt ran his hand over his face and scratched his messy beard. He was in desperate need of a coffee, a strong one. As he filled the empty kettle, he was grunting to himself as it meant he had to wait a little longer for the water to boil. He placed it on the base and turned it on. Looking around, he noticed that there was a note on the kitchen counter.

Holt,

I will leave you my number in case you need anything, or in case of an emergency. I don't mind being phoned on my personal number.

Lady.

He pushed the paper aside as he reached for some fresh fruit. He ate an apple and an orange because pills on an empty stomach was a recipe for vomit. He opened the drawer Lady organised the day before. He took out his morning medications, he swallowed them followed by a gulp of water straight from the faucet. After a hot cup of coffee, he made another and put it in his cup holder. The second spare room which was also the home office, had a pile of papers and books. Holt groaned as he looked at it all, he hated this part of the work. He emailed people instead of calling them because he didn't really like speaking on the phone.

He shook his head as he drank his coffee and forced himself to start. About fifteen minutes of trying to wrap his head around numbers, a car making a loud rattling sound pulled into his driveway. Holt looked out the window and saw that it was an old V8 Ute. He was familiar with this one, and it was a regular in his garage. Holt saw the smoke pouring out of it and he knew he was going to be busy for the day.

"Holt!" Frank, called out from his driveway.

Holt ran his hand over his face and threw down the pen he was holding. He gulped his coffee down, before yelling out for Frank to wait a minute. He tapped his fingers on the desk and then a lightbulb went on in his mind. Holt reached for his phone on the desk, he had memorized Lady's number and dialled it.

"Lady speaking." She answered, in her happy chirpy voice.

"Lady its Holt." He replied.

"Holt, are you alright?" She asked with concern in her voice.

"Mph," he groaned, Holt hated answering that question, so he deferred and asked, "How are you at Math?"

"Math?" Lady repeated, not sure why he would ask but she was curious. "Well, I'm alright, I'm not a rocket scientist but I can do basic-"

He groaned before she started to ramble, so he continued, "Are you able to do me a favour? I need someone to do the paperwork and books. I don't have the patience and I don't have anyone else that can help me."

"Holt, I have my son with me I -" Lady stuttered.

"Bring him over, I don't care!" Holt, cut her off.

Lady was a little nervous as she wanted to clarify, "I have to report any extra work to the agency." Lady said, as she didn't want to get in trouble by them.

"Fucking agency, it's not for them its private work, I will pay you, can you do it or not?" Holt was getting edgy.

"I can try, but you don't have to pay me." Lady assured him.

"Mph," Holt grunted, as he was running low on patience.

"Holt!" Frank, called again.

"I will pay your son then, see you soon!" Holt hung up the phone.

Lady was a bit perplexed as she stared at her phone screen. She looked at her son who was slurping on his breakfast.

"Looks like we have some work to do today." Lady announced, as she poured her coffee into her travel mug. "The grumpy man I'm caring for needs me to help him with boring math."

Bobby just smiled and hopped off his chair, grabbing his favourite toy, and put on his superhero mask that spoke, "Alright, ready for the action."

Chapter 3

Lady grabbed her bag and threw in some snacks and a drink for herself and her son. As they made their way into Holt's driveway, the garage was open. He was working on another car that broke down and they needed it fixed asap. Lady made sure that her son understood the rules before they got out of the car.

"Mask up." Lady directed.

"Yes, mummy." Bobby answered.

"Now, no bothering the grumpy man ok, his name is Holt, and we need to remember our manners."

Bobby rolled his eyes as he knew what that meant so he wanted to assure his mother that he would remember his manners. "Say please and thank you." Bobby said to her, as he pulled his mask back down.

Lady smiled as she could never stay serious with that boy, and they made their way to Holt.

"Morning Holt." Lady greeted as she walked up to the entrance.

Holt just looked out from under the car and cursed as he hit his hand on the axle, "Fuck!" Holt grunted.

"Mummy, he said the, f, word," Bobby whispered out from under his mask.

"Yes, thank you, sweetheart let's just make our way inside, shall we?" Lady said it loud enough so that Holt understood she could find her own way.

She put on the television for her son and made her way into the home office. She paused when she walked through the door and dropped her puzzle as the terror hit her. There were order papers, invoices, phone numbers and things scribbled all over the place. She grabbed the whole bundle and pushed it aside, just then Holt called out to her. Lady poked her head out the room with a look of confusion on her face.

"Where, exactly do I start?" She asked him.

Holt pushed himself into the room and turned on the computer for her, then he gave her his book from the garage. "Three months back, start from there, and then there is another book from the previous three months."

Holt pulled that book out from under the pile of papers as he continued, "I need to pay people and people need to pay me; I haven't checked the emails so there will be work there too. Write down your hours and do what you can, pay yourself, don't be a fool woman no one works for free." So, leaving it at that, he turned himself and went back to outside. Holt grunted and cursed under his breath as another car pulled up.

Bobby came into the room and plopped himself onto a pillow on the floor. He reached out and took some paper from a recycle box under the desk. Lady looked over at her son and she noticed that her son had come prepared. Bobby pulled out a few crayons from his pockets and started to draw.

"Grumpy, grumpy, grumpy." Bobby said, quietly as he started to draw a big car.

"Yes." Lady said as she solved her puzzle quickly before looking at the mess in front of her. "Grumpy indeed!"

Lunch time came around quickly, and there was a knock at the door. A delivery driver had dropped off food. The bag was big, and she thought Holt must have been hungry; so, she picked up the bag and made her way to the garage with her son in tow. When she reached the garage, Holt was already eating from another delivery bag.

"Is this extra for your fridge?" Lady asked.

"For you and the boy." Holt replied, as he took another bite of his hamburger with everything.

Lady was about to say, thank you, but Holt beat her to it, "Perk of the job." Holt told her, as he took a drink of his coffee.

"Thank you." Lady replied, as she opened the bag and saw a polka dot cookie and two party pies with a juice box. Pulling out her son's food, she passed it to him. Lady smiled when she saw what was waiting underneath, it was a hamburger and some fries big enough for two people.

"Eat." Holt said, as he finished his food and turned his back to keep working.

Lady didn't say anything she just sat down on one of the two fold-out chairs that were in the entrance of the garage. Bobby sat down next to her and started to chomp on his cookie first, then made a smiley face on his pie with the sauce. Holt looked over at the two eating; Lady took big bites into her burger and fries and sipped on her soft drink. She made small sounds that were the enjoyment of her food. While she ate, she spoke quietly amongst herself and her son and then while she was in the presence of Holt, as well as being on a paid lunch break, she needed to know some things. Perhaps he would be a little more open to conversation this time.

"Who did the books before, where is that person now Holt?"

Holt grunted before he answered, "Gone and moved on." Holt told her in a gruff tone.

Lady kept eating, reading the answer as a sensitive topic. "You should have a shop." Lady said, as she pushed another french fry into her mouth.

"I do, I just prefer to work here." Holt answered.

"Oh." Lady said, as she suddenly remembered Masons Auto, on the payment book.

"Masons Auto, that's your shop, I didn't realise." Lady finished her food and wiped her hands, and her sons face with a tissue from the bag.

"Yes, well it was mine and my brother's, but he shipped out and I needed money, so it worked out that way."

Lady could see the way his big hands worked around the twisted bits of steel and metal. Holt was a big man. He looked and studied everything that he did before carrying it out, every move he did was with a purpose and the stern look on his face was full of concentration. Lady admired him and she concluded he liked to do a good job and not a half-hearted one. Lady could have stayed there all-day watching Holt work, she was happy with staring out the window on rainy days, but she had plenty of work to do; so, she tidied up after herself and her son and said thank you once again as she walked inside.

Two hours later, Lady finally made piles of papers and filled envelopes with cheques and cash. She bound them together with rubber bands, payments were ready to be banked and the mess that was on the table was now all organised into date. Three main piles were made from the chaos she walked into; paid, to pay, and overdue. It was a big task in itself and she clipped everything together, the desk looked tidy, and she had made a list of people she needed to call and organised everything for the next time she would do the books.

Holt made his way inside and into the bathroom, where he wanted to wash his face. He called out to Lady asking how she was managing, and she told him that there was a bit more order in the chaos.

"I could use that for myself." Holt muffled it into the towel. "The couple of days you don't do the care work you could work here. I don't mind I'm working all the time anyway." Holt told her, as he kept cleaning the grease.

"It's a bit risky Holt, I mean, what if someone sees me, they might get the wrong idea and think I'm taking advantage of you somehow, I could get reported eyes, are everywhere."

"Fuck people! Who cares what they think, I don't give two shits who sees what, it's my house, my land, fuck everyone else!"

Holt couldn't see Lady as she was in the next room, but she covered her mouth as she laughed into herself. She admired Holt's attitude about the world, he was right after all and most of what he said had even been said by her mother, at more than one time.

"You do know how to answer people Holt, I give you that." Lady said, as she picked up her things and gathered her son's drawings.

"So?" Holt continued to ask, "Can you do it or not?"

Lady shuffled her feet and tilted her head as she was thinking of an answer. "I can, but it might get boring for Bobby, it's the days we usually spend together, I don't want to lose that time."

"One day then." Holt bargained; he wasn't going to quit. "Whatever time you have I will pay and pay it well."

Lady thought she could use the money, and her son could be baby sat at Matt's house the days he didn't feel like coming with her. He would have more fun with the two kids anyway.

"Deal!" Lady said, as she walked over to the doorway of the bathroom, she stuck out her hand.

"Good!" Holt shook her hand, which meant her hand and wrist were swallowed up by his big, long fingers which were soapy and full of muck.

Lady laughed as she realised Holt had forgotten he was washing his hands for a moment.

"Shit! Sorry," Holt mumbled, as he handed her a towel.

Lady didn't care about the dirty hands, she admired them, they had been busy working and working with care. "Alright, Holt, I will see you tomorrow then." And with that she made her way out.

Lady called out to her son, and he made his way outside with her. Holt could hear the little boy as he was happy, jumping and skipping around. As he sat and looked at himself in the mirror, he grimaced at the face he saw looking back at him, "Ugly, old bastard." Holt said to himself, as he ran his hand through his beard which was full and messy. He looked terrifying, so he reached for his shaving equipment but threw it back in the vanity as he didn't see the point. He didn't like holding scissors in his hand as it was intrusive thoughts of self-harm that would make him anxious. He could have seen a barber, but he didn't like going out in public; he was tired of the eyes staring at him and he would get overwhelmed when too many people would be around. Holt didn't like people or crowds; he was a very solitary man and he preferred it that way. He thought about how some home services have hair cutting skills, so perhaps he would ask Lady next time she came by. He was a little tired of the hair getting in the way when he worked, not to mention the oil and grease getting in there and causing the hair to stick to his face and scalp.

The next day Lady dropped her son off at Matt's house, her son was overly excited as they would spend the day baking and playing on the equipment in their backyard. The husbands had a big house and plenty of space for the kids as Mark was early retired. He had a large inheritance given to him by his grandparents and Matt only worked two days a week as a social worker with trouble and disadvantaged youth. Matt would be able to get things from Lady's house if he needed, as Matt had a key and could let himself in. When Lady arrived at Holt's door it opened automatically. She walked in and saw Holt drinking a cup of water in the kitchen, he was having a break as he started early.

"Good morning, Holt." Lady smiled, as she made her way into the kitchen. She set her bag down on the dining room table and turned her puzzle. His place was much cleaner, and she assumed that she should make her way into the home office.

"Good morning." Holt said, as he filled his cup again.

Lady stopped and turned around, she was surprised that he even greeted her, so she simply took it in for a moment.

Holt turned his chair and looked at her with uncertainty in his eyes, but he proceeded to ask her his question, "Can you cut hair?"

Lady smiled and nodded as she gave her answer, "I can cut hair, beards and anything you need, I taught myself, I'm not a qualified hairdresser or anything but I can get the job done."

Holt felt relieved. "How much do you charge?"

Lady frowned and screwed up her nose as she answered, "Charge?" Lady repeated, "Nothing! It's part of the care, I don't mind, and it won't take me long."

Holt scoffed. "You do too much for free Lady." Holt emptied his cup and put it away before voicing his opinion. "You should be paid your worth!"

Lady put one hand on her hip and stuck out her chin ready to answer him back, Holt thought she looked adorable, but he kept that to himself, it was so easy to get her revved up.

"Well, Holt, I don't see why I should charge for everything, I'm not about ripping people off." Lady retorted.

Holt held up his hand as he wasn't going to argue this early in the morning.

Chapter 4

He moved and made his way outside, where he had his hair cutting tools ready. Once they were ready, Lady asked him how much he wanted off the top and sides and started to brush and cut. Holt simply stared straight ahead, but that was a bit hard to do when she stood in front of him. Her summer dress was completely transparent from the sunlight behind her. He cleared his throat and closed his eyes as he had to keep his dirty thoughts to himself. He breathed deeply and just took in her scent as she moved around him. It felt nice having a woman touch his face and hair in featherlight movements.

He could feel her hands and fingers on the back of his neck as she zipped around with the scissors and comb. Her fingers were cool and soft, he didn't feel uncomfortable in any way. He wasn't sure if it was the early morning or the sound of the scissors clipping, but he suddenly had the urge to fall asleep. His head nearly bobbed down as she moved the beard trimming machine, his eyes snapped open as she gasped. He noticed that she stopped moving and had wide eyes staring at him, breathing heavily.

"Phew, that was close, I nearly gave your beard a mohawk, are you tired?" Lady asked and Holt frowned as he was getting irritated at himself for nearly falling asleep.

He shook it off and blamed it on the medication he was taking, but he knew damn well that wasn't the case. It was this woman in front of him, every single damn time she was around, all he wanted to do was fall asleep. She was a witch he thought, but he knew that was just ridiculous thinking.

"I think I need to see my doctor; I might have to change something; I get so tired on and off its not comfortable for me." Holt told her, as she was almost done.

Lady nodded and she said she would book him an appointment while she was around in the office room. Holt nodded as she looked at him once more and smiled wide at what she had created. Holt's hair was trimmed neatly, and his beard was two inches long and cut all in the right way. She laughed as she looked down at the ground, it was hard to believe all that hair was on this man's face and head.

"Woolly sheep." Lady said, giggling to herself, as she started to clean up around her.

Holt looked in the reflection of the glass door and he could see his face and hair was all clean. He was shocked at the face looking back at him, as it looked years younger and a somewhat friendlier. Right then he decided that only Lady would be cutting his hair and beard, as he looked exactly how he wanted. He thanked her as he moved away and told her that he would be in the garage if she needed anything. Lady just nodded and made her way inside the house.

As Lady kept busy, she called customers and managed to collect a long list of funds transfers that had been made that day. There was a whopping total of just over thirty thousand dollars. It was all well overdue, as some people had an account and others paid in cash. They would be making sure to pay as Lady wouldn't give up easily. One invoice made her laugh, as it was for a woman called Gladys Evens, it had the words Lasagne and Beef casserole, written on it and paid stamped across the page. There was only a guess that Holt's belly had a good week after fixing that car. Pleased with her work, she wanted to let Holt know the good news and how much he was going to receive in his bank account by the end of the week. She made her way outside closing the glass door. She noticed that the handle was covered in black muck again, and she needed to clean that day after next. As she made her way to the garage, Holt's helper had finished for the day and moved everything in the right place to be repaired.

Smiling she announced loudly, "Thirty thousand dollars richer by the end of the week Holt!"

She couldn't help but giggle as she heard what sounded like Holt's head smacking on something as he rolled out from under a car, Lady covered her mouth and then stayed composed.

Holt just looked at her with a frown as he asked, "What? How much?"

"Thirty thousand." Lady repeated, looking at him. "Seems like you were owed quite a lot after the past financial year."

Holt scratched his head as he had no idea how much money he had missed, but he wasn't struggling with the pay-out he got from the services after his injury. He was pleased that he had worked hard. Holt looked at Lady, and as he was looking up at her, she stood with her dress blowing in the slight breeze, she looked beautiful. He needed to know how long she would be contracted for, as it never occurred to him to ask.

"How long are you here for Lady? In the care department I mean?"

Lady seemed surprised that he wanted to know anything about her and so she answered fiddling with the small puzzle in her hand. "I'm here for the next six months and then I will be finishing my Doctorate at the University. I want to rent an office and start a counselling service for youth, I will be finishing on my birthday. It's kind of funny how that worked out, a big gift to myself, new beginnings and all the rest." Lady smiled, as she thought about her goals and what she had to do to achieve them.

Holt was unnerved by her answer, he thought that if she was studying full time she wouldn't be working and most likely be at home or in class. He was already dreading the day she would be done with him, and he didn't want anyone else around. Knowing his luck, it would be an old bossy nurse, or even worse, a big burly man. Holt frowned and scratched his hairy chin with the wrench as he had a loud thought, "So, you wouldn't be able to do the books then."

Lady shook her head slowly, as she wouldn't be able to work every weekend or late at night. Holt understood and thanked her for her time. He was about to pull himself under the car again when Lady mentioned one more thing, "I booked you a doctor appointment with Andrew Roberts this Friday, so I will be taking you at about ten, am, if you like, or you can use a taxi service as it was the only time, I could get you in."

Holt nodded his head slowly, he didn't like taxis and wasn't confident driving himself with the medications, everything was too much work. Holt stopped himself from grumbling and looked at her sincerely as he would try to get as much time as he could with Lady. "See you on Friday then." Holt said, as he moved back under the car and Lady started to make her way home.

As Friday came around Lady walked up the pathway of Holt's home, and just as she came to the door it was open. Holt was ready and dressed in a navy-blue polo shirt and black shorts covering his knees. He had his black sock covers on the bottom of his legs so that he wouldn't scratch them on anything. His hair and beard were clean, and he looked very smart and presentable. Lady stared for a moment and looked him over before grinning a huge smile and complimented Holt on how he looked.

"Wow! Looking handsome today, Grumbles, your limo is ready, shall we?"

Holt looked down at the first time she had a nick name for him, he didn't seem bothered at all, he actually liked it. He smiled so faintly that only a small dimple formed in his beard. Lady started to make her way back down the path and Holt followed her. He pulled himself into her car and Lady put his chair in her boot. When she climbed in next to him, she could see that his head was almost touching the roof of her car and he slightly bobbed in the seat. His long thighs stretched out touching the glove box and he moved the seat all the way back to make himself comfortable. It was going to be a forty-five-minute drive.

Andrew was Holt's friend from the service, he was near Holt in age and opened his own practice after he was finished. Holt didn't say anything as Andrew's identity had to remain a secret, due to the missions that he undertook.

As Lady pulled out of the drive, the small bump made her glove box fall open and it slammed into Holts covered knee joint. He hissed at the small pang of pain.

"Oh shit, I'm so sorry I have been meaning to get that fixed." Lady panicked and slammed on the brake. She started to reach across and fumble around at the papers that were flying out on to the floor, but Holt didn't mean to have seemed angry, it was an accident, and he wasn't annoyed at Lady at all. He reached forward and told Lady to drive as he said that he would have a look at the lock and clip on the glove box. He lifted the papers out and put them onto his lap and the other half onto the floor.

Lady seemed nervous after apologizing a million times and Holt only reassured her that it was alright, and she should stop apologizing. Finally, after taking a breath and pulling out into the street, she picked up her two by two and started to turn it as she drove. Lady could see that his attention was lingering on the letters in his lap.

"Oh, that's nothing there, I will sort them out later." She told him, as she took them and put them on the back seat behind her.

Holt noticed that Lady was uneasy, and he could see why. There was a name of a lawyer's company on the header of the letter. He only imagined perhaps she was getting divorced or something else was going on, but he didn't ask. He dug around and managed to click the lock, it closed again, and it wouldn't open. A temporary fix would do for now, as he would take care of it back at home. He moved the seat back and made himself comfortable again. Lady turned up the music she had playing, it was a mixture of rock and other music. As Lady turned up the music, she loved the song that was playing and Holt noticed how she sang as she drove, he admired the sight next to him, she was free of care and as it was her car she had every right to act and do however she pleased. He could smell her simple scent, no perfumes just simple soap on her skin, plain laundry detergent in her

clothes, and her hair had a soft smell of coconut and vanilla,
He looked away with his eyes as she turned to talk to Holt.

"So, Holt, tell me about the drum set, what songs do you like? Played in a band? Tell me about it, I love music."

Holt didn't really like small talk, but he also thought that he should share a little about himself as it was a bit of a drive, and he could see the traffic building up at this time of the morning.

"Played in a cover band, we usually played at pubs and small venues, and we managed to get the crowd rowdy every time; it was always great before my limb issues. I still practice drums, but the leg bass is taken by a second drummer; he needs to hit hard and fast to match my pace and it took a long time to find him. He does a great job, and we never need to talk about anything before we play, it's like we are thinking the same thing when it comes to music. The crowd always loved the show and it always made people smile."

Lady's face lit up; she loved the idea that two drum sets playing in tandem would be a hell of a show. "Sounds bloody awesome to me, I would pay to see that for sure, two drum sets and all that power on stage would be fascinating stuff." Lady couldn't help but smile as she imagined the show.

Holt's gaze lingered at her smile. He could see she was faithful in her words; he could sense her whole body was into the way she said them. He also noticed her cheeks flushed and for the first time he felt a slight flutter in his chest as Lady spoke. He moved his eyes to the road ahead and it made him smile under his beard. He thought he should take the leap and ask her to come watch him play sometime. Holt cleared his throat and built up the courage, as he finally spoke the question on his mind.

Chapter 5

"Might get the guys together then, it's been a while since we played, you should come watch us play, or we could go together. I think I would prefer being in a car with someone who is careful on the road and sober." Holt was relieved that he said something. He waited to see if it was taken on board. Lady blushed as she drove, she couldn't help but giggle at the thought of perhaps this was Holt asking her out on a date.

"Holt Mason, are you asking me out on a date, you cheeky thing?" Lady smiled, as she looked at him.

Staying casual, she realised that it was her way of coping with the situation, after all, she just said she would pay to see him play and he did ask her to watch, so she kind of got herself into this situation herself. There was only silence and Lady didn't expect Holt to answer her question, but as she came to a stop at the red lights, she looked at the brooding man who was sitting next to her.

Holt just looked at the stumps below his knees and thought inwardly to himself as to what woman would even want to be with half a man. Holt hadn't been with a woman for years; he wasn't happy with himself and didn't see the point of anyone fussing over him. He just wanted to go through life working and occasionally living, but he didn't really know how to do the latter. Lady noticed that he was distracted in thought, but she chirped up and made it into a positive situation, by answering his question.

"I would love to see you play Holt, I can pick you up and we can go together; I could only imagine your friends will be the rowdy type when they are all together."

Holt nodded his head slowly as he replied, "Yes the music and alcohol does that to a group of men."

Lady tapped her steering wheel as she smiled and spoke again.

"Done!" Lady said as she came to the entrance of the doctor's car park. "Let me know when and where, simple as that Mr. Mason."

Lady beamed a smile and for the first time in a long time, she felt like she had butterflies in her stomach.

In the waiting room Holt scanned the area with his peripheral vision. He kept perfectly still as he looked all around him. Faces were grim and even frowning, except for an elderly man who was fast asleep, waiting for his wife to come out of her appointment. Without moving his head, Holt looked next to him at the crunching puzzle being turned in Lady's hand. He found it amusing that people were so bothered by her turning it, even the receptionist glanced over her computer screen as she started to type louder and shuffle papers. Holt grinned as he leaned on his elbow and kept one long finger over his lips to hide the smile. Lady was so focused on the puzzle, and she frowned, as she looked at the colours. She noticed that it didn't seem right, she had done the turns thousands of times with the same algorithms and always managed to solve it. She checked it again and the noticed that one of the corners had twisted. Holt had played a joke on her without even realizing. When Lady was distracted while driving, she didn't notice that Holt quickly twisted the corner and dropped it back into her console of her car, as he made it look like he was fixing the glove box.

He wanted to see if she was patient and tested her in his own way. Just as she was about to shuffle the puzzle again, Andrew came out and called Holt's name. A unanimous sigh of relief was heard amongst everyone in the room and Lady put the puzzle in her bag. She went to stand, but then stopped as she realised, she didn't have to go in with him, so she sat back down. Andrew smiled at Lady and greeted Holt.

"Holt buddy, come on in, and you are?" Andrew stopped, as he stretched out a long hand to Lady.

"Lady Myne." She replied, then took Andrew's hand and shook it.

Andrew wanted to get to know this woman, so he asked her to come into the room. He could see that Holt was well dressed and groomed, and that was a huge surprise to his usual, dishevelled look.

"Please," Andrew said, as he stretched out his arm and showed them the way, "Join us Lady, I need to know a few things for Holt's file."

Holt just rolled his eyes and grunted as he pushed himself along. He knew that Andrew was talking garbage and wanted to be a sticky beak into Holt's life. Once everyone was seated in the small room, Andrew sat in front of his computer and asked his questions.

"Lady, how long have you been with Holt? He looks well, and I can't help to think that he looks happy today."

Holt shot a stoic look at Andrew, but he was immune to Holt's death stares. Lady smiled and answered that she had been with Holt for two weeks and that she works for a care agency, she was happy, and all was going well. Andrew then moved his attention to his friend and gave him the all-knowing look.

"Holt what can I do for you today?" He asked.

Holt grimaced as he answered. "I think my drugs need changing, I've been getting tired and sleepy past two weeks, and I can't sleep all day I need to work."

Andrew paused as he looked at the screen, two weeks Lady had been working for Holt and two weeks he had been tired. Andrew tried to hide a smile and made a professional act as he looked at Holt and replied, "Hmm wonder what we can do, I will have to examine you then and see what's happening, as for you, Lady, it was a pleasure meeting you, but I need to have a moment with Holt."

"Yes of course." Lady answered, as she grabbed her bag and made her way out of the office to the waiting room.

Andrew closed the door behind her and dropped the act. "Holt, buddy, it's good to see you man." He bent down as he gave Holt a manly hug and then sat opposite him.

Holt pulled his drawer open and got out the small shot glasses and homemade alcohol from underneath Andrews fake paper drawer insert. Andrew poured them both a drink and as they saluted each other they downed the small shot glass.

"So, have you been taking too many of the sleeping pills, or what is it? Talk to me, Holt."

Holt poured himself another, as Andrew went to his sink and rinsed his mouth out with mouthwash.

"I told you already, I'm tired."

Andrew sat in front of Holt and smiled as he spoke. "I can tell you why, it's Lady."

"What?" Holt said, as he stopped mid drink.

"Lady, believe it or not, you are so at peace and comfortable that you are able to completely relax, you don't realise it, but it's true, your tired because of her. I can't explain why because I'm not in your body, but that's why, nothing has changed with your pills so it's all I got for you Holt."

Holt studied his glass and raised an eyebrow in unexpected surprise about what his friend had just told him.

"So, I should fire her then." Holt said grimly and half sarcastic as he downed the shot.

"Dumbass!" Andrew said, as he slapped Holt on the arm.

Andrew put the bottle and glasses away, as he opened the door he reached down and shook Holt's hand.

"Holt, was good seeing you, but I hope I don't see you again soon, if you know what I mean in a medical sense."

Holt just pushed past him and flipped him off as he went to the waiting room, where Lady was waiting patiently.

As they climbed into the car again and were ready to head home, Lady looked around as she was amazed by a strong smell of alcohol.

"Wow, what's that smell? Did you get an injection?" Lady looked at Holt and checked to see if he was wearing any band aids.

"Oh?" Holt said, as he suddenly realised. "No, it's hand sanitizer, Andrew likes really strong stuff." Holt kept his face straight as he opened his window.

"I can tell." Lady replied, as she rolled her window down and turned on the air in the car.

She drove slowly and very carefully, turning her eyes from the road she looked over to the man next to her. He was mouth open, body limp, snoring in the seat. Holt had air blowing through his window into is face, and the music was blaring. Lady was amused that a man could sleep through the drive and not even flinch due to being completely unconscious; she could have driven over speed bumps and been through a police chase and he wouldn't have even noticed.

As they pulled up in front of Holt's house, Lady cleared her throat to see if Holt would wake, but he kept on sleeping, so then Lady honked her horn, and he woke up quickly and looked around himself.

"Sorry." Lady said, as she seemed bit guilty and sheepish.

"Was I sleeping the whole time?" Holt sneered at her, but he was angrier at himself.

"Yes, the whole time." Lady repeated, with a big smile on her face.

Holt sat up straight and opened the door, he made his way into the house and into the bathroom. He washed his face with cold water and splashed until there was no sleep left in his eyes. He could hear Lady going about her work and then with one last glance into the mirror at the awoken grump staring back, he grunted and made his way out to go back to work. Holt stopped as he could hear Lady humming, she was organizing laundry in his room.

"I will get that glove box fixed for you then." Holt told her, as he made his way out.

"Oh, thank you Holt, I appreciate it." Lady called out from the back room, "Just move the papers onto the floor and I will fix it when I get home."

"Right." Holt replied, as he closed the sliding door behind him.

Holt worked furiously and made sure that he was going to finish all of the work he had. As he worked on Lady's glove box, he noticed that the papers were still in the back seat. He picked them up and his curiosity got the better of him.

It was a letter covering the estate of her late mother and she had an inheritance that would surely make life comfortable for herself and her little boy, but as he flipped the page there was a real-estate notice and a contract that said all the money that was left to her was being gifted to her sister. Who in their right mind would do that? Was she insane? Crazy? he thought to himself, but then as he looked at the papers more closely, it made sense that Lady was taking care of her sister to make sure that she had a roof over her head. Holt bit back a curse as he could have imagined there was another reason.

A loud grumble came from his stomach as lunch hour was approaching. He moved everything back to where it was and made his way inside. Holt had a newfound admiration for this woman; she gave up money and easy living as a sacrifice for her sister. Money wouldn't mean anything, he thought that's why she gave it away. He had never met anyone like that in his whole life, and never ever would he meet someone like that again. She was a woman who deserved kindness and good, and anyone that would be responsible for hurting her would have Holt to deal with.

Lady was ironing some wrinkled shirts that were in Holt's wardrobe for a few days, she liked everything to be neat and tidy and she loved the smell of fresh linen. She hummed to herself as she worked, and Holt could see that she was smiling. Simply pleased, he thought as he told her that he had fixed her glove box.

Chapter 6

"A screw was missing, but all is well, and it won't be dropping open again." Holt called out as he made his way to the room.

Lady was happy that it was fixed, "Excellent!" She said as she moved more clothing. "And thank you by the way, I'm sorry it hit your knee, I feel bad, but good thing it didn't cause you too much pain."

Holt simply waved off her comment and said, "Forget about it already, or I will forever be known as the man who fixed the glove box."

Lady laughed as she folded the clothes and put them away. Holt looked around and realised that everything was organised in colour. Shades of darker colours were slowly morphing into lighter tones. Lady had taken all his clothes and turned his wardrobe into a boutique that you would see at a high-priced shopping mall.

"Quite the colour expert, if I didn't know any better, I would guess you like to do art." Holt scratched his chin as he was looking at the amount of clothes he had and never really wore.

Lady nodded her head as she moved some more laundry aside. "Well, I like to dabble in a lot of different things, life it's too boring every now and then, I like to keep my hands busy".

Without saying anything else, Holt simply nodded and moved down the hallway and into the kitchen. He opened the fridge and got out a platter of food that was delivered. It had small wraps with different types of fillings. He got out two plates and without asking Lady if she wanted any, he just felt like it was the right thing to do, and he didn't want to eat alone. Holt filed both plates full and moved to the small dining table in the kitchen. Lady made her way down the hallway and saw that Holt was waiting patiently at the table while pouring a drink for two.

She approached slowly and asked, "Are you having lunch with somebody?" She looked to the doorway and Holt only stared at her.

"You, sit!" Holt told her, as he went to start eating.

Lady was taken back by his mannerisms. "Don't mind if I do then." She said quietly, as she took her seat. She reached for the food on the plate and began to eat. They ate in silence and Holt was only looking over at her briefly, when he wanted to blurt out why the hell, she gave away money, but he had to stop himself and kept putting more food in his mouth.

"Mm." Lady said as she ate.

"This is so good, I will have to get this for myself sometime, where is this food from?"

"Rolls." Holt replied.

Lady knew the sandwich store but never thought of eating food from there, she always snacked on small foods during the day and saved her appetite for dinner later in the evening.

"Wow this is something." She said, smiling.

She picked another wrap and took the biggest bite Holt had ever seen, it seemed years since he had watched a woman eat and every part of her was enjoying the food. Her eyes were closed as she chewed and her fingers were dripping with sauce, she had food all around her mouth and her cheeks were plumped full like a chipmunk collecting acorns. Lady opened her eyes as she finished. It was the most entertaining thing he had seen in a very long time, but he didn't smile he simply stared at her. Lady licked her fingers and when she came out of her food coma, she noticed Holt staring.

"What?" Lady asked, as she wiped her face with the back of her hand.

Holt swallowed slowly; he saw she had sauce on her chin. He plucked out a tissue from the box that was on the table and went to wipe her face.

"Did you enjoy the wrap, Lady?" Holt asked.

"Oh yes, that was delicious." The smile beamed on her face as she licked her lips, they were full and red, her cheeks were rosy, and she seemed as though she was blushing. Very slowly and carefully Holt reached forward and wiped off a drip from her chin.

"Let me guess?" She continued, "I have it all over my face?"

A huff and almost what resembled a laugh came out of Holt's mouth and as he put the tissue down. He kept eating and recalling how it looked when she ate the food, it was brutal and adorable at the same time, so keeping his voice low and hiding his grin, he said, "Let's just say there wasn't any time for the wrap to feel pain."

Lady spluttered out laughing and went to take a drink to wash it all down. She plucked another tissue and cleaned herself up. As she stood and gathered the plates and drinking glasses, she thanked him for the lunch. Lady never really sat down during the day to have any kind of break. She liked to keep going and make sure that she worked diligently, although she would feel tired, she simply kept pushing through. She always liked the way she would sink into her bed after a full day's work, then she knew that she had worked hard enough.

Many nights of sleeplessness were behind her, she had so much responsibility and stressful times in her life that she found a way to make sleep a reality. She would work and work and work, only then when the sun went down and the day came to an end, she had made it through another day, and it was a good fight.

'Keep going and never give up,' was what her mother would say even when her bones were aching and she could barely stand, she pushed through and kept going until she had no fight left for the day. Right then Lady was taken out of her thoughts, as a plate clashed with another, and she shook herself out of her distracted mind.

"You alright?" Holt asked, as he noticed that her eyes dissociated from the world, and she was entirely in thought.

"Me? Oh, um, nothing I'm fine, I'm just day dreaming, it happens time to time." She replied, focusing again on what she was doing. She continued to rinse the dishes and put them in the washer, as it was full, she closed the door and turned it on.

"Done!" She said, as she clapped her hands together. "I guess I will go and do the books then, I still have an hour." Lady smiled and started to walk away.

"Lady!" Holt called out.

She stopped and turned to look at him, his eyes were serious, and he couldn't help himself any longer, he wasn't a liar, and he didn't like hiding things from people.

"I'm sorry you lost your mother; I saw an estate letter when I cleaned up the papers in your car." Holt was relieved.

Lady was touched by the sentiment, she didn't really care if anyone saw the papers, she just found it hard to talk about because at times, she would have to fight to hold back the tears.

"I appreciate that Holt, I really do, she was a beautiful woman and a good woman, I really just have a hope that I can be like her."

Holt had to hold himself back from confirming that she already was, as it would no doubt make her cry. He wanted her to feel more at ease around him, he didn't want to come across to people as the monster in the haunted house, he wanted to get to know her. Holt wasn't sure why he felt that way, she was a helper and a good one, but there was something different about Lady. Maybe if he tried a soft approach, Lady wouldn't feel like he was avoiding her. Holt didn't like people, but there were few people that he did. He had a very short span of patience, but that didn't mean he was a heartless man. So, keeping eye contact with her he spoke quietly.

"I'm sorry, I haven't been very good a talking with you, but I'm not much of a talker at all. Just know that I'm grateful that your here, even if I don't show or say it enough."

Lady's eyes started to well up, but she bit back the tears as she fiddled with the puzzle that was in her jacket pocket. She put on a smile to show that she appreciated him for saying those kind words. "Your welcome Holt, anytime you need anything you let me know and I will come to you." She turned away and went into the study to continue the work.

While Lady was working, she could only think of how Holt had wiped the food off her face. She was completely aware of his presence and the reason she didn't move was because she wanted him to be close to her. In all her years as doing the job she had never met anyone like Holt before. Usually, work was always old ladies and old men that needed her help, but Holt was a completely different case. He was handsome to boot and downright broody, everything that a romance novel was written about, although the thought went through her head that perhaps she might be thinking about it all a little too much. Holt was both polite and grumpy, thoughtful, and hardworking. She never really thought about a man for years after having her child.

When she was with her past boyfriend it was a time of her life when she was very happy, but then as time went on, they grew apart. It is in nature for people to change, and they do grow into different characters. Lady always loved Ryan and he was a wonderful father, but as times got tough, he worked in the mines another state away. He never really had the time to do the whole family thing. Ryan enjoyed freedom and going to work away from his loved ones and then only being home briefly for a two-week period. As time went on Lady wanted Ryan to stay and find work closer to home, but Ryan was adamant that he wanted to keep going with his life the way it was, so they separated, and Ryan sees his son when he returns from his shift.

Bobby loves his father and understands that both parents love him and that he will always have everything that he needs. Lady always made sure to explain to her son that he is loved no matter what. Their son was used to his father not being around since he was born, so to him nothing has really changed.

***

Later that evening, Matt was staring at Lady as she told him what occurred in the last couple of visits she had with Holt. He took a gulp of wine and started the barrage of opinions.

"Ok, so let me get this straight, he asked you to come watch him play drums at a venue that's not work related, he wiped sauce off your chin which you are very capable of doing yourself and -" Matt held up his fingers in the quotation for his final analysis, "He also bought you and your son lunch while you were working?"

Lady was regretting telling the story, but she also valued Matt's thoughts, so she went on the offense.

"Well, yes, but it's not a date it's just because he is -" Matt just started at her as she was trying to make an excuse, so she finally continued. "He is just lonely, and maybe needs some company, besides it wouldn't be just me at a bar you know it would be a whole bar full of people, even other women." Satisfied with her conclusion she sipped on her wine.

"Yeah, I bet Holt is thinking about other women." Matt rolled his eyes as Lady slapped him on the arm.

"Ouch! Why are you so mean? Don't get green eyed Lady." Matt tried make her feel guilty, but she didn't budge at all.

"Ha! The green-eyed jealousy monster you mean, nice try Matt, and by the way, even if he was in a relationship, it would be good for him. I think he has been in one by the sounds of things, and he still might be a bit sore about it."

Lady thought about the way he answered her question about the book work, perhaps Holt was still healing but the way his life seemed to her there was a lot of healing he had to do and what Lady could see momentarily was just the surface, of a very deep, dark, ocean of pain. After a couple of drinks and a much-needed laugh, Matt, Mark and their two children went home.

Chapter 7

Holt turned on the headset he wore when he played his electric drum set. He remembered the songs that Lady played in her car and wrote them all down, he was familiar with all the music, and he knew how to play it all very well. There was one song that he even sang and that was a collaborative one written about a beautiful woman. Coincidently the name of the song sounded the same as 'hers'.

Oh, Holt knew a Lady Myne alright, and she was starting to make her way into his life and his head more than he expected. His mind was occupied day in, and day out. But every time he thought that perhaps a rare opportunity had been brought before him; and it was his chance of redemption, he loathed himself.

Holt turned the music and drum sound up in his ears until the outside world was drowned out. He closed his eyes as he took a deep breath and began to play. Two hours past, as Holt beat the drums so hard his arms were burning, and he was sweating profusely. He missed the way it felt pounding away at the instrument in front of him and loved every second of it. He felt like all his anger and frustrations were coming out of his arms into the sticks and down onto the drumhead. Holt hit hard and fast and didn't stop until he needed a breath. He played every song Lady played in her car and one that he was fond of which reminded him of his time in service. It was a song about the way soldiers aren't praised anymore, all the fighting they do on the battlefield is in vain, and if they are brought to an untimely end while in service, they are shouldered, laid to rest, and then replaced.

Right then, a pain developed in one of Holts knee joints, and it was a pain he was very familiar with. It shot all the way up his torso into his spine and neck. He dropped his sticks and grabbed his knee trying to push on the nerve ending that was responsible. He was supposed to be getting surgery to remove it, but he didn't want to go under the knife again. Occasionally he would take a strong pain killer that would help with the ache that lingered after the pinch, but it was starting to cramp and get worse. He dropped to the floor in agonizing pain and then he pulled himself into the bathroom where the medication pen was hidden. He took it out of the cabinet, bit and spat out the protective cap. Holt waited for it to pass so he could focus before it would return.

He wished Lady was with him, but it was too late at night. He pushed the pen onto his thigh and pressed the button that released the drug. He waited, then slowly made his way into his bed, as it worked quickly, and he didn't want to fall asleep on the floor. He was exhausted from playing the drums and didn't mind the rest that would be coming. Laying on his bed staring at the ceiling fan, he thought about the surgery and that it would be painful in the rehabilitation process, but Holt knew that it would only get worse as time went on. He wasn't ready for the surgery, no, 'he wasn't brave enough', he thought. He frowned at his own self-doubt that started to creep into his mind, he closed his eyes, and his mind became silent.

***

It was Lady's day off, and Holt was still a little groggy from the injection. He only had a minor adjustment to make on a small car and then he would close for the day. After cleaning his shop, and rubbing grease off his tools, he went inside and changed his clothes. As he looked down at his thigh, he saw the injection site from the night before, it was a little bruised but that was normal. Holt settled himself in his lounge room and called his friend Andrew. Holt told him about what happened. After they spoke, Holt was defeated as he trusted him, and he would be the best person to take the medical advice from. Holt decided that he would get a cortisone injection that would last for six months and stop the pain. Andrew also told him that Holt shouldn't put off the surgery, as it would only get worse if he left it too long. The nerve was fusing against a piece of bone. Andrew told him the operation would be small and only take a couple of hours until it was over; there would only be small stitches once it was finished, and Holt would have a pain free time after.

While Holt was resting, he sat there alone, and his mind started to wonder. He was thinking about how he should go about it all, he knew the injection would be painful, it wouldn't take long but it was a long enough when its being put directly into the painful spot. He knew he would be very angry, but he also knew that he wanted Lady to go with him.

Surgery, he thought, what for? His own company, pain and thoughts was his way of life for years and he got used to it. It didn't matter if Holt was in a foul mood, or swearing at cars, there wasn't anyone around for him to offend. When Holt thought of Lady, he was a little confused as to why after all this time a beautiful woman like her was sent to him. He didn't want to be a burden to a partner or spouse. Being alone made it easy for him, with no small children under his care made life also easy, but as he thought about Lady's little boy and his kind and funny little nature, how he wished he had children of his own. With the thoughts of fatherhood, Holt was always in limbo, the constant sway, to and fro, of thoughts occupied his mind. What type of father would he have been in this situation? Would he have been any good at it? Would he be a role model? And more importantly, would it have been fair on his children to have an amputee as a father? Guilt and doubt about himself were enough to think he was better off not reproducing.

Holt's world was very small, he only had the few people he knew, and none of the opposite sex to become involved with. Sure, he loved women, many women, in his early days, but as he grew older and somewhat wiser, he knew that the right woman wasn't one you would find in a nightclub or bar. The care agency never sent out a person prior that Holt felt like he wanted to get to know and feel comfortable with. Holt groaned as he ran his hand over his face, he put the beer he was holding down on the table next to him and sat back. He was trying to watch the game, but she kept creeping into his mind over and over and he was annoyed at himself. Not only now was Holt getting used to Lady, but he also enjoyed having her around. Holt was also thinking about how miserable he was going to be once she moved on. The universe was surely having fun with him, he thought to himself as he picked up his beer and drank it empty. The universe was cruel, he started to blame his own existence but deep down he knew that wasn't the right way to think. He made his own choices not anyone else, he alone decided to join the army and go into service, he knew the risks being involved in the job. What a fool! He thought, as he believed that it was all for a good cause and then the life, he was living now was the reward for it all.

Countless times he wondered what the purpose of it all was, why he was left this way damaged and broken. He thought that Lady was able to put up with him because it was her job and she was used to it, but that wasn't convincing enough. He thought about her smile and the way she spoke, everything that she did, her patience and caring nature, that tiny puzzle she was always turning, why did she do that? Why was Lady doing her job? What was her reason to make that choice? Holt was surprised at himself for thinking about all these different questions, he never thought of wanting to know any answers about habits or hobbies people had, but this woman had his mind rolling.

Holt picked up a cushion from the couch and slammed it onto his face as he growled in frustration, then he threw the cushion across the room. He checked the time, and it was only seven in the evening, so he picked up his phone and stared at the screen debating on whether to call Lady now, or wait until the morning, but he was impatient with himself and dialled Lady's number.

"Hello Holt." Lady answered.

"Lady, how are you?" Holt asked.

"I'm well, is everything ok?" She asked out of courtesy.

"Dandy!" Holt answered with sarcasm in his voice.

Lady laughed a soft laugh, trying to get conversation out of him was like getting blood from a stone, so she asked, "What can I do for you Holt?"

Holt asked her about the appointment without hesitation. "Would you come with me on Friday to have a cortisone injection, it's going to be painful, and I wanted to know if you could drive me to Dr Andrew."

"Of course I will drive you, what time is your appointment?"

Holt could hear Lady flipping pages, she clicked a pen and got ready for the details.

"Ten thirty in the morning, it should give you enough time to take your son to school."

Lady wrote down the time humming to music playing in the background, she also wanted to know what the injection was for, so she was forward and asked.

"Cortisone is for slow release, is there something wrong, Holt are you in pain?" Do you need me to come over tonight? Are you alright?"

Holt was surprised at her firing away with the questions, so he wanted to ease her concern.

"No, no, I'm alright, I was in pain yesterday but I'm not now, I just need to do this, so it stops for a while."

Lady wasn't satisfied so she prodded gently.

"What stops Holt? What happened?"

Holt was trying to control himself; he didn't want to be rude, it's just that he didn't like people fussing over him, and he was a bit tired of always sounding like he was complaining, explaining about his problems was something he liked to avoid. Although Lady was concerned, and he was asking her for her help, so he tried to go out of his comfort zone and speak about himself. He took a deep breath to calm himself and stretched his arms out before answering.

"I have a nerve that's causing me problems, in the knee, its fusing to the bone and I need it to be fixed, but I'm not ready to have that done just yet." Holt was relieved after he told her and relaxed back in his seat.

"Oh dear, Holt, that sounds painful, I hope you put yourself first and make sure you get it taken care of, you deserve to be pain free, it's not fair to live in pain." Lady was trying to be encouraging, it wasn't her place to tell anyone what to do she just supported the idea of living without pain. Holt resisted the urge to grunt, he was getting ready for the call to end and as he was about to speak but Lady chimed in.

"What was your day like today, Holt?"

Holt knew that she was trying to keep the conversation flowing but he wasn't used to it, and it felt a little uncomfortable for him, but even with that feeling he decided to speak a little more.

"My day was quiet; I had a small job to do and then I closed for the day. I was still a little tired from the pain I had last night."

"Holt why didn't you call me?" Lady asked before she could stop herself, but she just wanted to reassure him that she was there any time he needed help.

Holt thought about how he wished she was there, when he was sitting in the bathroom with the pain pen, so he just answered.

"It was very late, and I didn't want to wake you or your son."

Lady was touched that Holt did have them in mind and for the sake of sleep he didn't want to bother her. She wanted to reassure him without sounding like she was putting on pressure.

"Holt, I just need you to know that you can call me anytime and if there is ever a problem, or you need help please don't hesitate, I -" Lady broke off for a couple of seconds. What was she doing? She thought, she should tread carefully as she didn't want to come across the wrong way. Holt could hear how she was taking a breath and pacing herself, then she continued.

"I know I work for an agency that provides care, but I don't mind helping you outside of work Holt, if you like that is, the offer is there if you need."

Chapter 8

Holt was pleased to hear those words and put aside any doubt that Lady was genuine, but as he looked down at his knees, he answered her the only way he knew how.

"I don't want to be a burden in all hours of the night, I've had to learn how to take care of things myself." Holt replied flatly.

Lady was silent, she was a little hurt by what he said, she even felt a little rejected, so she tried again gently.

"Please don't say things like that Holt, it hurts me to hear that you think you are a burden, you are not, and I would like to think that we are friends also and friends help each other when they need. I also understand that you are very independent and private, but you have helped me with extra work so I'm happy to return the favour."

Lady stood back and put a hand to her head she was showing Holt that she was grateful for the small job, but she also thought maybe she was being foolish and thought that Holt didn't want any new friends after all.

Holt took a breath and just stared at the screen, as he was understanding what was happening. He was gently being put in his place and gained an offer of friendship at the same time. He didn't mean to upset Lady as he spoke about himself, so he tried to ease her. It just that he didn't want to sound needy and was afraid of ruining the nature of how things were. He never thought about becoming involved with someone from a care agency before, whether it be becoming friends privately or even more, he just thought that if he did, he would no doubt make a mess of it later.

"Maybe your right." Holt said quietly.

"Mummy!" Bobby called out.

Holt could hear the boy calling for his mother in the background, he understood she had responsibilities, and he didn't want to hold her up any longer.

"Thank you, Lady, I will see you tomorrow for the bookwork." Holt reassured.

Lady smiled and Holt could hear it when she spoke.

"Yes, you will Holt, I will come by after school drop off."

"Goodnight Lady." Holt felt strange saying goodnight instead of goodbye, but it just came out naturally. Lady smiled and she had to stop herself from being giddy, so she pressed her lips together before she told him the same.

"Goodnight Holt."

***

Bobby needed a bath as he was covered head to toe in muck from playing outside in the sandpit. As Lady was washing Bobby's hair, he was curious about the grumpy man.

"Mummy what happened to the grumpy man's legs?" Bobby looked at his mother with his big blue eyes and Lady needed to be careful how she answered.

"I'm really not sure, sometimes people are born that way and sometimes they have an accident or have an illness that can cause it."

Bobby took his mother's answer as truth, but Lady didn't really know the full story of Holt or what happened.

"Why is he sad?" Bobby asked.

"What do you mean sad?" Lady asked, as she didn't see Holt as sad at all.

Bobby wiped bubbles out of his eyes as he answered, "He looks sad mummy; does he have any friends to play with?"

Lady was melting on the inside as his innocents came through, she was stumped for an answer so she thought she might try to make it into a positive.

"Maybe next time I see him, I will ask." Lady replied.

Bobby grabbed a toy truck that was floating in the bath and held it up as he spoke, "When I grow up, I want to fix cars too."

Lady froze as she bathed her son. Her little boy was fond of Holt, and this was his way of telling her. This was exactly the reason why Lady was never in another relationship, because if her heart would be broken then her son's heart would also be hurt in the process. After a good soak, her son was now clean and grit free. Lady pulled the plug out and dried him off, she hugged and kissed him, and he giggled with joy. This little boy, saw things that others didn't, such as Holt's sadness, and asking if he had any friends. Lady was proud of her son, and it made her feel like she had been doing a good job at being a mother. Lady doubted herself many times, finally after years of being mother she felt like she had done something right. Tucking Bobby into bed she kissed him goodnight, she sat in the chair next to him and held his hand while he chattered about his day, slowly his eyes grew heavy and then he drifted off to sleep.

As Lady was lying in her bed, she thought about her conversation with Holt. She was starting to think that maybe she was coming on a bit strong with offering her friendship to him. He didn't say that he didn't want to be friends but then again, she over-analysed every detail about the conversation. She thought maybe she was getting the wrong idea about it all and thought that she should be a bit more casual about it next time they spoke. After all she offered, and it was up to Holt to decide if he wanted it. She couldn't imagine what it must have been like for him after all these years, he must have been putting up with a lot of things alone, along with those thoughts of him being alone it made her sad. Lady also realised that perhaps he was the kind of man who liked being alone, there were many people she came across in her work that preferred life that way. Lady was glad that she met Holt, maybe there was something that she could learn from him. She understood that over the years of being in her job, she was taught a valuable lesson from every single person she worked with, and Holt would also be a part of that.

As tomorrow was a day in Holt's home office, she knew that it shouldn't take her all day to do the work she had. She thought maybe she could finish early and go for a long walk on the beach. It had been so long since she had time to do something for herself, so she thought it would be nice to get a coffee and sit on the sand. Watching the waves and debating in her mind was something she enjoyed. She managed to get a clearer picture after, and the things she was worried about or unsure of always cleared and sorted themselves out. Lady loved the water, and she was blessed that she lived close to it. Just then she thought of the pool that was in Holt's backyard; was he a swimmer or was it for rehabilitation? What did he use it for, or did he use it at all? Oh dear, the questions kept rolling again and she groaned into her pillow. Lady moved onto her side and looked out the window. What was happening? This was silly, she thought, she should never mix business with pleasure. Tapping her forehead, she wanted her mind to stop, she closed her eyes as she thought it was, best to keep it on a friendly and professional level and not get her heart bruised in the process.

First thing in the morning Lady woke up to a sneeze, she looked around her and saw her little boy rubbing his soft bunny on his arms.

"Oh no." Lady said, as she saw the runny eyes and nose. She checked his arms, her son had small welts that were coming and going in various places, his eyes were watering and he kept sneezing.

"Mummy I can't stop sneezing and my arm is itchy." Bobby told her with a sorry look on his face.

"Did you roll out in the grass yesterday?" Lady asked him, as he was beginning to look weepy.

"Oh, it's ok sweetheart, I will get your medicine." Lady kissed him on the cheek and gave him a cuddle as she threw the covers back and hoped out of bed. She couldn't send her son to school, it would take a while for the allergy medicine to do its work, so, she packed Bobby a bag including his bunny, his favourite soft blanket, and his tablet to keep himself entertained. An hour later his welts and sneezing calmed down. Once they were dressed and ready for the day, they made their way to Holt's home.

As they arrived, Lady looked behind her in the car and her son was fast asleep. He must have had a rough night, and the allergy medicine made him drowsy sometimes. She parked under some shade so the car wouldn't get too hot in the afternoon. Lady collected her things quietly and carried her son inside. Holt saw that there was a bundle in her arms as he worked.

"What's wrong with the boy?" Holt called out.

Lady answered him as she got closer.

"Allergies, he will be alright in a couple of hours, and I couldn't leave him anywhere. When he's not happy or well, I like to have him with me." Lady stroked the small boy on the cheek as he was snuggled in her arms.

Holt moved forwards to see him.

"That's fine, your welcome to put him on the bed if you like, he looks like he needs some rest." Holt told her, as he studied the little boy, he was peaceful and small, Holt didn't show it, but his heart warmed by the sight.

After settling her son, Lady remembered how she had plans to go to the beach, but she laughed at herself as she sat down at the desk. "So much for making plans." She told herself, as she knew better not to plan anything anymore. After a while Lady decided to make herself a coffee and went outside to ask Holt if he would like one too. She made her way down the ramp and saw that he was trying to work on something under a big V8 Ute. He was grunting and cursing then he stopped when he heard Lady's voice.

"Would you like a coffee? I'm about to make one for myself?" Lady smiled as she noticed that Holt bit his lip, he was about to swear. He ran his hand over his face as he was getting frustrated with the narrow spaces. When he looked at Lady's smile, he thought it would be better to take a break, as he started early in the morning.

"Think I might need one," he said as he put down his tools and wiped his hands.

He made his way back up the ramp behind Lady. Holt went to wash his hands, as they were slippery, and he didn't want to get grease on everything. He needed to change his shirt as it was soaked with sweat from the heat outside. He pushed himself into the bedroom, then he stopped and saw the tiny human in his bed. Holt quietly pulled out a shirt from his drawer and pulled it over his head. He sat there and started to take in the view. A child in his bed, so small and helpless, precious, and peaceful. He studied how the boy had strawberry curls, rosy cheeks and his mother's nose and lips. How lucky this boy was to have such a beautiful mother, he thought. Then with that thought he wondered what his own children may have looked like. He pushed that thought away as he heard Lady calling quietly that the coffee was ready. They both sat down and sipped at their drinks. Lady was writing in her diary and checking things to stay organised. Holt wanted to refresh the conversation about coming to watch him play the drums, but as the thought came into his head his phone rang.

"Damn!" Holt said, as he answered his phone quickly and didn't want it to wake the boy.

"Holt!" He said, as he took a drink.

It was his younger brother Finn; he was in the cover band with his brother and three others. Finn was the singer and he enjoyed moving around a lot, never really settled but enjoyed his life working and meeting new people. Holt put the phone on the table and put his brother on speaker.

"So, Big bro what's happening?" Finn asked.

"Oh, the usual just working on the cars." Holt replied as he drank.

"Nice! What's the latest sexy engine you're working on?" Finn asked sarcastically.

Holt grunted before he answered, "V8 Ute, big and old." Holt replied grimly.

"Oh, nice, just your type, huh?" Finn said, with a cheeky tone.

Lady nearly spit her coffee into her cup, but luckily, she managed to avoid making a mess. Finn continued as Holt stared at his phone with fury in his eye.

Chapter 9

"Well, you did ask about getting together to play, so lucky for you, I'm doing work down your way in about two week's time, want me to call the others and see if there are up for it?" Finn asked.

"That would be good." Holt answered gruffly then pushed buttons while he spoke. "I'm sending you a playlist now." Holt hit the send button and Lady heard the beep.

"Wait, let me see-" Finn said, as they could hear he was checking his phone, "Oh, nice choices bro, a bit different for you but it looks good to me, the place I'm working at is a pub, I'm sure I can get us in for a night."

"Pfft, Cock!" Holt mumbled into his coffee, as he knew that his brother was confident but sometimes a little too much. Finn had a way with people especially women.

"Ooff, now now." Finn said as he was getting under his older brother's skin.

"Need me to pick you up that night?" Finn asked as he remembered his brother didn't like driving.

Holt looked at Lady and she was smiling holding her cup to her lips, waiting for Holt to make the choice.

"No," Holt replied confidently, as he looked at Lady, "I will be going with Lady."

"Does this, lady have a name.?" Finn, misunderstood.

Lady laughed and chimed in.

"Lady is my name, Lady Myne."

"Oh, Sorry." Finn apologized, but he was very curious, so he asked the question.

"So, are you two-?" Finn trailed off before Holt intervened.

"Lady is from the care agency, I invited her to come watch us play, she loves music, and it might be a nice night for everyone."

"Right!" Finn said, as he knew his brother better than anyone and he defiantly knew that Holt never arrived with a woman before.

"Ok just let me know later." Holt told him, as he hung up the phone.

Lady wanted to know about Holt's family so while he was just about to finish his coffee she asked about Finn. "So, Finn, is he the one you had the shop with?"

Holt shook his head, "No, Roman, my older brother, he worked with me."

Lady's eyes widened with surprise, she needed to know more now. "How many of you are there?"

Holt turned the empty cup on the table before answering, "Three, Roman Holt Mason, he is four years older than I am, my full name is Holt Finn Mason, and then there is Finn Roman Mason, Finn is four years younger than me."

"Wow!" Lady said, at the discovery she was really intrigued. "I'm guessing that the names you all have are from forefathers then.

Holt nodded, "Yes, my father and his father."

"I really like that Holt, that's really nice to know, and I'm guessing your mother had her hands full with three boys," she laughed, as she only had one, and he was definitely keeping her busy.

"Yes." Holt replied, as he looked like he was thinking in the past.

"So where is Roman? Is he in the cover band too?" Lady asked as she thought that would be very interesting to see.

"No, Roman is always travelling for his business, he works with the mining industry, after his wife passed away, he stopped working in the mines and started to do the, behind-the-scenes work."

Lady's face fell on hearing the passing of the loved one. "I'm sorry to hear your brother's misfortune, it's very sad."

Holt continued, "Faye passed away ten years ago, and my brother never really got over it, Faye was very sick, she suffered for a long time with her health. It was overbearing to see her that way, she was a good woman, and we all miss her.

They didn't have any children because she wasn't able to, after all the chemical therapy from a young age."

Lady leaned on her hand as she looked at Holt when he spoke. Lady knew that Faye wasn't in anymore pain and that was a comfort to know. So, she added her thoughts. "At least Faye is resting now and there is no more suffering."

Holt looked at her and nodded, "It hardened Roman, he never speaks about her, it causes him too much pain." Holt said quietly, as he started to move his chair.

"Thank you for sharing things Holt, I like people's stories, you never know what you can learn from others." Lady stood and collected the cups so she could make her way back to work.

Holt looked down the hallway and saw the little boy watching his tablet on the floor.

"Hey, Champ." Holt called out, the boy turned and smiled at him.

Lady went to check on her son and she saw that his eyes had cleared up, his welts were disappearing, and he was in much better spirits.

"Oh, look at you." Lady said, as she bent down to give her boy a kiss on the forehead. Bobby smiled and asked if he could go outside and fix cars with Holt, but it was dangerous with cars and machinery moving around so his mother said that he had to stay here in the room or come into the office and sit with her while she worked. Bobby decided that he would stay in Holt's room and Lady made sure that she had her ears pricked the whole time, occasionally calling out to him to make sure he was still in the house. Lady worked swiftly, going through the overdue list, and then making sure things were in order, she had to make a few phone calls and got distracted with one of the customers on the phone, they both clicked when they were talking and then started to chat about children. Lady checked on her son, she saw his little feet in the doorway, and he was playing with his screen. After she hung up the phone, it rang again and she called out to Bobby, he said he was in Holt's room.

***

Holt was getting frustrated with his work; his hands were too big to fit into a small space and his arms were heavy and tired from keeping them stretched out above his head. His apprentice had gone home for the day, so he put down the wrench and looked at the small boy in front of him, suddenly, Holt had an idea, he leaned forward in his chair and asked,

"How big are your hands?"

***

Lady hung up the phone and she called out to her son, as there was no answer, she remembered the pool outside. In a panic, she ran into Holt's room and checked out his window the hard cover was still in place and the gate had the lock on it. She was relieved and decided to check the other room with the drum set, looking around calling for the boy, she heard a squeal and made her way out to Holt's garage.

***

Bobby squeezed into the small space above Holt's head, he lifted the boy with one arm, little feet were poking into Holt's face and beard.

"Almost, got it!" Bobby said, as he was doing his best to unscrew the tiny bolt.

Bobby used Holt's shoulders, face, chest, and head as leverage, he was wriggly and giggling, toes were going up Holt's nose, Bobby's other foot was kicking him in the eye, Holt grunted as he took the foot out of his mouth. Bobby squealed as Holt's beard was ticklish, and as they were just about done, they heard someone clearing their throat.

They both froze as Holt opened one of his eyes and saw the boy's mother standing in front of him, arms crossed, foot tapping; Lady waited for her son to realise that she wasn't happy.

"Is my mother looking at us?" Bobby asked.

"Mm hmm." Holt said, as his mouth was smothered in baby toes.

"I got it!" Bobby called out, then the bolt fell, and the boy made his way out. Bobby stepped down on to Holt's shoulder, then jumped into Holt's family jewels.

"Ooff!" Holt huffed, as he grabbed his crotch and bent over in pain.

"Good boy." Lady said and smiled at Holt.

To add insult to injury, a large wrench left on the top of the hood, fell, and hit Holt in the head.

"Ah! Ff, shit!" Holt didn't know what hurt more.

Lady thought karma was having a turn, she needed to clear the air about her son sneaking off. "Please let me know he is with you next time; I was very frightened for a moment."

Holt was nursing various sore places and choked out an almost inaudible, "Okay, sorry."

Lady looked at her son and now it was his turn. "Let's get you cleaned up mister." Bobby wanted to object but Lady pointed to the front door.

"I was fixing a car." Bobby told her, proud and covered in grease.

"Yes, well you need to tell me where you are next time." Lady ushered him in the house as he knew mother was in charge. Holt watched after them and then when they went inside, he looked up at the sky and asked, "Why?"

***

While Lady was inside scrubbing the muck off Bobby's feet, he was giggling and wriggling. When she looked into her son's eyes and saw his smile, all the frustration she felt disappeared, and she started laughing also. Bobby was so happy that he was able to help fix the car and Lady was delighted that her boy was so happy. She heard the front door open, and Holt pushed himself inside. Lady could hear him groan as he went to the kitchen and opened the freezer. Taking out two bags and red faced, he placed one cold bag down his shorts and the other on his head. The wrench was heavy, and a lump started forming. Lady and her son came out of the bathroom and Lady saw the wounded man sitting next to the refrigerator. Holt was resigned he had enough for the day, his mind was occupied with the appointment tomorrow, and he was dreading it.

Bobby jumped into the lounge room and on the couch, he used the remote himself and started watching a cartoon. Lady made her way to Holt and asked to see his head. He pulled the bag off his head and Lady noticed that there was a small wound that was bleeding. The pointy end of the wrench hit first, and she wanted to help.

"Oh, looks like you have a cut there, I will need to clean it, there is grease and dirt."

Holt winced a little as she moved his hair and automatically reached up and took her hand in his. He didn't need her to tend to it as he has had worse. He knew she was doing what her instincts told her, but this was really nothing. Lady thought perhaps he didn't like to be touched so she wanted to retract her hand, but Holt didn't let go. Holt looked up into her eyes, and for the first time she saw that they were green like blades of grass, she was a little stunned to see eyes so beautiful, they were almost like her mothers.

"I'm alright, Lady." Holt told her, as he almost smiled, he admired her nurturing nature, and wanting to jump into medical mode. Lady smiled as she felt his fingers move on hers and Holt released her hand slowly.

"Well, that's good then, it was quite funny." Lady had to laugh, covering her mouth as she was remembering what it looked like. Holt almost laughed but then grunted as he reached down and grabbed the bag from his shorts.

"I need a shower." Holt groaned, then in the likes of a limping soldier, he slowly pushed himself into the bathroom.

Chapter 10

A little while later, Lady decided that she would clean a couple of things before leaving. She would be busy tomorrow so she thought she could get a head start on a few things before the appointment tomorrow. Tending to her son's needs and putting on a load of laundry kept her busy enough. Lady cleaned the kitchen and sprayed some window cleaner on the back, glass sliding door, as the grease was thick, it was very difficult to clean because it kept smudging.

Taking a scrubbing brush in her hand she was starting to scrub away.

Holt finished his shower and put on some fresh clothes. As he made his way down the hall, he had a thought that he should lock the front door for the sake of the boy, then pushed himself in the lounge room. He noticed the boy was still watching television, and he heard a squeaking noise and scrubbing. Holt was still drying his hair, then after moving the towel out of his face he looked to the back door. The afternoon sunlight was shining directly through the glass and Lady's dress. He could make out the red and white polka dot underwear she was wearing and then she scrubbed so furiously that her hips and backside were wiggling around. Holt thought his mouth was wide open and his tongue rolled out onto the floor, he couldn't blink, he was in heaven. Then as she was about to turn around, he put the towel on his face and decided to move out of the room.

Packing up her son and making her way out, Holt was resting on his couch, she walked up to him and reassured him she would be back in the morning. Holt looked a little uneasy, but he had a hard day. Bobby chirped up with a question.

"Can I help you fix cars again?" Bobby looked at him with his big eyes and a smile on his face.

Holt was softened by this boy, so he looked at Lady and told him the obvious answer.

"That's up to your mother, but it's fine with me, maybe you could do my job one day." Holt looked at Lady waiting for her answer.

Lady couldn't help but smile at Holt as she answered.

"If you tell me where you are next time then it should be ok." Lady said it looking at her son and Holt at the same time.

Both had learned a lesson today, and when they looked at each other Holt held out his hand to Bobby.

"Thanks champ." Holt said, and Bobby's tiny hand reached forward and shook back.

"I will see you tomorrow, Holt." Lady gave him a soft smiled as she knew it would be difficult for him.

With loneliness in his eyes, he looked at her and as she started to walk away, very softly he had to tell her goodbye.

"See you tomorrow, and goodnight."

Later that evening, Holt was staring at the television blankly, there was a ball and people running but he didn't care. He was consumed in thought and regret, he didn't want to sit there alone so, he picked up his phone and called his younger brother.

***

It was a warm evening and Lady was trying to concentrate on her forms for her schooling. She was getting tired, and her mind was distracted by the day's events. She was starting to get aggravated at herself and wanted to push all the romantic ideas out of her head. She thought about how Holt's brother assumed that they were and item, she also remembered the way Finn said the last word of the conversation. It was as if Finn was not buying the story of how she worked with Holt and that maybe, there was something going on.

She pushed her papers away from herself and checked on her son and he was fast asleep. She leaned on the doorway and thought about how happy her baby was that he did a small job like unscrewing a bolt from a car. Lady started to feel regret about bringing her son with her to work, she didn't want her son to get too attached. Who was she kidding? She was getting attached herself and she knew it was unavoidable to romanticize things that happen between them. She thought about the way Holt's hand lingered on hers and the way his fingers caressed hers so gently as if to be unnoticed, but she noticed alright and she hoped that Holt was trying to reach out to her.

She wanted Holt to soften, and it seemed that perhaps she was making progress, but she had to remember that it wasn't her job to change people. Her mind tried to blame herself for what was happening, but she wasn't really doing anything. She was just doing her care work, and this was all happening out of her control. She wasn't going to go against the grain, she had done that long enough, so she thought that it was just how things were unfolding. She walked away sighing, going through the kitchen she opened her back door and sat down looking up at the moon and her mind went wild.

She thought about his beautiful eyes, they were magnificent. She imagined what it would be like to kiss Holt, how would his lips feel on hers? would he be rough? would he be soft and gentle? how would he love and show love? Her mind drifted to his body and his arms, what would his arms feel like wrapped around her body? what would he feel like when they were skin on skin? and then the most intimate of things entered her mind, what would it feel like to make love to Holt?

She put her hand on her face and rubbed hard, she was going a million miles an hour, but she was a woman, and it was natural to think these things. It was her own mind, her own thoughts. She had every right to imagine and think what she wanted in her private life.

"Oh, my word." Lady said as she was driving herself crazy, she needed to try and distract herself, so she went into the bathroom and splashed her face with cold water. Then as she looked up at her reflection, she spoke to the face looking back. "Open your heart to it."

She thought about how tomorrow would be, she was a little nervous and worried. Not for herself but for Holt, she was starting to take his pain and problems on her shoulders, she needed to make a stop to it, but why? She started to remove her clothes and she turned on the shower while speaking aloud to answer her own question, "It's our nature."

***

Holt was grunting at the poor pass of the ball while he watched the game and listened to his brother on the phone.

"Holt, you're making it sound like you have a situation, but I don't see the problem." Finn told him.

Before Holt could answer, Holt took a big drink from his beer bottle and then frowned when it was empty. "Well, it's not as easy as you think, she is doing the care work and the books for me plus, she has plans to open a counselling place after studying full time, which makes her sound like she won't have time for helping me or being around after that."

Finn just clicked his tongue before he voiced his thought.

"I just don't think there is a problem, she will be doing a different job, and she can work anywhere, you have the empty office next to your old shop; it was rented out all the time, plus you should be happy for her to reach her goals. Don't forget it doesn't mean you can't build something together later."

Holt resigned and simply answered with tired voice, "I guess you're right."

Finn continued, "Look, big brother, you need to try and live again your hearts still beating, isn't it? Fixing cars and being in your own company sounds like a lonely life if you ask me. Look at Roman, do you want to end up like him?"

Holt just scoffed before he mumbled a loud thought, "You mean, wealth and a private jet?"

Finn laughed, whole heartedly at his brothers, dour answer.

"Okay, so what? but have you ever seen him smile?"

"No!" Holt answered quickly and huffed a soft laugh.

Finn pressed on, "I just think you should let go a little, you deserve to be happy, everyone does, I know I'm not married but still, it's not a bad thing to find a bit of life and live it."

Holt was aware of how his younger brother lived life, he was always loving life and living it. Finn was a single bachelor and enjoyed it, but all three of the brothers were different and Holt was one who wanted to share a life with someone. Holt always admired the way his parents loved each other unconditionally. His father adored his mother and still does, spoiling her and cherishing her every moment of his life. Holt and his brothers were the legacy of his parents and Holt couldn't help to think that he would like the same someday.

Holt stretched out on the couch, he needed to sleep before the night got too late, "Fine! I guess I will work it out, and just take each day as it comes."

Finn sounded happy after Holt had a slight change of heart, "There you go, see, things are looking up already, I have to get this job done big brother, I'll see you in two weeks."

"Right!" Holt hung up the phone and dropped it on the ground. After thinking about the conversation, he just had with his brother he started to feel a little better. He needed to talk to somebody, and his parents were around but he didn't want them to get too excited that Holt was interested in somebody, so Finn was the choice he had left. Roman didn't speak to anyone and never about relationships, he had good reason not to. Holt turned off the television and then slowly, started to feel a small weight lift off his shoulders.

As the summer morning began, Holt was ready in a black tank top and black shorts. The morning was already very mild, and the warmth was creeping in quickly for the day ahead. He made his way to the front door and saw Lady was already waiting patiently. She had her car running with the air-conditioning on. Holt was taken back momentarily when she stepped out of her car. He caught a breath as he looked at her. She was wearing a dark blue paisley dress with pink and white flowers. Her hair was pulled back and she had loose strands of curls coming down out of the ponytail, her face was covered in a small amount of makeup and her eyes were adorned in eyeshadow and mascara. Holt couldn't help but stare at the beautiful ocean blue eyes and smile that looked back at him.

"Morning Lady." Holt greeted her when he finally managed to get his mouth moving.

"Morning Holt, we should get going. I think it's going to get hot, and we don't want to get stuck in traffic. People are angry drivers when its summer." Lady started to make her way down the ramp and Holt followed.

In the car they slowly made their way to the doctor's office and Holt was making sure that he didn't make a habit of staring. He kept his eyes straight ahead and then her phone started to ring.

"Oh Ryan." Lady pushed the button on her steering wheel and put the call on speaker.

"Hey hey, pretty Lady." Ryan said as she answered. Holt stayed composed looking at the road ahead.

Lady laughed as Ryan was doing a play on words.

"I'm well Ryan, busy busy, just taking a client to the doctors, I have you on speaker, so what's happening in your world?" Lady asked casually.

Holt noticed that she wasn't bothered by the call, and they seemed friendly. This was a good thing, Holt thought, as there would be nothing worse then, two parents screaming at each other. Not a very good environment to grow up in if you were a child.

"Nearly done with this shift, I wanted to take Bobby for a camping weekend, is that ok with you? And don't worry it's not far from hospitals and doctors in case, of an emergency." Ryan told her, as he knew that she would ask about that next.

Lady was at ease.

"He's your son too Ryan, as long as he is with you and safe, I'm fine with it." Lady kept her cool and didn't show her nerves.

Ryan reassured her that they wouldn't be alone in the middle of nowhere, "Its actually at a holiday camping place, there will be a couple of others from work taking their kids too, they are close to Bobby in age, and he won't be bored."

"That's Ok Ryan, I'm not worried." Lady told him, as she was really bouncing with emotions on the inside.

"Ha!" Ryan laughed as he continued, "Lady, you forget I know you, especially when it comes to our boy." Lady laughed as this was true and she was happy that Ryan wanted to spend time with his son. School holidays were close, and she wanted to remind him.

"Next week is his last week before the holidays, just make sure you're on time and I won't say anything in case." Lady made sure to add that thought as she was aware of the plans changing quite often when it came to Ryan organising this with his son. She only prayed silently that this time his plans would come through.

Chapter 11

Ryan cut off Lady as she was doubting him.

"I'm not going to change my mind, and nothing is going to change. I made it clear to work that I'm not working back this time. I booked it in months ago, I might even be coming back a few days early, because I have some time up my sleeve."

Lady was relieved and started to relax, "Good to know, I guess we will see you later then."

"You will mama, bye." Ryan ended his call, and Lady breathed a sigh of relief.

Lady looked over to Holt and gave him a smile, Holt just looked at her while he was leaning against the window with his finger on his chin.

"Sounds like a good guy." Holt said still looking at her.

"Oh, it's been a long journey for both of us, we were together young and very much in love, but things change," Lady shrugged her shoulders as she continued, "I'm glad he is going to see Bobby, the little one is always asking about his father, and I keep making sure he understands that he works far away, and he will visit. It's hard sometimes, trying to keep the world positive for him but I'm trying my best, sometimes I doubt my efforts about being a mother but it's a learning process from the moment they are born."

Lady came to stop at some red lights and looked over at Holt, he was looking at her like he couldn't comprehend what she had just said. He seemed a mixture of both angry and bothered. Lady wasn't sure what was so wrong with what she had said besides the truth. Slowly, Holt moved his hips, his lean, long, body started to stretch and move around, he looked like he grew a head taller, almost like when males in the animal kingdom are about to attack their prey or compete for a female. He adjusted himself in his seat and took in a breath all the while directly looking at Lady.

"You are a wonderful mother, don't let anyone tell you different." Holt held his gaze.

Lady just smiled she didn't know how to take the compliment, so she tried to make it casual, "Oh, that's a nice thing to say." She answered and tried to keep it light, but then she noticed that she only made Holt more vexed.

Slowly with purpose and poise, Holt reached up a long hand, to his eyes, took off his sunglasses and pushed them over this head, this time he leaned forward close to her face and looked her right in the eyes. With his elbow leaning on the centre console, he reached the other long hand forward and touched hers resting on her thigh, he caressed her hand gently and saw how Lady was in full attention and awareness of what was happening. Her breathing started to hitch, but she stayed still. Holt needed to make sure she was really hearing what he was going to say, he kept his voice low and then it rambled trough her when he spoke.

"It's not just a thing to say Lady, you are a wonderful mother, it's the truth, don't let anyone tell you different, ever!" Holt was just a short distance away from her face and they could almost touch noses.

Lady noticed that his lips were full, and his mouth was perfect in all its masculine glory. Her eye lashes fluttered quickly, and she could feel his warm breath over her lips as he breathed. Holt's eyes were like hot pins going right into hers, she never had chance to see him like this in full sunlight and not covered in grease and sweat. His skin was clean, and he smelled like warm woods and spices beard wax, which was making her senses go into overdrive.

Lady swallowed slowly as her mouth was suddenly dry, and even thought she was in full swing of emotions she managed to speak.

"Thank you."

A car honked from behind them, Lady jumped in her seat at the sound. They didn't realise that the lights had turned green, and cars were moving forwards around them. Holt released her hand and slowly moved back in his seat, he kept his gaze on her as he reached for his sunglasses and pulled them over his eyes again. Lady switched her attention to what she was doing, she cleared her throat and blinked a few times as she looked at the road again. In her head was only her own voice, "Focus girl, focus."

When they reached the doctor's office, Lady noticed that her puzzle she carried wasn't in the car and she remembered that her son was playing with it last time they were in Holt's home office. It made her feel naked and she didn't have anything to keep her hands busy, so she just kept playing with the small puzzle that was hanging on her key chain, it didn't feel the same and it was small and fiddly, but it would have to do for now. They were seated in the nurse's room and Holt was answering questions before his injection. Lady thought that she would wait on the chair outside the door, but when Holt was called in, he turned and called to Lady.

"Lady?" Holt was trying not to show his nerves and stayed calm, but he knew that he was going to be in a world off pain.

Lady looked up at him she could see that he was uneasy, he seemed a little pale and like a cold sweat was starting to fall. She leaned closer to him as he spoke quietly.

"Would you come in with me?" Holt asked.

Lady saw his Adam's apple bob as he swallowed hard, he was nervous, and Lady couldn't let him go in alone, "Of course, Holt."

Holt laid down on the bed, the nurses prepped his leg for the needle, it was going to be big, and Lady was starting to think that she wouldn't be strong enough to handle what was coming. A few moments later Andrew entered the room.

"Holt," Andrew greeted him and shook his hand, "You're going to need to bite down on something."

Holt pulled his shirt off over his head and Lady was in awe at his body. The entire bed was taken up by Holt's figure, his arms were long, and full, his chest was broad, and his stomach was like that of a swimmer, just all the correct size and perfectly formed for his height. She looked down the length of the bed, had Holt not been an amputee, the bed would have been much too short. His thighs were long and strong, this only meant that he was an extremely tall man at full body size. Holt rolled up his shirt and put it between his teeth, he gripped on to the bed post behind his head. His bicep was bulging, and his forearm was starting to form veins that were part of the adrenalin going through his body. The nurses were passing the needle over to the doctor and Lady was suddenly shaken when she saw the size of it. It was thick and would have hurt like hell.

Andrew started with instructions as he held it above the injection site.

"Holt, I need you to count down from ten when I put it in, try to breath slowly, and you can't hold anyone's hand because you might break some fingers."

Holt angled his head so that he was looking up and away. Lady turned away her face from the needle to Holt, when she looked at Holt her heart shattered. Andrew put the needle in Holt's knee joint. Holt's eyes closed, and he tensed and groaned out in pain. His teeth were biting down so hard on his shirt Lady could hear the material grinding and beads of sweat were coming down his forehead. His other arm gripped the handlebar that was hanging from a chain above his head, and he was starting to shake. Holt groaned out again, his neck was popping veins, and he was starting to go red.

"Eight." Andrew said, as he was moving it slowly.

Lady was horrified for Holt as she watched him suffer. His sounds of pain were tearing at her soul, so she did what felt right and comforted him as she would have done to any person in pain.

She wrapped her arms around Holt's shoulders, she pressed her cheek to his forehead and started to sooth him, "Shh. Its nearly over, shh."

Holt had a single tear escape his eye and his red face was starting to ease as the injection blocked the pain.

"Three." Andrew kept counting.

Lady looked at Holt, she wiped the tear off his cheek and kissed his forehead, soothing him still, "Shh, it won't hurt anymore."

Lady could see that Holt was opening his eyes. He groaned out in relief and started to calm and ease. Lady pulled the shirt out of his mouth and stayed close to him. Holt let go of the handle and wrapped both of his arms around Lady.

Andrew dropped the needle into the sharps box, and he took off his gloves. The nurses were cleaning Holt's leg and covered the injection site. Andrew was just as relieved that it was all over, and he was able to let his friend have some peace.

"All done Holt, you need to wait here for fifteen minutes and then you can go, you did well buddy." Andrew tapped Holt on the arm and then exited the room.

Holt didn't let go of Lady and they stayed like that in each other's arms until Holt was settled. There was no speaking, only silence and the noises outside of the room. Holt was catching his breath and Lady could feel his body relax while she was in his arms.

Holt was taking in everything about her, and Lady was doing the same, they were a comfort to one another, and they were simply just being. After a few minutes Lady lifted her face and Holt saw that she had tears in her eyes. He didn't know that she was crying.

"Lady?"

She looked like she was in grief and Holt reached up and wiped her big tears away.

"What's wrong?" Holt asked as he looked into her eyes welling up.

"I can't bear to see you in so much pain, it rips my heart out."

Holt pulled her face down onto his chest. Lady felt the warmth from Holt and his skin under her cheek, she could hear his heart beating and ran her fingers over his skin gently as she stayed there. She didn't want to move and was sad that she may never have the chance to be this close to Holt again. She was falling deeply, and this was only getting harder for her. Holt didn't let go and he couldn't remember the last time he had a woman in his arms like he did that very moment. It had been years, and it was something that he had craved for a very long time. Lady was calming herself and she only had one request, "Please Holt for your sake, please have the surgery. It hurts me to see you in so much pain."

Holt gently stroked his hand over her hair, and he touched his lips to her head when he answered in a whisper, "I will, soon."

A little while later the nurse knocked on the door to check on Holt. Lady turned her head to look at him and she saw that he was feeling much better, and Holt was relaxing with his eyes closed. They slowly released each other, and Holt pulled his shirt back on. On the way home Holt was resting in the seat, the treatment made him tired, and he was under instructions for seven days not to work or exercise. Lady was quiet and occasionally she would reach across and check his temperature, which was a habit that she had from being a mother.

As they pulled into the driveway, they looked at each other like it had been a long, stressful morning.

"Home sweet home." Lady said as she smiled.

The afternoon heat was well under way. Holt groaned as he nursed a sore knee, it felt a little bruised but that was normal after the injection. When they went inside, the house was nice and cool, and the air conditioner was going. She looked around with her hands on her hips and remembered that she had already caught up on the care work yesterday.

When Holt pushed himself into the kitchen, he saw that his phone on the counter was vibrating and flashing. A list of missed calls and messages in his answering service were all waiting for him. He grunted as it would keep him busy later. The sweltering weather was most likely the reason, causing cars to drop out one by one.

Lady already did the book work for the week, so she thought that to recover from the mornings testing events, it was best that she goes home. Doctor's offices, hospitals, and anything to do with medical treatment was draining, and it was the one thing she didn't like about her job. She remembered she needed to organise things for herself and her son. She knew it was only an excuse, but she was feeling a little awkward. Conveniently, her son had the school holidays and a camping trip that were coming up, so she ran with that idea. Even though in the back of her mind she always knew that the camping trip would be a never occurring thing she still thought she should keep her hope alive for her son.

Chapter 12

"Is there anything else you need Holt? I have some things I need to organise for the little ones camping trip." Lady was making notes in her diary about the day's work and the time she was finishing. She was a little tired and didn't mind having time to sit, she only hoped that Holt didn't have any more pain.

"What kind of things does your boy need?" Holt asked her.

"Everything." Lady laughed, as this was the first time Bobby was old enough to go on a camping adventure with his father.

"I guess you will have fun shopping then." Holt said as he sat in the kitchen, debating on what to eat.

"Yes, all the gear and no idea." Lady replied.

Holt slightly smiled as he settled for a cold drink instead. He pulled two glasses out of the cabinet and made his way to the table. Lady put away her book and pen and she saw that he was settling to share a drink with her.

"Would you like a drink?" Holt asked as he already poured the two glasses full.

"Do I have a choice?" Lady asked as she sat down.

"No!" Holt replied grinning, as he took a big drink.

Lady didn't like the silence, so she kept in her care mode.

"Are you alright now?" She asked.

Holt was just looking at her and knew that he didn't want to make her feel awkward.

"It's better now, I won't need to worry about it for six months."

Lady didn't want to mention the surgery, but Holt was already ahead of her.

"The surgery is something I have been considering for a while, but after this morning I think its best that I go through with it."

Lady wanted him to know that she would be there for him if he needed again, as she had once before, "I'm happy to help you whenever you need once you have it done, just remember that, Holt."

Holt nodded he didn't have anything to say and wasn't going to reject her, so he simply told her what he thought.

"It's good to know I'm not alone."

Lady wanted to reach for his hand, but she stopped herself.

"You're not alone Holt, I promise."

Holt needed to know more about her study plans, so he didn't hesitate to ask, "What will you do while you study?"

Lady couldn't help but think that he was fishing for information, but she didn't want to give too much away, because she wasn't sure herself, so she kept her answer open.

"I'm not sure, I don't really plan anything Holt. It's something I've learnt over the years. I'm hopeful that my studies will go ahead, but until things get moving, I'm not sure. I just go with the flow after having Bobby, I see it as the right way to go about things. I will be getting a loan for the schooling, but then possibly working to pay it back later, so ironically speaking, that is the plan." Lady sighed as she took a drink from her glass.

Holt wanted to know more about her, but he wasn't sure what to ask, it had been a long day and Lady would have to leave soon to pick up her son.

"What about you, Holt?" Lady asked, as she wanted to know his plans for the future.

"What about me?" Holt replied.

"Why don't you open your shop again, you could teach younger amputees how to become a mechanic."

Holt was surprised, he did think about it a long time ago, but Holt wasn't sure he had the patience to teach other amputees especially of an adolescent age. There would be a good chance that they would be the younger version of himself, and that was a very difficult time of his life, so Holt answered as best as he could. "It crossed my mind, but I guess time will tell." Holt simply left it at that.

The alarm went off on Lady's phone and she quickly noticed that the time flew by, and she had to go. She drank her cold juice finished and out of habit, stood up and went to pick up the two glasses, Holt reached forward and stopped her hands.

"You don't need to do that Lady; I can do the dishes."

Lady felt a bit silly but then nodded, "It's habit I guess."

Holt tightened his fingers on hers and pulled her a little closer. Lady was a little nervous, but she just stood in front of him and waited for Holt to lead the way.

"Thank you for coming with me today, I'm glad that you were there, and whenever I decide to have the surgery, I want you to be there too."

Lady was exploding with joy on the inside, but she dared not move. The man in front of her was finally opening a little, he let her in, and this was a huge relief. He accepted her offer of friendship and she was over the moon.

"I will be there with bells on." Lady replied in her usual quirky way, she smiled at Holt, and he softly smiled back. Lady needed her hands to pick up her phone and keys, Holt reluctantly released her.

"I will see you next week, then Holt." Holt was looking into her eyes as he nodded his head, this was his way of acknowledging Lady's pace.

"Next week then." Holt said quietly, as Lady made her way out.

***

"Aww." Matt looked at Lady as she explained the day's events at the doctor's office. He was already on his second bottle of wine with his husband and the kids were happy playing outside. "Sounds like you're in limbo." Matt said to Lady as he poured all the grownups another round.

"Limbo? I guess you could say that, but then again about what really? It was a comforting matter, and I was just emotional because I hate seeing people in pain." Lady tried to explain before she took a big gulp of her wine.

"Well, honey you need to remember that he is a man, and he sounds like he's been alone for a while, which means that he is making sure he won't scare you off."

"Scare me? No, he doesn't scare me at all, I just think that I want everything and too quickly, which wouldn't be out of the ordinary." Lady had a look on her face like she wasn't surprised at her own answer.

"Mm," Matt said, as he took another mouthful. "What do you think darling?" Matt turned to ask his husband, who was sitting opposite Lady.

"I guess you could say it's all like chess really, you need to take your time and make sure you observe before acting."

Matt rolled his eyes as he had to know what his husband was going to say, "Yes, dear but let's look at it like two humans, a man and woman for a change."

Mark sat back and thought before giving his analysis, "So, judging by everything that has been happening, it sounds like the King, being Holt, is working out the path. Everyone knows the Queen, in this case you, Lady, are able to move anywhere and do whatever you please."

"And?" Matt impatiently asked.

Mark continued after having a sip of his wine, while swirling it around in the glass.

"The Queen needs to keep doing as she pleases, then the King will decide, it really can't go anywhere else until he has more of an idea of which path to take."

"Hallelujah." Matt said as he gave a high five too his husband.

Lady was just looking at both and was touched by the way they were invested in her wellbeing. She thought about how it felt to be on Holt's chest again and the way his heartbeat, she was missing him.

She started to think about what he would be doing over the weekend and how he would be feeling, she couldn't help but have him on her mind. She sipped at her wine and then she noticed that she had zoned out of the company that she had in front of her.

"Oh no." Matt said as he looked at Lady,

"What?" She asked.

"You're falling for him, aren't you?"

Lady's eyes welled up and she held up her hand in surrender, "Of course, I am." Lady said as she looked out the window and watched the children play in the yard.

***

After a night of nearly no sleep and sheer frustration, Holt decided it was a good idea to distract himself by working on an engine. The day was cooler, and he was able to do light duties. He had the engine pulled out of the old V8 Ute and it was being held by chains that his apprentice had helped him with. There was a car that needed detailing and he wanted to be alone, so he sent his young helper away to have it completed. If distance makes the heart grow fonder, then why did this time apart from Lady, feel like his heart was in a blender?

Holt cleaned small parts as he was thinking about having Lady in his arms. He realised that not only was she beautiful, but he was also slowly getting addicted to her. His problems, and ailments were not so evident when she was around. Slowly, he was starting to see the silver lining, as nothing but dark clouds had been his company for several years. How was he going to tell her that he wanted more with her? How would she react? Every part of Holt's body came back to life whenever she was around and that was something he hadn't felt in a very long time. He thought about Emily and all the mistakes he made, but then without making those mistakes he wouldn't have learned the lessons on becoming a better man.

He looked out into the sky and saw how beautiful it was going to be, it was clear, no clouds in sight and a slight breeze came through the garage every now and again. What was he doing? he thought. Holt didn't ever look out at the sky and say to himself that it was a beautiful day. He was starting to see the world in a different light than he did before and it's all because of the woman on his mind. He hoped that he would hear from her at least once, or maybe he thought he should call her just to see how she was going with organising things for her sons camping trip, no, he didn't need to make it obvious he was missing her. He had to admit to himself first that this was a time he was wanting to have her in his life every day and not only on a part time basis. He thought about it all night as to how it would ever work between them. Lady told him that she liked to go with the flow, fair enough that was a casual approach to life, and he didn't see a problem with it. Holt even thought, she still held a torch for Ryan but maybe that was just the pessimistic way of looking at things.

As Holt started to screw things back into place, he heard his phone ring in the house, he knew he would miss the call, so he cleaned his hands and made his way back inside.

When he got to his phone, he saw that it was Lady's number who tried calling. Relief, happiness, and joy came over him, but then it quickly disappeared as he didn't really know the reason for the call.

Holt dialled her number and she answered, "Hey, Holt."

"Lady, sorry, I missed you; I mean your call, I missed your call." Holt frowned at his twisted greeting.

Lady laughed as Holt fumbled his words. "I just wanted to see how you were feeling today." Lady replied.

"I'm alright, just doing some small things, I'm not climbing around."

Lady wasn't surprised he was breaking the rules, "Well, you know you're not supposed to do anything." Lady told him remembering what the nurses had said.

Holt grunted before he replied, "Well I don't want to sit around, it drives me crazy."

"I can't blame you," Lady agreed before continuing, "It's such a beautiful day today, I was thinking of going to the beach for a walk on the pier, Bobby is having too much fun with Matts kids and Ryan is on his way to see him, so he wants to wait for his father, I get bored if I'm in the house too long." Lady waited to see that he caught on to what she was implying, Holt didn't need any encouragement as he wanted to see her again, so he asked,

"Do you want some company?" Holt asked staying hopeful.

"Of course." Lady replied quickly. "When would you like me to come get you?"

Holt looked at the small amount of grease on his hands but there wasn't any hard labour that made him as grubby as any other day.

"I'm ready now." Holt told her, as he wiped his hands with the cleaning cloth.

"Alright I will see you soon then." Lady confirmed.

"Well alright then." Holt replied, before they ended the call.

Chapter 13

As Lady appeared in his driveway, Holt was ready in a navy surf tank, his arms were bare, and his legs were covered. Lady stepped out of her car, another beautiful dress patterned in green leaves and small flowers. The material was hugging her figure, and she flashed her cheeky smile to complete the look.

"Ready?" She asked as she got the car ready for Holt.

"Very." Holt said as he got ready for the ride. Holt looked at Lady while they were driving, and he couldn't help himself any longer he needs to let her know what he thought about her appearance.

"You look beautiful Lady." She smiled, keeping her eyes on the road as she came to the corner, before driving on the main road,

"Thank you, Holt, although I must say you look devilishly handsome today." Holt hadn't received a compliment for years and he smiled this time almost fully.

When they pulled up to the parking lot at the waterfront, it was very busy, bustling with boats, bikes, people playing ballgames and music coming from a small cafe that was directly at the water's edge. Holt had to stop himself from groaning as he wasn't fond of crowds, but he had to remember that he was here with Lady, and he needed to ignore what was going on around him. Lady parked under the shade and made sure that it wasn't far for Holt to push along, although she didn't mind pushing the chair for him occasionally, if he let her.

When they made their way out of the car and started walking, Lady sniffed the air and looked around, "Mm coffee," she said as she looked at the coffee van that was next to the park equipment.

Without telling Lady, Holt turned his chair in the direction of the van and people in the queue made way for him quickly he got to the front right away. He held up two fingers to the owner and he handed Holt the drinks.

"Holt, thank you." Lady said, as he handed her the hot drink.

Holt put his in the cup holder on his chair and stared at her while she took the first sip.

"Really, Holt, thank you." Lady smiled and licked her lips.

"You're welcome." Holt replied, as they made their way to the pier.

They walked slowly, Holt was experienced enough to push himself along with one hand and drink with the other. He looked at the woman next to him and couldn't remember the last time he had been here. This was nice, Holt thought, being with Lady and not in a garage or working or talking about work. Just two people spending time with each other.

As Holt looked around there was no-one staring at him like he imagined just people going about their business doing what made them happy. When they reached the end of the pier there was a bench and a beautiful view of the ocean Lady sat down and Holt sat next to her in his chair.

"Thank you for coming with me, Holt it's been a very long time since I was able just to have some time and not worry about anything."

"I'm glad you called." Holt said as he finished his coffee and dropped the empty cup in the holder.

"You're glad?" Lady asked, as she lifted her sunglasses to look at him.

"Yes." Holt answered.

"Why is that, Holt?" Lady pressed on.

"Because I was thinking about you." Holt answered and looked at her as she put her glasses back down.

"I was thinking about you too." Lady answered, as she looked out at the water.

Holt felt like he wanted to kiss her all over her face, but he wasn't in the right place just yet. He didn't know how he could voice his desire to have more between them, so he went for the softer approach.

"You know what I think about?" Holt asked, "Why you always have puzzle in your hands." Holt noticed that she had a bulge in her dress pocket.

Lady laughed as she pulled the larger puzzle out and started to turn it.

"Why I have a puzzle in my hands?" Lady repeated, she looked out at the water and turned the puzzle at the same time. "I guess it's a problem and its one that I can solve." She looked at it, as it was scrambled, then turned it so it was solved.

Holt wasn't sold on the answer.

"Elaborate!" Holt said plainly.

Lady held it up to her face and really tried to think of a way to answer, then after a moment she tried to explain it as best she could. She scrambled it and held up for Holt to see.

"When it's mixed like this, its chaos, I need to turn it and look at it from every angle, then I can start to look at possibilities of slowly turning it back to the way it was." She started to turn it piece by piece until half of it was solved. "I try and do it slowly, so that if I make a mistake I can go back and try something else. Eventually every problem has a solution, it's just a matter of patience, discipline, and effort to make it work. I like to think that life is the same, it's just a matter of time before it falls into place and out of chaos, I can make order."

Holt was thinking that he was like the puzzle, and she was working on him to get back some kind of order. He also thought that she was using it as a metaphor for her own life, so he asked her, "Pretend I'm a puzzle then, and tell me what you see?"

Lady looked at him and she put the puzzle back in her pocket before she answered, "I don't see a complicated puzzle, all I see is a man, a good man, one who needs patience and understanding."

Holt nodded his head as he was finally seeing the world through hers and that it probably wasn't as bad as he always thought. Lady had her arm leaning on the top of the bench, so Holt reached out and took her hand in his, he intertwined their fingers and rested their joined hands in his lap.

"Do you think that there could be more between us in the future Lady?"

Lady looked at him and smiled, she was wondering what to say as she didn't want to come on too strong, so, she kept it light.

"I hope so." Lady said as she could see that Holt was relieved with her answer.

The sound of giggling and small feet running came up from behind them and it was her son Bobby and his father Ryan.

"Mummy." A little voice called out, and several women turned around.

"Sweetheart, what are you doing here?" Bobby threw his arms around his mother which meant that Holt had to let go of her hand.

"Hey pretty Lady." Ryan said, as he walked up to where they were sitting.

"Matt told us where you were." Ryan said, as he leaned forward and gave Lady a kiss on the cheek. Bobby's hair was wet, and he looked like he had been in the water already. Wearing sandals and his swimming outfit, complete with floaties. Lady saw the two men looking at each other and she was about to introduce them when they took care of it themselves. They shook hands and turned their attention to Lady again.

"Matt is always blabbing my secrets." Lady said, as she tickled Bobby and he giggled with delight.

Ryan decided to break the ice.

"So, what are you two up to?" Ryan asked, looking at both Holt and Lady and wiggling his eyebrows at her.

"We had a coffee and a chat." Lady said, as she was keeping things neutral.

Bobby was always moving and made Lady a bit nervous on the water's edge.

"Come here and sit down please." Lady kept saying, while Holt and Ryan were starting to talk about the camping trip that was coming up. Holt kept his eye on the boy and Ryan was also.

"Daddy, look, this man has fish." Bobby said excitedly, as there were a few people fishing. Lady stood up and took Bobby by the hand so that he could have a closer look.

"I want to go fishing." He said, as they were swimming around in the bucket.

Lady looked at Ryan and Holt as she knew, Bobby had no idea that they would be on someone's dinner plate later.

"Maybe buddy." Ryan answered.

"Ok let's go back Bobby." Lady gripped her son's hand and tried to make her way back with him.

Very quickly the boy pulled away from his mother's grip and ran over to another bucket, he lost his footing and fell over the edge.

"Bobby!" Lady screamed and ran to the water's edge, she was just about to jump in when she heard water splashing, she turned to look behind her and Holt's chair was empty. She saw him gripping Bobby in his arm and pulling him on his back. Bobby was coughing a little and crying but Holt moved through the water with ease and used breaststroke as he made his way to the stairs at the end of the pier. Lady took Holt's chair and held it in place.

The boy was crying and a little embarrassed. People were bustling all around them, but they could see that no harm had been done. Lady scooped Bobby in her arms and checked him to see if he was ok, Bobby wrapped his arms around her and wanted to hide from the people around him. Ryan helped Holt out of the water and positioned his chair so that he could seat himself again.

Cold and wet, Holt grunted at the water in his chair and started wheeling himself away. Lady saw how Holt was leaving to go back to the car and she started to walk after him, with Bobby in her arms.

"Holt!" Lady called out, but he didn't stop.

"Holt, Stop!" Lady tried again.

"What!" Holt grunted loudly as he turned to look at her.

"Where are you going?" Lady didn't understand why he was angry.

Holt didn't answer, he just wanted to get away from everyone and that's what he did. Once Bobby was settled and changed into dry clothes Lady took him by the hand to say thank you to Holt for saving him form the water. Lady made sure that Bobby was told once and for all never to run away again and he understood this time.

When Lady and her son approached Holt, he was sitting in the shade, he had taken his shirt off and had it hanging over his shoulder.

"Holt," Lady said as she reached him. "Bobby has something he would like to say to you."

Bobby looked at Holt as he took his sunglasses off and put them on his head. Bobby let his mother's hand go and walked towards his chair. Holt looked down at him, but he wasn't angry at the child. Bobby climbed into his lap and Holt helped him up.

"Thank you for saving me." Bobby said, and kissed Holt on the cheek.

Holt wrapped his arms around the boy and held him there for a minute. Holt's anger and frustration melted away and he squeezed the boy a little tighter.

Holt tapped him on the back and offered his advice.

"Next time your parents say something you need to listen, okay?"

The boy nodded, kissed Holt again and climbed down. Ryan walked up next, he thanked Holt and reached out to shake hands, but Holt just started at him.

"Ryan, can't swim." Lady said quietly.

Holt softened, reached out his hand and shook.

"We will see you at home." Ryan said, as he picked up Bobby and left.

Chapter 14

Lady was upset and she felt like everything that her and Holt had shared and felt had disappeared. She felt alien and Holt was as cold as ice. Once they were in the car Lady wanted to ask what was wrong, but Holt looked out the window, so they drove back in silence.

When Lady reached Holt's home she turned her face to him, but Holt was already opening the door and turning to get out. Lady helped with the chair and Holt started to make his way inside so he could take a shower, as the sand and salt was starting to irritate his skin. Lady followed to the door, but Holt needed to be alone.

"You should get home to your boy; he seemed upset and needs his mother." With that, Holt went through the glass door, and it closed behind him.

Lady stood outside watching him as he went into the hall and out of her sight. Lady felt lost rejected and hurt. She got back in her car and tried to fight the tears that were growing in her eyes. She didn't want to cry, but Holt had a hold on her heart, she was only human. After a few deep breaths, she let a tear fall and wiped it away then she started the car and drove home.

Holt stared at the wall in shower and thought about what it would be like if he was at full body. He hated that he was in a chair and even though he was too agitated at the time he realised that people were patting him on the back as he came out of the water with the boy. Hero? He thought grimly, what kind of hero could he possibly be, he was in a wheelchair, the only reason he dove in was because; not only was it the right thing to do, but he was an expert swimmer and was able to handle any kind of water.

Holt turned off the water and dried to get dressed while he sat in his room. He saw that Lady had cleared some things and noticed the long metal case that was in his wardrobe. It was covered in other boxes and all kinds of belongings; he pulled it out and placed it on the bed. He ran a hand over the top and took a deep breath before opening the two clips. When they popped open, he let the lid fall, and saw the two, carbon fibre covered prosthetics that were in the box. They were very advanced in technology and had mechanical fixtures that made them look like they moved naturally.

He sat back in his chair and looked out the window of his room as a slight breeze came through his curtain. His mind was taken back to what happened the day he nearly lost his life.

***

"Holt, stay still." Will yelled.

"Ah! Fuck! Hurry up!" Holt screamed out, he was limited on movement because of the prison barb wire wrapped around his legs.

"Get down Will!" Holt screamed, as he pulled his friends head down, Holt shot two more enemies that were coming right for them.

Gun shots rang across the sky, bloody war was all around them and it was a brutal time.

"Almost." Will said, as he had to cut Holt's boot free.

"Take cover!" Will said, as he blocked Holts body from an explosion that was nearby.

The adrenalin was going into overdrive and Will finally cut the last strand holding onto Holt's leg.

"Ok!" Will said, as he tied off Holts Legs with Holts belt and his own.

Will helped Holt to his feet although he was bleeding heavily, they couldn't stop. Another explosion came as a grenade went loose and was aimed directly at them.

"Man down!" Will screamed into his radio, as Holt was trying to hold his gun and shoot, Holt dropped to the ground almost to faint to keep his strength up, Holt heard a shot and Will fell on top of him.

"Fuck!" Holt yelled, as Will was bleeding from his stomach.

Holt called it in on the radio and tried to cover Will's body with his own.

They were trapped and an air strike was coming in, "Copy Mason, on our way." The radio called back.

Holt could see in the distance that the air strike was coming fast as the radio called out to him again, "Mason, you need to get out of there now!" The radio called again.

Holt grit his teeth as the pain was excruciating and he needed to get Will and himself out of the brutal battlefield. Holt screamed as he got to his feet and pulled Will up, now both men were limping and trying to cover each other.

Planes and choppers were shooting and coming closer, "Mason, get out!" Again, the radio called.

Holt was limping and screaming as he saw an enemy in the corner of his eye, he had to drop Will and aim quickly, Holt took the shot, and it landed as there was no more shooting from that direction. With loud bangs and the ground vibrating under him the air strike began. Holt shielded Will's body with his and tried to pull him out of the way. Holt was gasping for breath, he was feeling weak and started to think the end was close, as he knew they were sitting ducks. Closer and closer the explosions came until Holt couldn't run free. He pushed Will down into a ditch and just as he was about to pull himself over, Holt grasped at the ground to crawl but there was an explosion behind him, then he was flying through the air.

"Mason! Holt!"

Barely able to open his eyes, he could see blurry faces, muffled voices were all around him and he knew he was in a chopper, he was looking at the blades turning and then saw the sun come through the clouds and smoke, pain was gone, and blinding light was the last thing he saw.

"I'm sorry Holt but there wasn't anything more we could do."

The doctors walked out of the room, and he didn't want to look down at his legs. He had his head back on the pillow and stared at the hospital ceiling. He closed his eyes and wanted to scream, he had tears falling and was in too much emotional turmoil to bear. Will couldn't be saved, and Holt tried so hard, he was his best friend, and this was a torture that he couldn't handle. Holt screamed out and tore out the needles, plugs and anything else that was attached to him, he fell to the ground and started throwing things around the room. He tipped over the bed, threw the machines around and when he saw staff coming in, he was enraged even more.

Holt threw punches, and attacked the male nurses that were coming to restrain him. He punched two of them and wrestled with another. The alarm was raised, and many more nurses and security came into the room, Holt was screaming, swearing, biting, and wailing. Holt wasn't a small man, and his strength was astonishing. Another nurse came in while they took turns holding him down. Holt's face was being held to the floor and he felt a needle go into his backside. Slowly, the world went dark, he was pain free. He closed his eyes and hoped that death was coming to collect him.

Opening his eyes, he could hear the light buzzing above him. Holt tried to move his arms but then saw that he was strapped to a bed and had been sedated to calm him. He needed to be restrained as his outbursts were deadly, both to himself and others.

"Oh Holt." Emily said as she looked at him on the bed.

"What are you doing here?" Holt snapped.

"Holt don't be like that please." Emily pleaded with him and was starting to think that the man she loved had disappeared, never to return.

"Get out." Holt ordered, as he looked to the side and not at his long-time lover.

"Holt, you have no right to speak to me like that." Emily said as she had tears coming down her face.

"I said leave!" Holt said angrily, and through gritted teeth as he was in complete misery.

"What's happening?" Emily asked him, as she looked at him and didn't want to leave.

"I want to be alone Emily, I said get out!" Holt yelled at her, and this time Emily stood up and walked out of the room sobbing. Holt slammed his head back onto the pillow and prayed that this was all a bad dream.

After many months of therapy, and rehabilitation, Holt was being taken home by his older brother Roman. As they pulled into the driveway, Roman helped Holt with his chair and all his belongings. When Holt entered the house he saw his younger brother Finn, doing some alterations to accommodate for Holt's chair. There were tools everywhere, the smell of sawdust was in the air and building materials placed in piles on the ground. Finn walked over to his brother and gave him a hug.

"Welcome home buddy." Finn slapped his big brother on the back. He was happy and cheery to see Holt again in his own surroundings.

Holt went to settle into his room and Roman helped him unpack, then Finn walked in and handed Holt a letter, that was on the kitchen counter for months.

"It was from, Emily." Finn advised, before Holt took it from him and opened it.

Dear Holt,

After the last we spoke, I decided it was best if I took the job interstate. I know we had plans, to go together, but it seems that fate has had other ideas. I know you were angry, of course, not at me, but I did take your advice and do what has made me happy. I will never forget you and hope that one day you will come and visit me, you have a long journey ahead of you and I know you will get through it. You are a hero in all our hearts.

P.S. My address is on the back if you want to write, and I wish you love and happiness in the future.

Love always,
Emily.

Holt saw the date it was written, and it was well over a year ago. He never spoke to Emily after the day he was strapped to the bed, and he was ashamed to ever show his face around her again. Holt screwed up the letter and threw it in the paper basket next to the door.

"Thank you, Finn." Holt said as he was happy, he was home.

From that moment he vowed that he would try and be a better man. He didn't like who he was and didn't want the past to interfere.

"So old man?" Finn winked at Holt as he was directing to Roman.

"What?" Roman answered gruffly.

"I could use some help over the next couple of weeks, are you free?"

Roman shook his head. "No, I'm due in Peru, there is a new mine that they want searched, I have to go." Roman finished unpacking and lifted the suitcase into Holt's wardrobe.

"Okay." Finn said as he just nodded and pulled his pencil out from behind his ear.

"More work for me then." Finn whistled as he exited the room.

Roman held out a set of keys to Holt, they were from the Auto shop. While Holt had been in rehab, he decided it was best to set up Holt a space at home to work as he thought it would keep his brother out of harm's way.

"I set up the equipment in your garage, it's all ready, so when you're feeling up to it again you can keep the money coming in for yourself. I won't be returning for a while. I made the decision that running the mechanic shop from here, would be better suited for you."

Roman was stern and authoritative, he took after their father and always had the family's best interests at heart. Holt looked at the keys and reached out to shake his brother's hand. Roman shook back and had one last parting word for his younger brother.

"Promise you will behave, or I will come back and kick your ass myself." Roman slapped Holt on the back and made his way out.

Holt watched after him as he left and realised that he was lucky to have such a family. The three brothers always took care of each other, it was drilled into them from baby's age. Their mother and father made sure that it would be hell to pay if they didn't do as they were told.

Chapter 15

Holt closed the case and put it back into the wardrobe, he had come a long way from how his life was, he was grateful that he was still alive, but will always carry a grief for his friend he couldn't save. Holt knew that Will would never blame him for anything, and both men knew the sacrifices and repercussions of war. It took Holt a long time to forgive what had happened so that he could move forwards.

Holt thought about what happened at the beach, and how it was to be out in public after a long time of being at home. It was strange, but Holt was originally there with Lady, so he focused on that rather than others. The moment the little boy threw his arms around his neck to thank him, was the moment he realised that he can't stay angry at himself the way that he used to. Holt despised the way he was bound to a chair, he felt like he could never fit in with other people. He would always be an exception to things and events and it's not how he wanted people to see him.

He didn't want special treatment, but he also had to accept, that if he was going to have some kind of life, he would have to make room for it. Holt remembered what Lady said on the pier, she saw a good man, who needed patience and understanding. Holt agreed in his heart that she was right, and he also admired how she said she didn't see a complicated puzzle. He only hoped that when Lady looked at him, she did see a good man because that's what has taken him years to try and become.

As Holt thought about the way he last saw Lady, he felt guilty about the way he spoke to her. He only hoped that Lady would be patient and understand, that diving into the water today was a big step for him; as he hasn't been in water for years, and this was to save a little boy that Holt cared deeply for. Granted her son was safe and well afterwards, it still didn't atone for what happened to his friend. Holt had lost his self-confidence, although hard work and discipline was something that he knew from the army, so he has had to find a way to bring that into his everyday life. He didn't want to be the man who pushed people away again, so he needed to put a stop to it before it got too late, to make things right.

Holt went into the kitchen; he took his phone off the counter and dialled Lady's number.

"Hello Holt." Lady answered, her voice was a little flatter than usual, but Holt didn't let it get to him.

"Lady, I just wanted to see how your son was feeling." Holt asked, as he was concerned about the little boy.

"Oh, he's fine, he had a warm bath, and I checked his chest with my stethoscope, and it was all clear. Ryan has taken him for the night, he still wanted to spend time with his father. I think they were going to see a cartoon movie or something."

Holt was glad that the boy was already putting the day's events behind him, so now he wanted to know about her, "Lady, are you alright?" Holt asked as he knew he was trying to ignore an apology.

"I'm alright, I was a bit confused when I spoke to you last, but I'm alright now that you called." Lady's tone was quiet and sounded like she had been sleeping.

"Did I wake you, Lady?" Holt asked as he didn't want to disturb her.

"No, Holt I'm fine, are you alright? I should ask, I'm a bit concerned because you seemed upset before I left."

Holt realised this was his chance, "I'm sorry about before Lady, I was just trying to digest what had happened, it's been a long time since I've been out in public." Holt looked out the window as he wasn't settled on the way he apologized; it was a cheap cop out to what really happened.

"Well, I'm glad you were there, I am a good swimmer, but I would have had a bit more difficulty keeping Bobby calm and out of the water, I think you did everything perfectly, and like I said already Ryan can't swim, and the fishermen on the pier didn't look like they would have been comfortable in the water."

Holt realised that there was more going on around them, but he didn't even notice that when he was there.

"Thank you, Holt, and just to make it clear I have banned Ryan from taking Bobby to the pier, he can stay in the shallows but that's about it."

Holt was glad to hear it, "I'm glad that you pulled the mother card."

Lady laughed and understood that she did have the upper hand, especially when it came to taking her son near water.

"Are we alright Holt?" Lady asked, as she was spending a lot of time thinking about what went wrong.

"What do you mean?" Holt asked.

"I mean you and me, we were holding hands and sharing things and then it all disappeared after we got Bobby out of the water."

Holt understood that it may have seemed that way to her, but he just needed time on his own,

"We are alright Lady, like I said, I didn't realise that it was a good thing I was there, I was just a little overwhelmed with all the people that were around. I did have nice time with you, and I wanted to know if you would still go with me to the gig that we will be playing next Saturday."

Holt thought it would be nice to reassure her that he still fancied her, and he wanted to make it up to her.

"Of course, Holt, and I'm relieved to hear you say that I was dreading that maybe you hated me for taking you to the beach today."

Holt groaned as he knew she was talking jargon, "Hate, is a strong word, and I could never hate you, Lady, if anything I was starting to think, that I scared you off."

Lady laughed as she was waiting to hear those words come from Holt himself.

"No Holt, it's going to take a lot more than a grumpy attitude to get rid of a person like me, I solve puzzles remember?"

Holt nearly smiled as he was relieved.

"Well, I'm glad that you do, you might have to twist and turn me bit more until I start to make sense."

Lady was laughing uncontrollably as she had a visual of Holt being a human puzzle and she was trying to solve him, "That's a picture I won't get out of my head for a while."

Holt let out a small chuckle as he imagined what she was thinking, "It's nice to hear you laugh Lady."

Holt could hear Lady as she had a sip of a drink before she continued.

"Well, I guess I am still trying to get you to laugh, I really don't know what you would sound like, but again its part of the human puzzle I guess, you'll see Holt just give me time." Lady teased him, as she was sure she would get there.

"I look forward to it." Holt told her, as he realised the day had gone and it was dark outside. Lady yawned and she heard Holt do the same, she was tired, and her brain had been going into overdrive, she wasn't sleeping when Holt called, she was sobbing.

"I guess I will see you later Holt, you're still on house rest, you can't play the drums if you hurt yourself. I have some things to organise for my course, and I have the little one, on and off, so I trust you will be alright without me until then."

Holt felt a little low as he realised, he would be on his own for a few days, but he had practice and small jobs along the way. He could always call Lady if he felt the need to, he didn't want her to worry about him, "Yes Lady." Holt answered as he was slowly moving down the hall.

"Well alright then Holt, goodnight for now." Lady said as she yawned again.

"Goodnight Lady." Holt waited for her to hang up and after putting the phone down, he felt better after speaking to her.

***

Lady was still feeling grief for her late mother, every now and then it all came back how she felt losing her. It was something she never thought would happen in her young age, not only had Lady lost her mother, but she was also her best friend. She could talk to her about anything, and her wise advice always helped her out of problems. Lady thought about her little boy and how much her mother had missed out on, he was growing into a little man, and she would have adored him. Lady had moments of feeling like she was trapped in her problems because she always relied on her mother to help her through it. When Lady was at her lowest, her mother always picked her up, dusted her off, and set her on the right path again.

Guidance and wisdom are extremely important to Lady, and she was in desperate need of it now. As she was staring at the television, she remembered how her mother laughed and smiled, she remembered her gentle touch and caring nature. Lady sighed as she felt like she was robbed of her mother too soon, and she had to find her own way in the world, a very difficult world. She tried to listen for her mother's voice in her head, for what she would have thought of Holt and what advice she would have given, but there was no answer.

Everything was so hard, and Lady stared to feel turmoil bubble up inside of her, oh how she missed her and everything they shared. Lady pulled the blanket off the couch and lay down to sleep. Bobby was at his fathers and the house was dismally empty, she hated being alone because her boy always kept her mind occupied and busy. It felt like time was moving too slow, she was getting impatient with herself and hated feeling that way. She thought perhaps starting the course early would be better. There was an intake opening three months ahead of what she had originally planned, so she decided perhaps it was best she take it. She had saved enough money to be covered for a while and she would just work it out along the way. She could always apply for studying online, as it would drag the tuition out a little, but it was looking like the best option. She could study both in class and at home and find a small job to have some income. She reached for her laptop and opened the website, after she filled out the details and hit send, she was relieved. She needed a change, she needed to move forwards. So, after receiving the confirmation email, she closed her laptop and turned off the television. She closed her eyes, and in case her mother's spirit was around, she whispered out softly "I love you."

***

Lady fixed the big gold hoops in her ears and looked over herself one more time before she was ready to watch Holt play. She sprayed a perfume that she adored called 'Fire and Ice.' She walked around in circles in front of the mirror at her doorway and looked over the black dress she had on. She dressed it up with heels and put her favourite gold curb chain around her neck, she dressed her wrist with a simple gold bangle and added a clutch that she would use to carry her phone and keys.

Matt came into the room and whistled at her, "Hey, look at you mama, doesn't your mama look beautiful?" He asked Bobby, who was ready for the sleep over with Matt's family,

"Yes." Bobby agreed, as he grabbed his bag and stood on his tippy toes, giving his mother a kiss.

"Love you baby." Lady said, as she squeezed him tight.

"Love you, mummy." Bobby replied.

Lady was excited, nervous, and a bit sad all at the same time. She hadn't been out for an evening for years and this was all a bit new. Lady watched her boy walk out with Matt, as he walked past Lady he whispered in her ear, "Go get him mummy."

Lady laughed as they walked out, and she was ready to have a bit of fun.

Chapter 16

Lady was parking in Holt's driveway, when she saw him ready and waiting. He was wearing a black figure-hugging shirt and mesh shorts; his legs were covered in black pullovers to protect them and hide his scars. When she approached him, she could smell a delicious aroma of male scent. Holt had groomed his face, and had his hair was out of his eyes. He looked amazing in the evening light, he looked mysterious. Holt looked at Lady up and down, as she made her way over to him, hips swaying, with a seductive walk, slow movements, and a grin on her face that he knew all too well.

He was feasting with his eyes when he greeted her, "Wow!" Holt said quietly, as he ran his hand over his beard.

"Wow yourself." Lady replied, as she took his chair and put it away.

As Lady sat in the driver's seat, she turned to look at Holt, only to be surprised by a big kiss on her lips, and then he released her.

"Mm very nice." Holt said with a drawl, as he licked his lips, tasting her raspberry lip gloss.

Lady blushed, as she thought it was endearing for him to steal a kiss. She pulled up her dress to free her legs a little and Holt looked down at her thigh that was showing. His eyes followed down, to her beautiful knee, then calf muscle, lower to her small ankles and her heels with beautiful feet, and painted toenails.

"My my." Holt said as he put on his belt and stretched out his arm behind Lady's seat.

Lady was well, aware of what was happening, so she laid down the law, "Well, that will have to do for now, you need to concentrate." Lady gave her cheeky grin as she knew he was distracted.

Holt shook his head and opened his window, as the car was getting very warm. When they arrived, there were people everywhere, and Holt told Lady to drive around the back, where they would go inside. Once they arrived at the door, security greeted them and directed them. Lady said she would watch Holt from the crowd, as she didn't want to miss anything. Holt went into the back rooms where all the instruments were, and he needed to do some warming up. Lady sat at the bar and ordered herself a drink, she was more comfortable out with the crowd and thought it would be better for Holt to focus on his own.

About twenty minutes later, the lights dimmed, and then Lady saw that there were people getting ready on stage. She saw Holt being helped by a man who looked very similar to him only younger. That was Finn, Lady thought, as she watched the brothers communicate with each other.

Finn was tall and she could only imagine what their father would have looked like, as these two of the three brothers, were fascinating creatures. Holt was seated and his partner drummer was beside him. Lady could see Finn, in full view when he stepped into the light, taking the microphone in his hands. He had black hair like his brother, it was cut and styled shorter, he was broad and a little slimmer figure wise. He looked as though his arms and shoulders were strengthened by manual labour, but like his brothers they were strong. Finn wore a black tank and blue bootcut jeans, along with brown leather scuffed boots with a heel; making him gain a little height. He also had long thighs like his brother and slim waist. She couldn't see his eyes, but she imagined they must have been the trademark green like Holt's. The biggest give away was the grin, he pulled the microphone closer to his mouth and delightfully winked at the ladies.

Lady finished her drink and squeezed her way to the front. Holt had a look on his face like he was searching and when he made eye contact with Lady, it was his turn to grin. Finn looked at Lady and gave her a wink too, then he looked at Holt and he was eyeing off his younger brother.

Finn just laughed and addressed the crowd, "Well, hello everyone." The crowd cheered and whistled as Lady realised, they were in for a treat.

Finn continued, "I think I see my future wife in here tonight." Finn smiled, as the crowd erupted, every woman screamed, cheered, and blew kisses at him.

Lady held up a hand to her cheek and looked at Holt, he was grinning as he shook his head and readied himself to play. As soon as the guitar riff started Lady was ecstatic, it was the song Holt heard her play on the first day she came to care for him. and she was smitten with joy.

Lady was in awe at how Holt played, letting herself move with the music she sang, danced, and clapped her hands, all the while exchanging glances with Holt. He was in a different world, and she could see that on his face.

Holt was not thinking about pain, being an amputee or sitting in a wheelchair, he was free. Lady was in love with everything about the way they played, and she was taking everything in as it was happening around her. This man that she cared for was a different person in the night, and behind a drum set. When it was time for another song, Lady cheered and blew a kiss to Holt, he reached up his hand, caught the kiss and put it in his pocket.

"This song is for a very special Lady in the room." Finn looked over at Lady.

Lady was smiling so much her face was hurting. As it came into the second verse, she noticed how Finn lifted the microphone and put it in front of Holt. Lady was gobsmacked, Holt's voice was booming, and he was magnificent. Every woman screamed in the room and started to blow Holt kisses, they danced wildly and clapped while jumping to look at him. Finn laughed and cheered on for his brother also and then the microphone was passed again, Holt made eye contact with Lady before the words left his mouth.

Lady felt like she was glowing and realised that she was staring with her mouth open, she was hypnotised with the way Holt said the words and she felt like she was the only woman in the room. She looked around her when she finally managed to have the courage to look away and was wondering if anyone could see her blushing in the dark. The night was full of beautiful songs and as they were nearing the end of the set a drunk intruder was starting to make his way over to Lady.

Using brotherly communication, Finn signalled his brother to look out into the crowd, Holt smacked one of his sticks on the rim of the drums as it was already hanging by a small splinter. The drunk intruder was trying to chat up his

Lady. She was doing her best to ignore him, and when the lights went out, Holt slammed the splintered stick on the crash cymbal, it broke and flew across the room, smacking the unwelcome man in the nose. Lady turned around and noticed that the man was leaving, but she kept dancing and clapped her hands.

As the show was ending, it was time for the final song, and Finn dedicated it to his brothers, whom he no doubt saw as his heroes. The music started to play, and she recognised it right away, her heart warmed, goosebumps crawled up her arms, it was a beautiful song. This was a song that both men played with full hearts. The words were so powerful, and Lady could feel tears coming down her face. She looked at them as they played and sang, they were a powerful duo with their voices and the way the music was played by the other members was making its way through her bones. Holt was glancing at Lady as he played, and Finn was fully consumed in the music as he sang. It was so wonderful and beautiful; Lady would never forget what she saw this night.

This man had etched his way into her heart, and she knew that she would never feel the same if she couldn't have him in her life, she would keep the friendship as long as Holt wanted, and this would be a learning experience she would cherish. Never did she feel this way about anyone before. A stranger, who she had never met was a gift given to her, and she would be forever grateful. She had to make sure hear heart would be strong and take what was coming.

When the bar was closing, Lady met up with Holt outside the front of the venue, lots of people wanted to shake his hand and thank him for the wonderful music he played. Finn had already left as he had a long drive for a job he had to get to. As Holt waited, he saw Lady approach him, she had a big smile on her face and Holt looked at her with love in his eyes.

"Looks like you had a good time, Lady." Holt said, as he was handed a beer by someone from the crowd as a thank you.

Lady just stood there and looked at him, he was so beautiful, he was relaxed and looked like he was carefree, but just as she was about to speak, something hit Holt in the shoulder.

"I think this is yours, asshole."

Holt looked at the broken drumstick on the ground and turned his attention to the drunk jerk who was no doubt the troublemaker of the venue. Holt just popped his beer open and saw that the security guard was already getting ready to usher the man away. Holt had a big drink as he earned it after all the work he just did for the band.

After he swallowed, he thought he would admit that it was his drumstick.

"It is, I was wondering where that went."

This enraged the drunkard more and he pointed his finger at Holt, "Well looks like your all out of ammo, come on wheels, show us what you got, oh that's right you can't do much from down there."

Holt raised his eyebrow at the security guard and even though Holt was in a chair, the guard knew exactly who Holt was and thought it would be best to intervene.

"Sir, I've told you not to come here you should leave." The guard waved down a taxi and wanted to escort the man to the car.

The man stepped away staggering because of all the alcohol he consumed, as he moved from the guard he stepped right in front of Holt. Lady stood behind Holt's chair and as she was just about to push him away, Holt dropped his hand and held the wheel so the chair couldn't move.

Holt drank his beer empty and waved his finger for the man to come closer before he spoke to him, "Want me to show you what I can do?" Holt asked the man.

"What?" He slurred, in drunken spray.

In lightning speed Holt's fist flew into the man's crotch, and just as he bent over wallowing in pain, Holt spun his beer bottle in his hand smacked it over the drunk fool's head. Rolling on the floor the man was wallowing in pain, and even though the bottle didn't break, he would definitely feel it in the morning.

Holt looked at Lady with a big grin on his face, and then spoke to the man as Lady pushed him away, "A four-year-old, taught me that move."

On the way home Lady couldn't stop talking about how wonderful the music was, she was smiling laughing and always telling Holt how amazing he was. Holt just looked at her and while she was talking, he saw the smile on her face and couldn't hear anything, he was just in awe at this beautiful woman and how happy she was. Holt was the reason for it, and he had never been able to remember the last time he made a woman this happy. He never thought that he could make a difference in someone's life before, but as Lady was talking using her hands even singing various parts of her story. Holt didn't realise that he was smiling. Lady stopped at red lights before they turned off into Holt's street, and she had to do a double take as she looked at him. Her eyes widened and she was completely struck by the unbelievable surprise that was on Holt's face. She stopped talking and just started at him, his face was beautiful and the smile he had was one that she had never seen before.

Chapter 17

"Holt you're smiling." Lady wanted to let go of the steering wheel and kiss the beautiful man but then a car honked them to move on.

When they arrived home Lady turned to look at him, she thought he might kiss her but then she didn't want to make the atmosphere uncomfortable, so she went outside to organise things for Holt instead. Lady didn't want the night to be over, but she thought about her little boy and sent Matt a text to see if everything was ok with her son, Matt texted back as it was only eleven-thirty, pm and she knew that they always stayed up later.

"Oh, that's a relief." Lady said, as she put her phone away.

Holt was unlocking his front door, and he didn't want the night to end either. Holt turned to what Lady was talking about, "All, ok?" Holt asked.

Lady smiled, "Yes, he is fast asleep, the kids had a busy time and it's nice to know that he is peaceful."

"When is your son going on the camping trip?"

Lady dropped the phone back into her clutch and zipped it a little harder than needed before she answered, "Oh that, well, plans changed, Ryan had to go back early, he will be spending time with Bobby tomorrow, so he will be picking him up from Matts house in the morning."

Holt grunted as he was disappointed for the boy, Holt thought that it was all set-in stone, but obviously there must have been something that Ryan found more important than spending time with his son. Holt let Lady go inside first as he still remembered his manners.

"Probably best if Ryan leaves then no need to disappoint more than he has." Holt said it sternly, as he made his way to the kitchen for a drink, he got out some cold water from his fridge and poured them both a drink.

Lady knew what Holt was getting at, but she was also let down by the way it was all, "organised" and planned, but she knew Ryan, and she was lucky she didn't say anything to her son. Lady had a drink and changed the subject.

"So, tell me what are you working on outside?"

Holt knew she was just filling in the air between them, but he wanted to please her, so he pushed a button on his phone and then Lady could hear a click from the back door lock.

"Take a look." Holt said, as he made his way out the back with her.

When they reached the garage, Lady walked inside, and Holt turned on the lights. The old V8 Ute needed work and he was waiting for parts to arrive. Lady thought that she finally had a chance to ask her questions, "When did you discover you wanted to be a mechanic?"

Holt just looked at the old V8 Ute and shrugged his shoulders before he answered, "I was always interested in cars, even from a young age, my grandfather would always keep us around him when he was working on the engines and showed us how everything worked. All three of us know the ins and outs of an engine, but Finn liked different work in the end, and it stuck with Roman and I."

Lady looked at the machine and she would never be able to make sense of it, she didn't know anything about cars, "So, it must be the loud sounds of the engine then, or the way to get the ladies."

Holt smiled a little, as he rubbed his thumb over his beard before he continued, "The happy memories we have, or I have, fixing cars, keeps them fresh in my mind and takes me somewhere I don't have to worry or think about anything. I know how to fix it and I found that I didn't need my legs to keep myself happy when it came to choosing a career. Doing this, is from a time when things were good, before they went bad."

Lady looked at Holt as it was the first time he had really spoken about his past, being a child, mentioning his grandfather and the love for the cars, was the first time she understood that it was from family his happy memories were built upon. Lady watched as Holt moved around the car and looked at everything. She thought she should tell Holt that she was starting her course early, this was a time when he seemed to be most at peace, so she wanted to share a part of herself also, "Holt I've decided to start my course early, it would be better if I get started asap so that I can finish it, it's been on my mind and I'm eager to get things underway."

Holt moved out from under the car, "Ok so when will you be starting?" Holt asked calmly.

"Two weeks from now." Lady replied.

Holt scratched his chin as he was uncertain where this would be headed, "Just seems that its sudden to me, what's going on Lady?"

"Nothing." Lady tried to say in a convincing manner.

"So, when your busy I guess I can call you, and see how you're going then." Holt said in a low bothered tone.

"Well, it's just -" Lady wanted to try to explain.

"Just what?" Holt asked in a stern voice.

Lady shuffled her feet and shook her head before answering, "What are we Holt?"

Holt looked at her grinning as he answered her silly question.

"Well last I checked, I'm a man and you're a woman."

Lady wasn't amused so she played along.

"No! Really?" Lady rolled her eyes and dropped all guards to speak the truth.

"It just seems that every time you and I get close there is-" She stopped again. She wanted to say interruption, but she doesn't feel like her responsibilities as a mother are an inconvenience.

"A complication." She concluded.

Holt rocked his chair back and forth and he cleared his throat, he knew this was coming, so he wasn't going to avoid it, as he wanted to know for himself. Holt ran his tongue over his teeth, as he repeated what she said.

"Hm, complication." Holt locked his long fingers and rested his hands in his lap, he raised an eyebrow and partially grinned as he spoke.

"Well, we wouldn't want to complicate our perfect little lives now, would we?"

Holt watched her as she tapped her feet and started to get a little restless, she was playing with her necklace and then sighed as she dropped her arms by her side and looked at Holt before she spoke.

"Holt, we never discussed what we really want from each other, or where this, whatever this is, might be headed."

Holt was always fascinated with the way she was able dance around certain topics in a very polite and clever way. He kept his gaze on her, she was very, very, clever. She was waiting for Holt to take the lead and despite pacing himself for her, he decided that he would answer her honestly.

"Well!" Holt started, as he raised a hand and pointed out with a long finger flipping it between Lady and himself.

"This is what it looks like when one person is in a wheelchair and the other isn't, this is what it looks like when one of us is respectfully going at the others pace and waiting to be fit into the other persons schedule."

Lady frowned as she was momentarily offended, "What do you mean fit in-" she wanted to retort back.

"Lady!" Holt stopped her. "When was the last time you did something that made you truly happy?"

"Well, I am happy." Lady replied, very quickly.

"Right!" Holt said, while flashing his beautiful teeth, although he wasn't convinced, Holt sat himself up and leaned on his arm rest before he spoke.

"I will explain it to you in a way that you will understand then. When I look at you Lady, I see a scrambled puzzle. You carry the weight of the world on your shoulders and try to fix others because it distracts you from working on yourself. You know exactly what you want, and what will make you happy, but you put it all in a small box, and placed it on the highest shelf; because you don't think that what you want really matters, on account of others and how they might feel. It's either that or you are still in love with Ryan, and you're just passing time; keeping things casual because it makes everything easier for you and your son."

Lady was momentarily cut by the sharp ending of his answer, but she looked to the ground instead of letting a temper flare inside her, she sighed because Holt was right, every word was the truth, he knew her like he knew his engines. She surrendered, temper disappeared, and she lifted her head to look at him, Holt needed to know the truth about Ryan, or this would always be an interference in any life they would try to have together.

"I guess your right on all accounts accept one; Ryan is engaged to be married at the end of this year, he has two children with a woman that he met while working, one is

Bobby's age, and the other is on the way. It took me a long time to digest that I wasn't the only woman in his life, but my love for him was shattered the day I got the phone call from his mistress. Ryan and I have no future together, we try to stay civilised around our son, and communicate on the grounds of what's best for him. It hasn't always been easy the love and trust I had was all disposed of, there is no love there."

Holt wanted nothing more than to have a one on one with Ryan for taking advantage of the beautiful woman in front of him, his rage was clawing at his stomach.

Lady continued after pausing for a moment, as it took a lot for her to speak those words, "Once the baby is born, I'm well aware, that he won't be returning for many months, and my son will be going through a hard time, and I will have to pick up the pieces that will be left behind again. I thought that I could move things along by applying early and then I wouldn't have to rely on Ryan for Bobby's needs. Meeting you was unexpected Holt, I didn't think that I would find myself in this position and I'm not fitting you into a schedule, I just have my son's interests as a priority over mine."

Holt could see she was searching for order in the chaos, but there was one side of her scrambled thoughts he wanted to solve so he asked, "Where will that leave us Lady."

She couldn't find an answer, the only thing she knew was that Holt was a man that she wanted to have in her life, and deep down she wanted more, much, much, more. Lady decided to throw the ball and let Holt take the lead, as she was unsure what to do or say.

"What do you want Holt?" Lady asked, with all sincerity in her eyes and voice.

Holt slowly moved his chair forwards and reached out his hand and took hold of hers, he locked their fingers together. Lady smiled as she met his gaze, he pulled her closer and then lifted her hand up to his mouth and playfully nibbled on her fingers. She took another step forwards and Holt wrapped his arm around her waist, pulled her onto his lap and cradled her in his arms, with a low rough voice he spoke softly, "Do you really want to know what I want?" Holt asked while nipping at her hand.

"Yes." Lady whispered as she was overwhelmed with desire. He lowered her in his arms, and he kissed her cheek and moved to her ear, gently rubbing his chin on her face as he spoke.

"I want to stop talking, I want you to stop thinking." He ran his lips over hers and nipped at her chin.

"I want to take off that pretty little dress." Holt's eyes were green emerald and glowed as Lady was feeling her skin blush. Holt kissed her earlobe and made his way down her neck; his hot breath made her shudder with anticipation as he kept going.

"I want to tease you." Holt ran his hand up from her feet to her calf, he massaged it gently and continued to run his hand up her thigh and over her belly and hips, he moved his hand to her chest and snapped the buttons open on her bust, he pushed his hand in the gap and found only Lady underneath. He cupped her breast and ran his thumb over her nipple, he looked into her eyes and then in a low rumbling voice he finished his request.

"I want to be inside you."

Chapter 18

Holt closed his mouth over hers, still fondling her chest, Lady wrapped her arms around his neck and ran her fingers through his hair, she kissed him back hard and even nipped at his beard, messing his hair, she was grabbing his thick mane with greedy hands. Holt slowly made his way up to the back door, trying to find his way was bumpy, he was crashing into walls and missing turns as they were both kissing furiously and feasting on each other's mouths. Holt was pushing them along with his hands, Lady nuzzled into his neck and ran her tongue over his earlobe. Holt could hardly breath he was so aroused, and his blood was boiling over, he could only mutter, "Dear God." He used walls, door jams and anything he could find to pull them along, it was the longest, complicated, and fumbling trip to the bedroom he ever had. He stopped in front of the mattress and Holt lifted Lady by the hips on to the bed. Holt moved himself on top of her and they rolled around gripping at clothing, kissing, touching, gasping, moaning, trying to breath, they were both frantic with demanding chemistry.

Holt removed his shirt and threw it on the floor, he pushed his shorts and underwear off to free himself. Holt easily lifted Lady onto his lap with his strong and long arms, so she was straddling him. Holt cupped her bottom and squeezed. Lady was wrapping her arms around his neck and kept kissing him more. Holt took hold of her dress and spread it open, buttons popped and flew across the room. With one swipe of with his hand the small lace underwear she was wearing was pulled off and thrown away. Lady was too busy kissing his arms, shoulders and neck all the things she wanted to feel and thought about were being fulfilled, she was just as demanding as he was, and they had the same pace in showing it.

Holt pushed her down onto her back with her legs still spread around his hips, he ran his hands up her sides and then lowered himself onto her, he kissed her from her hips up to her stomach, he moved slowly towards her breast, he looked into her eyes as he ran his lip over her nipple and then opened his mouth and moaned as he took her into his mouth. Lady threw her head back and gasped out loud as he played with her, she writhed under him as he fondled her with his tongue, he teased, nipped, and suckled. He wanted to eat her flesh and bone, bite after delectable bite. He ran his long rough hand down her stomach, Lady was panting with pleasure and the heat that was rushing through her, this was something that she never experienced before. This was all different, this man, this feeling was all so overwhelming with pleasure.

Holt let her breast go, gently pinching her nipple between his lips, he looked into her eyes as he gently spread her thighs with his hand, he moved his fingers to her wet, hot centre and he cupped her, they both moaned in pleasure. Holt bit his lip as she was ready for him, and he kissed her deeply groaning in his throat. He licked her lips and her cheeks, as he spread her open with his fingers. Holt stropped and looked into her eyes as he gently pushed a finger inside of her and Lady arched her back as the feeling of his hand was sweet torture. Holt ran his teeth along her jaw and was in feral heaven, he moaned and then pushed another finger deep inside her.

"Mm fuck." Holt whispered, as he buried his face in her neck and nipped at her skin.

He was a starved man, and this woman was his very own, all you can eat buffet. Lady was losing control, thrusting her hips and needy, she was clawing at his shoulders, she called out his name as she was going to go over the edge.

"Holt! I need you inside me."

Holt only thrusted his fingers more, harder, and faster, as she was fighting the ecstasy that was ready to erupt, he nibbled at her ear and growled at her.

"Let it come baby, come for me." He grinned, ear to ear as he said it.

Holt ran his tongue into her mouth and Lady tried to gasp as she was going over, she arched her back and tried to call out in pleasure. Holt was taking her puffs of breath, screams and moans into his mouth, as he enjoyed the way her body rocked for him. When she was coming down, he released her mouth and looked into her eyes, they were deep pools of blue, he flashed his grin while saying, "Yes, that's it baby." Holt drawled the words, as he was pleased with himself.

He pushed his hips between her thighs and lifted her legs so that her feet were over his shoulders, he braced himself on top of her with one arm and his thighs. He reached down to take hold of his hard shaft, and he softly, slid himself up and down her wet entrance to make himself slick for her. Lady moaned and closed her eyes at the feeling of him, he wanted to watch her as she would take him.

"Look at me Lady!" He said in a gruff tone.

Lady opened her eyes to look at him and then he pushed himself inside her only a little. Lady threw her head back gripping the sheets and Holt's shoulder, she gasped at the feeling of him, thick and hard, he was wonderful. He filled her with his large body, and he moved his hips slowly, pulling in and out until he was fully submerged to the hilt. Holt licked his lips as he watched her, he was primal and loved it. Holt lowered himself and kissed her deeply, he was hanging on to a hair thin tether as he didn't want to lose control. He moved his hips back a little and with one long hand he pushed down on her belly, catching his breath, he needed her to hold still, she was teasing with her cheeky grin, so he lifted her head and took her bottom lip between his teeth. He held it there as he snarled at her.

"Don't move!"

Holt was going wild on the inside, she wrapped her legs around his waist and Holt lost the ability to think, he pushed her down, and threw her ankle behind his shoulder, then he gripped the back of her thigh and spread her wider. Like a wild animal he mated with bruising grip on her skin, he looked down at the glorious view of himself going in and out of her, he thrust hard and fast, he feasted with his eyes as her breast bounced up and down with his movements. He so desperately wanted it to last forever, this feeling of being inside her. Holt closed his eyes and tried to control the beast, but it wasn't possible. He gripped her hip, and he swore out loud as he was going over the edge, he grabbed a fist full of her hair and rubbed his teeth along her throat.

Moaning, heavy breathing, hips pumping, the smell and sounds of sex filled the room. Holt pressed his face against her cheek he was baring his teeth when he told her what he wanted.

"I'm want to come inside you!"

Lady only screamed out the word, "Yes!" As she wanted to feel everything.

Holt kissed her hard and growled as every muscle in his body went rigid, he filled her and thrust until he was empty, this woman was grasping his very soul and tearing it out of him. When he was spent, he collapsed on top of her and fought hard to breathe. Lady wriggled, as she was fighting for air herself. Holt moved them, so they were facing each other, and when he looked at her lazy smile and rosy cheeks, he was happy and content.

In the morning Lady woke to Holt lightly snoring, with his body wrapped around her. She wasn't able to move. She smiled as she looked around her and thought how peaceful it was and loved the way his body was close to hers. She wriggled a little, as she reached for her phone, she wanted to check for any messages that might be waiting in her inbox. There was one from Ryan saying, that he would be bringing their son back after lunch time. Lady put her phone down and Holt stared to stir as he woke slowly. She rolled to face him, and he turned to look at her gently caressing her arm.

"Morning Lady." Holt said, quietly as he still looked sleepy.

"Morning Holt." Lady replied, and she could only smile as she looked at the man she adored.

He kissed her and held her until he was fully awake, laying in his arms was wonderful and she closed her eyes as she took it in. The sounds of birds chirping, and a light breeze coming through the window, feeling the rise and fall of Holt's chest and listening to his calm and relaxed breathing. It was all something that Lady had hoped for and more. The sunlight was working its way through the morning clouds and shining beautifully through the window, it was the start of a nice day ahead.

Holt pressed his lips to her forehead. "Did you sleep well Lady?"

She just looked up at him and played with his small chest hair. "Yes, very well." Lady replied.

Holt had the same smile from the night before, and she ran a finger over his lips.

"You have such a beautiful smile Holt, I'm glad I got to see it."

He kissed her again and, he took in a deep breath and stretched. Lady could see the muscles and fine details of his body, there were small scars and dents on his thighs and torso, a long thin scar between his thigh and hip. She never saw those before, but she was able to see everything in the clear morning light now. She was in awe at his beauty, his broad chest, and shoulders, his strong stomach, all perfect down to his naval. Lady couldn't help but giggle as she looked at his hair, it was tasselled and stood up in all different directions. Lady only imagined that her own hair was looking just the same. Holt picked up her hand grinning widely and kissed it, he was in desperate need of a shower and food.

"Come shower with me, Lady." Lady only smiled and followed.

As Holt sat on the shower bench, he turned the water on and took Lady's hand as she stepped in. She sat on his lap and started to take the body wash and sponge to clean them both. Holt enjoyed her spoiling him and he also enjoyed the view from behind as he scrubbed her back. When she reached up her arms and washed her hair, he was admiring the way the soapy bubbles slid down her curves, he enjoyed seeing her like this, it was almost like watching a goddess bathe in milk and flower petals. He turned her to him, took hold at the back of her thighs and pulled her on to his lap so they were face to face. He couldn't get enough of her and was wanting more. Lady slowly rocked her hips back and forth teasing him as she kissed his cheeks and neck. Holt only tightened his grip on her thighs and ran his mouth down to her breast. Lady arched her back a little, so she could enjoy the view of the man in front of her. He was looking into her eyes as he played with her.

Holt saw that her lips were full, and her cheeks were flush, she was growing the need in her blood again and she wanted him all the same. His arousal made him hard, and she was bracing herself with her hands against the walls. He ran his hands up her thighs and cupped her bottom, he lifted her and slowly lowered her onto him, they both moaned out loud, as she was being wrapped around him again, she rode him slowly and he fondled her breasts using his mouth and tongue.

He adored this woman he could feel the same appetite rising that he had only hours ago. She was picking up the pace and he leaned his head back against the wall as he held one of her legs up and placed it on the bench, he wanted to be deep inside her, she was moaning and beautiful, she was seductive and sexy, as the water ran down her body and her hair was slicked back.

He gripped her hip and wrapped his hand around her neck, holding her back softly as he wanted to see more of her, "Beautiful, Lady," he whispered as he watched her move.

"God that feels so good." He said, as he licked her chest and teased.

"Oh, Holt," she said, as she gripped his shoulder, Holt grinned as he knew she was close.

"Holt, I'm coming." She gasped, as she held onto his shoulders and rode harder, she cried out in pleasure.

Holt was pleased and loved it when she came for him.

"Yes! That's it come." Holt whispered, as he slapped her backside playfully and ran his rough hand all over her body.

Lady opened her eyes and looked at him she was sighing with pleasure, as he moved his thumb over her lips and kissed her hard. He was pulling and pushing her, as he wanted to feel more.

"You feel so good." Holt said, as he kissed her neck and licked her skin, he was drowning in pleasure.

"Yes, that's it baby." Holt whispered into her mouth before he kissed her deeply.

She moved faster again for him, and Holt looked down seeing them joined. He leaned his head against the wall as he looked into her eyes and spoke.

"I'm going to come baby." Holt groaned, as he gripped a little harder around her neck and hip.

He groaned out as he filled her again and nipped at her breast as he was overcome with blissful pleasure. Lady looked into his eyes and saw the green glow, she smiled at the sight of his masculine body, as she ran her hands down his chest. Holt pulled her close and wrapped his arms around her, they stayed joined, and he kissed her until he receded.

Chapter 19

After a long shower, Lady wrapped a towel around herself and went to her car, she always carried spare clothes. Her dress did its job she thought with a smile on her face, as she remembered the crumpled heap of material on Holt's bedroom floor. When she went back inside, Holt was sitting on the bed dressing himself and they both heard his stomach growl. Holt couldn't help but chuckle at himself.

"Oh hungry? "Lady asked, as she removed her towel and pulled on her bra and underwear.

Holt pulled her close, and he kissed her chest grinning ear to ear.

"Very hungry," Holt replied, as he tilted his head back and looked into her eyes.

"I want you to stay with me today, Lady, no work, just stay."

Lady ran her fingers through his hair and looked in his eyes lovingly.

"I will Holt, I'm not leaving." Lady smiled at him and was so happy with him wanting her to stay.

Holt kissed her chest again.

"I'm cooking you, breakfast," he grinned, as he slapped her backside playfully.

"Oh, what service, sounds good to me, chef Holt." Lady said, smiling.

Lady could hear Holt start to move around as he got busy making a meal for them both, bacon and eggs with toast and big cups of coffee was on the menu. Lady could smell the delicious food as she changed the sheets and made the bed. She carried them into the laundry and turned on the machine. When Lady walked into the kitchen Holt shook his head at her.

"What?" Lady asked.

"No work!" Holt told her, as he flipped the bacon.

"Oh grumbles, it's just habit and I know where everything is." Lady replied.

She sat at the table and watched Holt in his domain, he cooked with care and placed everything on the table, he was very hospitable. She felt special and enjoyed being waited on. Holt sat next to Lady and told her to dig in. Lady couldn't help but take huge bites of everything, she was starving and made small happy noises when she drank her coffee.

"Oh Holt, this is wonderful," she said as she scooped up more eggs and chewed with delight.

Holt just looked at her while she ate, she was a woman who showed no mercy when it came to food. He took a sip of his coffee and was grinning again because she was happy.

"Your welcome Lady, I thought it would be nice to have someone take care of you for a change." Holt scooped up his food and started to eat.

Lady swallowed and looked at Holt as he said those words, never in her life has a man ever said that to her, and the love she was feeling for him was exploding on the inside. She dropped her fork and reached for his hand while she stood up from her chair. Holt wasn't sure what was happening, so he moved his chair back, Lady kissed his hand and crawled into his lap, he wrapped his arms around her, and she hugged him tightly, she desperately wanted to say I love you, but she didn't want to look like a fool, so she kissed him instead.

"Thank you, Holt, you don't know how much it means to hear you say that."

Holt held her face and saw she was overwhelmed with emotion, her eyes were looking into his deeper than they ever have before, Holt ran his fingers over her cheek.

"You deserve kindness and the best Lady, don't let anyone treat you different."

He kissed her and she released him to go back to her chair.

After the wonderful meal Lady was tempted to help with the dishes, but Holt made her another coffee so she could sit and enjoy it while it was hot. She watched him clear up and admired the view, his long arms and strong back, they were so beautiful, Holt just turned around as he caught her staring.

"Day dreaming?" He asked her.

"Oh, I could just sit here and watch you do the dishes for the rest of my life." Lady replied, in a sigh and blank look on her face.

Holt paused momentarily as he was drying a plate, he put it away and with a soft smile he looked at her. Lady's eyes suddenly widened as she realised what just happened.

"Did I just say that out loud?" She asked, then panicked and stood up. "Oh, dear I meant -, It was more like -"

Holt just held up his hand to stop her as he made his way over to her, he reached out and took both of her hands in his to calm her. "It's alright Lady, I didn't mind."

Lady kept trying to soften what happened, "It was more like a sudden thought- Like a daydream-" She was rambling.

Holt stopped her again.

"Lady!" He said, as he held her face in his hands, "I didn't mind." He said again and kissed her lips.

"Ok." Lady said and sat down again to finish her coffee.

As Holt went back to his duties, she drank her coffee cup empty then her phone beeped loudly.

Saved by the bell, she thought, as she was a little embarrassed about what she said before.

"What?" She said, as it was midday already on the kitchen clock, "Where did the day go?" She had a look at the screen on her phone, she saw a message from Matt, he said that Bobby was crying, and she needed to come home, "Oh no," she said as Holt was still moving around the kitchen, "I'm sorry, Holt but Bobby is crying, I need to go."

Holt closed the fridge as she seemed unnerved.

"Alright, do you need me to go with you?" He asked.

"No, no it's alright, I just need to see what's happened, I will call you later. I had a beautiful time."

Lady walked over to him and kissed him, Holt didn't want to let her go, but he knew she couldn't stay. Holding on to her fingers, he slowly let hers slip out of his grasp as she was leaving.

"I had a beautiful time with you Lady, let me know later." Holt said softly.

"I will." Lady replied, as she walked out the front door.

When Lady arrived home Bobby ran to her, and Ryan was still there, "What's going on?" Lady asked, and Ryan walked over to her and tried to explain, "I told Bobby about the baby, and he thinks I don't love him anymore."

Lady ruffled her son's hair as he was hugging her legs, "Bobby that's silly," she kneeled and hugged her boy.

Ryan was getting frustrated and tried to assure his son he would be back, but Bobby didn't want to speak to his father, so he ran inside to his room. Lady stood up and Ryan saw she was upset, "Lady, I know it's hard."

"No, Ryan, just go!" She said in a low tone as she didn't like yelling and screaming, even though it was hard to fight the urge to really voice her thoughts, she thought it would be best to go inside and started to walk away.

"Lady!" Ryan said, as he wanted to try to clear his mind. "Lady, stop!" He said as he held her arms and tried to speak.

"No, you stop!" Lady said, as she moved out of his grip. "You are unreliable and break every single promise you make."

"Come on, Lady." Ryan said as he tried to be blameless.

Lady took one look at his grin, and she grew angry, she pointed out her finger and stood right in front of Ryan's face.

"You lied to me, you cheated on me and still lie to my face, you said you were taking him on a trip and cancelled again, I never told him because I knew it would never happen, I'm tired of patching up your mistakes and seeing our boy get hurt because of your lack of commitment."

"I don't need this." Ryan scoffed, as he turned to leave but Lady wasn't finished.

"I'm done with picking up the broken pieces Ryan, and I sure as hell mean it, you can count on that."

Ryan turned around with a whirlwind of anger in his eyes. He took two steps and lowered his face to hers. "What do you want me to do? Leave and never come back?"

Lady smiled and stood tall as she was waiting for this very opportunity.

"Only come back when he can see you, wherever and whenever, he needs or wants to, but until that day comes Ryan, don't bother!" Lady turned to walk away, and Ryan shook his head, he knew exactly what she meant.

It was back to the beginning, being closer to their son, it was all the same argument, only this time Ryan knew she meant it. Ryan slapped his thigh as he was out of any defence. He looked around at the house and waved to his son who was looking through the window, only Bobby didn't wave back he just closed the curtain, so Ryan ran his hands over his face and turned away.

As Lady heard Ryan's car leave, she wouldn't have been surprised if he never returned. She had put her foot down, and one day she would explain it to her son when he was old enough. Bobby needed to understand the whole story, it just wasn't time yet. She went into his room and sat on his bed. Bobby was playing with his toys and didn't seem upset anymore. Lady moved onto the floor next to him and Bobby crawled into her lap and stayed there. She reached behind her and pulled the blanket and pillow off the bed, wrapping him in her arms she had to be strong and comfort him despite how she was feeling.

"Did you dance mummy?" Bobby asked. Lady was relieved that he was happily talking and not crying anymore.

"Yes, who told you I was dancing?" She asked with a smile on her face.

"Matt told me you went dancing." Lady had to laugh and kissed his head.

"Yes, I was dancing it was fun, Holt plays the drums very well you would like it, maybe he can show you someday?" She said as she pushed back a little curl from his eyes.

"Is Holt happy yet?" Bobby asked innocently, but Lady was trying hard not to laugh.

"Yes, he is happy." She said trying to stay serious.

"Does Holt have babies?" Lady just froze as she didn't want her son to be thinking about things like that, and she didn't really know the answer.

"I'm not really sure sweetheart but, I don't think he does." She said, as she cuddled her son closer.

"I want to fix cars again." He said with a smile as he played with his mother's hair.

Lady thought about Holt and the way he spoke about becoming a mechanic, she couldn't help to think that her son was finding joy in cars like Holt did, and it was causing her to think too much again.

"Maybe someday, I'm starting my course soon and we will be together again during the day isn't that good?" Lady said to try and change the subject.

Bobby nodded and yawned as he was tired from being upset, he closed his eyes and Lady stroked his cheeks as he started to breathe into sleep. She stayed there and touched her lips to his forehead. She took in the smell of her son's scent, he still smelled like a baby to her, and she never wanted to give away these moments. She wrapped the blanket around them and closed her eyes and fell asleep.

***

Holt grew restless as he moved out from under the car, he picked up his phone and called Lady.

Chapter 20

"Hello, Lady's phone." Holt frowned at the very new and unfamiliar voice that answered.

"Who is this?" Holt asked, with a temper flare.

"Oh, it's Matt, I'm Lady's neighbour, she was asleep, I will get her for you," Holt could hear how Matt went to Lady and passed her the phone as she stepped out of the bedroom, "It's Holt Lady," Matt said as he handed her the phone with a wink and smile on his face. "Oh gosh!" She said as she took the phone, "Holt, I'm so sorry."

Holt took a breath as he was relieved, she was alright, "Lady what's happening?" He asked and started to continue to fix the car he was working on.

"I don't want to bore you with the details but, Ryan and I had an altercation, Bobby was sad, and I cuddled with him and then we both fell asleep. Matt let himself in to check on us, but we are all alright, so you don't need to worry."

Holt grunted.

"What kind of altercation?" Holt asked as he thought it would have been best, he didn't go along for Ryan's sake.

Lady sighed before she answered.

"Ryan told Bobby about the baby on the way, and then he thought that his father wouldn't love him anymore."

Holt ticked his tongue in sympathy, as he was feeling anger for the boy.

"Bobby ran into his room and then Ryan wanted to try and start a spiel about things, but I put my foot down and asked him to leave."

Holt was happy Lady stood up for herself.

"Well sounds like it's for the best then." Holt replied as he kept his eyes on the work.

"It's just small things, when I was holding him in my arms, I just stayed with him it happens when you're a mother."

Holt shook his head as he didn't want her to feel like she had to make any kind of excuse.

"Lady it's alright you don't need to explain."

Holt said as he trusted her fully and never questioned her loyalty.

Just then Lady thought that perhaps the cars Holt was working on might help.

"Maybe tomorrow or during the week, I can bring him to look at the cars it, might cheer him up if you don't mind."

"Of course you can Lady, you're both welcome here anytime you should know that already." Holt wiped his hands as he was ready to move on to the next task.

"Thank you, Holt." Lady wanted to tell him that she missed him, but she just said pushed that thought away.

Holt heard Lady giggle as she sounded busy.

"Well, I have things to do here as I skipped my own duties yesterday." Lady smiled with the cheeky memories as to why she skipped cleaning her own home.

"I understand that." Holt replied as he couldn't help but smile also.

"I will see you tomorrow then Lady, have a good night with your boy."

"I will, goodnight, Holt." Lady told him and hung up her phone.

Holt stopped to think about the time he had with her, he couldn't help but replay the entire night and morning in his head. He was smitten with her, and he knew there was no way out of it. Even though they hadn't known each other for years, it had still been enough time to fall for her. Love was something he thought was out of his reach for a long time, but when he thought about the very first day, he met Lady, and the time they had shared together, he knew his life would never be the same without her.

The next day, when Lady arrived at Holt's home, she sat in her car and took a deep breath. Making her way out she he opened the back door and let her son out of the car. Holt was already working, and she was a little nervous, once she walked over to him, she wasn't sure what to do, so she kept watching him to try and read his body language.

The moment Holt saw her, his eyes lit up and he made his way over to her, even though her son was with her, she couldn't ignore how she was feeling about him. She could see Holt was happy, and then he reached out for her. Holt didn't hesitate to pull her into his lap, he wrapped his arms around her and kissed her on the mouth.

"Morning beautiful." Holt's voice was soothing and the feeling of his body touching hers again was instantly calming. Holt had no problem greeting her warmly and Lady wrapped her arms around his neck happily.

"Morning Holt." Lady looked at her son and Bobby only smiled.

"Hey champ." Holt said as he held out his hand to the boy.

"Hi." Bobby said and wrapped his little hand in Holts to shake.

Bobby was young but he could see that the adults were close, and Holt was happy, so seeming unbothered by the greeting, Bobby walked over to the cars in the garage.

"Can I help you again today?" He asked, as he was looking at the car on the hoist. Lady only smiled and nodded at Holt before he answered.

"Of course you can, I might need your little hands again, the part I was waiting for finally arrived."

"Yay!" Bobby jumped with joy and Lady stood to go inside.

"Don't worry Lady he will be fine." Holt assured her and she had no doubt that her son was in safe hands.

"Okay." Lady said and walked to the front door.

As Lady was having a quiet moment, she could hear the laughter and giggles from her son. She imagined what it would be like to experience this all the time. She was thrown into confusion about what she wanted, she thought about the years she was on her own with her son, and realised she never really had the full family experience. She was never married and never experienced a husband that would come home from work every day. There was so much she missed out on, but maybe it just wasn't the right time.

She didn't really know how things were supposed to work, how were her and Holt supposed to spend time together, or did Holt still want to see her every other day. "Just go with the flow," she thought as she looked at the pile of paperwork. It wouldn't be long before this would possibly be done by someone else or Holt himself. Then just like a lightning bolt, she remembered she stopped taking birth control years ago. Panic struck her, she picked up her purse and keys and went outside.

"Holt! Lady called out walking quickly.

"Yup." Holt called back, as he was distracted with Bobby's feet on his face again.

"I have a quick errand to run, would you be alright with the little one for ten minutes?"

"What do you need?" Holt asked, out of interest.

"I need to make a quick trip to the pharmacy." Lady said, as she looked restless.

Holt stopped and lifted her son to the ground again.

"Everything alright Lady?"

"Oh Holt!" She said as she lightly stomped her foot on the ground. She took her phone out and sent him a message saying, she wanted to get the morning after pill.

"Check your phone." Lady told him and crossed her arms.

Holt frowned as he pulled his phone out of his pocket. When he opened the message, he didn't show any expression, instead he asked Bobby to go fill up a bucket with water out in the front yard. While the boy was busy, Lady walked over to Holt. He took her hands in his and with a sombre expression on his face he spoke very quietly.

"Lady, I'm not worried about anything."

Lady shook her head, "I need to be responsible Holt." She looked over to her son who was splashing in the water.

"Come here." Holt said as he sat her down on his lap, he pressed his cheek to hers and he put his mouth to her ear to whisper.

"The impact that I suffered, caused damage to different parts of my body. After they stitched me back together a few times, I was told that there was a very high chance I wouldn't father any children."

Lady's heart sank and Holt only wrapped his arms around her.

"I'm sorry Lady, I wanted to tell you earlier but-" Holt's words trailed off as he couldn't find any more to say, he only shook his head and tightened his arms around her. She moved her head so that she could look into his eyes, Holt' s green, emerald eyes, looked like they were in world of pain. Lady glanced again at her son, and he was happily floating sticks in the small bucket.

"Holt, I'm so sorry." Lady said as she caressed his face.

Holt just pressed his forehead to hers. "Lady, I understand if you see me differently-"

Lady kissed Holt to silence him, and she wrapped her arms around his neck and pressed her cheek to his. "It doesn't change anything for me Holt, I can promise you that."

Holt sighed as he buried his face in her neck, then he took a deep breath before releasing her.

"Holt, you can talk to me about anything, just remember that." Lady kissed him again then she slowly stood up. She still had work to get through, so she made her way inside. Holt was relieved although he still had some fear and doubt lingering.

As the afternoon approached, Lady could see that her son was growing restless and started to get anxious for his evening routine. Lady packed things away and started to round up her things go home. Holt had been busy, and the V8 Ute was finally done. As Lady made her way out to the garage, she could see Bobby in the driver's seat, his tiny feet were dangling as Holt was pushing on the gas pedal with his hand.

"Turn it over." Holt said, and Bobby's tiny hand turned the key.

A great roaring noise came out and smoke from the exhaust pipe. When Lady looked at her son's face, he was smiling so big it brought a tear to her eye. Once the car had been turned off again, Holt gave the little boy a high five and thanked him for his help. Holt made his way over to Lady, as he could see she was ready to leave.

"All fixed?" Lady asked as she could see Bobby jumping and skipping with happiness.

Her son was covered head to toe in grease and every other element there was, and when she looked at Holt, he was wearing the same look.

"I fixed it mummy." Bobby said as he walked over to her.

Lady just laughed and looked at Holt as he was happy the boy could take all the credit. Lady walked over to the tired man in the chair and bent down to give him a kiss. Holt, as filthy as he was grabbed Lady on the face and kissed her hard.

"Oh no." Lady said as she giggled, and Holt kept kissing her and smearing his face on hers. Bobby was laughing and found it funny because his mother was covered in muck.

"Ha ha, you look like us now mummy." Bobby said, pointing and laughing. Holt released her and Lady just slapped him on the arm playfully.

"Yes, think we all could use a shower." Lady said as she looked at Holt raising his eyebrows at her.
"Can we come back mummy? I have holidays now." Lady looked at Holt, but then smiled as she was trying to find an answer.

Chapter 21

"How long are your holidays?" Holt asked, the boy.

Bobby looked to the sky and scrunched up his nose as he wasn't sure, so Lady answered for him.

"Two weeks." Lady said, as she wiped her nose with her tissues. "We were waiting for the weather, before making any plans, as it can change from one moment to the next, especially here."

"Hm, two weeks." Holt repeated, before he continued, "If it's alright with your mother, we might be able to have a day trip somewhere."

Lady nodded her head as she did want to take her son to a beautiful surf beach, it was a bit of a drive, but it was the one beach that had beautiful stones and shells which she liked to collect. It had been years since she had been and really wanted to go back.

"Well, I need to check and see what we can do, and then we will be able to sort it out." Lady said as she winked at Holt.

"Okay." Bobby replied as he wasn't really bothered by the answer, he was just over the moon that he fixed a car, and Holt just nodded at Lady waiting for her to spill the beans.

"I do have one thing I would like to do; would you really like to come along?" Lady asked as she was a little surprised that Holt mentioned it.

"It was my idea; I want to spend time with both of you." Lady felt a flutter as he said the words, she was only questioning it hours ago and like someone could hear her thoughts, she received an answer, but then she remembered that Holt had work, so she was momentarily confused.

"But, Holt, what about your business?" Holt just grinned as he looked at her.

"It's my business, that's the beauty of it, I can work when I want." Lady smiled as it was the truth.

"I like that answer." Lady said with a smile as she hoped that maybe one day, she would be able to do the same. Holt reached out for her, he wrapped his arms around her and pulled her into his lap, he pressed his forehead to hers and closed his eyes. He was hopeful that what he told her earlier wouldn't change things, so he decided to stay optimistic and kissed her goodbye.

"I will speak to you tomorrow then, Holt." Lady said, as she smiled at him and touched his cheek while he released her.

Lady wanted to step away, but again, he was holding on to her fingers and he let hers slip slowly. She laughed as she knew this would be how they would part all the time. Holt was inwardly entertained as he watched them both fussing around the car, the boy was cheeky and made his mother run around in circles, while she was trying to stay serious and get him in the car.

"Phew." Lady said, in the distance as she was seating herself for the drive home, Holt waved to them both as Lady drove away.

As the evening approached and the sun set, Holt was thinking about the day and how nice it was to have company. He enjoyed having Lady and her son around. He couldn't help but think he was getting attached to the little boy. When Holt thought about how he was helping with the car, it brought back a lot of happy memories he had when he was the same age. Holt's grandfather was a patient man and explained everything slowly and showed how to do things carefully. Holt found that he was doing the same today and was happy that he was able to display the same manner as his teacher once did.

Even though Holt didn't have children, he was starting to feel like he was growing a connection with Lady's son. When Bobby asked to help with the cars, Holt felt as though it was the boy's way of having a nice time and keeping busy and distracted, despite everything that was happening in his life with his mother and father. Holt thought about the way Bobby smiled whenever he completed a task and thought about the way he asked questions because of his innocence and never-ending curiosity. Holt smiled at the way they worked together, and Bobby wanted to try and do things after Holt had done them, so that he could show Holt he understood what he was trying to teach. There was so much that Holt didn't understand about children, but then again there was so much that he did. It was the male way, when life had its problems, the body likes to keep busy, so that the mind can work itself out along the way.

Despite knowing it wasn't impossible for Holt to have his own children, he just understood that it was all out of his hands. For a long time, he gave up hope and thought that he had been on his own for so long, that he was being punished for something he had done in his past, be it with Emily or taking lives as a soldier. If there was ever a woman who he wanted to have a child with, there was only one beautiful woman he had on his mind and in his heart.

The next morning Lady was thinking that she would go ahead with her plans and call Holt to organise a day at the beach, but what better than to invite those she called family. Lady asked Matt first via text if they wanted to join them, with quick replies of yes, and thanking her for the idea as the kids were getting bored Lady decided to call Holt next. As she dialled Holt's number, Lady took a deep breath as she was hopeful that she wouldn't have to experience the same let downs that she had been all too familiar with when she was with Ryan.

"Hello beautiful." Holt answered, in his gruff morning voice, it made Lady have butterflies in her stomach.

"Morning Holt, am I calling too early?" She asked out of courtesy.

"No, I'm up before the sun on most days." Holt replied.

Lady let go of her doubt and jumped into the conversation.

"I thought about taking the kids to Torquay beach, it would be a nice day and they would sleep through the night."

"Kid's?" Holt repeated.

"Yes, Matt and his husband Mark and their two children would like to join us."

Holt didn't mind as he thought perhaps it would make Lady more comfortable to go in a group instead of just the three of them.

"Sounds good, whenever you're ready then." Holt replied.

"Excellent!" Lady said, "We will see you shortly then."

When Holt put his phone away, and he tapped his fingers on his thigh, he remembered that Lady had never spoken about her family. Holt assumed it was a sensitive topic for Lady as he already knew a few things, but he never wanted to push and waited until she would start the conversation on her own. Holt wondered if there was a bit of mystery about it all. He started to understand that Matt and Lady must be close, and like family, Matt was important to her, so it was probably her way of introducing him to people who she cared deeply for. Holt grabbed his backpack and packed some things for the day, he pulled out his phone and looked up a nice hotel with facilities for himself and Lady's son. He thought he might surprise her and booked a place that had two rooms and proper shower and bathroom for himself it was an almost a two-hour drive and depending on the day he didn't want Lady driving to late in the evening. Holt pressed the confirmation button as he thought about the boy, it made it easy he was on school holidays, and it would be a nice way for them to spend an evening and night together. It was the first time, Holt had done something like that for over seven years, and he decided that he needed to show Lady and her son how much he enjoyed their company.

As Lady pulled into the drive, another car was waiting further down the road. Holt made his way down the ramp and could see that Bobby was super excited about the day. Holt made his way over to her car and when Lady stepped out, he was gobsmacked. She was wearing a wave printed bikini top, her hair was tied up into a messy bun, as his eyes made their way down her beautiful hips and thighs were covered in a small, almost see through sarong skirt which was tied at her waist. Her feet were bare, and her skin was olive in the sun.

"Oh my God!" Holt said as he looked at the goddess walking towards him.

"Hello handsome." She said as she bent down to give him a kiss. Holt pulled her by the hips into his lap and cradled her in his arms.

"My God! Lady." He said, as he kissed her hard.

Lady only smiled her cheeky grin.

"Ready?" Lady asked him.

Holt looked up at her son who was calling out to her to hurry.

"Oh Lady," he said grinning, "I'm ready."

When everyone was seated, Holt held his hand behind him to greet her son, Bobby shook it. Out of sheer excitement, the little boy was talking a million miles an hour, about all the things they were going to do. Lady turned up her music and with a cheeky grin pushed her sunglasses up her nose and stated to drive. Holt looked over at her and remembered that they were in young company, so he took her hand and held it for the drive. Even though they assumed it would be a long time in the car, they managed to get a good run of traffic. When they arrived in the small busy town it was bustling with people. Holt could see that all kinds of people were there, and he wasn't bothered or thought he might stick out in the crowd. Lady squeezed into a parking spot under a shady tree, it was close to the ramp from the grass to the water. When they got out, they all stretched from the long drive and like family, they all gathered around together. Matt and Mark with their two children, came walking up to greet Holt. Lady took the introduction first as she held out her hand at her two friends.

"Matt and Mark this is Holt."

"Well look at you handsome devil." Matt said in his cheeky, sorry not sorry way.

Mark held out his hand first, being proper and like a gentleman. "Holt you will have to excuse my husband, he is very unapologetic."

Holt shook Marks hand nodded.

"I'm Matt, we've spoken on the phone." Matt held out his hand and Holt shook it also.

Matt picked up Martha and played with her chin as he introduced his children.

"And these two little precious gems are Maddison and Martha."

Holt just looked at the two children and understood that they were adopted without any explanation.

"Ok, formalities out of the way, where are we going?" Matt asked, as he looked around. Lady pulled on her backpack and took her son's hand.

"Oh, it's this way." Lady said, as she took the lead.

On the way down to the sand the view was beautiful. Cliffs in the distance and beautiful blue waters crashing on the shore. The air was clean and there was no sign of any kind of debris on the white sand. Holt looked around and noticed that from a distance the beach looked full, but it was and illusion as the families were all evenly spaced out and had plenty of room for privacy. When they reached the sand Holt stopped and Lady turned to look at him. Like a leader she called out to everyone.

"We need to stay close to the path guys." Lady told them, and everyone followed.

Chapter 22

Holt waited for people to clear and slowly got out of his chair and crawled a little so that he wasn't in anyone's way coming down the path.

Holt just watched as Lady got busy, she put towels down, opened umbrellas and unpacked all kinds of things from her never-ending bag. Holt sat in the shade and as he looked around, he didn't feel like he was being watched at all he just enjoyed being included.

"Ok time for a dip." Matt said, as he pulled off his clothing.

Holt tried not to look, but both Mark and Matt, wore tiny swim togs that didn't cover much. Holt covered his mouth and looked to the side as he tried so hard not to laugh or say something silly. He looked over at Lady next to him and she was putting sunscreen on her son and herself.

"Allow me." Holt said as he took the sun cream and grinned as he was massaging it onto Lady's back and shoulders, Holt moved closer to her neck as he didn't want to miss any part of flesh that might get burned. Holt kissed her behind the ear, and she started to get goosebumps.

"Not in front of the children." Lady said, quietly laughing, as she stood up and gathered the small humans around her.

Holt took his shirt off and covered his knees from the curious eyes that might be glancing over the path handrail. He leaned back and watched everything arounds him.

"Well, well, Fabio, eat your heart out." Matt said, as he looked at Holts bare chest. Holt just grinned as he understood that there was no filter. Mark only pushed his sunglasses higher on his nose, ignoring his husband's comments.

"Come on kids." Lady said, as she held tiny hands and made her way to the shallows. Mark joined her and Matt sat down next to Holt.

"So, what are your intentions with my girl?" Matt asked as he was curious about the mysterious man next to him. Holt understood it was time for the interrogation, but he remained unbothered.

"Only good." Holt replied.

"Well, that's a relief." Matt replied, as he took a drink of water.

Holt could see Lady, she was happy and running around with the children, it suited her so well being in their company.

"I can tell you one thing, that girl," Matt pointed at Lady, "She's a diamond you'll never find anybody better in this God forsaken place. She's got the biggest heart in the world, she takes after her beautiful mother, God rest her soul."

Holt found his queue.

"What do you know of her family?" Holt asked quickly.

"Well, you're looking at it." Matt pointed to himself and the others. "Her father-" Matt waved his hand as it wasn't even worth the breath or an explanation.

"Her sister is occupied in her own world; they see each other a few times a year but that's it. Her mother died the same year her son was born, so it was a horrible kick in the teeth and bloody heart breaking for all of us, but she keeps going, and it's all because of that little boy of hers." Matt took another drink and applied sun cream to his arms.

"That little man is so much like Lady," Matt continued, "Nothing like his father that's for sure. We all grew up together, Lady's mother was everyone's mother."

Holt realised that Lady's life was a difficult one, and she didn't have the kind of family he did. Holt's heart grew more and when he saw her and the boy, he wanted them both to be his. He understood that she had lost more than two limbs, she had lost the very foundations of family. As Holt looked at the group, he understood that this was a tiny clan that leaned on each other when in need. Holt began to become protective of all of them, it was his nature, he was once a soldier after all.

For a long time, Holt thought he was the one who had lost everything and was alone to get on with life, but no, that was not the case. He gained more than he could have ever imagined, he was always meant to meet Lady and her son, he was always meant to be exactly where he was this very moment. When it all clicked into place, Holt felt peace inside his heart and mind, there was no more war inside him as it all faded away. Lady loved all these people with her whole heart and accepted them exactly as they were.

A few hours later, tired children were ready for rest and food. Everything that was packed had all been eaten, so with bags packed and children in tow, everyone made their way back up the ramp. Mark and Matt were trailing behind huffing and puffing, as they were carrying their children on their backs. Holt had Bobby on his lap and Lady was helping push Holt back to the top. For a moment it all seemed easy, but after seven minutes into the walk, they realised it was longer and harder going uphill.

"My glutes are broken." Matt said, as he tried to pull himself along the handrail.

"Nearly, there." Lady puffed, as she fell to the back of the line and was being pulled along by Matt.

Mark was holding on to Holt's chair for support as his legs were giving out. With arms burning, gritted teeth and hands slipping on the wheel grips, all three children were sitting on Holt's lap, as he was pushing with sweat beading down his brow.

"Woohoo, Faster Holt." Bobby cheered and the other two children were clapping their hands.

With a huge sigh of relief, they reached the top and when they got close to the car, they all dropped their gear and slumped onto the cool grass under the big tree. Holt was exhausted and lay down on the ground next to Lady and he reached out to her to lay on his arm.

"Well, that was very relaxing." Lady said, as she cuddled her son next to her.

Holt only wiped the sweat off his face and started to smile. Holt thought about how it would have looked with everyone struggling, he wished he had a camera. Holt was glad that he booked a room, never in his life did he experience a day like this, and as fate would have it, the unthinkable happened, Holt started laughing.

Lady rolled onto her side and looked at him, his chest was rising and falling, and he was wholeheartedly laughing from his stomach. Lady held her hand to her mouth as she thought he had the loveliest, deep masculine laugh she had ever heard. Holt moved his head as he wiped a tear from his eye and pulled her close to him. Lady looked at his smile and she kissed him.

"Was that a laugh, Holt Mason?" She asked as she looked into his shining green eyes. Holt only kissed her back as he waited for his laugh to subside.

"Yes!" He said and finally and caught his breath.

"Well, I never!" Lady said, as she remembered that she said she would hear it someday.

Once Matt and Mark packed everything away, they said they would be going back home and getting food along the way. Lady thought it would be a good idea, but Holt pointed to a hotel that was across from the beach.

"We will be staying there tonight."

"Wow!" Bobby said, as he looked out the window wide eyed.

"Oh, but I can't afford-" Lady started to speak but she was cut short as Holt held up his hand.

"It's my treat for both of you." Holt said, as he took her hand in his and kissed it.

Although Lady was tired, she really didn't feel like driving, so she started to get excited as she had never stayed anywhere like that before.

"Thank you, Holt." Lady leaned into him, and Holt pulled her close and kissed her.

When they opened the room door, Lady saw there were two rooms and a large bathroom. She dropped her things and laid down on the bed.

"Oh, Wow." She said as she rolled all over the bed.

"Yahoo." Bobby said as he was jumping on the bed in the second room.

"Careful Holt, I could get used to this." Lady said as she sat up and grinned at him. Holt just looked at her and smiled, he couldn't help but think that he had made her son the happiest boy in the world.

"Happy, little man?" Holt asked Bobby who was snooping in the hotel room already.

"Yes." Bobby answered, as he was preoccupied opening drawers and wardrobes.

"Well, I'm starving." Lady said, as she rubbed her belly.

"Me too." Bobby agreed, as he ran to the other side of the room.

"Hm-," Holt said, as he looked around.

"I want pizza." Bobby said, as he jumped onto the bed again.

"We can do that." Holt said as he pulled out his phone and picked the biggest feast with everything. "Done!" Holt told them and threw his phone on the bed.

"Yum, Pizza!" Lady said as she started to move the bags around and settled her son's things into his room. Holt smiled as he watched her and started to unpack a few of his things also.

After a few pizzas and lots of laughs, Lady bathed her son and shortly after he fell asleep. Lady smiled as she moved a curl from his face and stroked his little cheek, she laughed quietly about the way her son looked when they had dinner, the little boy's head was bobbing from exhaustion. Lady could hear his little snores and they were confirmation that he was retired for the evening. Lady closed the door a little, so he wouldn't be disturbed by light or noise. Holt made his way into the large shower and Lady followed.

"Today was so lovely." Lady said as she slowly washed her body and her hair. She sighed at the wonderful feeling of the water running down her body, and she was smiling as the day played through her head. Holt only agreed, as he was preoccupied with thoughts about the conversation he had with Matt.

"Thank you so much for this room, Holt." Lady said, as she kissed him and made her way out of the shower.

"You're welcome." He replied as he watched her dry off. Holt scrubbed all the sweat and sand off his body, he turned off the shower and Lady handed him a towel. Moving to the bed they both sighed as they climbed in and Holt pulled Lady over his chest, they lay there in silence listening to the sounds of the night.

Feeling relaxed they rested, caressing each other, and exchanging kisses. Holt moved his head and looked at her. The moonlight was shining through the window, and everything just seemed perfect. She looked beautiful, her long hair that tumbled across his chest, the curves of her face and body. He loved how the soft light shined on her skin and he ran his fingers down her arm. He thought about everything they had experienced together and the way she was resting in his arms made him feel like he never wanted to be without her again. Holt remembered his life and the way it was before Lady walked through his front door. Holt always thought that love at first sight was just a fantasy, but as he looked at her and stroked her cheek and watched her lips curl into a small smile, he was struck with a realisation that she was his purpose. Holt's thoughts moved to her son who was fast asleep, and he remembered the way Bobby smiled when Holt told them that he was treating them for the night. Lady and her son deserved the best, love and so much more. Holt felt like the old war dog that was trapped inside of him was forever baring its fangs and gnashing at its leash, but in the last three months the beast was calmed, soothed, and finally set free. Holt closed his eyes and took a deep breath, as the feeling he was waiting for set in, he was finally home after being lost for far too long.

Chapter 23

Holt moved Lady so they were facing each other, and he kissed Lady deeply, he held her close as he rolled on top of her, craving to be skin on skin once more. Lady moved her hips and wrapped her legs around his narrow waist. She sighed at the wonderful feeling of his weight on top of her, she adored the way his thighs felt, his long arms, being chest to chest and the way they looked into each other's eyes. Holt was warm and big; it made her feel safe. She could feel Holt growing with need as he deepened his kisses, gripped her thighs, and ran his tongue over her bottom lip. Lady writhed under him as his shaft was pushing on her belly, he kissed her face and her cheeks he needed to tell her what was on his mind and in his heart. He couldn't fight it any longer the wanting, the need, she was all he ever wanted in a lover and soulmate. It all came down to this very moment, this woman, he craved her and wanted her to be his forever.

He lowered his hips slowly and Lady closed her eyes as she started to breath deeper, her small sighs of pleasure increased Holt's desire. Holt licked her lips as they were full and welcoming, he moved, raising his body, he braced himself on top of her and he let out small shallow breaths and closed his eyes as he gently thrust himself inside her. Once he was submerged, he lowered himself and locked their fingers together, he thrust more deeply and slowly, he kissed her eyes, nose, and cheeks.

Taking a breath, he was moving to her earlobe and jawline, Lady was drowning in bliss, and he could feel her moving her hips with his. It was their very own sacred dance of pleasure, a secret they shared deep in the night. Holt started to want more, he looked into her eyes, and it was this very moment he was wating for so long it felt so natural, it was all so right. He surrendered, just as taking a breath or the beat of a heart, he looked deeply into her eyes and let his heart, body and soul speak,

"I love you, Lady Myne."

He thrust again and kissed her cheek, he felt freedom and peace, he needed to tell her again, he touched his lips to hers as he repeated the beautiful words, he so adored, "I love you," he said quietly and then he covered her mouth with his and kissed her deeply.

Lady closed her eyes, and she moved her arms to wrap them around Holt tightly, she was silent and overjoyed, she couldn't fight the emotion and a single tear fell down her cheek. As Holt intensified his affection, he was whispering repeatedly, "Oh Lady, beautiful Lady, I love you." It was his very own mantra.

Lady was focusing on the very moment not the past, and she wanted to tell him how she had felt for so long, as she was rising for the explosion of pleasure, Holt could feel her climbing with him, he could feel her in his heart and soul.

He was kissing her all over, running his big hands up and down her body and breast. He looked into her eyes as he knew she was reaching the top with him.

"Yes Lady, yes that's it, I can feel you baby." He said, as he thrust more deeper and harder.

"I love you so much Lady." Holt said again, as he was riding her passionately, he was equal with her on the blissful ladder.

He looked at her again and as she was holding back, she gripped his shoulders and arched her back, Holt looked into her eyes and Lady set her heart free.

"I love you, Holt."

Lady closed her eyes, and he kissed her more, grasping at her hair, hands, and anything in his reach. Holt needed to hear Lady say it again as it was the very fuel, for the fire in his heart.

"Say it again Lady, say it when you come." Holt kissed her neck wildly.

"Yes," Lady said as Holt moved to lick her lips and nipped at her chin. "Oh yes, Holt," Lady gripped his hair and resisted the urge to scream.

"Come with me baby." Holt whispered into her mouth.

"Holt, I love you." She gripped his hair harder as she wanted to cry out, but Holt crushed his mouth onto hers as they both experienced two worlds colliding and becoming one. Holt thrusted deeply; he was at the complete mercy of the intensity of their love coming together. Lady moaned and Holt held her close, now they were breathing as one. Holts body became hard, and Lady held him tight as he filled her, she tilted her hips higher, as Holt emptied himself inside her, she loved how it felt and wanted him fully and everything that he was.

He released her mouth as he needed air, he told her again as he ran his mouth down her cheek and locked their fingers together once more, "I love you."

Lady wrapped her arms around his neck and kissed him, as she was smothered and loved it. Holt moved them on their side to let Lady breathe. They stayed joined at the hip and wrapped in each other's arms, never wanting to let go.

As they grew weary, their hearts and breathing synchronised. The tidal wave of love they just travelled on together, took them slowly into beautiful blissful and peaceful sleep.

Epilogue

After her son's school holidays Andrew called Holt

and told him there was an opening for his surgery and that he

should take it asap. Lady was anxiously waiting for a nurse to

tell her that Holt was in recovery, she was nervous as she

listened to the conversations of doctors and nurses all around

her. She started to fiddle with her new puzzle that Holt

bought her, it was a lot more quiet and very modern.

Just as she was about to scramble it again, a smiling

nurse approached her, and she led Lady to where Holt was

resting. As Holt opened his eyes, he looked around him. He

was back in a hospital bed; he was sick of being in one, as most of his life has been doctors, hospitals, and therapy. As his senses woke more, he could hear breathing next to his ear; he turned his head and saw that Lady was asleep next to his shoulder. He gently stroked her cheek, and she opened her eyes, she smiled as she saw Holt looking at her.

"Hey, you're awake, finally."

Holt just swallowed as his throat was a bit sore from the breathing tube, he tried to speak but coughed instead.

"Shh!" Lady said, as she touched his lips, "You need to rest."

Lady leaned forward and kissed him. Holt was happy that Lady was with him, and he wrapped his arms around her and didn't let go. Lady crawled onto the bed and snuggled into his side.

"I hope you're feeling better soon." Lady said, as she laid on his shoulder.

Holt managed to get out some short words, "I will be." Holt moved his head closer to hers and he kissed her on the forehead. They held each other like they did so long ago, they just enjoyed the silence and comfort they were for each other.

"I love you, Lady." Holt told her, in a dry raspy voice and he squeezed her tighter.

"I love you, Holt." Lady replied, as she was listening to his heartbeat and feeling his warmth.

***

Three months later.

A delivery arrived at the door of Holt's home; he tried his best to take quiet steps in his mechanical prosthetic legs. When he answered he signed for the package and had a look inside. He placed it in the side pocket of his empty wheelchair and made his way to the soft sofa Lady was asleep on.

Holt stood there and smiled as he looked at her and could hear her small sleeping sounds. She was as beautiful as ever, resting peacefully with one hand on her three-month pregnant bump. Holt found her more irresistible than ever, and let his gaze move to her beautiful leg hanging off the edge. He bent down and woke her gently rubbing her hand kissing her forehead.

"Lady, wake up baby." Holt said, quietly.

She stirred and slowly opened her eyes. She smiled as she saw that Holt was looking at her.

"Hey there." Lady said, as she ran a lazy finger over his beard.

Bobby came into the room and asked when his mother's birthday gift was arriving. Lady frowned and was confused as she thought they must have had a secret they had been keeping from her this whole time.

"Your mother's present is a ten-minute drive from here."

Lady looked at Holt and saw that he wasn't in his chair.

"Holt! What?" She opened her eyes wide as she looked at him and couldn't believe what she was seeing.

"Oh my, Holt, you look wonderful."

Holt stood up and helped Lady to her feet, she was in awe at the beautiful man in front of her; he was incredibly tall, and she was falling in love with him all over again. She held her hands to her mouth and wiped away the tears that were falling.

"Come here baby." Holt said, as he reached out to her and held her close.

"It's the hormones." Lady sniffled, as she started smiling and looked at him again.

"Can we go now?" Bobby asked, as he wanted to see the gift and was getting impatient.

"Yes, we should." Holt answered as he walked over to the front door and held out his arm for Lady. Once outside they waved to Matt and Mark who were tending to their new garden; they moved in next to Holt a month after Lady and her son joined him. Lady smiled as she saw their new car, it was a large black V8 family car, and Lady picked the beautiful custom red colour. Holt decided he wanted Lady to have the car she always dreamed of so, he bought her one. Even though Lady did drive it sometimes, she enjoyed being passenger more than anything.

When she looked at Holt climb in next to her, she smiled at the beautiful long thighs as they stretched out and Holt knew she was having her dreamy moment; he picked up her hand and held it and they made their way to the gift that was waiting.

When they arrived, Lady saw they parked by a beautiful modern building. She looked at the sign and saw "Masons Auto," with a beautifully landscaped office building next door. Holt parked out the front and Lady was starting to wonder.

Holt made his way outside and took the chair out of the boot placing it by the office door, he took it because it's better to have back up but not for himself, for Lady.

When Holt helped Bobby and Lady out of the car, he walked her to the office door; he opened the package and took out the keys, he took Lady's hand in his and closed her fingers around the tag.

"Happy Birthday, Lady." Holt kissed her, and Lady was speechless.

Bobby grew restless and wanted to go inside, Lady put the key in the door and when they walked in she was amazed at the beautiful modern design of the office; it was large and was all set up with computers and phones, there was a waiting area with a sofa and television, beautiful art of the ocean decorated the walls, and the smell was fresh paint and carpet, as Lady could smell everything she could even smell the small tinge of sawdust. She noticed there was another door and Holt just tipped his chin at the keys she was holding in her hand.

When she turned the key and opened the door, it was a small, homely area; complete with kitchen and bathroom an area to eat and even a small room with new bed. Lady looked at Holt and before she could say anything, Holt handed her a card. Sniffling, smiling, and tears flowing from her eyes, she opened it, it had a message and three signatures.

Dear Lady,

Happy Birthday!

We hope you enjoy your new office.

Love always,

Roman, Holt and Finn.

"Oh my gosh, Holt this is too much." Lady was losing her balance and Holt pushed his wheelchair under her. He got down on one knee to speak to her as he could see she was overwhelmed.

"Lady, I love you, you deserve all this and so much more." Holt kissed her and she started to smile with joy.

"So, this is for when I finish my doctors? Lady wasn't sure, she was a scrambled mess, and couldn't think.

Holt just smiled and held her face in his hands. "It's yours right now Lady, you can fill it with puzzle's, turn it into a craft house, paint in here, or turn it into a bookstore, I don't care baby." Holt smiled as he spoke and enjoyed seeing her so happy.

Sobbing, Lady had to laugh at Holt's answer.

"I just want you to do what makes you happy." Holt said as he kissed her again and pressed his forehead to hers.

"Happy Birthday."

Holt pulled out one more thing from the side pocket of his chair, and it was a small box, he held it in front of her and opened it.

Lady's eyes widened as she looked at the gold and glitter. It was an eighteen-carat gold band with a tall three-pronged claw; it was holding six stones set in the way of a puzzle. Lady sniffled and held her hand to her mouth, as she looked at the ring and back at Holt.

"I love you Lady Myne, I need you to be close to me; since the day I met you I knew I would never feel the same if you weren't going to be in my life." Holt held a hand to her belly as he continued, "This little bump here, Lady, you've made me the happiest man alive; you taught me how to live again, and I want to be by your side forever."

Lady was laughing and crying with small squeaks, as she was overwhelmed by the words Holt was saying.

"Marry me, Lady Myne, please be my wife?"

Lady was only able to choke out words, as she was trying to comprehend everything. She nodded her head and managed to say the words, "Yes, yes, Holt, I will marry you."

Holt took the ring out of the box and placed it on her finger, he stood up and lifted her out of the chair cradling her in his arms. He kissed her while pacing around the room to hold his balance. Lady wrapped her arms around his neck tightly and looked at the ring on her hand she was able to stop the tears and smiled so much her face hurt. She pressed her face to his and laughed with joy.

"I love you, Holt Mason."

Holt looked at her again and smiled, as he could see she was over the moon. "I love you, Lady."

Lady looked at Bobby who was sitting on the big office chair drawing a picture; strangely he was quiet and keeping out of trouble. Her son was sorting through brand new pencils, then he looked at his mother and smiled. Holt put Lady down and they both walked over to him. When Holt sat on the table in front of her son, he held up his hand and Bobby tapped the high five.

"Wait!" Lady said, looking at her son and then Holt.

"Did you know about this?" Lady squinted her eyes at her cheeky boy.

"It's secret man's business." Bobby replied.

Holt grinned and Lady could see that devilish dimple on Holt's cheek.

"Does this mean we are a family now?" Bobby asked, as he looked at both of them.

Holt wrapped his arms around them, he squeezed them tightly and kissed them both on the forehead.

"Yes! Yes, you are my family."

END

Roman's Lust

BOOK 2 OF THE EMERALD EYES TRILOGY

F.L. MOON

<u>Never abandon hope or forsake love.</u>

<u>F.L. Moon</u>

Prologue

Two boys were prospecting with their father, Roman, an eight-year-old, was searching for hours in the quiet stream near their home. His younger brother Holt was busy splashing water around as he waded in some shallows and giggled as he played with his mother.

"Look dad is this a good one?" Roman asked, his father as he was hopeful that he would find treasure.

Sondre Finn Mason, just grinned as he looked at his young son's large eyes full of joy.

"Well, I think you found a piece of gold, well done son."

"Mum, look I found this for you." Roman handed the tiny piece of glitter to his mother and she kissed him on the cheek.

"My my, well done son, I will make sure I keep this in my treasure box." Roman's mother Lysindra Mason, winked at her grinning husband, as she knew it would be impossible to keep the tiny treasure safe.

A few hours later digging and grunting Roman wouldn't give up until he found more treasure. Roman stayed behind as his younger brother Holt went home with his mother, he was only four and grew restless and bored. After another hour Roman's father was holding gems, he had found under a light as the evening approached and he noticed that there was something blue and shining sticking out from the rocks that Roman was digging in.

"Roman, look here dig a little more." Sondre was happy that his son had unknowingly unearthed a small gem.

Roman pulled the small piece of gem from the stones and washed it under some water.

"What have I found dad?" Roman brought the piece to his father and smiled so big he looked like he had a tear of joy gleaming.

"Well, that is a fine piece of sapphire son, well done."

Roman was so excited that he grabbed his father's torch and shined it on the stone he looked at it as he was sure that he was falling in love with the beautiful treasure he had discovered. Hours of sweat hard work and patience finally paid off and he was so proud of what he had achieved.

"Wow, I'm going to be rich someday." Roman placed the stone in a special case his father had, and they gathered their tools and made their way home in the dark.

"I'm very proud of you son." Sondre tapped his boy on the back and enjoyed seeing his boy so incredible happy.

"Good things like these treasures take time, sometimes you have to go through hell and hard work before you get your reward, remember that and never give up hope on something you love, and your reward will come to you."

Roman nodded his head as he looked at his father and understood that he would try his best to always work like he did today, and use it as a valuable lesson and cornerstone, for the rest of his life.

Chapter 1

Roman placed a single, red rose on the grave, looking down at the headstone, he ran his hand across the name of his lost love, Faye Mason. He looked out to the distance and saw so many loved ones that had passed. They had all been brought here, to this beautiful cemetery. It was full of life despite all the graves that filled it. Many animals found this place to be a haven for all their needs. All matter of birds and small creatures moved around, gathering materials, and feeding on the flowers, nuts on the trees and fruit that blossomed. Many types of fish filled the small ponds and were tended to, a small family of ducks made their way over to the water feature that had been a special burial memoir for a loved one. The small ducklings hopped in the water one by one and picked around for food that visitors had dropped for them. Families gathered and had picnics alongside their lost loved one's grave, and laughed as they told stories keeping the memory of them alive. A small feeling of relief went through him, as he realised that he wasn't the only one feeling this loss and grief. He kissed the head stone and stood, he started straightening his clothes and took a deep breath as he made his way to his work that waited.

Shelly was wiping away tears as Roman came through the office door. She was packing her things as retirement was on the agenda. Her smudged mascara, and white curly hair looked frazzled, as she was a bundle of emotion. She wiped her tears away with a well-used, tissue and straightened her work blazer and blouse.

"I sure am going to miss you." Roman told her, as he stretched out his arms and gave Shelly a big hug goodbye.

"Oh, Roman, you handsome devil, don't get all teary eyed." Shelly tried to be strong, but her smile wavered.

"You beat me to it." He replied, as he bent down to give his long-time work college a kiss on the lips.

"Oh, Roman, you are a charmer." Shelly smiled, as she squeezed his face tightly.

Roman reached forward and wiped away her tears before he took her hand and lead her to the glass cabinet in the office.

"I have a parting gift for you, take your pick, Shelly."

"Oh, my word, I couldn't it's too much." Shelly replied, but Roman knew that she adored the rare and running low, Tanzanite.

He put the code into the security lock and opened the door taking out the precious gem. It was in a beautiful leather and gold foiled box, he dropped in a card of a specialty jeweller, and then handed it to Shelly.

"Happy retirement, Shelly, this will keep you covered if you choose, or turn it into whatever you like."

Shelly took the box and opened it; she was overwhelmed and threw her arms around Roman.

"Roman, I do hope all good things come your way, you deserve it." Shelly released him and ran her hand over his cheek with parting words.

"Do me a favour love, find yourself a beautiful woman and enjoy life with her. Spoil a special someone and treat her like a Queen, Faye would want you to be happy too."

Shelly said the words as she could see that Roman was only thinking of the one woman he loved. She kissed Roman one last time and picked up her bag placing the precious gem inside. The door opened and Shelly's husband Frank stepped inside, he greeted Roman and held out his arm to his wife.

"Ready, Shells?" He asked her, as she looked one more time at Roman before she turned to walk out.

"Goodbye, my lovely, Roman." Shelly blew him a kiss and smiled as she turned away.

"Goodbye, Shelly." Roman told her, as Frank opened the door for his wife.

"Take good care of her Frank." Roman called out, as they left.

"Oh, I will, you take care now, Roman."

As the couple walked out, Roman watched them leave arm in arm. He only had a small glimmer of hope, that one day he would experience the same. As he watched the world become busy outside, cars and traffic was building up. The workday was over, and the clock was ticking over to five thirty. He sat down in his office and started to check through messages that Shelly had left him. She had tried to sort through over two hundred, applications for her replacement, but as she wasn't sure what Roman was after, she left the big pile of papers on his desk to make his own decision. He moved the papers aside and clicked on the emails that were flooding the inbox with questions and orders. Roman grunted at one of the emails, as he knew that it was a hustler that liked to try and sell fake stones that were imported from overseas. While he worked in the mining industry, he oversaw, making the place safe for the workers who would risk their lives to try and dig out stones people used as a luxury item to look wealthy. He wanted to make sure the stones that he was selling were real and he asked a very real price for them. His part share in the mining business meant that he had good men and women who relied on him for a paycheck, and he made sure they were taken care of. Roman fell in love with gems ever since he was a little boy, and slowly it became an obsession. While his wife Faye was at home Roman went to work in the mines for many years and brought home gems that were used as payment for the chemotherapy his wife needed. She had a long battle with a rare type of blood cancer. He promised her that he would find enough one day to get her the best medical care, but as time passed no amount of gold or jewels could save her. She lost her battle and was laid to rest ten years ago. Roman never remarried, he was in too much pain and grief for years and tried to find himself after losing her. He began to build up his collection, and with that a wealth also. He started at the bottom and made his way up the food chain. Blood, sweat, and tears were paid, to be where he was today.

After managing to get some work done, he went into the spare room, which was more like a private dressing room. He took off his slacks and shirt, and exchanged them for a pair of joggers, pants, and tank top. As he kicked his work shoes aside, he pulled on his running shoes and enjoyed the feeling of the comfort. He stretched out his long lean legs and arms as he warmed up for the run home. Running was a way for Roman to gain focus he enjoyed the way it made his body work. He even thought of it as a kind of sweet torture but even though his home wasn't very close by, it didn't deter him from the hobby. As the security guards made their way up and down the street, patrolling the area, he locked his office and began the journey home. Night-time was amongst him, and he ran fast and slow to get the best out of the exercise. After thirty minutes of running, he took his tank top off and used it as a towel to wipe his face. He hung it from his pants and kept going as the home stretch wasn't far. Every day took at least an hour, depending on the weather. If it was raining, he would run faster if it was clear he would run slower. He didn't have a specific timetable that he kept to. He just went with nature and how he was feeling. Being out in nature was something that he enjoyed, especially if there were pretty stones to be found.

As he walked up his driveway, he unlocked the security door to his home. Finn his youngest brother helped him refurnish it and he didn't need a high-priced building to sleep in. The ranch style home was perfect on the large block of land that he owned. He didn't like being close to neighbours, Roman was very solitary and enjoyed the peace and quiet. He didn't own any animals as he was never home much to take care of them. It was a lifestyle choice that he saw fitting for himself. As he walked through the threshold, the night was cooling. He picked-up logs and started the fire in his living area and sat down on the sofa. He reached over to the small wooden table that held a decanter full of whisky.

He poured himself a drink and sat back watching the flames flicker and move. On the stone mantle above the fireplace, he looked at a photo of himself and his wife, he saluted her and finished the drink. Roman began to think about Shelly, he wished her the best and she deserved it. Her kind nature and loving heart were going to be hard to replace. He felt like she was the only person who understood that he did have a softer side. Her last words played over in his ears, and he was thinking that perhaps it was time he chip away at the stone wall he built around his heart. It didn't matter how many beautiful things he collected, there was still a dark void in his heart that needed to be filled. Giving in to his tired body, he took a shower, cooked himself some food and then went to bed thinking about how tomorrow would be a new and very different day.

As the sun began to rise, Roman nodded his head at fellow joggers as he ran to the office. Once he arrived, he greeted the security and bid them a goodnight as the shift was now over. He entered his building and went into the large bathroom which was also a laundry. He peeled off his sweaty clothes and threw them into the washer. After a shower, he dressed in black slacks, a long sleeve shirt and plain black shoes. He shaved and tidied his beard; he also groomed his short business style hair that had length on the top. Roman's dark black hair was sprinkled with the wisdom whites that were coming through. Granted he was only forty-nine, he certainly didn't look his age. He had his father to thank for the good strong family genes that were passed down to himself and his brothers. He stood in front of the full-length mirror attached to his wardrobe door, smoothed his long, big hands over his clothes and fixed his collar into place. The Mason men were all tall, broad in the shoulders and chest. They carried long strong arms and stood strong with long lean legs, slim in the waist and the trademark grin finished the look. All the men had emerald, green eyes that twinkled when they smiled. Even though Roman rarely smiled, meaning almost never, he did smile faintly when a new shiny treasure would catch his eye.

As he made his way into the office, he sat in the empty reception chair and turned on the computer. A strong wind came out of nowhere and he saw that the weather had a sudden change. The clouds were grey, it was howling and raining. He rubbed his hand on his beard in confusion, as he thought it was very strange. He didn't think that the beautiful sunrise he witnessed this morning would turn out so bleak, so quickly. The bus pulled up outside at the stop and a people were getting off. He heard a shriek and then saw papers flying around in the wind and rain. A frantic woman wearing a hat was running around. Trying to pick up all the papers she had dropped. People were trying to help her, but they gave up quickly and kept walking.

Pages were flying out into the street, up in the air and falling into the puddles that were forming on the ground. Roman picked up and umbrella from the holder and made his way outside. He started to search and pick up papers, keeping a grip on the umbrella he decided it was useless as the wind was blowing wildly, so he closed it and threw to the ground. The woman was running in circles and managed to pick up a few sheets but gave up when she found that many were blown three blocks down. Roman made his way over to her and noticed her glasses were fogged and dripping with rain, small curls of strawberry red hair were hanging below her hat and he didn't see much of her face because of the wide brim.

He assumed she was an older lady as she was wearing the same kind of clothing. A long skirt to her feet and colourful blouse, pink, knitted cardigan and silk scarf around her neck. Her height was two heads shorter then Roman and he saw that she had wide hips when the wind blew her clothing tight against her body.

"I think these are yours." Roman addressed the woman, as she looked up at him with her fogged glasses.

"Oh, thank you, I guess I will have to re-write most of it." She wiped away rain from her check but when Roman looked closer he could see that they were tears.

"Perhaps we should go inside where you can dry off in front of the fire for a while and sort through what you managed to salvage." Roman opened his door and held out his arm for her to walk through as she was welcome.

"That's very kind of you, thank you." The woman made her way inside and started to put down her things in the foyer as everything was dripping wet.

"I have towels for you, please have a seat." Roman showed her the sofa and she sat down with a big sigh as she was upset, she lost her papers.

When Roman went into the bathroom, he picked out two large soft towels and a hair dryer that Shelly used to use. He thought perhaps she might like to try and dry the pages that were wet. Roman dried himself with a towel and handed her one.

"Oh? Are you sure? I don't want to be a bother." She started taking off her scarf and hung it over the sofa arm then removed her cardigan.

"It's no bother at all. Please take all the time you need." Roman plugged in the hair dryer behind the sofa.

"Use this if you like, to dry what you can."

Roman dried his face and was about to turn away when he was suddenly star struck, at what he saw next.

The woman took off her glasses, keeping her face down and then she slowly removed her hat. One metre long, gold, and dark red hair draped down in thick locks around her diamond shaped face. Like a waterfall of fire it looked like long thick curtains, landing in her lap. She looked up at Roman and her eyes were the colour of lemon amber, her mouth was full and her pink flushed cheeks, looked like they had been airbrushed onto marble fair skin. Small braids were twisted into parts of her hair and were held together with leather ties and beads on the end.

"Thank you, my name is, Freya, by the way." She held out her hand to Roman.

Roman felt like he had found a treasure in the form of a woman, he was a little stumped to speak, but then managed to say his name and shake her hand.

"Roman, is my name, it's a wonderful pleasure, to meet you, Freya." Roman held her hand and felt the smooth marble skin on her fingers. He didn't realize but Freya was waiting for him to let go of her hand.

"Can I have my hand back now?" Freya asked, as she smiled and had to laugh a little.

"Oh, yes forgive me." Roman said, as he took the towels and made his way over to the fire. He placed them on the ground and the heat from the flames would help in drying her work. He reached for some of the sheets and without asking he wanted to place them down.

"Oh, no you don't need to do that, I will be leaving when the next bus comes. I need to restart this whole day."

Roman turned to look at the clock and it was going to be at least an hour or more for the next bus. She didn't reach out for her work, but Roman started laying them on the towels.

"You may need to wait for the bus, knowing this weather, it's probably thrown the traffic into chaos this morning. I was about to make myself a coffee as I just started the day myself, would you like to accompany me with a warm drink?" Roman patted the paper down and then stood waiting for her answer.

"Well, you are correct, a coffee would be lovely, just however it comes is fine with me."

Roman nodded his head and made his way into the back room. He changed his clothes and made his way out to the kitchen but stopped when he looked at Freya. She was frowning at her papers on the ground and keeping warm in front of the fire with a towel draped around her shoulders.

"Freya, if you like I have a dressing room full of clean, spare clothing from a retired work colleague. She completed her thirty years yesterday, and before I donate the clothing, you are welcome to change if you wish, or keep whatever you like. I am hopeful there will be things you may find appealing."

Freya smiled and stood in her bare feet, as her shoes were soaking and kicked off by the doorway. Her frown turned into a smile as she did do all her shopping for clothes at second hand stores. She didn't mind and it was cheap, as she didn't have much of an income. She decided to accept his kindness and pulled her small glasses back onto her face and walked over to Roman where he was waiting in a hallway.

"Oh, I do love collecting preloved clothing, are you sure you don't mind, I can pay you some money-"

Roman held up his hand to stop her, as he didn't want anything. All he wanted was to make her comfortable. Freya closed her mouth and then beamed a smile at him. It had been such a long time since she had any new clothes, as she only had a very small collection.

"Second, on the left." Roman told her, as he made his way back into the kitchen.

When Freya walked into the room. Her mouth fell open when she saw the Hollywood lights around the mirror and dressing table. It was complete with makeup shelving, storage, and a vintage chair from the Victorian era. Next to it was a vintage style vanity with sink, covered with gold tap wear and cupboard knobs, it looked like it was all designed for a wealthy family in the renaissance age. There was a double door, floor to ceiling wardrobe, that was covered in full length mirrors and a coat stand covered in all kinds of scarves and hats. A shoe rack stood next to the doorway, that was three tiers high, full of all kinds of strappy shoes and warmer boots. There was second dress rack next to the door, it was full of expensive looking dresses that glittered, and they were all covered in dry cleaner plastic bags.

Freya turned on the light switches and the room came to life; she instantly fell in love with her surroundings. She closed the door behind her and walked into the centre spinning around in circles like a princess in a dream. She could have lived in this place, it was beautiful, magical, and full of wonder. It was almost bigger than her living area and kitchen combined, and she imagined what it must have been like to work here. After sorting through the beautiful clothing, she went with a light blue ankle length, paisley dress, leather waist belt and light grey crochet, knee length cardigan. She pulled on some black ankle boots that were her size and pulled up her hair in two long thick brides that fell down her shoulders. She cleaned up her face with wipes and sprayed some perfume on her neck and smiled at the wonderful smell it reminded her of a mixed bouquet of flowers. She found a plastic bag and used it for her old wet clothing, and one final turn in front of the mirror, she opened the door and walked out to the waiting area.

Chapter 2

While Roman was waiting for the coffee machine to finish, he heard footsteps behind him. He turned to look and saw that Freya had changed her clothing as she walked past the doorway.

"That was Shelly's favourite, she purchased it ten years ago." Roman called out as he lifted the two coffees from the machine and saw that Freya stopped to look at him, in the hallway.

"Thank you, it is very lovely. There is so much beauty in there it was very hard to make a choice." Freya smiled, as she took the coffee from Roman's hand.

"Let's take a seat, there is something I would like to speak to you about." Roman said, as he headed towards the small coffee table with two chairs against the wall in the waiting are and pulled out a chair for Freya to sit.

"Oh, alright." Freya sat crossed her legs and sipped at the coffee.

As Roman sat opposite her, he looked her in the eyes and couldn't help to think he was drowning in them.

"What do you do for work Freya? I have a space here that I would like to fill, and I need someone to take Shelly's place. I can see that you enjoy writing, and you have excellent knowledge and skills of the English language. You possess the attributes for the position as an assistant and granted, you present yourself immaculately in that outfit alone."

Freya wasn't sure how this came about; she wasn't currently employed and only did volunteer work. She had some savings from the previous novels she had written but it wasn't enough to last for a very long time.

"Well, I'm just clear of a terrible job. They treated me like I didn't matter, they spoke all the wonderful jargon in the interview process but then three months later it all went sideways. I do enjoy writing; I have a few novels that I have published and they are selling quite well online. I haven't really investigated the working market as such, but I was even happy to work at a fast-food chain if I needed to, to pay the bills."

Freya sipped at her coffee and noticed that Roman seemed like he wasn't happy with the answer she gave, but then he drank and took a deep breath as he asked her the next question.

"As a writer, it comes from inspiration does it not?" Roman looked at her as he knew how to work around her doubt.

"All creative art comes from inspiration, although sometimes I'm writing stories I thought of as a young teenage girl, but I never had the resources to make my stories a reality. I grew up in a foster home and the people who took care of me couldn't afford a computer. Then later I supported myself and went my own way, sometimes I still like to use my typewriter."

Freya looked around and finally noticed the cabinet with the precious gems inside. Her eyes glittered as she noticed that she was in a room full of beautiful stones and rough uncut clusters on shelves and behind glass.

"What do you do here exactly?" Freya asked, as she slowly stood from her chair and walked over to the glass cabinet.

"I work, within the mining industry, involving safety amongst other things." Roman knew his job was complicated but he kept it simple to avoid confusion.

"There is travel involved and the days and evenings can be long depending on what needs doing. This place however is what you would call a 'side hustle' it's more of a hobby that involves the market of precious metals and gems. People make me offers and vice versa, there is always questions that need answering from people who have just found a stone while they are out prospecting, and they come to me for advice and the right connections."

Freya turned around as she had never seen a placed like this before.

"So, all of these are a part of your private collection, then I take it?" Freya asked as she was intrigued.

"Yes." Roman answered as he finished his coffee.

"Wow!" Did you find these yourself?" Freya asked.

"Many of them I did, and some I purchased." Roman said quietly, as he could see her amazement.

Freya turned around and then sat back down and finished her drink. She wasn't sure why he would ask her of all people who are more experienced in the field.

"I don't really know anything about precious stones. Did you advertise, for the position?" Freya was trying to avoid giving him a direct answer as she wasn't sure she would be good enough.

"Yes, but I'm not impressed easily, I have a very specific type of list that needs all the boxes ticked." Roman wasn't going to give up, and he wanted her to realise that he didn't give up easily over anything, ever.

"And I tick all the boxes?" Freya asked in a doubtful tone.

"We are discussing topics over coffee; the atmosphere is comfortable. You have enquired about the business and what I do, which shows you have an interest. Both you and I are asking questions and giving each other honest replies. Sounds like it is a job interview, does it not? Also, I have told you the qualities you possess, are what is required." Roman held up his finger and did a tick gesture in an invisible box after he spoke.

He grinned only slightly, and looked at her as he leaned back in his chair, he moved one arm out and rested it to the side, his long legs moved and stretched out, shoulder width apart. He took up the space with a type of flair and style that was extremely masculine.

Freya couldn't help but look at him sitting there and noticed his long and tall handsome figure. She was a little uneasy and believed that it was all too good to be true. She turned the cup on the table and thought that realistically she didn't have anything to lose. What would have been the harm in trying to find work that wasn't too far from where she lived? She would be earning a wage and could slowly start to work her way up and publish more books than she had previously. She was a fast learner and could pick up things quickly, but she wasn't quite confident enough to give an answer.

"Freya, the reason why I'm asking you is because, I see great potential in you. I have scanned over some of the writing you have on the floor over there and granted I have not read any of your books, I believe that you are a great author. I value a person on their talents and their nature. You are writing in the old shorthand and use cursive, those written languages are a dying art, but not for you. You have some old-fashioned qualities that are rare to come by these days. I understand that you have been mistreated in the past when it comes to employment, but I can promise you that you will not be treated as such here. On the days when it is quiet you are more than welcome to use the resources here to write if you wish, I have no problem supporting you in your own work and career. I just ask for your help in return and any support that you can give me. We would both be supporting each other as business associates."

Freya understood that Roman was very professional when it came to his work and he did strike some of her own personal boxes that were ticked when he spoke. They both stood and Roman showed her where she would be working. The desk was very large it had all the newest and up to date equipment a long screen that could be used for multi-tasking, everything was set up ergonomically for support of the persons health that would be sitting at the desk for long amount of time. There was a cupboard next to it for personal belongings and a bar fridge to the side for personal food and drinks. The chair was very hi-tech and moulded to her back when she sat in it. There were small things that needed tweaking to make it her own but when she thought about her small, old kitchen chair and work desk at home, she felt like she was betraying herself.

"It all seems lovely, when would you need someone to start?" Freya asked, as she made her way to the fireplace and collected her things.

The clock was ticking over, and her bus would be arriving soon. She suddenly wanted to go home as she was a little intimated by everything. She tried to hide her unease, by placing a smile on her face and placing everything quickly in her bag. She looked around to see if she had forgotten anything, but all she could see next was Roman walking towards her. He was stoic and seemed to have a hard exterior, but she didn't feel like he was lying. Freya had lost her trust in many people, but at times she felt like she was just best left to her own devices. Roman stood in front of her and handed her a paper with information about the job and its entitlements.

"Freya, please take as much time as you wish to think it over. It would be a great pleasure to work with you, whenever you are ready." Roman looked at her eyes one more time as he had a feeling that he would never see them again.

Freya took the paper and put it in her bag.

"I should have an answer by tomorrow, I appreciate everything that you helped me with today. Your kindness and hospitality have been something that I find very rare and hard to come by." Freya smiled nervously.

Roman held out his hand and Freya gently placed hers in his. They kept eye contact and Roman could only concentrate on the way her smooth skin was feeling between his fingers, then as the bus pulled up outside, he released her hand slowly.

"Enjoy your day, Roman." Freya said, as she walked out the door and headed towards the bus.

Roman watched her board the bus and kept his gaze on her while she was seated. He felt his heart drop into his stomach as he was afraid that he would never see her again. He realised that she was uneasy at the end of their conversation, and he was hoping that she would give him an answer. Other than his previous love, this woman that he met today was the rare time he was struck with awe and carried into the undertow of beauty, at first glance. Her lemon amber eyes were something that he had never seen. Her hair, face, and china doll skin had his mind occupied with the wonder of where she came from, and who her family were. In all the time he had been in this building he had never seen her before and wondered that perhaps they had crossed paths many times but never had the opportunity to meet. He thought that perhaps nature had its way of making things happen, perhaps the leaving of Shelly shifted all things into the next chapter of his life. He trusted nature and always relied on it, rather than the human word.

As he was about to unplug the hair dryer, he noticed that there was a paper poking out from under the sofa. When he picked it up, he saw the shorthand and knew that it was Freya's. He took it into his office and started to decipher the script.

It was a page about a woman who travelled to a different time, and she had fallen in love with a great King. The woman needed to return to her own time to save his empire and people, using any means necessary; including using herself as the sacrifice if that was what was required. Her love for the King in the past time was greater and deeper than any love she had ever experienced before, and if she could not be with him, she had never wanted to love another again.

When Roman finished reading the page, he leaned back in his chair and made up his own theory that the woman in the story was an avatar that Freya used for herself and the King she fell in love with, was a man who she only dreamed about and didn't exist in her world. He also thought that perhaps she had been heart broken and misunderstood and was writing the story to console herself. Roman always enjoyed creativity, he remembered taking his wife to the orchestra and other artful events. Creativity in Romans world was important, as he needed inspiration himself, to design some rings and items of jewellery for others and have them made by talented craftsmen to satisfy his clients and fulfil their hearts desire.

Freya would be a great asset to him, and she would be his muse, so to speak. Her personality, imagination and talent would be the very signature of such fine treasures. When he turned the page over, he tried to find any kind of contact information but all he could find in the bottom corner was Freya Lust printed on the page. He wondered if that was her pen name or birth name. She was a mystery that he hoped would find her way back to him. Roman hoped that he was worthy of having her in his life whatever form it may be.

He checked on the book websites for her work and found a large amount of romance novels and all fantasy, love fiction. He added whatever he could find to his cart and checked out all the books. Roman did enjoy reading and he thought that perhaps he could get a deeper insight to what kind of woman she was by looking at her work. He checked the express box, and they would be all delivered in the morning. When he checked any social medias there was nothing available nor any videos with information. So Roman decided to call a friend and get them to do some of the searching on his behalf. He wanted to know everything, and he wouldn't settle for less.

***

As Freya arrived home at her little cabin in the holiday park, she collected her mail and checked on the book sales in the small convenience store which was also the office. She saw that the books had been restocked, and she smiled as she knew that they would sell like hotcakes in the park. She loved living there as she never really felt alone. It was its own small community, and she was one of the long-time tenants along with others who rented a caravan or cabin.

"Restocked them this morning, lots of mothers on holidays with their kids said they need something to read." Mary poked her head up from the computer as she just finished booking people in to stay.

"Well, it's kind of the targeted audience, so as long as they keep selling, I'm happy to write them." Freya beamed a smile at Mary, as she loved selling her books here.

The whole thing just worked, and it made everything more comforting.

"What's the newest one honey, and when's it coming out?" Mary raised her eyebrows and winked at Freya, as she was trying to get some information.

"It's a secret, shh!" Freya tapped her nose and walked out through the park.

When she greeted everyone, she knew she walked up the three wooden steps to the cabin she opened her door and let the fresh air inside, as she dropped all her things on the floor and decided that she needed some more coffee. She wiped her hands over her face as she remembered her work flying away in the wind and was dreading the process of re-writing it all over again. As the kettle boiled, she turned on her old computer and let if fire up slowly. She kicked off her shoes and looked at the mess that was falling-out of her bag. Tipping it upside down, she sorted through the pages and tears came to her eyes when she saw the way it had all been battered by the wind and rain. She put them in the best order that she could and put sticky notes with the page numbers missing in-between. There was a total of thirty pages that needed replacing and she wasn't worried about someone stealing her work. She was more worried about not being able to fully complete it with the same emotion and love.

When she started writing the story it was a life's work that she started many years ago and kept adding to it and changed things as she went. Every page and word were influenced by things that had happened to her in her life at that particular time. It wasn't just a story; it was more like a personal diary of sorts, a fantasy that fulfilled every desire and dream she had. Piles and piles of papers were stacked on the table next to her and they all belonged to the same story.

It was a piece of work that needed time and if the heart wasn't in it then she wouldn't work on it.

A buzzing sound came from her computer and then a pop. She looked up as she could see a small thin wave of smoke come out from the old speaker vent and the screen had a white line going through it. In a panic she went to unplug it from the electrical point and then she just stood there with her hands on her hips. She always saved everything on USB and made copies, but this was just the final straw for her day. She took the computer and threw it outside. It crashed down the stars in a miserable heap and then she threw the keyboard out after it. Roger who was the greens keeper and maintenance man, was driving past in his small truck. All he did was stop and take one look at Freya and he knew that it was not safe to ask questions. As she walked back inside and slammed her door behind her, Roger got out of his truck and picked up the broken machine.

"I don't know what you did, Mr Computer but your time is over." Roger dropped the rubbish into the back of his truck and without question he drove away.

As Freya sat on her kitchen chair sipping on her coffee, she looked at the work contract that was sitting on the floor. She picked it up and decided to give it a once over, the amount that would be paid was more than plenty and she even saw that there would be a month's advance. Company credit card and choice of company vehicle would be included. Freya frowned at the last part as she didn't like cars. She did have a license, but she had a fear of being behind the wheel as she had a small accident many years ago and was never brave enough to drive herself after that.

The accident wasn't fatal, but it was enough to write off her car that she spent a long time saving for. Small cuts and bruises and a sprained wrist kept her in hospital for a few days after the accident, but she only had herself to blame, as she was fatigued from writing to much and ignored her body's need for sleep. The fact that she had a nasty break up a week before didn't help, but it was a blessing in disguise as the accident was a big wakeup call and she changed many things and the way she lived her life.

Chapter 3

Two days passed and Roman was growing restless. Even though he was a patient man he was starting to think he should interview anyone from the pile of papers that was left on his desk and give them the job.

As he was sitting with his feet on the desk, crossed at the ankles, he had been thinking of a way to find the woman that walked into his life and then disappeared. Just when he was about to turn the page on the last chapter from the tenth book that he was reading, his email tone went off on his computer and he grunted as he didn't want to be disturbed during the final chapter, He placed the book down on his chest and had a look to see what the message was. To his pleasure, it was from the investigation into contact details for Freya.

He clicked on the mouse with his shoe and then he grinned as he was finally put at ease. He was a little surprised when he saw that she lived in a holiday cabin park which was only a ten-minute drive from his office. He folded the page that he was in the middle of reading and put the book down on his desk. Picking up the phone he dialled the park number.

***

Freya was folding her laundry when she heard a knock at her door, Mary had come to see her, and told her that there was a phone call from a Mr Roman Mason, at the office.

It surprised her as a little bit of fear mixed in with her emotions. She almost told Mary that she didn't know the name, but when Mary told her that he had found a few of her story pages, Freya was relieved and made her way to the office.

"Freya, speaking." She answered.

"Freya, Roman here, it's nice to hear your voice again."

"Oh, thank you." She replied.

"I have some good news for you, I usually jog to and from work every day and I have managed to pick up fifteen pages of your writing that I have found. I have them safely here if you would like to collect them, or I can mail them to you if you like?"

"Oh my, thank you so much, I'm so relieved to hear that, I was starting to think I would have to start it all from scratch, but what you have told me has certainly lifted my spirits. I will make my way there today and should arrive in the afternoon if you are still open?"

"Yes, I will be here all day, and I don't usually go home until later in the evening."

"Oh, that's good to know, sometimes public transport can be unreliable."

"Have you given any more thought about the job, and taken a look at the information I gave you?" Roman asked hopeful.

"Oh, yes, I have been meaning to speak to you about it, but I have been a little nervous about it all, and that's me being honest. I thought perhaps you were being kind to me because you felt sorry for me."

Roman was silent as he had realised, she had completely misunderstood, he needed to reassure he that he was genuine.

"No Freya, I am definitely interested in having you work by my side, and I was honest when I told you that I see great potential. I didn't feel sorry for you, as you have just said, I have been very genuine in all my intentions. As a matter of fact, I have been reading your books and am very amazed by your creativity and imagination. I could definitely use your creative gift here."

"Oh, well that's a lovely thing to say." Freya replied shyly.

"It's not a thing to say, Freya, I mean it, you are gifted, and I would like to see you again at your earliest convenience."

"I don't live very far. I should be there in about twenty minutes or so, and then I'm happy to talk to you further." Freya replied happily.

"I look forward to seeing you then." Roman replied softly.

"See you soon, Roman."

Freya jumped for joy when she hung up the phone and gave Mary a hug even though she wasn't expecting one, she hugged Freya back.

"Oh, I'm so happy, pages that I lost have been found, it's such a relief." Freya said, as she squeezed Mary tightly.

"Yes, well Roger told me that your computer was kicked out of the park the other day I was starting to worry that there wasn't going to be any more stories coming."

"Oh no, don't you worry Mary, there is definitely more coming your way." Freya released Mary and giggled as she saw that her glasses had been squashed off her face.

Humming to herself she put on a denim skirt and boots along with a black tank top and threw a cardigan over her shoulders before leaving for the bus stop. Freya collected her purse for the bus ride, she stopped at the door as she almost forgot the work contract.

***

As Roman had finished the final chapter he threw the book in the box full of the ones he had completed. He was confused as the endings were always left open and he was feeling like he was being cheated. He wanted to know, full stop if there was a happy, forever after.

Roman wasn't a movie fan, but he did enjoy a good story. He used to spend days on end watching movies with Faye when she was in recovery, and somehow, he was always the one who got sucked into the story and wanted to know how it ended.

Freya's books did have happy endings, but he felt like it needed a bit more of a final kick at the end, a bit of spice, 'the big bang' so to say of complete finalisation with a declaration of love.

Just as he was about to pick up the next book, he heard the doorbell as someone had made their way inside.

"Hello, Roman?" A familiar voice called out and as he made his way to the front of the office, he was once again taken into a trance, as he set eyes on the mysterious beauty.

"Freya, it's good to see you again." Roman said, with a soft smile as he approached her slowly.

Roman held out his hand and Freya shook it. He was trying to stay composed as he was full a strange energy he hadn't felt in a very long time. He suddenly remembered he forgot to hide the boxes of her books he ordered. As he saw them in the corner of his eye. Roman tried his best to keep her attention averted from the packages.

"Please, have a seat, and I will get your pages for you."

"Oh, thank you, I'm a little excited, I'm happy to stand." Freya replied, as she was looking around.

She looked at her surroundings and saw the boxes piled up against the corner by the front door. When she looked closer, she recognised the name of one of the bookstores, and she was a little suspicious.

"Here they are, I'm sure I may even come across some more as I go about my travels." Roman told her, as he walked out with the pages in his hands.

"Oh, thank you." Freya went to take the pages but Roman pulled them back and she frowned at him.

"Roman, please what is this?" She asked him, lifting her eyebrow and smiled.

"I'm afraid, I'm going to need your answer." Roman said, as he stood there looking directly into her eyes and didn't move.

"Oh?" Freya crossed her arms and tapped her foot as he held the pages, Roman tapped them against his thigh.

"Alright already." Freya threw her hands in the air and gave in.

They exchanged papers but Roman didn't let go of the pages in a playful way as he enjoyed seeing her tiny nose scrunch when she started to pout.

"Thank, you!" Freya said, in a small aggressive manner as he let go of the pages and she flipped through them to see what was found.

"You have missed a page." Roman said, as he pulled a pen out of his shirt pocket and handed it to her to sign.

"Oh, I don't like driving." Freya replied honestly.

"What do you mean?" Roman asked her.

"I have a fear of driving. I was in an accident a few years ago; and I don't like to be on the road behind the wheel."

"Oh." Roman said, as he looked at her and was grateful that she was still alive.

"That's something we can work around." Roman told her, as he initialled the page and rolled the papers putting them onto the reception desk.

"When will you be jointing me, Freya?" Roman looked at her and saw that she was defeated as he kindly and cleverly bargained.

Freya squinted her eyes, and she tipped her chin up at Roman with a small grin on her face.

"How did you know where I live?" Freya asked as, she nibbled on her bottom lip.

Roman simply ran his hand over his thin beard as he realised, he had been caught out.

"I had done some research." Roman lied.

"You mean spy?" Freya concluded.

"Not, directly." Roman replied

Freya just threw up her hands as she didn't really think the conversation was going anywhere, so finally gave him the answer he was after

"Yes, Roman, I would like to come work here. My computer died two days ago and my funds a are running dry. I could really use the support and I do appreciate it."

"Very well then. Please come into my office, and we can discuss a few things."

Freya followed and she almost tripped over another box before she sat in the big chair opposite Roman's desk.

"Well, looks like you have done some book shopping." Freya announced, as she looked around his desk.

Roman pulled out his chair and kicked the box of open books under his desk so she couldn't see before he answered her.

"Yes, there was a new array of germ stone books that caught my eye, and I was going to do some research."

"Oh excellent. Maybe I can use them to get a bit of background knowledge for myself." Freya replied happily.

Roman ran his tongue over his teeth with his mouth closed, and groaned as he realised, he was going to have to do a lot of book shopping when he got home.

"Yes, they should come in handy, and it will be a useful tool for you." Roman supported her comment.

"Great!" She said, as she laid her hands in her lap.

"So where do we begin?" Freya asked.

"At the beginning." Roman answered.

He pulled out his drawer and handed her keys to the building. He made a couple of quick phone calls and organised all the financial things she needed, as well as handed her a credit card with five thousand dollars as the month advance. Freya just stared at the card in her hands.

"What? Are you sure?" She asked, wide eyed and smiling.

"Well, yes, you need to set yourself up for the job." Roman encouraged her.

"I will need you to organise a phone for yourself, and there will be communication from your home if you wish to work at home on some days, the choice is yours."

"Oh." Freya just thought about her computer.

"My computer-"

Roman stopped her by raising his hand while looking at his screen.

"I have one unused and unopened in the back room, you can have that if you like?"

Freya was amazed at this wonderful man that was giving her everything she would ever need. Never had she been treated so well in any workplace.

"Roman, I really must thank you again, it's very much appreciated."

But then she frowned as she remembered she had no way to get the computer home.

"I can't carry it on the bus though." Freya scratched her nose in confusion.

"I'm happy to drive you this afternoon if you wish, or I can have it delivered to your home if you prefer." Roman offered, as he was curious to see where she lived.

He always made sure to give her options that she would feel comfortable with. He didn't want to come across as the kind of man that was forcing his way into her life.

"Oh, that would be wonderful. I would like it if you could drive me, there is a lot of sneezing going on in the buses lately, and I don't really want to get a cold while I start a new job."

Roman just nodded his head slowly as he looked at her beautiful eyes. He could see her lips moving and was in a daze. She could have been talking about how ants migrate into colonies, and he would happily look at her and nod his head all day long.

"I'm just so happy that you have found my pages, it's just such a relief." Freya finished, as he didn't hear the rest of what she was saying. So, he grasped on to the last of what she had said and went on from there.

"I have been changing my course every couple of days, and I am confident that there will be more. It's just a matter of time before the pages find their way back to you,

I'm sure."

Freya nodded at the optimism, he was already a great

help, and she was excited, nonetheless.

"So, tell me, Lust?" Roman queried.

"Oh, no its more like 'L-oos-d' the 'u' is dragged out,

and the 't' is pronounced more like a 'd'."

"L-oos-d." Roman repeated. "It's a very unique

name."

"It's a name I gave to myself when I was old enough."

Freya smiled as she looked down at her hands.

Roman wanted to ask her what her name was at birth,

but he thought that there was a reason she no longer wanted

to carry it, so he dropped the thought of asking. Roman

clicked on his mouse and all the front doors and window

shutters closed and locked. He stood from his chair as he

began the beginning of her employment.

"Let's get you set up, shall we?"

Roman stood by his office door and waited for Freya

to exit the room first. As they walked down the hallway,

Roman asked her if she wanted to take anything from the

dressing room as it would now be hers and she could change

and do what she liked to suit her taste and take whatever she liked. Freya accepted his generosity and filled bags with clothing and loaded them into the back of the large, and very shiny black pick up that was parked behind the building. Freya watched Roman as he lifted the heavier items such as a new chair and cabinet on to the back tray of the car, he added boxes of paper and other supplies that she may need at home. Once they were ready Freya directed Roman where to drive and he parked out the front of her cabin.

"Home sweet home." Freya said, as she climbed out of the tall car.

Roman looked around and noticed that it was a very tight knit community. Everywhere they turned people greeted Freya. She smiled brightly at everyone and even small children that rode their bicycles past her home called out to her by name. She greeted them the cheeriest and pretended to chase them as they came closer. The children squealed with delight and kept going around the park.

"You seem popular." Roman said, as he grinned a little and lifted things on to her veranda.

"Oh, the kids are gorgeous, I love them." Freya smiled, and her cheeks were pink with love as she said the words.

Roman enjoyed seeing this, as he loved and regarded a woman very highly especially if they were of a maternal and nurturing nature. Freya unlocked her front door and Roman slowly made his way inside. As he looked around, he saw that the place was very small and a little on the chaotic side. Although it was clean there was a living and kitchen area then a short hallway that had a bathroom with laundry, and then at the end of the hall there was a bedroom. There wasn't much in the way of storage but as Freya was on her own, this small place seemed fitting for her needs. He looked over to where there was a small coffee table in the kitchen section and then there was a table that seemed a bit larger in the living area against the wall and that was where all the stacks of papers and manuscripts were piled up. Roman started to move around and he assumed that the computer would go on the larger table, so he started to unpack and watched Freya move things to make room.

"You could use some shelving." Roman told her, as he connected wires and plugged devices together.

"Oh, yes, I was looking around for furniture, but I couldn't find anything small and cheap enough." Freya moved her stack of papers and wriggled past Roman as she cleared more space.

"I am happy to organise some for you if you wish, I have time on the weekend if you are free?" Roman tried to ignore the feeling of her backside against his leg as she was reaching for more paper.

"That would be wonderful." Freya replied, as she turned and found her face against Roman's chest.

She slowly looked up, and they stared into each other's eyes.

"Sorry, it gets crowded in here." She smiled, shyly but she also noticed that Roman didn't move even though there was space behind him, he just kept looking at her. She looked at his mouth and saw that there was a slight curve of a smile, but she was preoccupied with the way he towered over her. Never had she been in the presence of such a handsome, masculine male.

Roman held up the plug from the computer and kept his voice soft as he spoke.

"Tell me then, where do you want it?"

Chapter 4

Freya looked at the plug waving passed her nose, and she pointed to her left.

"On the table." She replied, as she swallowed hard and then decided she needed a drink.

She hopped and leaped over her papers and made her way into the kitchen.

"Would you like a drink?" Freya asked out of courtesy.

"Not at the moment, thank you, Freya." Roman replied, as he set up the computer.

Freya opened a bottle of water and leaned against the sink as she was admiring Roman's backside, narrow waist, and long legs. She sipped from her bottle slowly and she couldn't help the 'Mm,' sound she made, as her view influenced a loud thought.

Roman turned around slowly as he went to reach for more equipment out of the box and Freya put the bottle down.

"That's good water." She said, then made her way back outside to get some fresh air.

After a few hours the workday was over. Everything was set up and Roman brought out a tape measure. He took his time and accurately measured small spaces, her walls and anywhere else he could see potential for storage. He wrote numbers down on a note pad, and Freya was surprised at the way he was very precise he measured everything a few times before finalising his drawings for some shelves and small bookcases. Freya was overjoyed with the way he was so helpful and prompt in doing things. He didn't mess around and was straight to the point. He seemed experienced in many things; he was domesticated which showed in the way he tidied up after himself and even used the dustpan a broom to clean up the mess that accumulated from unpacking and moving things around.

"How much do I owe you for the shelving?" Freya asked, as she was a little nervous about the pricing.

"Nothing." Roman answered, as he put the notepad in his back pocket.

"Why? I mean, it's for my home so-" Freya replied, but then stopped as Roman started to move out of the room.

Roman didn't mean to ignore her, he just didn't feel like explaining anything, it was a quirk he had. When he wanted to do something out of the goodness of his heart to help someone, he didn't want the offer of money or questions. Freya understood that Roman was the one who brought up the furniture and she also knew that Roman was aware that she didn't have much in the way of money, so she decided to stop the questioning of the kindness and just accept the help.

"Thank you, Roman." Freya held out her hand to him.

"You're welcome." Roman seemed pleased that she didn't continue with her questions, so he shook her hand and packed up his car.

"I will see you in the morning." Roman called out from his car window as he started the engine.

Freya nodded and waved as he drove out of the park.

In the morning, Freya made her way outside and as she closed her door behind her, the black pick up stopped in front of her cabin. The window rolled down and she saw that Roman was waiting for her.

"Um, Good morning?" Freya said, as she was a little surprised.

"Morning, Freya." Roman replied, as she slowly made her way to the car.

She scrunched up her nose as she was about to ask what he was doing in front of her home, but Roman beat her to it.

"I have some materials to collect this morning for your shelving, I thought I would give you a lift to the office, as it is on the way if you like?"

Freya was unsure, but she just smiled and thought that out of the good nature she would prefer to be driven, as the morning transport was always packed full.

"That would be lovely." Freya replied.

Roman reached across and opened her door for her. She handed him a coffee in a travel mug, and he helped her place her things inside so she could climb in and sit.

"Oh, I could get used to this." Freya smiled, as she looked at Roman.

"My own private chauffeur." She said in a cheeky way, and then they began to move.

"I am happy to drive you if you like. I never really have a use for the vehicles otherwise." Roman leaned back in his seat and turned out onto the road.

"So, how do you travel? You don't run everywhere, I'm sure?" Freya wasn't sure, but she was intrigued.

"No, I have a private driver that takes me to functions if I require him to, but having said that, I usually run everywhere else or have things delivered."

Freya sipped on her coffee and smiled as she enjoyed the idea of having such a life.

"Sounds like you are spoiled for choice, a private driver. Wow! That would be exciting." She looked ahead as she noticed that Roman turned on the radio.

It had been a long time since he had been in a car with a woman and the morning commute would be slow, so he thought background noise would ease the strange feeling he had sitting next to her.

"It is good to have options. I find it uncomfortable to drive in black tie." Roman leaned his arm on the window and held his finger to his chin.

"Black tie?" Freya asked.

"Yes, there are functions for charities that happen a few times a year, and I have always sent Shelly and her husband to a few of them, as I didn't really like to attend. If I would have to attend it would be rare."

"That sounds lovely that you are involved with charities, what happens with these events?"

"They have a formal ball once a year, and then smaller events that are more in the way of dinners and meetings with others. All the proceeds go to research and any charity you choose. The ball is dancing, dinner and small auctions, as well as a small dancing contest. The winners are awarded five thousand dollars to donate to any charity of their choice."

Freya was amazed at what she was hearing and she was even more struck with the way he said he would send his past employee with her husband on his behalf.

"Why did you send Shelly and her husband? Are-, are you married? Or in a relationship?" Freya asked honestly, as she wanted to know more about him.

"Once, and no." Roman replied, as he pushed the indicator stick down with a little more force than it needed.

He always knew the question would come but he was able to answer things about himself briefly, he had lots of practice at it over the years.

"Oh, forgive me, I didn't know." Freya said, as she realized his tone and noticed the body language when he drove the car.

"There is nothing to forgive." Roman said, as he looked at her.

He pushed a door button as he pulled up at the office garage. Freya made a mental note not to harp on any relationship conversation around Roman she took his word as it was given to her and accepted the answer. There seemed a mystery about Roman but Freya enjoyed the unknowing parts, as it made the experience of being around him more welcoming. She thought perhaps that he may have been divorced or widowed. Roman didn't wear a ring but there was a dent in his finger that showed a wedding band had been there for a very long time. She assumed then maybe he was a wealthy Batchelor and could pick and choose female company when he wanted it or desired, but then she thought about the way he presented himself and the way he helped her and that thought slowly faded away.

As the day progressed there was lots to do, there was work that needed catching up on. Freya was busy organising her desk and a phone for herself. Roman was busy with people that came in and asked his expertise about the stones they had found. Freya stood next to him and made notes as he explained things and showed her what to do. There was a lot of information to take in and she was trying to make sense of the mud that was in her head.

The first day at a new job was always overwhelming for the senses and she was grateful when there was a moment for quiet as she wrapped her head around everything. Roman sent her to the grocery store across the road, he gave her a list of food and drinks he enjoyed. The refrigerator was running low and he asked her to pick whatever she desired for herself. Once the kitchen was restocked and the small, odd jobs of steaming shirts and taking things to the dry cleaners was done, the clock was ticking over to the end of the day.

Roman came out of his office as Freya was packing up her bag, and he noticed her bare feet.

"Shall I drive you home, Freya?" Roman asked her, as her hair was more frazzled then usual and she had a small slouch in her posture.

"Please." Freya's tired smile and glasses slipping down her nose were an endearing sight for Roman to behold.

She had worked hard and very well for her first day. As she made her way passed him without her shoes on, she was much shorter and Roman admired the way her wide hips swayed when she was walking down the hallway. When she reached the garage, she looked over to the side and saw that there was wood piled up. She assumed that it was for her shelving.

"Is that for the shelving?" Freya asked. Roman nodded as he opened her car door for her. "It's a lot more than I imagined." She said, as she put her seat belt on.

Roman grunted and closed her door to avoid any more conversation about the wood and then climbed in the driver's side.

"Does this weekend suit you?" Roman asked Freya plainly.

"Yes, I suppose." Freya answered, as she could see that Roman wasn't going to be swayed about his offer.

"Very well then, I will come by tomorrow at nine am if you like?" Roman asked, as he drove her home.

"Yes, that would be great, thank you." Freya replied, as she wiped her hand over her tired face.

Freya wasn't much of a talker on the way home. She was tired and run off her feet. She was looking forward to a hot shower and food, pizza would be the order of the day and then typing up of her notes. It had been so long since she was so busy and had new things to learn. She felt like it was her first day of school all over again. Roman came to the entrance of her park and he turned to her as his curiosity got the better of him.

"Tell me Freya, what is your relationship status?" Roman asked formally.

"There is no relationship status." Freya replied and then started giggling and snorting with laughter. "There hasn't been one for a very long time."

She opened her door and slipped down the seat, planting her feet on the ground. "Thank you for everything today, Roman."

Roman nodded and she closed the door. He stayed until Freya climbed her small steps, he enjoyed looking at her little feet and big thighs as she walked. Once she was inside Roman turned the car and drove home.

Freya sighed when the hot water ran down her body, she was smiling to herself at how lucky she had been to meet such a man as Roman. She started to think about the story she had been writing and thought that she had some things she could add as she had been inspired by the last week. When she was relaxed, she sat in her bed and grabbed her notebook, she started to design a character that had the same background as herself and then one like Roman. Even though she didn't know that much about him, she decided that it would be another work in progress, and it would evolve along the way, like her other story had been over the years.

She was thrilled with anticipation about where the characters could lead the story, so she came up with a few names and then crossed off the ones she didn't think matched together. She decided there would be no harm in using the first names as they were, as they made a fitting match when they were written on paper. Roman King and Frey-Anna Quinn, she scribbled on the page. It was the first time she had written her real name on a page, but she felt a sense of nostalgia when she looked at it. The name given to her at birth and then as the little girl grew, she was sent off to a boarding school and never returned home. Never visited by her parents and never collected for holidays, she remembered the night she ran away and went to a homeless shelter where she was taken in and cared for. Freya nearly had a tear fall from her eyes as she ran her finger over the names but then she decided that it was time to give the little girl she once knew a happy story.

She got more excited, and more ideas ran through her head as she jotted down rough notes about what the story would be about and then as the inspiration hit, she climbed out of bed and sat at the new computer. She was in love with the way it was perfect in every way and so much easier than her nineties edition that she threw down the stairs. She became addicted and before she knew it was daylight outside. Not sleeping much was second nature to Freya, but she decided that she would be able to have at least a couple of hours before Roman showed up at her door. Typing the last paragraph, she looked at the clock, it was coming up to six am and so she saved her work and went to bed.

***

As Roman finished another of Freya's books he was already on his third coffee. He grew restless and grunted as he looked at the clock on the office wall. Wearing his bootcut ripped jeans and a form fitting t shirt, he uncrossed his ankles and put on his steel capped work boots that he used when he helped his younger brother Finn with carpentry. He turned the book and saw the title called 'The Love Slap, By Freya Lust'. He thought that it was another ending that could have used a bit more juice. Fair enough the declarations of love were great, but it just lacked the depth in the words and chemistry. He started to wonder if perhaps Freya wrote her love scenes from experience, and then it made him angry when he pictured with another man in her bed. Pushing the thought out of his mind, he wondered that perhaps because she said that there was no relationship status; that she had never experienced the real heart, body and soul, love that he had earlier with Faye.

He grunted as he looked at the artist cover with the man, bare chested and all muscles with the fair maiden and her voluptuous breast and dress pulled off her shoulders. It was very fair to say that she had a wonderful imagination, but why did the characters always have to be so typical? He threw the book in the box and made his way outside where he had worked on some shelves through the night. He never went home because he was too preoccupied with keeping busy. He cut materials in all hours of the night and bolted certain pieces together so they could be added to Freya home without complication. He ran his hands over the wood and made sure that everything was correctly cut and planed. He put together a few small narrow bookshelves and then added small dowels so that he could save time later. Once he had completed everything, he needed, he loaded up the work horses that he would use to cut materials on as well as, tools and all kinds of other things he used were added also. By the time he was done it was time to leave. He collected two cups of coffee on the way as he imagined that perhaps Freya would like one and then as he pulled up to the front office of the park, he waited for the gates to open.

***

Freya woke up in a startling mess when her alarm went off. She jumped out of bed as there was also a heavy knock on her door. She reached for her glasses and was trying to put them on while blowing her thick hair out of her face. She managed to stumble to the front door and pull on her dressing gown at the same time, she tripped over a box that she didn't see and swore under her breath. When she opened her door Roman grinned at the adorable sight. She was sleepy eyed, and her glasses had been knocked sideways. She was fiddling with hair that was stuck in her mouth and tangled on her glasses. Thick long curls of her hair were in all directions.

"Morning." Roman greeted, as he held a cup of coffee under her nose.

Freya sniffed through her hair and finally cleared her vision.

"Morning, are you early?" Freya asked, as she turned to look at her clock.

It was right on the dot, and she understood that this man was extremely punctual.

"You look like you could use a coffee." Roman said, as she gladly took the cup from his hands.

"Absolutely, thank you." Freya replied, as she sipped and jammed open the doors for Roman to begin.

Feeling a little sleep deprived she was wincing at the noise of the tools; the loud saw was grinding through her brain and she jumped whenever Roman used the nail gun.

She noticed outside that residents were trying to see what all the commotion was about and as it was a small neighbourhood; there would no doubt be gossip later. She swallowed two pain killers for her silly writer's headache. She realised that the computer lights were something she wasn't used to and she almost felt hungover. To get away from the noise she gathered baskets of clothing and decided to use the laundry that was for residence. She needed her headache to settle and then she would be able to think.

"Roman!" Freya tried to call out, but the loud saw and the noise kept going.

Because Roman was wearing his sunglasses, she saw that he almost looked like he was grinning and as she opened her mouth, he started the saw again. Freya gave up and then walked over to the public facilities.

Chapter 5

Roman worked diligently, it had been so long since he had the chance to please a woman. As he measured and cut wood, he enjoyed the feeling of being useful, he remembered what it had been like many years ago doing things around the home for his wife. He built her a hobby room and anything her heart desired. As he looked into Freya's home, he enjoyed the small space and understood that she was a woman who didn't need much to be happy. He didn't want to change that about her either. He hoped that she would stay true to who she was; even though Roman wanted to spoil her rotten, he made sure that he did everything with care and with his heart.

As he worked, he noticed that the people were very friendly and were quick to welcome him. They came and had a quick chat to him asking questions and even asking if they could pay him for some favours. He made sure to give them his brothers number and they were just as grateful.

As Freya woke from a quick nap on the laundry courtesy bench, she was relieved that her headache was gone. Her laundry was clean and ready to be taken back. Feeling refreshed she made her way back to her cabin and properly noticed Roman this time.

She saw his casual clothing and that he was wearing a tool belt. The look suited him well and if she hadn't had met him before, she would have assumed he was a full-time carpenter. It seemed that he moulded in well to be a businessman and a handy man at the same time. His build and the way he managed things suited both roles perfectly. She felt lucky that he wanted to help her and so she managed to give him a smile as she made her way inside.

When she walked in, she could see that he had completely transformed her tiny space into a haven. There was storage everywhere and she imagined that once she had sorted everything, it would be even more spacious than it was. Her smile was beaming and she had to thank him.

"Oh, my, Roman, you are a wonder, it all looks fantastic thank you."

Roman actually gave a soft smile and nodded his head, as he walked over to her and took off his sunglasses.

"I'm glad you like it, there are a few more things I can add into your combined bathroom and laundry, then you will have even more space."

"Oh, I'm so grateful, that would be fantastic."

She almost jumped for joy as her tiny home was looking almost brand new.

"You are a talented man, what else can you do?" She asked not expecting him to answer but he did.

"I'm also a mechanic." Roman looked at her as his eyes glowed even more brighter green then before.

"Wow! You are a jack of all trades, I'm speechless, you have really taken me by surprise, I must say!"

"I appreciate that, Freya." Roman tried to hide his grin as he felt a little happier about himself.

"It's true, your fabulous." She said and stood on her tippy toes and gave him a quick kiss on the cheek.

Roman looked down as he was a little surprised, but he curled the corner of his lips into a small smile and turned back to work. Freya didn't care that she kissed him, she was over the moon and he deserved it. She tidied up her fresh clothes and then started to move about in her home. She moved things, cleaned things, and filled the shelves. When she was done in the first half of her home, she stepped back and saw that it looked like a masterpiece. As the day progressed, Freya wanted to offer a warm meal, as she was at home she enjoyed cooking. Instead of asking Roman, she would just begin, and she started cooking for two. Roman was doing her a favour and so she would return one. She cooked a lasagne and made a fresh salad. Once the food was ready, she called out to Roman.

"Lunch is ready, when you are, Roman."

Roman stopped his work and then made his way inside.

"Smells very lovely." He said, as he went to sit down at her small dinner table.

She put the food in front of him and served them both drinks. After she sat down, she noticed he didn't start eating until she did. Freya was enjoying her food and looked around at her home smiling. Roman took a mouthful and closed his eyes as he tasted the food.

"This is lovely, Freya, thank you."

"You're welcome." She replied, and she understood a little more about how Roman worked; don't question his offers of kindness, and he won't question yours. She ticked a mental box, and she was glad she had understood the man at her table.

"I received an Email this morning, about a ball that is coming up soon, I was wondering if you would like to accompany me for that evening?" Roman asked her, as he lifted his glass to drink.

"I have never been to a ball, I'm sure I could borrow a dress from Shelly if that works for you."

Roman shook his head.

"Not for this ball, it's very much a formal ball. You will need a new outfit and accessories to match."

"Oh, Roman, I wouldn't know where to start."

"I know a fashion designer, who was and old work colleague many years ago, I'm sure she can help."

"Freya stopped as she was thinking about the small fortune it would cost.

"Oh, but I don't think I could afford-"

Roman held up his hand as he cleared the air.

"My company, will pay for anything that you need, including attire for functions and meetings, that's how Shelly grew her ever growing collection, the things that were still at the office were her third refill." Roman almost smiled to his eyes, as he drank from his glass.

Freya noticed that Shelly must have enjoyed going shipping with Roman's credit card, then she laughed as she had the epiphany.

"Oh yes, now I understand, well, in that case I would love to go to the ball with you. It would give me inspiration for my new story, I'm sure." Freya widened her eyes as she looked at her food, she didn't want to give anything away about her new book.

"What is the new story about?" Roman asked, catching her out on her own slip.

Freya smiled as she knew the question was coming.

"Well, I'm still sketching out ideas, but it will be a good one."

"I do enjoy your books, I have read quite a few. Tell me, where you write from? is it experience or only imagination?"

Roman sat back to let his food settle, as he wanted to know the answer to the question, he was asking himself this morning.

"Well, I guess it's mostly imaginative, because most of the intimacy in my stories, which I'm sure you have come across, doesn't really exist in the real world."

Roman studied her face as she spoke, and he noticed that she was almost nervous and a little shy. He sat up straight and stretched out his long legs and they reached all the way across to Freya's side.

"How do you know it doesn't exist?" Roman asked her.

Freya drank deeply from her glass, and then wiped her face as she was debating on how to answer.

"Speaking from the past relationships, I've had, I can only say that it certainly doesn't exist."

Roman understood that she had been mistreated; and that her idea of what love should be like, has never been returned.

"How do you think it would affect your writing, if it did exist." Roman asked her.

"Well, I probably wouldn't sell any books, because fantasy is what's fulfilling the readers appetite. I can only imagine that there are many readers who think that it would be nice if it was real, but its most likely not, that's why they buy the books and read them to fulfil the fantasy and have a mental picture of a story with a happy ending. It's a substitute as there are many real-life experiences, that are not happy in the end or satisfying."

Roman was impressed with how she answered the question, and she did hit all the points well, but then he needed to get to the part that was bothering him.

"Suppose a man was to declare his love for a woman, what would be the ultimate ending for you?"

Freya looked into his eyes, and she wasn't sure why he would ask such a question, but she was understanding that maybe he was questioning her style of writing.

"Well like you have read, that my stories end with happy times of the people becoming lovers. I suppose if I finalised all my stories with marriage, it would be too much of a big jump and then the readers wouldn't be able to make their own conclusion. I guess it's also because I have never been married or had a proposal offered to me, I can 'imagine' what it would be like, but as far as the actual act goes, I always struggle to put it on paper."

Roman was settled that his theory was correct. She had never experienced the kind of deep love that he knew, and he almost found it unbelievable that such a beautiful woman has never been made a wife.

"I appreciate your insight Freya, thank you, and for the food it was lovely." Freya looked down at his plate and it was spotless.

"I'm glad you enjoyed it, a favour for a favour." She told him, with a large smile as she went to stand and collect the dishes.

Roman moved his legs slowly out of her way and he enjoyed seeing her in her kitchen. She had the nature of a real woman and it warmed his heart as it was a view he hadn't seen in a long time. He pushed in his chair and started to make his way back to work.

As the evening approached, Roman had completed all his set tasks for Freya's home. His stomach growled, he was dirty and dusty. As he loaded his car and thought he would take the leap and ask Freya to join him for dinner. She had already cooked lunch, he didn't deem it appropriate that she take the task of creating a meal for a second time. He washed his face and hands using the tap in the front garden, sawdust was irritating his eyes, and he took off his shirt to wipe himself down. When he was done, he tucked his shirt into his pants and walked into the door.

"Freya?" Roman called out for her.

"Yes?" She answered, as she came out of her bedroom.

"Would you like to join me for dinner this evening? There is a restaurant not far from here, I can bathe and change at the office and pick you up in an hour?" Roman leaned against the door frame as he looked down at her.

Freya tried not to stare at his bare chest that was on display, so she stared into his eyes a little too hard not looking past his neck.

"Sounds lovely, but is there something we need to discuss for work?" Freya asked as she was a little nervous.

Roman shook his head slowly as he gazed at her.

"You cooked a meal for me today, it would be a favour for a favour, as you put it and having said that, I would like the pleasure of your company." Roman looked at her and saw she was a little restless, she shuffled her feet and played with her hair as she gave thought to his request, so he added some insight to make her understand.

"I haven't been to a restaurant in many years, nor had the company of a beautiful woman such as you, it would make an old man such as myself a very happy one if you would join me."

Freya looked at Roman and could see the sincerity in his eyes, she was understanding that Roman had been alone, as she had assumed when they met, so she calmed and smiled as she gave her answer.

"Dinner would be lovely, Roman, and for the record, you are definitely not old."

Roman grinned as he rubbed the dust of his arm. "I will see you soon then, Freya."

"Thank you, Roman."

He walked back to his car and Freya watched him as his long legs and sensational masculine figure sauntered to the driver's side. After he climbed in, she closed her door and peeked through her curtain as she watched him drive away. She sighed as she realised that perhaps she was becoming attached to his company and there would be a possibility of them spending more time together other than for work. She felt blessed in both ways but deep down, she hoped that there would be more between them in the future, but until then she would have to go along the course nature had intended. Slapping her hand on her head as she thought about what he would look like naked, "Don't be stupid!" She told herself and then she went to get ready for the evening.

As Freya braided her hair and hung it over her shoulder she heard a knock at her door, she slipped into her small heels and went to answer. Her eyes widened when she saw Roman, and his widened when he saw Freya. Both of them were going to complement each other at the same time but they both stopped and Freya laughed.

"Good evening, Freya, you look lovely." Roman greeted her.

"Good evening, Roman, you look wonderful." Freya replied smiling.

Roman looked at her black curve hugging dress and grinned at her little feet in heels.

"Shall we?" He inclined his hand to the car and opened her door for her.

Freya admired his black attire, he looked powerful in his trousers and shirt, clean shoes, and groomed features. He wore a thick gold watch and cufflinks, his scent was rich in dark spices that were warming, and her favourite part was the small strand of hair that fell forwards from his brow. As he helped her in the car, he took her hand for balance and made sure her dress was free of the door, after he climbed into his side, Freya noticed he has soft music playing and she couldn't help to think it felt a lot like a date.

"So where is this restaurant?" She asked.

"The Shining Hearth." Roman replied

"Oh, yes, I have walked past it but never been brave enough to go in."

"Well, you will today." Roman said, as he drove out slowly.

"Are you comfortable, Freya?" Roman asked, as he moved switches for air.

"Yes, it's all perfect, thank you." She replied and sat with her hands in her lap.

She noticed that he slightly tapped his finger on the steering wheel to a song that came on the radio. It was a love ballad about a man who is uncontrollable when he is away from the woman he loves and adores, it also mentions the way she affects him and how he needs her to feel whole.

"This is a beautiful song." Freya said quietly.

"That it is." Roman agreed and looked at her as they approached a red light.

She noticed that his eyes floated from her face to her hair and then to her mouth he looked extremely masculine with the way he leaned his hand on the centre console.

"You look stunning, Freya." Roman said, as his emerald eyes glowed slightly.

She couldn't help but smile and look to the road, she wasn't used to such compliments.

"Thank you." She replied softly, as she could see out of the corner of her eye, he slowly moved his attention to the road again.

When they arrived, they were seated in a quiet area, heads turned as people looked at Roman and Freya, both looked beautiful and complimented one another, they were admired by many in the restaurant. Freya sat as Roman pushed in her chair for her, and then they leisurely looked at the menus. Freya's eyes widened when she saw the price of the food, but Roman told her to order anything she wanted. Once the food arrived, they happily ate in silence, and Freya was scribbling wildly on a small note pad. Roman enjoyed seeing her in her own world and the small smiles she made when she wrote, it was in shorthand but Roman was able to make outs few words.

Chapter 6

"Seems you have been struck with inspiration."
Roman said, as he grinned while eating.

"Oh, very much." She replied. "This place is the
reason, so I have you to thank."

Roman sat back as he finished his food using his
trademark stretched out arm and legs crossed at the heel in
Freya's direction, she glanced at him as he was looking at
her.

"Don't suppose you can tell me what you're working on?" Roman asked, as he lifted his glass of wine once more.

"Well, it's almost an autobiographical, fictional story, if that makes sense."

Roman actually, chuckled at her answer and Freya smiled as she looked up at him.

"You have a beautiful laugh." She told him.

He nodded his head in an appreciative manner. As he looked at her, Freya admired his beautiful emerald eyes as they sparkled in the soft light.

"You have the most beautiful eyes, Roman; I've never seen a green like that ever."

He wanted to say the same as he looked at her lemon amber eyes, but he shifted the focus.

"My father, passed them down to us."

"Us?" Freya asked.

"Yes, I have two brothers, both younger than I, Holt and Finn."

"Are they all as handsome as you?" Freya asked as she couldn't help but giggle.

Roman grinned as he appreciated the compliment, he answered in the typical male pecking order.

"I'd like to think, I gained all the best genes." He chuckled again, as he waved down the waiter for the check.

Freya waved her hand and laughed at his answer, as she knew there was some male competition when they were growing up. Once they finished, Roman drove them to a quiet spot at the beach. He helped her out of the car and gave her his coat for the leisurely walk.

The park at the beach had a beautiful walking track and he thought it would be a nice way to end the evening. As they strolled, he held out his arm for Freya to take and he enjoyed listening to her speak about the plans she had for becoming a well-known author. He stopped her at a bench and they sat.

"The cabin you have, are you renting or is it yours?" Roman, asked her.

"Oh, it's on a loan and in another fifteen years or so it will be mine." She laughed at the financial misery in her answer.

"Are you happy there?" Roman asked, as he moved a stray curl from her cheek.

"Yes, it's surrounded by people that have become like family. When I was in need they helped me, so I have never left."

Roman ran his finger down her cheek gently and then withdrew his hand. Freya stayed still as she enjoyed his touch.

"Where do you live, Roman? Tell me about yourself." She directed the questions back at him.

"I live in a renewed farmhouse, on a large block of land, it's quiet, no pets, no farm animals, or children, only myself."

Freya nodded as she understood he was a solitary man.

"Are you happy there?" She asked him, just as he did before.

Roman looked out at the distance and then turned to her.

"I've gotten used to it." He answered, as they both stood to make their way back to the car.

When Roman brought Freya to her home, he walked her to her door.

"Thank you for joining me Freya, it was a lovely evening." He took her hand in his and kissed it.

"Yes, it was." Freya replied, as she leaned in to kiss him on the cheek. He kissed her back then they both stared into each other's eyes as she unlocked her door.

"Goodnight, Freya, see you next week."

"Goodnight, Roman." Freya replied, as she walked in and closed her door.

As Roman walked down her stairs he took in a deep breath and looked around the park, everywhere lights were on and small voices were audible. As he drove out, he noticed how both cramped and private it was. It was a big difference to where he lived. As he pulled up to the office garage, he locked up the car and changed his clothes. It was coming up to late hours, so he stared on his jog home.

The next few days were a part of a new routine for both. Roman would collect Freya from her home in the morning and then he would drive her home when the day was done. As time progressed Freya became more confident in her work and was able to complete tasks on her own. She managed to take care of things without Roman's assistance or help. When Roman would have to go to meetings with shareholders or business associates from the mining industry, it would usually be long lunches and Freya would go with him as his assistant. She would take notes and minutes of meetings on the new laptop that Roman bought for her. When they would return, she would be busy writing up reports, mostly involving numbers that she didn't really understand, but Roman assured her that she didn't need to make that part of her everyday work. She enjoyed being useful to him and she always tried her best, making sure everything was completed on time. Occasionally they would share lunch together, taking turns preparing each other food in the kitchen at the office and then Roman would treat her to dinner a few times a week as it would make their lives more convenient.

Freya wouldn't need to worry about cooking or getting home late and Roman would have company which was something he appreciated. It was a win for both and they enjoyed each other's company. The conversation topic of the coming charity ball would be brought up, and Roman was in a waiting list for Freya to be fitted for a dress of her choice, by the very busy fashion designer. There was at least a month's wait and the ball was in two months' time. As more time past, Freya found that she was able to speak to Roman more openly about personal affairs and this made Roman start to speak more of himself.

He told Freya how his brother Holt, had recently married and they have a baby called William. Roman showed Freya photos of the child and he noticed how her face lit up and her maternal side made itself evident. Roman also shared some stories about how all three of the Mason brothers became mechanics and how their grandfather showed them the workings of an engine. Finn was a topic of conversation as Roman always liked to tease his younger brother. Freya admired the way he regarded his family and enjoyed listening to his stories. Even though Roman didn't mention his wife, marriage or personal relationships, Freya wondered if that perhaps he would speak about it someday. Freya was only limited in information she shared also, as she wasn't really around her family since she was a little girl. Last she heard her parents lived in Italy, or some far off place, but Freya had no desire to contact her parents. Freya always held to the story of living in a foster home as it made everything easier. Her life wasn't easy when she ran away from the boarding school. She moved from place to place and made sure never to stay long. She did however tell her parents many years ago that she was safe and happy, but she also told them that she had no desire to see them. Freya was torn a few times between trying to convince herself that perhaps her parents should be forgiven for sending her away, but then she decided that she was better off without them in her life. Over time she grew into a mature young woman and her 'non-legal' foster parents that cared for her, did a good job in looking after all her needs but, the way she was adopted wasn't in any legal form, she was taken in by a couple who found Freya hiding in their garage, when she was fifteen years old.

They had many children in their home of all kinds of backgrounds and so Freya was happy and stayed with them. Freya refused to speak when she was younger, and she gave a false name. She refused to be photographed and taken anywhere that had to do with public law, and over time she managed to gain a confidence and find work at a café and was a dishwasher, so she didn't have to speak to people. When she was old enough, she moved out of the home and came to the cabin park, staying there ever since. She went to the public records office and was able to get copies of her certificates. She paid for everything herself and then got her driver's licence shortly after. She avoided credit cards and anything where she would have to give identification and when Mary and Roger took her in at the cabin park, they made deal with Freya, that she could work at the park, and have small payments taken out of her wage for her cabin. Mary and Roger wanted her to be safe and thought a cabin would suit her better. They did lay down some rules for her and made sure she would stick to them.

Working two small jobs and making some income, she wrote her first book and sold it online with Mary's help. It became popular, and so she decided to write another and then another, making it her work and hobby. She was offered an advance from a publisher with her fifth book, and then she was able to set herself up more confidently. Mary and Roger helped her wherever they could and started to sell her books in their small store office as well as share it with others they knew. Freya loved their loyalty and looked up to them as her role models.

It was all information about a patchy past that she didn't want Roman to know about. She just thought it was all best left behind her. Freya was very much a free spirit, but her imagination and creativity was what gave her that peaceful freedom. She was happy to spend hours, writing and reading, she didn't need a social life, or needed a group of people around her. Her own company was enough, and it made her happy.

***

As another day ended, Roman had received a message from his sister-in-law saying that it was William's baptism this weekend and that they all wanted him there for the occasion. Roman got up from his desk and walked out to Freya where she was busy typing away on her story.

"Are you free this weekend, Freya?" Roman asked, hopeful that she would be.

"Yes." Freya replied, as she stopped typing to look at him.

"My nephew, is being baptised this weekend, and my family members wanted to know if I would like to attend, but I would also like it if you came with me."

Freya smiled as she was happy to be invited, but it was very much a family event. Not only did she want to go, but she also just thought perhaps she wouldn't fit in, as she never really knew a proper family lifestyle or environment.

"Are you sure, you would like me to go?"

Roman walked over to her slowly and took her hand in his as he took the leap with hope of swaying her decision.

"I am asking you, because it would mean a lot to me if you were there, and to share in the occasion with me and my family."

Freya smiled as she looked into his eyes, and she was jumping on the inside that he asked her and not anyone else, but she wanted to know what was really on his mind and she didn't like to be left in limbo. Their time together had blossomed over the few weeks they had known each other, but she needed more from the man of few words.

"Well, Roman, I need to be frank; and ask would it be like a plus one, or a date?"

"Both!" Roman replied, quickly and without hesitation, as he turned her hand in his and kissed the top of her fingers.

Freya blushed as she looked at him and he grinned when he saw that her cheeks turn red.

"Yes, Roman, I would love to go with you." Freya replied as she tried to control the butterflies in her stomach when his lips touched her skin.

"Very well then, thank you, Freya." Roman said with a grin, as he turned to go back to his office and answer the ringing phone.

After Roman locked the office and climbed in the car with Freya next to him, he looked at her as she was running her fingers through her hair and kicked off her shoes. She folded her knees up and took a deep breath as the day had been busy and she was ready to relax for the evening. Roman noticed that she looked as though she was in deep thought, but he didn't want to pry in her private business, instead he reached across and took her hand locking their fingers together.

Freya looked at him and smiled softly as she had the small flutters of butterflies in her stomach again, the electricity that she felt from their hands meeting was something that she had never experienced before and Roman was a great comfort to her. As he started the car, he didn't speak, he was just happy that she was by his side holding her hand the whole ride to Freya's cabin. When they arrived, he pulled her hand in towards him and looked into her eyes.

"You are such a beautiful woman, Freya." Roman kissed her cheek and lingered with his mouth close to hers, Freya seemed a little nervous and he only touched his lips to hers in feather light movements as he spoke.

"I will pick you up tomorrow for the baptism in the morning."

Freya could feel her eyelashes flutter as he spoke his breath was warm against her mouth and then Roman closed his mouth onto hers.

He held her face in his hands and he pressed his lips more firmly, sliding his tongue into her mouth. She felt heat rush through her at the sensation of his tongue moving with hers, his lips and everything she could feel was blissful and arousing. Freya moaned at the new and strange feelings of her body come alive, as their tongues were dancing, the warmth of his mouth and the way he moved it was all so delectable. After a few moments Roman pulled back from the kiss to pace himself and he watched how Freya slowly opened her eyes as she came up for air with him. Her eyes turned into pools of molten gold and Roman was delighted with the effect he had on Freya. He looked at her lips and they were red and full; he loved her pink cheeks that flushed. He reached past her and opened the door. She sighed as she needed to use self-control and show that she was going at the same pace. Roman released her hand as she collected her things.

"Tomorrow, then." Freya said, as she made her way out of the car.

"Tomorrow, Freya." Roman replied, and then he watched her as she made her way inside her cabin.

After Roman returned the vehicle back to his office, he changed his clothes and began on his run home. He was full of extra energy he had not felt in a very long time and found himself thinking about Freya and how happy he was that nature had brought her to him. As he ran, he noticed papers under a thick set of bushes and shrubs, they were poking out from underneath. He stopped and pulled them out, sure enough it was Freya's work and there was a total of five pages. He ran around the same area and searched high and low but there were no more to be found. He ran down an alley way and noticed that there were some water washed pages next to a dumpster, three more sheets were found, and hence he pushed the dumpster forwards and found five more.

He saw that some of them had been a little damaged, but Freya would still want them returned to her. Roman had found a total of twenty-eight pages, and he was glad that he almost completed her lost work. As he ran home, he made sure to keep her pages safe, he folded them and placed them into his deep pockets of his sweater and zipped up the pocket.

Once he arrived home, he had completed all the evening rituals and then sat down and read through the pages. He noticed that there were some words that he couldn't make out, but it seemed like it was a chapter that had an open ending. The woman in the story who fell in love with the great king; became pregnant with his child before he marched away to battle. Roman was getting intrigued by the short snippets of the story and he thought that he would ask Freya about it when he saw her next.

Roman was also thinking about how he would be seeing his brothers and sister-in-law. He adores his nephews and Lady; both of her boys were taking after Holt, and it was showing in the photos she had sent to him. Roman walked over to the cabinet in the living area and pulled out the box that had his wife's name on it. When he sat down, he pulled out the last note she wrote for him before she became too sick to move. Roman ran his hand over the paper as it was becoming thin and had been read so many times. It was something he used as a healing tool in the years after her passing it was her final instructions for him. He took a deep breath as he opened it and smiled softly when he saw her beautiful words.

My Love,

It is not good for a man to be alone. You may, miss me occasionally, you may, grieve only a little, but you must, live and love, as long as you are able.

Forever yours,

Faye-Lynne.

As Roman ran his fingers over the words he looked into the box. He picked up the small jar with the ashes of her beloved pet that she had when she was younger. He held on to these small mementos because they made him feel like she was still there when he needed to feel her presence. It seemed that no matter how much time passed he felt like he would never get back to a normal life, but this time when he took the items in his hand, he didn't feel the overwhelming grief that he always had. He seemed to think that becoming closer to Freya helped him become stronger to manage his emotions and help him overcome the past pain.

As he put the box away, he sat and went into deep thought as he watched the flames of the fire. Perhaps it was the small amount of joy he was feeling that was helping him gain strength and will power, to adjust to the changes that were happening in his life.

Chapter 7

As he thought about Freya, he couldn't help but feel
that there was a small part of her that seemed so very
familiar. Freya and Faye were both very different women,
but yet something about her nature was so similar and so
comforting. Roman had a hard time putting his finger on
what that might be. It's almost like when people say that the
'eyes are the window to our soul' Roman saw a small
familiar part of her that he swore, he had known his whole

life. The invisible connection he felt to her ever since the first time he saw her come off the bus was too coincidental. Like the pages that he had found from Freya's story it was like there were things moving in a circle and it was only a matter of time before it all fell into place.

Roman knew that there would be questions tomorrow about who Freya was and why he was bringing her along. Roman hadn't been seen with any woman for ten years and he hadn't spoken of one either. Hoping that his brothers would understand, he had no doubt that they would make Freya feel welcome, and he had no doubt that his sister-in-law, Lady, would put them in their place if they did otherwise. Even though Roman grinned at the thought that Holt had a swimming pool, he would have no hesitation throwing his brothers in the water if they tried to be smart about anything. Roman was equal in size to his brother Holt, whereas Finn was more on the smaller side. A touch shorter then Roman and thinner in build. This didn't stop Finn from making him good competition, but as his older brother he always knew how to handle his younger and sometimes very annoying sibling.

Roman grinned at the times their mother and father would pull them apart when they would have a brawl. His mother would pull them by the ears and their father would grab them by the scruff of their neck and toss them into the mud puddles to cool off from one another when things got heated in the back yard. All three boys would be punished with chores if they didn't listen to what they were told, and even thought they had stern parents, they were also fair. Everyone made sure to keep to their responsibilities. Their mother would say 'don't worry about finding the right girl, you need to concentrate on becoming the right man first.' It was something she would always tell them, and it stuck with all three.

Respect and discipline were something that Roman always took in high regard and he made sure to carry it through his whole life. He always looked up to his father and grandfather. Both were wonderful role models, displaying patience, kindness and authority when required. Roman strived to become like them, and as he thought about all the times he had helped his younger brothers, he was pleased that he was able to without excuse or hesitation. Roman was grateful for the family and upbringing that he had, then he thought about Freya and how she said she grew up in a foster home. He began to wonder if perhaps she was hiding something from him, but then he disregarded the thought as he thought over time, she would begin to share more about herself when she felt more comfortable to.

***

When they arrived at the church Roman walked hand in hand with Freya towards his family who were waiting outside. They all gathered and then greeted each other lovingly. Lady was quick to welcome Freya and Roman. The brothers all looked very smart and devilishly handsome in their formal clothing. Freya was a little nervous to meet Holt, as he was the most frightening looking of the brothers with his scowl, beard and narrow eyes. But as she was introduced, she noticed that Holt's features changed, and he was no more than a gentle giant. Holt and Finn were extremely handsome and she only looked in awe at all three of the men when they stood together and marvelled at what their father and mother must have looked like.

Tall, dark, broody and very handsome, was the only way to describe what she was witnessing with her own two eyes. Using her imagination, she could easily see them as main characters in love stories and heroes just as much. Finn on the other hand was more open and very affectionate towards Freya, he held her tightly and kissed her on the lips, as he had a knack for moving quickly. When Finn went to give Roman a brotherly hug, Roman grinned as he squeezed the air out of his younger brother's lungs, noticing the kiss he gave to Freya. Finn managed to gasp as he was released and made sure to keep his distance from Roman's woman.

The baby boy was adorable, little William was a happy bundle. He had the same green, emerald eyes that his father had and he had his mother's cheeky smile. His tiny head was covered in thick black hair that had small waves in it, which was a mixture of features from both parents. It wasn't difficult to tell who this baby belonged to, as he was very much a Mason's son. All of the brothers became the God Fathers, including Matt and Mark who were so dear to Lady and were her close family. As the words were spoken by the father of the church and the baby giggled at the cold water that was poured on his head, all involved were quick to pose for photos which would be hung on their walls.

When Roman held the child, he fit the tiny baby into one arm, and he stroked his nephew's cheek feeling the soft skin. He was taken by a moment of thought as to how lucky Lady and Holt were to have such a beautiful boy. Roman had a moment of weakness as he held the child, he was feeling guilt that he never fathered any children, but it quickly disappeared as he looked at the beautiful woman he brought with him. Deep down in his heart he hoped that nature was smiling upon him and would grant him the same blessing someday. He hoped that his time had not yet come to a close to become a father.

Finn picked up Bobby who was growing bigger and posed with him, easily throwing the boy over his shoulder in a funny photo. He was the more kindred spirit when it came to being with the children, as Finn was still very much a 'man-boy' himself. He adored all the kids as they were gathering around him for their own funny photo opportunity, and he was creative holding one by its feet and then the other upside down and tossing the other into the air. Squeals of happiness and laughter was all around Freya and she was taking everything around her. She was almost going to let the tears go, but she remembered that today was not about her, it was about this little soul that had been welcomed into the world.

Freya was asked by Lady to hold her son as she quickly had to sign some papers with her husband. Freya didn't hesitate as she reached for William, she smiled so widely and became instantly motherly. She was cooing with the boy and smothering his small cheeks with kisses. Roman saw how happy Freya was with a child and it made him surer that Freya was just the type of woman he had been waiting for. She played with the tiny fingers and baby toes. She made up her own baby language and the smile on her face only became bigger when the baby smiled back. He reached out his tiny hand and hung onto her curly hair and laughed as it tickled his nose. Freya was so clucky that she had to try to contain her own tears of joy, as the baby was making her one with her female nature.

When she was able to finally pass him back to his mother and father, Roman wrapped his arms around her waist from behind and he kissed her cheek as he was smitten with the beautiful woman.

"Have I told you how beautiful you are?" Roman whispered into her neck as he nuzzled her.

Freya smiled and giggled a little, as his lips tickled her skin.

"Well, I can never hear it enough." Freya replied, as she loved the way he was easily comfortable with her in public.

In her past relationships public displays of affection were a never occurring thing. It was almost like the partner she had didn't believe in making her feel any kind of love in the public eye. She only rested her head against Roman's chest as he held her and they looked at all the people around, un-phased by the way they fancied each other. Love should always be displayed and that was something that she always believed with her whole heart. The world was so full of hatred and negativity that it seemed rare to find people who showed that they liked each other in any kind of affectionate way.

After the event, they all returned to Holt and Lady's home to enjoy in some celebration. Wine bottles were popped open and many stories were shared. Finn danced with the children to the music playing outside, Mark and Matt were asking Freya a million questions about her beautiful hair and eyes.

Lady was busy keeping an eye on everyone and Roman was busy talking to Holt about his mechanical business. After the men had a few more drinks, Finn decided it was a good idea to try and push his oldest brother other in the pool, but he ended up in the water on his own. Fully clothed and somewhat drunk, he ended up staying in the water as it was helping him to sober. Holt decided to try and help his younger stumbling brother out of the water, but he ended up being pulled in. As the two men started cursing and wrestling, Roman pulled off his tie with a dangerous grin, he couldn't resist the rough play that began. Roman enjoyed nothing more than a good barrage of knuckles on flesh with his brothers. As Finn said something Roman didn't like, the wrestling became more serious, and water was flying everywhere. Finn tried to scramble out of the pool and reached the edge, he thought he was clear of his brother's wrath, but a big hand came up from the water and pulled Finn by his long black hair back into the water. Laughing and grunting, limbs were flying up and down and then Lady's oldest son decided he wanted to join in on the fun.

"Bombs away!" Bobby called out, as he had his floaties on and decided to run up from the back of the yard to the deep end of the pool.

Lady only gasped and all the grown men stopped and swam as fast as they could to the deep end, catching the boy by legs, arms, and torso, he was suspended in mid-air and opened his eyes as he hadn't hit the water.

"Hey!" Bobby called out, as they all lowered him, and Holt pulled him onto his back.

"We know about you and water." Holt said, as the boy hung on to his stepfather tightly and giggled as he used breaststroke around the pool.

Freya was a little more than tipsy when she made her way to the pool. Roman noticed that she was walking gingerly and had misplaced her shoes. She was laughing as she was splashed by Holt and then she removed her glasses as they were foggy and smudged.

"What time is it, Freya?" Roman asked her loudly over the voices and music, as he hoped she would come closer. He tried to hide his grin as she was perfectly falling into his trap.

"I'm not sure." Freya replied, as there was water on the face of her watch, and she couldn't see properly.

She lowered her wrist to Roman so he could have a look. Just as she was about to pull out of his reach, she shrieked and was already on her way into the water. A flurry of hair, woman, and dress, was all Roman saw as she splashed in. She spluttered as she was taken out of her alcohol impaired state.

"Roman, you beast!" Freya said, as she slapped him on the chest playfully.

She was still holding her champagne glass, and frowned as it ended up full of pool water. She spluttered and laughed as he helped her to him. She pulled the hair out of her eyes and Roman held her closely. After dipping her head under she was able to see better and she looked even more beautiful in the water. Roman thought he was seeing a beautiful nymph goddess in front of his eyes. He held her against his body and kissed her deeply he didn't care if anyone was watching as he was completely taken by her. He deepened the kiss and ran his hands up and down her body in the pool before he let them come up for air. Freya was in a daze and Roman only wanted to spend more time with her.

"Get a room!" Finn said, as he made his way out of the pool and splashed water at them both.

Roman shielded Freya as he held her, he was able to reach the bottom, but Freya could not.

"I'm so glad you came along, Freya." Roman told her, as he wiped the water out of her eyes.

Without her glasses on, Roman noticed how the evening light brought out more colour in her eyes. She was magical and he was treasuring everything about her.

"I'm so glad I came too. You have such a beautiful family, all of them are so lovely. To be honest it's the most fun I have had in a long time around a family environment."

Roman kissed her and she nuzzled into his neck as he brought them closer to the pool stairs. After drying off and letting the alcohol wear off. Lady and Holt gave some of their clothing to the guests, as they hadn't brought any with them. Before everyone said their goodbyes, Finn pulled Freya aside and Roman noticed that he was leaning in close to Freya. He knew his youngest brother was cheeky, but he didn't let it bother him as they both looked at Roman and smiled. Freya hugged Finn and then they all made their way home.

As Roman pulled up at Freya's cabin he couldn't help but hold her in his arms and kiss her in the front seat. The heat and passion was all around them, but then they stopped as they didn't want to rush into anything. The chemistry was there, and they needed to pace themselves. Roman was growing hungrier for her, as he kissed her again and again, and Freya was finding it hard to resist him. Roman didn't want the first time to be in a car or a cabin park as she meant more to him than a one-night lover.

Roman was a man and if he made love to a woman, it would be in his own territory and privacy would be needed, he wanted to make sure that there was freedom for them to express themselves as he imagined that Freya would want the same. He was groaning as he buried his face in her chest and she was running her hands up his torso under his shirt, her touch felt like fire, and she was completely overcome with the need of a man.

"Freya!" Roman groaned deeply, as he pulled back from her.

"Yes!" Freya stopped, as she looked at him.

Roman just kissed her softly as he looked into her eyes. Freya understood that Roman was feeling the same as she was, but she nodded her head as she knew he was struggling with words.

"It's alright, Roman, we should pace ourselves, and I have had a fair bit to drink." She giggled at herself trying to stay serious. Freya kissed him gently and Roman reached for her door.

"Yes, you are right." Roman agreed, as he made his way outside with her.

He kissed her hard one more time and took a deep breath of the night air. He put his hands in his pockets as he let her walk up her stairs and watched her from behind.

"Goodnight, Roman, I had a wonderful time."

"So did I." Roman replied, as he was beginning to calm down from the fire that was burning inside him.

"Goodnight, Freya." Roman said, as she opened her door and closed it behind her.

After returning the vehicle to the office, he splashed his face with cold water and changed into other clothes, he thought that a jog would help clear his mind and work off the sexual tension he was feeling for Freya. As he ran, he pushed himself harder and harder so that he wouldn't stop. He could feel the alcohol leaving his body and started to feel more energy as he kept going. He enjoyed looking at the beautiful moon and the stars as he came into the clear nature section of his run. He thought about all the wonderful things he had experienced today with Freya and could only remember feeling those things when he was very young and in a relationship. It had been so long for Roman to actually enjoy the company of a woman he admired. For years since the death of his wife he had stopped himself from experiencing that joy, and it was all because of pain and sadness. He started to feel lighter in his heart and realised that there are wonderful things in life that still are worth living for.

So much time had passed that he thought perhaps it wasn't in his future anymore, but he needed to understand that it could only work if, or when, he was truly ready. Roman was never one to treat women as disposable objects, and in the modern society relationships had become just that. He was very much the old-fashioned kind of man when it came to trying to woo a woman. He thought that perhaps Freya was also of the same breed. Judging by her writing and the things she would say, he thought she presented it all in her books, in the ways that she wrote about love and commitment. As Roman reached his home, he took a shower and laid down on his bed. He was glad that he and Freya had decided not to let their chemistry blind them, into making a quick decision and letting momentary lust overcome them both.

Lust and desire were human feelings, and it was present as it plays a part in a relationship, but as he thought about her more, he didn't want her to think that she was only a quick catch and release to warm his bed. As he closed his eyes, he thought about how it felt to hold the baby in his arms and the way Freya looked when she held him also. She was beautiful and it suited her so well; she seemed a natural around children and this was more striking than ever in Roman's mind.

***

As Freya thought about how nice it was to be included in the family event, she thought about how lucky they all were to have each other, and she wondered if it would be like that all the time. When she thought about how the brothers were wrestling in the pool, she had to laugh at the memory of them and the way they roughed around. It was proof that men never grew up, and that they would probably have a rumble no matter how old they were, as the saying goes 'boys will always be boys.' The whole day was beautiful, and she was happy that Lady welcomed her to the baptism of her child. She thought about Holt, how he was in a wheelchair and wondered if anyone had recorded his story and that it would be a great legacy if someone took the opportunity to have him tell the tale. She thought about how perhaps he survived a great struggle, heartache and pain. She wanted to make sure to meet with them again, as she was interested in the love story that Holt had with Lady.

As she thought about Roman and the way he kissed her in the pool, she was never shown that kind of tenderness before. She adored the way it made her feel like a teenager again, and that it was a reminder of just how precious time and life really is. With smiles and laughter going through her mind, she closed her eyes and went into a peaceful rest.

Chapter 8

When the new week began Roman and Freya had may things to work on together. They had meetings with shareholders that were partnered with Roman and also met with people form a sister company that specialised in the same safety industry. They had many days that were full of lunches, late meetings and lengthily conference calls. It didn't give them much time to share any intimate moments together. Many came in and out of the office with their enquiries and

Freya was run off her feet with her normal daily tasks. As the week rush slowed towards the weekend, Freya, and Roman spoke about the lovely time they had with his family and the baptism. Freya also mentioned to Roman that Finn advised her that it was the first time in a very long time that Roman had female company in a family event. Freya didn't notice that Roman was short in his answers and took it as his normal nature, but he was a little disappointed at his brother for opening his mouth, even though Finn always had his best interests at heart, he knew there were boundaries. Roman was pleased that his brothers were excited but, as the minutes passed, it was the slow prodding from Freya about his wife that made him uncomfortable.

"I really am sorry to hear of the passing of your wife Roman, if anything I would encourage you to speak about her, someone once told me that talking about things helps the healing process." Freya smiled brightly as she spoke, in the hopes that Roman would engage in conversation.

Roman was sorting through some papers and shuffled them in a rough manner as he answered her.

"Yes, so I've heard." He replied, in a stern voice.

"What was her name and where did you meet?" Freya asked innocently but Roman only grunted and walked into his office.

Freya went against her instincts and followed him in continuing her questions.

"Where you high school sweethearts? It would make a beautiful story." Freya was speaking from her heart as she wanted to know more about him in a bid to understand him better, but Roman was growing more tense.

Roman took a deep breath and thought he may try to answer a little.

"She was in the same street, we met when we were children."

Roman hoped that it would give her enough information to quench her curiosity, but he groaned when she kept mentioning more. Roman opened his cabinet drawer and filed away his papers, hoping that the phone would ring, so that she would become distracted. He walked out into the waiting area and tried to find something to do but there was nothing, so he leaned on the table and tried to think of the best way to keep Freya from continuing.

"Finn said that you never speak about her, he said he was concerned for your happiness."

"Why is everybody so quick to judge me?" Roman asked the question as he looked at the table, tempted to let out his anger on it.

"Please Roman you can speak to me." Freya said softly, as she was hoping he would.

"I encourage you to set your heart free of the weight that you carry, I would never pass judgement if you wanted to speak to me about your past love, ever, I promise, cross my heart hope to d-"

"NO!" Roman thundered the word so loud it made her jump.

He turned to face her, but Freya was having a hard time deciphering all the emotions in his eyes.

Roman was breathing heavily and he looked as though he was growing taller. His chest heaved as his eyes glowed, he managed to calm himself and then speak in a softer voice.

"No, don't say that Freya, don't ever say that."

Freya understood that she had made a mistake and stayed silent, she closed her eyes and tried to stay strong. She gave him the time to speak, as she realised, she may have pressed too much. Roman walked away from her and then moved around the room.

"My silence is always mistaken." Roman said as he began pacing by the fireplace.

"Roman, what do you mean?" Freya whispered, as she was fearful, she was losing all connection with him.

He whirled around and had fury, grief, and pain in his eyes.

"My silence is always taken as though I have no grief, I do not wish to speak about the heartache and the tragedy, of what I have lost, why can no one ever understand that?"

Roman moved in-front of Freya and stared at her golden eyes, that were filling with tears. She carefully held out her hands hoping that Roman would take hers.

"Roman I don't know what it's like to have lost a beloved like you have, I can't put myself in your shoes, but I do know what it is like to be in the complete agony of love."

Roman's eyes softened then Freya reached down to take his hand, Roman curled his fingers around hers, and he looked deeply into her eyes as she continued to express what was on her heart.

"I have loved and do love so deeply, that it tears my heart out every day, it's the love that is out of my reach, and all I want to do, is have it in my arms." Her tears fell like a waterfall as she continued to speak.

"It's like a void, that is impossible to fill. I encourage love and to love. I encourage to speak about it, to feel it, to have it, and dream about it. That's where all my writing comes from, a love I have never had in my life, and hope that it-" She stopped as she dropped her gaze to the floor, Roman lifted her chin slowly.

"I hope that it will find me, Roman, someone once said that hope is all we have, when everything else is lost. I do have hope, please open your heart to it as I have." She stepped forward and placed one hand on his cheek as she continued to speak in a soft tone.

"It's in our nature, Roman, it's what makes us human, we always know the risks that come with love, but we still welcome it bravely and willingly."

Roman lowered his brow to hers then went to hold her face in his hands. He looked into her eyes and realised that he had been defensive, but he didn't mean to hurt or frighten

Freya. She was right and Roman needed to make room for change.

"Please, Freya, understand that I am not shutting out love, or abandoning hope."

Freya nodded as she understood that Roman was on her side, and he just needed to be understood.

"I know that Roman." She said, as she closed her eyes.

"Just know that I am on your side." She said as she tried to smile through the tears.

"I know you are, Freya, and that's where I want to keep you." He closed his mouth onto hers and kissed her briefly, then he wrapped his arms around her holding her close.

"I wish, to put this behind us." Roman said, as he released her slowly.

Freya stepped back and tried to ignore the pang of pain she was feeling, she didn't want him to let her go. She had a small feeling of fear go through her, as she was worried that she had ruined any chance of a future between them. She went with her best defence and thought that perhaps they had been overlapping each other's company far too much, and that it wasn't helping on the stress levels of their feelings for one another, she needed some space as she was sure perhaps Roman needed the same.

"I need to make my way home, and if you don't mind, it's been a long and stressful day, I think we both could use some alone time to re-collect." Freya smiled faintly, as she wiped the tears away from her face.

"Goodnight, Roman." Freya told him as she opened the door and walked to the bus that just pulled up.

Roman walked into his office he placed his hands against the cabinet to try to gain focus he was in complete turmoil of what was happening inside him. He didn't want to betray his love for Faye, but he knew that he could never fully love another if he didn't free himself from the cage that was wrapped around his heart.

He knew that he couldn't keep Freya at arm's length and he didn't want to, he needed to make peace with himself, not Faye not Freya, but his own heart was fighting against him. He went into his dressing room and changed into his joggers clothing. After locking up the office he ran so much that he almost collapsed when he arrived home. He lay down on the grass and looked up into the night sky, thinking about everything that Freya had said, and he knew that she was honest and speaking truth, she was always right. It was well past any reasonable hour to call and speak to somebody like his younger brothers, so he dragged himself up to stand and went into his house.

As the new day dawned Roman arrived at the office, he decided that today would be different and both he and Freya needed to get out of the workspace. He booked two seats for the orchestra that was playing, it would be a nice day in the city and he wanted to give Freya the opportunity to dress up and make herself happy. After he changed and cleaned up, he made his way to Freya's cabin. When he pulled up, he saw her come out slowly. She seemed a little shy, but he got out of the car and reached out his arms for her. Roman gathered her lovingly and held her tightly. He took her face in his hands and kissed her deeply. Freya didn't like holding grudges and she was put at ease as her thoughts were going a million miles an hour the night before. She was having doubts about her and Roman and that they wouldn't be able to get over the small obstacles in their young relationship.

"Good morning, beautiful." Roman said, as he stroked her hair and her cheek.

"Good morning, Roman." Freya replied and took a breath before she spoke.

"I'm sorry about yesterday, I didn't mean to push you into speaking about anything you didn't want to. I just hope that it doesn't deter you from pursuing us, or me."

Roman held her closely as he kissed her forehead.

"There is nothing that could deter me Freya, please understand that. You and I are going through minor issues, they are small obstacles in the path that can be overcome. If you haven't noticed already, I don't give up easily on what really matters and brings me happiness."

Freya smiled as she looked at him and felt like they had reached a truce and they could finally move past their misunderstanding.

"Roman I just need you to understand that I want to understand everything there is about you and sometimes the past can help, of course our past doesn't define us, but it does 'refine' us, if you understand what I mean?"

Roman nodded his head as he led her to the car.

"I understand a thing or two about being refined in this life, Freya, there are things about myself which I am working on, it has been a long and difficult journey. Not only do I need patience with myself, it is the patience with others also that I am trying to better myself with."

Once they were in the car Roman took her hand and made his way slowly out of the park, as he continued to assure Freya that that the previous day would not interfere with the future.

"I understand you have many questions and as I said previously, I am not abandoning hope or forsaking love, it is like you said, 'agony' is a very apt word for it. It is love that has the biggest effect on the decisions I make and sometimes it can be overbearing when I am torn between what my heart and mind want. Over time perhaps you and I can find a solution for the discrepancies together and then we will make our way from there. I was wrong to raise my voice at you, I'm sorry, Freya, and I hope you can forgive me."

Freya knew that Roman was full of emotion and he was not angry at her, he was in pain and this she understood.

"There is nothing to forgive." Freya replied, as she held his hand tighter.

"We will be going to the office to get ready and then in a couple of hours we will make our way into the city." Roman said, as he pulled up in the garage.

"The city?" Freya asked.

"Yes, today we will be spending the day together, no work, today is about you and I spending quality time together." Roman kissed her hand and he felt peace that their issue had been dealt with and resolved.

After Freya got changed and picked a beautiful gown that was from Shelly, she twirled around in front of her mirror and made her way passed Roman's door.

"Lovely." Roman said, as he looked up from his screen.

To fill in the time Freya typed a few pages and did some correcting so that what she had written made sense. Then as she was sitting at her desk, she received an email from Mary at the cabin park. It was a letter saying that there had been a payment made for her cabin. She saw that the payee was Roman Mason and there was no more left on her loan. She was surprised; but then she also felt like it was all too much. She wanted an explanation but also knew that Roman didn't like being questioned, so at the risk of making a mockery of the day, she picked up her courage and went into Roman's office.

"Roman, I have an email saying that my cabin has been paid off and it says that you paid it?" Freya looked at him with the paper in her hands, and he only moved his gaze to her from his screen. He controlled his reply and sat back nodding his head.

"Yes, that's correct." Roman replied, with a stern look on his face.

"But, why?" Freya asked him.

"Why not?" Roman replied.

"Roman, I can't accept it, it's too much, it's too-"

Roman stood very slowly from his chair and he could see that she was overwhelmed, but he didn't want to take back what he had done. He moved to stand in-front of her and placed his hands by his side.

"Are you questioning my kindness, Freya?"

She looked at him like she was getting in trouble from a parent, but she wasn't going to let that stop her from answering.

"Well, I'm not questioning, I just think it's too much, I-, you didn't have too-"

Roman stepped towards her and placed his hands on her shoulders, she was taken back by what had been done, but she was also very grateful. It was just confusing as to why he would go to that length, she took a deep breath and then steadied herself.

"I just don't understand, why you would do that?" Freya was stuck for words and couldn't think.

Roman just placed one hand on her cheek and looked into her eyes as he answered.

"It makes me happy to help you, Freya, I only want to do what I can to make you happy."

"But it's so much money, how can I pay you back?" Freya said softly, as she was feeling the sting of tears in her eyes.

Roman only looked at her and his green eyes flared. Freya could see that he was irritated by what she had said, but then Roman softened as he understood that for Freya, it was a very large sum of money, as for himself it was not. Freya leaned against the door frame, her gaze fell to the floor as she dropped her shoulders, she didn't know what to say. He picked up her chin gently and he could see that her eyes were shining with tears that she was fighting to let go. Slowly moving closer to her he reached out for her hand and lowered his mouth to her ear; he moved his arm around her waist and gently pulled her closer to him. Freya closed her eyes as she could feel his breath on her skin and then Roman touched his cheek to hers as he spoke softly in a deep whisper.

"Let me take care of you, Freya, let me do these things that bring me joy." He ran his lips softly over her earlobe.

"Let me, make you happy." Roman continued, as he gently took her lobe between his lips.

Freya felt a heat rush through her as he spoke and her body was coming alive as he moved his lips on her skin.

"Please, Freya, say thank you." Roman gently squeezed the lobe between his lips and held it until she spoke.

"Say it." Roman told her again quietly.

Freya leaned close to him and realised he wouldn't stop until she did what he asked her to.

"Thank you, Roman." Freya whispered quietly, as she was melting against his body.

"You're welcome." Roman replied and released her lobe from his lips.

When he looked at her, he could see that her eyes were pools of yellow gold, and he enjoyed seeing her this way. He understood that she didn't mind the affection, so he ran his finger down her cheek.

"Now, with that out of the way, I would like to take you out for lunch."

Freya only huffed out a small laugh as she was being spoiled rotten. She was also feeling a small amount of fear that it was all too good to be true.

"My cabin is paid off, and now you would like to take me to lunch, Roman this is all too good to be true." She spoke the exact words on her mind.

Roman only grinned as he looked at her confused and dazed state.

"Perhaps it is your turn for good things, Freya, have you ever thought of that?" Roman asked her as he tried to turn her to the optimistic side of things.

She smiled as she looked at him and Roman could see that she was sincere when she spoke.

"I do really hope so, Roman." Freya smiled, as she wriggled passed his close body.

She went to collect her small clutch and take one last look in the mirror before they made their way out.

After they ate a lovely meal, they went to the orchestra which was playing at a beautiful cathedral. The music was bone trembling and Freya could feel goosebumps on her arms and all over her body. The music was so deep that she could feel the drums beating in her chest and the beautiful sounds of the violins and organs brought tears to her eyes. They played a mixture of favourites, themes from famous movies and classical songs with a twist of modern sounds. Roman looked over at Freya as she gripped his hand when one of the climatic verses was played and he could see tears rolling down her cheeks. He reached into his pocket and pulled out a clean handkerchief and wiped her tears away. Freya was smiling and her emotions were heightened as she listened to the music. Roman sat closer to her and wrapped his arm around her holding her tightly.

Chapter 9

He kissed her as the music had an effect on him also and he was so glad that he was holding Freya in his arms. It was difficult to hear but Roman asked her if she was alright and Freya only nodded with a big smile as she could imagine that it seemed backwards to him. Roman knew that only certain people were able to feel effects by music, it communicated with their bodies in a different way than others. He knew that Freya was a creative person, so she would have gained more from the sounds and the experience than himself.

Freya was trying to make mental notes of the ideas that were constantly popping into her head with the music, they were a mixture of different scenarios. She imagined angels flying through the air at war and protecting humanity, she imagined a scene for the woman in her story going through a portal and flying with powers and speed to her King that she loved so much. She also imagined beasts flying through the air and women warriors going to war. Her favourite was a scenario that a man and woman made love so strongly that they felt like the ground shook underneath them.

When the music came to a close the sounds were more of a sombre nature and she imagined herself as a little girl watching the wonderful orchestra play. She saw the little younger version of herself smile and she was so happy. Freya cried most when she saw this in her mind and she made sure that she would add it to her private story she was working on, as it would have a very important role later.

Once the show finished Roman waited for Freya to collect herself. He sat waiting for her and made sure she was ready to walk. Roman was able to see the way her eyes had widened and she was fully aware of her surroundings.

"Did you enjoy that, Freya?" Roman asked her, as he held her face in his hands.

"Oh, yes, very much." Freya wiped away the last tear that fell as she answered.

Roman kissed her and she pressed her face into his cheek.

"Thank you, Roman." Freya told him, as she hugged him tightly.

Roman smiled softly as he could hear in her voice the depth of her appreciation and when she said the words, they were from her heart and soul. Once they climbed back into the car Roman pulled out a brand-new leather notebook from behind his seat and gold pen. He handed them to Freya and she was over the moon. She kissed him on the mouth before she started to write down everything she had thought of.

Once they returned Freya frantically typed away at her desk, while Roman decided to do some work out the back. He had some more ideas for Freya's home and then as evening came, he started to feel the drop in his stomach. He was going to have to bid Freya goodnight, but he didn't want to be without her, he wanted to show her just how much she meant to him.

"Freya?" Roman called out, as he changed his clothing and washed his face.

"Yes, just one moment." She answered cheerily, as she was finishing a paragraph that was fresh in her mind.

Roman came out behind her and kissed her neck as she was trying to concentrate but she gave in and he whirled her chair around to face him. He kissed her and whispered into her mouth as he nuzzled and enjoyed her lips.

"I'm hungry." Roman grinned, as he made his way to her neck.

"Yes, I think I can figure that out." She started to laugh and try to playfully resist.

"Have dinner with me." Roman told her, and she only nodded as she was hungry herself.

When they arrived at the restaurant Roman sat down and Freya started to jot down some notes in the new black leather book. She was happy to point at anything on the menu and Roman ordered for both of them.

"I have given thought into what you said earlier, about understanding me and I'm open to welcome that." Roman took her hand as she stopped writing and looked at him with big eyes. She didn't want to get ahead of herself, so she wondered how to go about it.

"So would you be comfortable, if I asked you questions about your lost love?" Freya could see that Roman was thinking but he was fair in his answer.

"You may ask, I will try my best to answer, and you will have to forgive me if I am brief or if I don't give a story or memory to some things." Roman felt pleased with the answer he gave her, and then he studied her as she drank from her wine.

"Well, I'm very happy, and I'm not going to ask for anything too overwhelming. If I did ask, it would be more along the lines of happy things and memories. I would never want to cause anyone grief." Freya smiled, as she looked at him and he nodded his head slowly accepting her comment. Freya took a bite of her food and was patiently pacing herself between eating and small conversation.

"Roman, if I did have a question, it would be something as simple as, what was her first pet? Freya kept eating, staying casual.

Roman grunted as he bit into his steak. Freya could see the cogs turning in his head and he looked into the distance as though he was in thought.

"It was a rodent." Roman answered her shortly.

Freya smiled as she took a drink from her wine, she assumed he didn't like the animal. She watched as he remained unbothered and calm, he reached forward and sipped on his wine, then he emptied his mouth to speak.

"He was a wretched beast."

Freya's smile turned into a soft laugh; she held her hand in front of her mouth as she was hoping he would continue but she didn't prod.

Roman looked at her, and grinned before he continued.

"You want to know the story, don't you?"

"Please?" Freya said, as she wiped a tear of laughter from her eye.

"Very well then." Roman wiped his face with a serviette and leaned back on his chair, he didn't want to say Faye's name as it would cause him pain, so he used her nick name which was Lee.

"Fatty Rat was his name he was a hideous rodent. Lee found him when he was a baby in the vegetable garden that her mother used to have. He was small and weak, so she picked him up and took him to her mother. Lee was so taken by the small creature that she managed to convince her mother to nurse him back to good health, over time he grew into a very large and ugly animal." Roman almost smiled at the memory as he spoke.

"One day she was sick at home with chicken pox, we were twelve at the time. So, I visited her and kept her company in her room, she had the rat on her lap and pet him while we spoke and watched television. I went to put my arm around Lee's shoulders as I admired her and wanted to get closer, then the rat jumped up and bit my hand hard, sinking his teeth deep into my skin. Lee tried to get him to release his bite, but it only got stronger. I screamed and ran into the kitchen and her mother pushed me out the back door into the vegetable garden, he let go and jumped into the thick of a bush and scurried away to hide."

Freya was almost balling, but she stayed composed as Roman continued he had another drink and showed her the scar between his thumb and first finger, it was deep and looked like it needed stitches.

"Oh, no!" Freya said, as she dabbed her cheek with a tissue.

Roman began to smile but only a little.

"Lee was upset with me and blamed me for him running away."

"Oh, poor thing." Freya sighed as she took another sip.

"After a doctor's visit, stitches and needles in my backside, her mother asked me to try and find him."

"Oh, that sounds difficult." Freya sympathised.

Roman shook his head and flashed his beautiful teeth in a wicked grin.

"Oh, I knew where he would be. I went home and asked my mother for fresh vegetables, I opened the compost bin and threw them in there, in the morning sure enough when I lifted the lid, he was looking at me with his red eyes and creepy fangs. He was hissing at me while he ate."

Freya took off her glasses as more tears fell her down her cheeks, they were sore from laughing and Roman finished the story.

"I went to my father's garage and put on his welding mask and leather gloves. I grabbed the beast by the tail and scruff of his neck, then took him inside to Lee and dropped him back in his cage."

Roman chuckled as he refilled his water glass and seemed relieved once he told the story.

"After that she said I was her hero and she wanted to marry me."

Freya was all but falling off her chair. She tried so hard to laugh quietly and compose herself, but she just had the visual of a young teenage Roman in battle with a giant rat.

"Oh my, Roman, oh dear, that is a funny story. I'm so grateful you shared that with me."

Roman just smiled as he looked at her and took her hand in his.

"You have a beautiful laugh, I'm glad I was able to make you happy."

"Oh yes, I haven't laughed so hard in so long, dear Roman and Fatty Rat, that is a good story."

As they exited the restaurant Roman stopped before he opened Freya's door he gently reached out and took her face in his hands, all he felt was joy and freedom after the dinner and conversation. Roman leaned in and kissed her on the mouth, he angled his head and Freya parted her lips to welcome him. He kissed her deeply, slowly and Freya moaned as their tongues danced. He wrapped his arm around her waist and pulled her closer as she wrapped her arms around his hips.

Roman felt himself come alive and his arousal was felt by Freya. He was feasting on her mouth and felt like he was able to express himself fully without restriction or hesitation. His body became hard, and he felt his blood pumping viciously, the pleasure of kissing her, tasting her, and feeling her was blissful, the wall he had around his heart was slowly crumbling. Roman welcomed all the sensations, feeling her, touching her hair, and ran his hands up her arms and shoulders. He groaned at the feeling of her smooth china doll skin, he adored her and wanted more. After he let them come up for air, he didn't want the time with her to end. He needed to make peace with his past and understand that life and time was still moving and on his side. He kissed her cheeks and then moved his lips close to her mouth as he spoke quietly and softly from his heart.

"Come for a drive with me, Freya, please let me have more of you."

She opened her eyes and seemed dazed, but when she saw the green pools of desire in Roman's eyes she could only agree as she was feeling the same.

"Yes, I want more of you." Freya replied and Roman touched his lips to hers before he opened her door.

As they drove, Roman pulled into a long driveway. Freya saw a farmhouse and smiled at Roman.

"Whose land is this?" Freya asked nonchalantly.

"It's my land." Roman replied, as he drove out to a beautiful lake that had a fireplace.

When they parked and made their way out of the car, Roman opened the boot and Freya watched as Roman laid out a soft mat and picnic blankets. He helped her on to the back of the big tray and made the fire so they would have warmth and comforting sounds. Freya loved the way it all looked and felt, the nature was beautiful, the lake was clean, and birds sang their evening songs. Once the fire was set, Roman climbed in next to her.

"This is very beautiful, Roman, it would make a perfect place to come and write."

Roman nodded slowly as he took off his shoes and admired Freya in the evening light. He reached forward and looked deep into her eyes caressing her face gently with his fingers.

"You are such a beautiful woman, Freya." Roman said softly, as he kissed her cheek and made his way down her neck.

"Mm, so beautiful." Roman continued to whisper the words nipping at her soft flesh gently and running his lips and tongue along her skin.

He wrapped her in his arms and laid her down, as he deepened his kisses and ran his hands up and down her body. Freya was kicking off her shoes and Roman started to grasp at her dress as he reached for her breast.

"Mm, Freya, so beautiful." Roman repeated over and over as they both grew hungry with arousal and lustful need.

Freya was fighting the urge to break away from the kiss, as she was at her wits end, with heat, demanding chemistry, and desire, she was becoming greedy grabbing at his body and his shirt. She was sighing and breathing more intensely as Roman moved his hands over her body and showed her how much he treasured her. Freya was riding the inevitable waves, over and over on the inside from one moment to the next, of pleasure, arousal, need and wanting. She felt like she was on fire and needed to have a release.

"Please, Roman, make love to me, make love to me now."

Roman didn't need any more encouragement as he lifted her, he pulled her dress off over her head then he pulled his shirt off and fumbled as he tried to take off his pants. The belt got stuck and he ripped the damn thing loose. Finally free of clothing and they were blissfully naked, he laid her on her back and kissed from head to toe. He was lapping, licking, nibbling, and tasting every inch of her skin. He parted her thighs and kissed her slowly from the knees moving to her centre. He looked into her eyes as she was breathing heavily with anticipation, her eyes were pools of gold, and he parted her pink flesh with his hands then he licked his lips as he looked into her eyes, he was dangerous and a hungry primal male. Roman moaned as he dipped his tongue inside her. He groaned loudly at the pure taste of woman, he had missed out on it for so long. Freya fell back and gripped at the blankets, gasping at the feeling of his mouth on her.

"Mm, you taste so good." Roman whispered, as he lapped more and teased her.

"Fuck, you taste so good, Freya." Roman continued in a deep feral tone and deepened his mouth even more. He pushed her knees down and spread her wider as he moved faster. How could he have denied himself this pleasure, how could he have been so cruel to himself. He felt like the richest man alive, and this was his kingdom.

"Oh, Freya." Roman moaned, as he could feel her moving her hips to him.

"Oh, Roman, Oh yes!" Freya called out, as he found her sweet spot and kept playing with her.

To please them both he gently pushed a finger inside her and she started to moan as he could feel her coming.

"Yes, baby that's it, I want you to come." Roman said, as he kept going, he didn't want to stop, he wanted her to give in to him and to surrender.

"Oh, Roman, I'm going to come, please come inside me." Freya gripped at his hair and tried to sit up but Roman pushed her down with one hand on her chest as he kept going. Freya was trying to prolong the feeling, but she could feel herself start to take the fall.

"I'm coming!"

"Yes, that's it." Roman grinned and moved harder and faster.

She called out his name and cried in pleasure, her body quaked and shivered in ecstasy and carnal bliss. Roman only continued until she was done, he loved how she was wriggling and trying to move but still he held her down. Roman kissed her thighs as he made his way higher and then he slowly moved his body between her thighs. She looked at him as she was trying to catch her breath and he was only pleased at the rosy cheeks and golden eyes that had been tamed.

"Now you are ready for me." Roman said, as he kissed her deeply, he lifted her legs and prodded her wet entrance with his hard tip.

"Oh, Freya, oh yes, your mine." Roman grit, his teeth as he thrust inside her, he hissed at the heat and pleasure. He kissed her hard as he submerged himself deeper, she gasped in his mouth at the size of him, he was filling her fully and he closed his eyes at the feeling of her. He couldn't breathe completely drowning in her beauty, he released his soul and he let all guards down and became one with nature, one with being a part of the animal kingdom.

"Fuck, you feel good." Roman grunted loudly, as he thrust slowly and wrapped his arms around her tightly, he licked her neck and took her skin between his teeth as he was riding her.

"God you're beautiful, Freya."

He was in a dirty world; he was a man and he was viciously hungry. He loved the sensation of her, she was slick, hot, and tight, it was everything a man could dream of. He pushed his hips harder and the feeling of her thighs against his skin was glorious. He was taking and taking and didn't want to stop, Roman was kissing her neck hard and being feral as he took her skin gently between his teeth again.

"Mm, baby I'm going to take my time, I'm going to fill you, and I'm going to come inside you."

He thrust harder and faster and he even lifted her leg above his shoulder to gain more depth. Freya was clawing at his shoulders and loved the blissful torture, Roman looked at her and loved her breath against his skin. He grinned as he saw her deep gold eyes and kissed her deeply sucking her tongue, he was throbbing and grew harder as he climbed the mountain of pleasure.

"Freya, beautiful, Freya." He told her again, as he kissed her deeply and ran his hands over her breast.

"I want everything!" Roman said, as he pulled out of her and rolled her onto her belly.

He lifted her on to her knees and parted her legs with his, he gripped her hips and slowly pushed himself inside her, wrapping his arm around her waist and nipped on her back while he thrust. He moved to look at them joined, himself inside her and her beautiful backside bare and smooth. He became one with his inner beast as it was lying dormant for a long time, he wanted her and he was claiming her, marking her with his scent.

"My God, your beautiful." Roman repeated, as he licked her back and nuzzled his face in her long hair.

He loved her beautiful curves and gripped her hips as he moved faster and harder. He grit his teeth and felt his blood pumping with feral desire.

"God, your sexy baby." Roman licked his hand, from palm to fingertip and smacked her backside hard. The sound of flesh smacking rang out across the quiet land and he loved how she cried out for him.

"Oh, yes, Roman."

He grinned loving the sounds and the way she rocked for him.

Freya smiled as she knew it was from her book 'The Love Slap' and she adored his attention, quoting it in their love making. It was endearing and she treasured him even more. He could feel himself coming and looked into the reflection of the car window as it added to his arousal.

"Look up, Freya! Look at us!" Roman ordered her.

Freya lifted her gaze slowly and a smile curved on her lips when she looked into Romans eyes.

"Oh, yes, Roman, yes."

Freya moaned the words, as she was admiring the man behind her, he was strong and powerful as he pumped, groaned, and bared his teeth.

Roman loved seeing her breasts move and the sound of their skin meeting, it all seemed so deviously blissful to him, out in nature, a man and woman freely expressing their natural mating ritual, his primal need was being fulfilled and he loved it all without any guilt or reserve. Only she made him feel this way, only Freya, unleashed this from deep within him.

"Oh, that's it, Freya, I'm coming beautiful." Roman gripped her hair and hips harder.

'Yes, Roman, come please, come inside me." Freya told him, as she was pushing harder into him.

Roman looked at her in the window and groaned as he pumped hard and the stars exploded in his head, he moaned loudly and his toes curled as he tried to prolong the pleasure. Every muscle in his body was as hard as stone and he pulled her close wrapping his arms around her as he filled her. He growled softly while he thrust, emptying himself inside her completely. Freya only sighed at the wonderful sensation of feeling his climax for her.

"Oh, Roman." Freya whispered, as she moved her head to the side and he kissed her from behind.

Roman still held her as he was slowly being released from the blissful current, he was catching his breath and felt like he had been reborn after a long sleep.

This is what he was created for, this was his right of passage as a man. He grew weary as his strength began to waver and softly, he collapsed with her as he was completely drained. He laid behind her and he caressed her skin and kissed her shoulders and neck. Silence was all he had in his mind and heart; it was a feeling he had not known for so long.

As the evening cooled, he could smell rain was coming, but

he didn't want Freya to leave.

Chapter 10

"Come home with me, Freya, please stay with me tonight." Roman nuzzled her neck as he was seducing her with his voice and charm.

Freya smiled as she was hoping he would ask; it wasn't difficult for her to answer his request.

"Yes, Roman, I would love to stay with you."

Without care they drove back to his home naked. When they stepped inside Roman's home, he took Freya's hand and lead her to the bathroom and into the big double shower. Freya tied up her hair and he held her in his arms as the beautiful hot water soaked their bodies. He took the pleasure of washing her with soap, he loved the view of her all soapy and wet, he admired the bubbles as they slid down her hips and all the beautiful curves of her body. Roman grinned and even got down on his knees to wash her beautiful legs and feet. Freya giggled as he played with her toes and massaged her calves with his big rough hands. He enjoyed looking at her from underneath and he wrapped his arms around her and kissed her thighs and belly. Freya hugged him and ran her fingers through his hair, he was so beautiful, so large in size, masculine and handsome. She explored the strong features of his body and gently kissed his arms and chest; she played with his hands and ran his fingers over her face as she loved the way they felt. Roman closed his eyes and took a deep breath, he was happy that she was in his arms and he never wanted to let her go. Once they were clean Roman led her to his bedroom and they cuddled under the thick warm blankets. Roman pulled her across his chest and she smiled as she played with his short chest hair, the fireplace was illuminating beautiful warmth and light and

Roman only laid quietly appreciating every single detail as he held her in the night.

"This place is so beautiful, Roman, it's so peaceful and yet so full of life." Freya smiled softly, as she listened to the noises of the night and took in the smells and wonder of the room. Roman kissed her forehead as he nodded in agreement.

"It is now." Roman said quietly and closed his eyes.

Freya nuzzled into his arm and she closed her eyes as she listened to his heartbeat and felt his chest going up and down as he breathed calmly. Soon after, the sounds of the fire and the soft rain falling, sent them both into a quiet sleep.

***

Deep black water engulfed Roman he was searching for Freya and couldn't find her he swam in the dark water as she came into view, he tried to swim to her, but he only felt like he was going further away. He was running out of air and tried to swim to the surface, he couldn't move he struggled and didn't know which way was up, he needed to breath his chest was heaving-

***

Roman sat up and wiped the sweat off his brow, the room was dark and only dim moon light was what he could see and heard the rain tapping on the window. He pressed his hands to his eyes as he tried to gain a clear vision. Small glowing embers from the fire were coming clearer into his vision as he steadied himself. He reached next to him and felt Freya as she stirred and rolled on to her back. He moved next to her and stroked her cheeks kissing her gently and slowly, he started to bring himself back to reality as she opened her sleepy eyes and lifted a hand to his face.

"Are you alright, Roman?"

He kissed her and pushed her covers back running his hand over her to see if she was real and safe, he nodded and pressed his forehead to hers closing his eyes in relief.

"Yes, Freya." Roman whispered, as he kissed her again and ran his lips down her neck and over her chest.

"I need you, Freya, I need you now." Roman was overcome with desire and he let it take him.

Freya gladly opened her arms to him and he moved on top of her gently. He licked his fingers and parted her folds between her legs, she was already aroused from their previous encounter and he kissed her deeply as he lowered himself on top of her.

"Oh, Roman, yes." Freya sighed, as she welcomed him, she lifted her legs more and moving his hips lower he pressed himself inside her gently, then thrust slowly and kissed her deeply.

"I need you, Freya." Roman whispered, "Oh, Freya, I need you."

He repeated the words over and over as he moved his hips. He rolled her on top of him and she sat up to ride him, her beautiful thighs straddled him and she looked down at his glowing eyes and smiled at the beautiful man she couldn't get enough of.

"You're beautiful, Freya." Roman told her, as he played with her breast and tugged gently at her nipples.

"Oh, Roman, oh, yes." Freya called out, as she moved her beautiful hips, her hair made her look like a wild warrior and he adored her on top of him.

"That's it baby, that's it." Roman encouraged her, as he gripped her thighs and reached up to her neck.

"Oh yes, Roman." She rode faster and harder, gripping onto his chest, her hair was falling on to his body and he adored the feeling.

"More baby, come on, let go, Freya, show me who you are." Roman told her, as he slapped her backside playfully.

She became vocal, moaning loudly and calling out his name, expressing her need.

"Yes, that's it." Roman encouraged her more, as he thrust from underneath.

"Oh, Roman, you feel so good, oh my, I'm coming." Freya moaned out aloud as she gripped his chest harder, digging her fingers into his skin.

"Yes, come, Freya." Roman grinned, as he loved her going wild, he sat up and buried his face in her breasts nipping and teasing. He groaned like a beast at the pleasure of her giving in to his demand, he wrapped long fingers around the back of her neck and watched her as she was going over the edge.

Freya threw her head back and cried out into the night, the orgasm ripped through her, and Roman slapped her bottom to add to her pleasure.

"Good girl, that's a good girl." Roman said, as he gripped her hips and flashed his beautiful teeth. He pushed harder and deep for her.

"Roman!" Was all Freya could manage, as her breath was taken from her, she was completely overwhelmed by the strength of the climax and then she threw her arms around Roman neck as she went limp.

He rolled her onto her back and rode her on, he was needy and demanding, he threw her ankles over his shoulders and pumped like his life depended on it, he was wild and vicious, this was his woman, his territory, his home, and he was marking her again.

"Mm fuck, you're so good baby." He gripped her wrists and pressed his face against her cheek.

"I'm want to fill you again baby, I'm going to come hard." Roman snarled the words, as he ran his teeth along her chin.

"Yes, come inside me, please." Freya pleaded, as she loved the way he told her what he wanted.

"Yes, say it again." Roman told her as he buried his face in her neck.

"Come inside me, Roman, please." Freya looked into his eyes as he kissed her deeply and she was captivated by the green glow of his eyes.

"I'm coming now baby." Roman crushed his mouth onto hers and loved her puffs of air as he thrust.

He pumped, moaned and groaned as he kissed her and licked her lips. He growled into her thick hair and she wrapped her arms around him as he gripped her hips while he filled her again, she lifted her hips as she loved him inside her and she wrapped her legs around his waist. His body was both free and uncontrollable, as he emptied himself once again.

After a few moments his body went lax and he slowly caught his breath as he kissed her. As they held each other, Roman could see Freya smiling because she was completely and blissfully exhausted.

"You destroy me, Freya." Roman said, as he kissed her and held her in his arms.

"I hope that's a good thing?" Freya implied, as she wasn't sure.

Roman chuckled lightly and nipped at her lips as he threw back the covers to feed the fire and get them a drink.

"Yes, yes indeed it is." Roman replied, as he walked over to the fading light.

Freya leaned on her elbow as she admired his naked masculine figure, he threw the logs on the fire and he looked confident, comfortable and at ease. She took in the way he moved in the soft light and everything about his hard exterior seemed softened in the night. It all seemed so whimsical and yet so real, the rain hitting the widow, the sounds, the smells, it was all like a fairy-tale and she was making mental notes along the way.

Roman moved back to her side with a cold drink, he handed her the glass and clinked hers before he drank. After they sipped, he curled up behind her and held her close.

"How will we get any work done, Freya?" Roman whispered into her neck, as she could feel his lips curved into a smile.

She laughed and only shook her head at the events that had taken place, she wasn't able to give him a definite solution, so she laughed softly as she answered the best way she knew how.

"I'm sure, we will come up with something." Freya replied, as she made herself comfortable.

"Goodnight, beautiful, Freya." Roman said, as he kissed her shoulder and intertwined his fingers with hers.

"Goodnight, Roman." Freya replied, as she snuggled lower and smiled while gently caressing his arm.

As the sun began to creep over the land and birds were singing their morning songs, Freya slowly woke to Roman stirring beside her. As he opened his eyes and stretched, he was taking up most of the bed and Freya was only smiling as she looked at his long lean body next to her. He was a big man and very handsome in all his morning glory. Roman grinned at her when she saw that she was staring at his appendage, but he didn't mind and only flexed himself to make her laugh.

"Oh my, Roman you make me blush." Freya couldn't help but giggle as he pulled her towards him and gave her morning kisses all over her face and neck.

"Good morning, beautiful." Roman's deep husky voice only made her blush more and she was in desperate need of a cold shower.

"We have somethings to organise today." Roman told her, as he nuzzled her neck.

"Oh?" Freya was distracted but she was able to keep her mind from being completely discombobulated.

"Yes, you and I have some dance lessons today, for the charity ball." Roman reminded her, as he thought that she had well and truly forgotten.

"Oh, yes the ball." Freya said, as she tried to wipe the long hair out of her face that Roman was nuzzling into a mess.

Roman was only able to chuckle deeply as he was admiring her curves and body, he was loving the way she was melting in his hands again and he desperately wanted her.

"Oh, dear Roman, I don't think I will be any good at dancing if you turn my legs into spaghetti." Freya was going cross-eyed as she was feeling the arousal hit her again and Roman wasn't going to stop.

"That's alright, Freya, I will carry you around the dance floor, if I have to." Roman crushed his mouth onto hers and Freya only moaned as she tried to wriggle her way out of the bed. Roman understood that Freya was correct, so for both of their sakes he helped her to stand and they both went to take a long, well-earned shower.

Afterwards, they were on their way to the dance studio that wasn't very far from the office. They were greeted by a few people and when everyone was partnered and ready,

Freya was trying her hardest to remember everything the dance instructor was saying but she was confused and only looked at Roman.

"Come here." Roman said, as he was looking into her eyes and held her waist and hand in the ready position.

"Don't look down at your feet and just move with me." Roman grinned, as he could see she was trying to not look down and was confused.

"Alright, don't move at my feet, and look with you."

Roman chuckled at her confusion and when the music started, he took the lead for them both. He moved so fluidly over the dance floor and Freya had no fear at all of falling or losing her balance. He held her hand and moved her with him and she was sure at one stage she was floating as Roman whirled her around in the waltz. Freya closed her eyes after the second round of practice, as she was taken to another place in her imagination. She saw herself in a ball room full of beautiful men and women all wearing gowns that glittered and she was being held by Roman. When Roman looked at her face, he could see that Freya was in a blissful thought as her lips curved into a smile. Roman only felt as though he was smiling with her and didn't realise that all the people in the dance studio had moved to give them space and watched them as they took the whole floor. When the music stopped Roman dipped Freya and she slowly opened her eyes to see the beautiful prince in front of her. When they stood to bow everyone clapped their hands and Freya looked around surprised that they were all watching.

"Roman, what just happened?" Freya smiled nervously, as they all smiled and cheered for them both.

"I think you captivated everyone with your beauty." Roman took her hand in his and kissed the top of it as the dance instructor came to stand beside therm.

"Now, I hope everyone saw these two beautiful people, that is what love looks like on the dance floor."

Freya blushed as she only kept her gaze at the ground but Roman didn't seemed at all bothered by what was said, he only smiled at the instructor and then everyone made their way home.

Once they returned to the office, Freya needed to have some time for her writing, Roman could see she was growing restless and almost suffered withdrawal from her keyboard. Before he took her home though, he was sure to christen his office desk with their love making, this only led to the dressing room, pull out couch and even in front of the fireplace in the waiting area. As it was the weekend to come, there wasn't anyone coming in, so Roman didn't care if people walking on the footpath could hear the happy sounds they were making. He only wished that he didn't have to let Freya go, but he knew as they were both adults and had responsibilities, being naked and pleasing each other was something they couldn't do all day long, well, their bodies needed rest but still, Roman had other plans.

"My word, Roman, you destroy me." Freya said, the same thing he did the night before, as she was catching her breath in front of the fireplace.

"Excellent." Roman said with a grin, as he picked her up and carried her into a shower.

"Didn't you say you had some more ideas for my cabin?" Freya asked as she stepped into the shower and started to soap up her body.

"Yes, I would like it, if I could spend the rest of the day with you, I enjoy working on your home, while you type and let your creative mind work."

"Really?" Freya asked, as she wiped bubbles out of her eyes.

"Of course, it's a comfort to me, I enjoy time with you." Roman only grinned, as he had other things on his mind.

"I enjoy you too." Freya opened her eyes from the water, and she could see that Roman looked into her eyes sincerely, he pulled her towards him and kissed her deeply.

"You make me happy, Freya, very happy." Roman said, as he held her in the water.

"You make me happy, Roman." Freya whispered, as she held him and rested her cheek on his warm skin, but as the tender moment lingered, Roman's stomach grumbled loudly.

"And food, makes you happy." Freya said, as they both laughed, and stepped out to get dressed.

Once they arrived at the cabin, Mary came to visit Freya as she was concerned that she didn't come home last night but Freya pulled Mary aside and told her that she was spending time with Roman. Mary felt like she was responsible for Freya she had known her ever since she was just nineteen years old. But when Mary stepped inside to see the way Roman had made her home look, she was put at ease and made her way back to the office.

Freya had more inspiration than ever as she typed away without stopping and Roman kept himself busy, working around her. Food came to them that Roman had ordered and they had a short break to eat together. Freya enjoyed seeing Roman in her kitchen as she had been alone for a long time and this was a nice change to her small home. She didn't want to get ahead of herself and understood that these things took time. They had a lovely time together she wasn't prodding Roman about his past, she was just happy that he was being himself and she appreciated everything that he did.

At times she started to let the fear and negativity go about being with Roman and having all these wonderful things in her life, but every now and then it came creeping back. Almost as though Roman could read her thoughts or feel her emotions, he came to her and kissed her or held her in his arms. She felt as though they were tuned into each other in a strange way, but she didn't understand how after a short time of knowing each other. She just decided to take every moment as it came and was grateful for the experience she was having.

Chapter 11

As the ball was approaching, Freya was getting excited for the fitting of their outfits as the fashion designer was due to come into the office. Freya wasn't sure what sort of gown she should choose but then as the large bus pulled into the rear of the office parking lot, she was amazed at the size of the boutique on wheels.

"Oh, my word, what a way to work." Freya gasped, as she couldn't believe what she was seeing.

When the door opened, she was greeted by the most stunning looking woman, she was wearing a black fitted suit, big sunglasses covered her eyes and her hair and make up looked like they had been done by a graphic designer program. Everything was perfect and Freya felt like she was looking at a masterpiece in human form.

"Roman, my darling how are you?" The woman said, as she made her way over to him and kissed him on both cheeks.

"Very well, you look stunning." Roman told her, as she patted him on the chest.

"I always make myself look the best for you, and who is this stunning woman?" She asked as she walked over to Freya.

"Verika, this is Freya, we worked together a long time ago and after a while Verika decided to chase her dream in fashion."

"My my, what a magnificent looking creature." Verika said, as she pursed her lips and walked around Freya.

Roman looked at Freya with a soft smile as he knew Verika was very taken by her beauty.

"Raymond?" Verika called out, clicking her fingers and a man with a tape measure stepped out and made his way to Roman.

"You will need to work with Roman inside, as for me, Freya and I will be very busy out here." She took Freya by the hand and led her into the bus.

As Freya walked up the steps it was the most amazing thing she had ever seen, there were gowns and a changing room a make-up and hair station, as well as a small bar and kitchen. She had never seen anything like it before in her life.

"Wow!" Freya said, as she was captivated by the experience.

"Take a seat darling." Verika told her, as she readied herself for her work.

Freya sat in the chair and Freya wasn't sure what was happening but after a few moments, make up was applied in a testing manner and then colours were smeared all over the fashionista's hands, she whirled Freya around to look in the mirror and she was amazed at how her face had changed.

"You are an absolute Goddess!" Verika said, as she looked at Freya in the mirror.

Freya touched her face and looked deep into the reflection; she had never thought makeup could enhance her beauty, but this woman was an artist.

"That's amazing, how did you do that?" Freya asked bewildered.

"Years of practice and failure, only the best know failure the most." Verika replied, as she continued her work on Freya's hair.

"No! this hair will be down." Verika said, as she turned Freya's chair and led her to the dressing area.

"Now, with those eyes we need shimmer and shine." Verika tapped her finger to her lips as she inspected the gowns.

"Ah, yes, the Bella and her beast." Verika said, with a sudden moment of realisation.

Freya noticed how she went into a different closet and pulled out a dress from a large box, when she held it up Freya gasped in awe.

"Oh my!"

"Yes, this thing hasn't been given a home, but it has now."

When Verika held it up against Freya and looked in the mirror, Freya felt like she was in a fairy-tale. It matched her eyes and hair, the gold and lemon amber tones on the long soft layers of materials reminded her of the old tale about a stunning beauty and a man which was a beast, and she was in love.

"I made this dress years ago and not one single person has ever done it justice, this is a one-of-a-kind piece. I'm so incredibly happy I never opened it until now."

"Are you sure?" Freya asked, as she was very shy by its beauty.

"Absolutely! now let's get you changed and do a twirl to have a look."

As Freya stepped into the dress and it was fitted into place, she ran her hands over the beautiful material it was so perfect and sat beautifully on her curves. Her bodice was covered in small flecks of gold and as Verika held her hair back and cleaned her curls to a smooth finish Freya felt like a princess in a story. Verika walked around Freya as she studied her creation and thought there was something missing. She walked over to her drawer and pulled out a gold and yellow diamond necklace it was the biggest jewel Freya had ever seen and when Verika put it around her neck, it brought out Freya's eyes and it was as though the entire outfit was meant to be. It was complete and perfect.

"Fabulous! that's what you will be wearing." Verika clapped her hands together as she looked at her work.

"This necklace is beautiful." Freya said, as she was too nervous to touch it.

"Yes, well Roman and I were digging in the mud a very long time ago and we came across this stone, there was enough of it to make two cuts, Roman has the other and I have this one."

"So, you and Roman worked in the mines, as in digging for gold?" Freya asked with astonishment.

"Yes, we became friends many years ago, we were much younger and braver, but as the time went on, we decided that it was time to step out of the dirty work boots and go into the other direction. I was working in a division as Roman is now but then when my riches were accumulated, I decided to go where my passion was and here we are." Verika smiled, as she could see that Freya had no idea about what Roman's past was.

"That's a wonderful story. I would very much like to hear more about it some time."

"Well, when there is time, I can share a story." Verika had to laugh at the pleasure of being so busy and she helped Freya out of her outfit.

As Freya went to hand back the necklace, Verika placed it in a black box and gave it to Freya.

"These will be staying with you darling; I won't be having them back."

Freya was in shock as she couldn't believe what she just heard.

"Oh no, I couldn't take this." Verika squeezed her hands around Freya's.

"Oh yes you can. I know Roman and he pays for the best." Verika winked as she continued, "and my work is the best."

Freya was speechless as she took everything with Verika and walked into the dressing room in the office. There was a safe in the wall and Verika placed the precious yellow diamond in and closed the safe door.

"Roman can't see this before the ball, he asked to leave it all until the evening comes understand?"

Freya nodded as she was still trying to wrap her head around everything.

"Yes, I understand." Verika gave Freya a kiss on both cheeks and squeezed her tightly before she walked out.

"Thank you." Freya said, as she was only able to think of those two words to say.

"Your pleasure is mine, so enjoy!" Verika replied.

As Verika walked out into the office and her phone was buzzing in her pocket.

"Raymond?" She called out and clicked her fingers as they walked out into the giant bus to make their way.

Roman walked out to Freya and saw the bewildered look on her face.

"And? how was it?" He asked with a twinkle in his eye.

Freya was unsure how to answer so she just replied in a very shocked manner.

"Wow!" Was all she could say and then Roman pulled her into his arms and kissed her head.

"Well, Verika, must have a big surprise in store then."

Freya only laughed as she tried to hide her secret.

"Let's just say, I'm surprised." Freya replied.

Roman picked Freya up and carried her into the dressing room and closed the door behind them, he was kissing her neck and Freya started to laugh as she knew what Roman had in mind.

"Give me a clue?" Roman whispered, as he nibbled on her ear and he lowered her onto the pull-out sofa.

"You know I can't." Freya said, as she was being held captive. Roman looked at Freya as he had a dangerously devious grin on his face.

"Very well then, Freya, let's see if we can try and get something out of you."

Freya moaned as he started to kiss her and hold her in his arms, she was fighting the urges, but she was able to keep everything close to her heart.

"No, I can't, Verika said its top secret."

"Oh, Freya you shouldn't have said that." Roman said, as his eyes were glowing with heat and passion for the beauty he had in his arms.

They both chuckled as Roman pulled his shirt off and pushed a button on the wall that locked the office.

***

Once Roman arrived home, he was restless that he was away from Freya. He tried to make sure that he was well drained from his day to sleep, and after a long hot shower he sat in on his large sofa and thought about the ways Freya had been changing his life. He was becoming surer that this feeling he had for her was growing, or already had grown into the most delightful feeling in his heart that he had missed for so long.

When he took a sip of his whisky, he reached for the small box of mementos from his wife again in a test to see if it would be easier than it was the last time. As he opened the lid and held the well-read note in his hands, he only found that he smiled and didn't feel any more grief or pain in his heart. Roman looked at the photo on his stone mantle and he was sure that he could feel his wife's spirit looking down on him, encouraging the joy he was feeling.

"Thank you, Faye." He said quietly, as he put the small box away and realized that she was right to give him instructions as she did.

For the longest time Roman always thought he would never be able to fulfil her wishes for him to 'live and love as long as he was able,' but as he looked into the fire and the flames were flickering, he could feel the stones falling away from the wall around his heart even more and there was life beginning to beat once again.

***

Freya had found it very difficult to stop smiling as she was typing away at her story. She was really beginning to think that she had found her forever happiness, as she kept moving her fingers over her keyboard. She was thrilled that the characters in her own private story were infatuated with each other and this was possibly blossoming into love. Freya never thought she could be so happy. She paused as she sat back in her chair and put her feet up on her small desk. She sipped at the cup of tea she was holding and looked around looking at the beautiful way Roman had transformed her home. She thought about what her life was like only two months ago and then compared it to the overwhelming change that had happened. She never thought stepping off that bus would ever bring here to this chapter of her life. She replayed the entire moment she laid eyes on Roman and remembered how beautiful his eyes were, his figure his stature and his demeanour, were all so perfect. When she was a little girl, she always wondered if the fantasy of meeting the perfect stranger was ever something that happened to people in real life. Freya thought about the way he made love to her and the wanting and passion she could feel in his touch and kiss. She closed her eyes as she thought about the very moment, he kissed her for the first time and the way he made her head spin. The depth of complete and utter joy she felt was something she had never experienced before in her life. As she returned to typing, she wondered where the story would lead next. Freya also thought about the beautiful gown she was given for the charity ball and how Verika told her that her and Roman were once work colleagues. What was Roman like as a young boy? she thought, when did he find the love for gems and jewels?

These questions went through her mind and she wondered if Roman would ever share those stories, or if they were locked away as a memory in his heart never to be retold. She didn't mind that there was the 'always wondering mystery' about him, but she adored his ways and wanted to know more. As the clock was ticking over to midnight, she started to think that the story she was writing would be something she would have to keep to herself and eventually in the future, she would be able to share it and then make it into a book.

There were times when Freya thought she should tell Roman the story of herself, but she was afraid that it would make Roman see her differently and then even change his view. Although Roman was never easily swayed as he had told her, there was the lingering doubt that perhaps her past as a runaway and mischief maker was better left as a learning experience for herself only. After all, in her story it would make sense for a runaway who didn't have much, to fall in love with a rich and handsome man.

When Freya thought about the way she would write her characters showing their affection for each other, it was something that she only thought was in fantasy, but then as she replayed every time her and Roman made love, she realised that it was something that had been kept from her as he was a wonderful and fantastic lover. Never had a man showed her body appreciation and praise the way Roman did. She felt spoiled not only with material and physical things, but she was beginning to be spoiled in the absolute pleasure he had given her own ego.

Freya always wondered if a man would ever hunger for her the way she would write about in her books but as she kept typing, she smiled and thought, oh yes, there was a man who hungered for her the way she had been dreaming of.

When she was about to save her work, she thought about her mother and couldn't help but feel an empty part of her heart sting with hurt. Freya always wanted a mother and father to walk her down the isle of her perfect wedding and this she thought was something that she would never have as she thought about all the times, she told her mother she didn't want to see her.

They abandoned her she concluded, as she made her way to the bedroom, but then she wondered if they ever thought about her or what she had become? was it too late for them to make amends and then would they even want to?

Chapter 12

As Mary made her way to the back of the cabin park, she was holding a new copy of Freya's book that had been out of stock for a while. When she reached the door of the old cabin that had been here since the seventies, she knocked on the door three times and then pushed the bell.

"It's only me" Mary said, as the door opened, and she stepped inside.

"Hello, Mary, is that the new book?" A voice asked from behind the door.

"Oh, Anna, when are you going to tell her?" Mary asked Freya's mother who had been living at the park for the last ten years.

"You know I can't do that; I see her from time to time and that's enough for me."

Anna took the book and passed Mary the money from her purse.

"And how long do you think you can keep hiding that you're here?" Mary asked as she put the money in her pocket.

"Oh, as long as I can, eventually there will be a day when I will have to tell her the truth but it's just the fear of her rejecting me that is what's keeping me from saying anything." Anna turned on the kettle as she was about to make them both a cup of tea.

"Anna, please don't be like that you know as well as I do that daughters are a handful, we know as mothers they never really mean what they say, especially if it is along the lines of, I hate you." Mary and Anna laughed as they hugged each other and sat at the small coffee table.

"Yes well, Mary, there are things that I still have to deal with don't forget I'm hiding from that money hungry wolf that tried to track down the half fortune I was rightfully entitled to, and besides I'm glad that I can have Freya close to me. I feel like I still have her in my life even if it is in small moments and glimpses."

"Yes, well there was quite the buzz about the incredibly handsome man she met a couple of months ago, he is very rich and a wonderful carpenter." Mary spoke as she made her way to Anna's kitchen and took a ginger cookie from the fresh batch that Anna made in the morning.

"Yes, I have heard many things. I think I may have caught a glimpse at him myself, but it was crowded there a few weeks ago, people at the park were asking him all kinds of questions and he seemed a little short tempered." Anna laughed as she made the tea.

"Well to top it all off he gave Freya a job with him and there has been rumours of lots of happy sounds coming from the office in town." Both women cackled as they began to drink from their cups.

"Oh yes, I guess she gets her flamboyant ways from her mother." Anna said, as she grinned and sipped.

"It would be so lovely if you could patch things up with her, from the looks of things they may even be very serious, he picks her up, cares for her, drops her off, renovated her cabin. There is so much going on in her life that I'm sure she would love to share with her mother." Mary sat back as she warmed her hands on the cup.

"Mary, I understand you only mean well, but I find that if I am close to her this way, then it gives me a chance to start fresh with her, even though I do it in disguise, it's still nice for me as a mother."

Mary tapped her cup with her fingers as she thought about what Anna was saying and agreed that it wasn't her call to make about what to do.

"Fair enough I guess." Mary sighed as she drank.

"So, what does he look like, is he handsome? Do you know what he does?" Anna asked as she ate a cookie.

"Well, his name is Roman Mason. He works in the safety business of the mining industry. He has two brothers, but I can't remember their names and he was also married but now widowed." Mary realized that her words made Anna freeze as she was biting into a cookie.

Anna jumped up from her chair and went to her bedroom where she scrambled through a drawer of papers and photographs, she pulled out a card with photos inside and went back to Mary.

"Mary, I need you to look closely at this picture and tell me if this is the man."

Anna handed the photo to Mary and as Mary looked at it, she saw a beautiful young woman and a handsome man. The young lady looked like Anna and she imagined the man a little older.

"That's him, are you telling me that this was Faye's husband?"

Anna began to cry and nodded her head. She started to smile and put her hands on her heart.

"Oh God yes that's him, they were married, Faye's adoptive parents sent me photos of her from their wedding day, Faye never knew that I was speaking to them via the mail, but this in unbelievable. He was such a wonderful man, he loved Faye so much and he made her so happy. My beautiful darling girl was so tiny and sick, not a day goes by that I think about her, I was only fifteen when I gave birth, her father was never in the picture, but this is one-of-a-kind news you have just told me Mary."

Mary moved her chair next to Anna and hugged her.

"Anna, this is something you really need to think about, you need to tell her, not only for Freya or Roman or

Faye, but for yourself. You have loved ones right in front of you and you all deserve to be together, don't leave it all too late."

Anna tapped Mary on the hand as she nodded. Mary was right but Anna had so much she needed to make peace with, and this was getting more harder as the moments were passing.

"Oh, my darling girls, Mary, this is a mess that I feel like I am fully responsible for, what can I do to make it right? I wish there was an answer."

Mary plucked a tissue form the box on the table and passed it to Anna as she wiped her tears away.

"Anna, you can't blame yourself for Faye your tiny baby was so sick and you were so young, you were a child yourself. Don't blame yourself for anything, she had a wonderful life, full of care and love, you know for yourself she was taken care of. Faye had the best medical care money could buy, love form a wonderful man, happiness and anything her heart desired. Your daughter will always be loved, fully and completely. Don't ever blame yourself for the decisions you made when you were thrown into a situation beyond your comprehension at such a young age."

Anna nodded as she wiped away her tears and poured herself another cup of tea.

"Mary, you speak the truth. I guess there are lessons that are still being learned no matter how much time passes, but this with Freya and Roman, oh my, what a wonderful occurrence this is."

Anna pressed her hands to her heart as she sat down and smiled through the tears as she sipped at her drink.

"I suppose you will have to buy some new wigs if you plan on dragging this out longer." Both Anna and Mary looked over at the stand behind the door and laughed in amusement when Anna nodded her head.

"Yes, well they are getting a little old, but I am a master of disguise."

Mary only nodded as she reached for the blonde wig that had red highlights and playfully plopped it on her head.

"Oh, the days when I was so much younger." Mary laughed, as she stroked the wig and looked in the mirror behind the door.

"You can have it if you want?" Anna laughed, as she could see the joy in Marys eyes.

"Hmm, I don't think my husband would like the red, he always loved my blonde which is now a little more silver." Mary placed the wig back on the shelf.

"So, what will you do if this man is the forever after for Freya?" Mary asked Anna as she stood to rinse out her cup and made her way to the door.

"I guess I will need to have a good stern talking to myself but please, Mary, don't say anything to her. I promise you that it will all be put to rest and behind us, but I just need time. And as time would have it, there are new developments that the universe has created, I believe that it will fall into place, I'm just waiting for the right moment."

Mary nodded as they embraced briefly.

"It's alright Anna, my lips are sealed but I don't know how much longer I can keep them that way."

Anna nodded because she agreed that she was keeping Mary in her complicated loop, and it wasn't fair.

"I know, Mary, just a little longer, I promise."

"Okay, I will see you on Friday, Roger is making a roast it will be ready at dinner time."

Anna smiled as she put her cup away.

"I will be there with wig's on." Both laughing, Mary exited Anna's cabin and made her way back to her house.

After her talk with Mary, Anna started to feel a little weight lifted off her shoulders. She thought about how things had progressed for Freya and she was happy that Roman had come into her life. Anna was afraid that perhaps if she did intervene that things would change for them both and that Roman would break Freya's heart out of grief for Faye. Anna paced up and down her kitchen as she was holding the new book close to her chest thinking about how she should go about letting Freya know that she was only a few steps away from her.

This was a situation she never thought was so wonderful and complicated at the same time. Perhaps there was another way or method that they could all be in each other's lives once more. Even when she looked at her photo of Faye, she held it in her hands and she had tears well up in her eyes, but then it started to grow into joy as she realised that as such a young teenager giving life, Faye was a gift and she was given the best possible care Anna could never have offered her.

Anna sat back down and looked into the small envelope of cards and photos of Roman and Faye along with others she had of Freya. Anna knew that it was always something that would need changing and she decided that perhaps there would be a time when Freya would reach out to her. Mary was right in the sense that raising daughters was a very difficult task at times, but she also knew what it was like to be a teenage daughter and have moods and temper that flared at her own mother once upon a time.

The day Anna found out that Freya had run away from the boarding school Anna decided it was time to leave her husband that had turned Anna into something she never wanted to be. Anna thought about how young and naive she was when she met Antonio and thought that he was the only person she would ever need in her life. Even though he treated her like a Queen and gave her everything her heart desired, it all changed when they moved to Italy after leaving Freya at the boarding school. Anna always made sure to send money and anything that they needed to care for Freya but in the end, it was Antonio that more or less, made her separate from her daughter. If Freya would have been his, he would have treated her differently but in the end, he persuaded Anna that she would have a better education and chance at life if she stayed back. Antonio was very good at manipulating Anna's mind and promised her the world. He also told her that after a short time they would return back to collect Freya, but he grew stubborn and they would argue about returning.

Anna wouldn't give in and when Freya had disappeared, Anna left Antonio and then a messy legal battle, as well as residency drama occupied most of her time. The never-ending lawyers and trouble she had to go through to be free of him was a nightmare and she decided that she would start to disguise herself as Antonio still had family on the outside of this town.

It wasn't that she was afraid of him he never had a violence driven demeanour it's just that Anna didn't want questions and people meddling in her life. After a while Anna found Freya's foster parents. They put out a report without Freya's knowledge but also because she was already sixteen, she was able to have her own rights of where she wanted to live. Anna always made sure to send them money every week and stay in contact with them in the hopes that Freya would want to see her again, but she started to give up hope as all she got in return was hate mail from her daughter. Over time

Freya stopped communicating with her and Anna ran her fingers over the box of letters she had. She remembered what it was like to open each one with the anticipation that her daughter would tell her that she needed her in her life.

As evening started to creep over the sky and the day was coming to an end Anna sat on her back porch. It was enclosed with a tiny garden, and she didn't have the need to hide her face. She lit a candle and held paper and a pen in her hand. She hesitated to write over and over she would hold the pen to the paper and then move it away again. This was silly Anna thought, her daughter was right there in the same park, after all this time why bother writing a letter? Anna put down the pen and paper and decided that this was something that she needed to pluck up the courage to do herself. There was no need for a post man to be the in between person for this issue, it was time for her to take responsibility and be accountable for what had been done and try her best to make it right.

***

Early in the morning Freya went to the public laundry as her washer and dryer were much too small for the amount of clothes she had accumulated over the past week. She grinned at the outfits as she had fond memories of her intimate encounters with Roman and remembered how each dress and top had looked like a crumpled ball on the office floor. She hummed to herself when she sneezed and started to feel the tickle of a small cold coming on. She wiped her nose with a tissue and then sat down as she waited for her laundry to finish.

"Morning, Freya, you're up early." Lynne greeted Freya. She wore a black curly wig and big sunglasses that covered her face.

"Morning, Lynne, how are you?" Freya greeted her back.

"Oh, just cleaning up before the day gets too warm to do anything else.

Freya smiled as she looked at the woman and studied her small frame and fair complexion.

"I like your hair is it a new look?" Freya asked, as she was aware for the ever-changing styles she used.

"Yes, well this old thing could use a freshen up. It's starting to get a bit difficult to maintain."

Freya only smiled as she checked on her laundry and then sneezed.

"Oh, my are you feeling alright?" Lynne asked Freya.

"Oh, yes, but I think a sniffle is on the way, I don't usually get sick, but I have been around a fair few people so it's inevitable I guess." Freya blew her nose, and it made a small trumpet like noise.

"Oh, my you sound like you could use some home remedies to clear that up."

Freya only nodded before she agreed.

"Yes, I could use some ginger cookies, but my mother was the only one who had a special recipe that made me feel better." Freya sat back down and checked her watch as there was still time before Roman would come to collect her for an outing they had planned for the day.

"Well, I would be delighted to bake you some and bring them over this evening if you like."

"Oh, yes they are the ones that Mary keeps raving about, she brought me over some last week, they tasted wonderful and took me right back to my childhood, well, my happy time of being a child anyway."

"I can drop them off at seven if you like and I will be making another batch for Mary and Roger while I'm at it."

"That would be lovely, thank you." Freya removed her clothes from the washer and put them in a basket to hang up at her cabin.

"I will see you then, have a beautiful day Freya."

Freya laughed as she tried to talk back but only started to sneeze uncontrollably, so she waved as she made her way out of the laundry.

As Anna made her way back to her cabin, she closed her front door behind her and held her hands on her heart. She beamed a smile as she remembered the times she had with her daughter when she was a little girl and they lived in a small bungalow she rented. The time of her young motherhood came back to her and the way she used to eat the ginger cookies with delight.

Anna started to get her things ready, along with a large amount of ingredients in her kitchen. She hummed to herself and smiled as she turned on the oven, she knew that the smell would be travelling through the entire park and there would be people asking for her famous magical cookies.

Chapter 13

When Roman arrived at Freya's cabin, he usually would meet her by the stairs but then he noticed that she didn't come out, so he went to her door and knocked. As Freya answered Roman could see that she wasn't her cheery self, as her eyes were watery, and her nose was red.

"I would say good morning, but it seems you are not having a good morning." Roman grinned as he opened her door and went to hold her in his arms.

"Oh, I have a stupid cold, it's getting worse every minute, I know we had plans today, but I don't think I'm up for it, you will have to forgive me Roman, I'm so sorry."

Roman wasn't anywhere near angry or upset. He grinned as he saw her ruffled hair and slumbering look. Roman took off his tie and untucked his shirt, kicking off his shoes at the same time. Freya was about to speak and sneezed instead, so Roman picked her up and carried her to her unmade bed where he lowered her and climbed in next to her.

"Please, Roman, I don't want you to get sick, go save yourself." Freya laughed as she sneezed again and reached for the box of tissues on her bedside table.

"I don't get sick and I'm not leaving." Roman said, as he kissed her on the mouth.

"Your brave." Freya replied, as she snuggled into his side.

"So, Freya, what will we do today? daytime television or online shopping?" Roman asked, as he stroked the hair out of her face.

"Just leave me here Roman, go about your things, you have a company to run."

Roman only chuckled as he pulled his phone out and ordered some breakfast for the two of them to be delivered. Freya looked like she could have used a fresh juice and everything that went with it.

"My company, my rules." Roman said, as he flipped through the menu.

Freya only stayed quiet as she could feel him beside her, and she was glad just to be with him in silence.

"Have I told you how wonderful you are Roman?" Freya said, as she looked up at him.

"Yes, now close your eyes and rest we will be eating breakfast in bed soon."

"Yes, Roman you are wonderful." Freya said, as she wiped her nose and listened to him make the order on his phone then he switched on the tv with the remote.

After lots of snuggles and lazy time, Freya began to feel more like herself. She went to the bathroom and washed her face as she looked in the mirror, she was happy that her nose was not as red as it was earlier in the day and her appearance seemed to be better. Gladly she was happy that it must have been a quick bug that had been making its way out of her system. As she made her way back to the kitchen, she saw that Roman was coming back from his jog.

He had been running around the park and the closest streets keeping up with his own therapy and relaxation. Freya understood that he needed his time for himself, and she was most happiest that he was returning home to her cabin. Just as Roman was climbing the stairs a woman greeted him and he helped her up by extending his hand out to her, so she didn't fall, as her hands were full with the plate of cookies.

"Oh, thank you kind man, it's a bit of a struggle, climbing stairs with limited movement, especially when you are in your sixties."

"You're welcome, if I didn't know any better, those are for Freya, she has been talking about cookies all day." Roman grinned, as he opened the door for the woman and they both stepped inside.

"Yes, I don't mean to brag, but they are famous in this park."

"Lynne, you made it." Freya greeted her, as she walked towards her and the cookies were passed to Freya.

"Yes, I have been busy, but I have baked enough for just about everyone and the bake sale for the small children at the school that they are having. Some of the mothers asked me as they are not keen or confident cooks." Lynne turned towards Roman and looked at him up and down, as she moved around Freya's kitchen.

Freya picked up one of the cookies and made sounds of happiness as she ate. Lynne studied Freya and she could see that Freya was smiling with her eyes closed and then opened them as she looked at the cookie in her hand.

"Wow, Lynne, thank you so much, I feel like I am getting better already."

Lynne only smiled as she wanted to reach her hand out to touch Freya's brow like she did when she was a child to check her temperature, but she only placed her hands in the pocket of her apron instead.

"Lovely, I'm glad to see you are getting better, was nice seeing you, Roman a pleasure." Lynne turned as she wanted to leave but Roman never introduced himself to her by name.

"Have we met?" Roman asked, as Lynne stopped at the door she turned slowly and realised the mistake she had made but then she turned and thought of a quick way out of it.

"Oh, no, Mary told me your name, there was a buzz around the park a while ago and people told me that you were working on Freya's cabin, that's how I found out your name."

Lynne fiddled with her earing's as she hoped that it would be a good enough explanation. Roman only looked at the woman in front of him more closely and he could see that there was a nervous way about her. He wasn't able to make much of her face as her sunglasses covered most of it, but he looked at her hair and her complexion and understood the hair was a wig.

"Yes, very well then, I imagine news travels quickly in this place." Roman offered a small smile, as he didn't want to make anyone feel uncomfortable.

"It does." Freya agreed, as she picked up another cookie.

"Enjoy!" Lynne smiled, as she made her way out of Freya's cabin.

Roman stayed with Freya the whole night. He made sure that she was comfortable and safe. As they were sleeping, Roman had a dream about the woman who brought Freya cookies. He saw her again, only this time he focused more on her. He looked to her neck and saw the small gold and sapphire necklace she was wearing. Roman concentrated on it, and then he realized that it was a stone he had unearthed a very long time ago and it was the necklace he had designed in his younger years.

Roman opened his eyes and stood quietly, he went into Freya's bathroom and looked in the mirror as he washed his face. He knew right then that the necklace was the one that was part of Faye's collection. In her last will and testament, she gifted some of her jewellery to her foster mother and birth mother. Roman drank water from the faucet and wiped his beard with a towel as he went to turn to go back to bed with Freya. As he climbed in, he was in a daze that this woman was in the park, and it was very possible she was the mother of his wife.

Roman remembered that he had papers from Faye at his office and he would look at them again in the morning. He remembered that there was information that Faye had a sister by her biological birth mother that she had never met. Could it have been that this woman was both the mother of Faye and Freya? Roman closed his eyes and looked over his memory of the woman he met earlier in the day, her skin complexion and mannerisms were familiar to both Faye and

Freya. He thought about the large sunglasses she wore that covered her face and he understood that if she had light coloured eyes, they would be sensitive to light. But then again, he thought that perhaps they were to hide the familiar features of both of her daughters. He remembered that her eyebrows were of a light strawberry blonde colour and her lips were red and full. Her high cheekbones and diamond shaped face were also similar to his wife and Freya and if he didn't know any better, he guessed her eyes would have been the same dark amber colour as Faye's were.

Roman was afraid that if this was the case that Freya would think it changed everything. But Roman only held her tighter as he lay behind her and took in her scent. He curled his fingers around her hand and feeling the warmth of her body against his made him feel like the luckiest man in the world. He was being pulled in more and he knew that there was no escape for his heart. Every moment he spent with her he was becoming more free and he never wanted that feeling to end. As he closed his eyes, he thought that if his assumptions were correct, then it truly was a miracle at work that he has been given this beautiful woman. Roman only hoped that it was true because then it would make sense as to why he felt like he had a special connection with her that he wasn't able to decipher any other way. If Freya was the sister of his lost love, then he would surely become complete once again. Having Freya in his life was like a presence of his wife's soul that he could feel and sense with every part of his being and he was terrified that he would lose it again. As Freya stirred and rolled to face him, Roman stroked her cheek as a small smile curved on her lips and she looked so peaceful. She snuggled closer and rested her head on his chest and Roman only kissed her forehead as he listened to the sounds of the night. Roman understood that all the years he spent on his own had been worth it. He never regretted waiting until he met Freya to become involved with a woman. Roman has always been a faithful man and it was something he was taught by looking at how his parents loved each other. He remembered how it was when he first met Faye and he knew he was smitten with her from the day he saw her beautiful dark amber eyes and her long blonde and red streaked hair. Faye's features were small and petit, and she had the flair of a beautiful woman in the making even from a young age. There would be no escaping his further and thorough investigation and he was going to make sure that he would understand everything there was to know about the beautiful women that had entered his life.

In the morning Freya was feeling better but she still wanted to rest for the day. Roman jogged to the office and he went about his usual duties. After he had completed the main tasks, he had to catch up on, he made a few phone calls to people that could help him with information that he was seeking. When Roman pulled out Faye's original certificates, he understood that her mother's name was Anna-Lynne and this made Roman think about the name the woman used at Freya's park, she called herself Lynne. Surely this wasn't a coincidence but Roman had to make sure. He looked over Faye's will again and sure enough the items of jewellery were signed and handed over to the people that she wished to have them. Along with the law papers there were signatures of her biological mother and it all made sense that this was a definite positive for Roman. He needed more information about Lynne, so he made sure to send in requests for her papers and after a couple of hours he received an email giving him the answer he required.

Anna-Lynne Mira Quinn, mother of Faye-Lynne Mira Quinn she had another certificate that showed she was married, and her daughter was Frey-Anna Lust Quinn.

Roman took in a deep breath when he read the papers and ran his hand over his beard as he was taking in the words on the page. Freya had named herself Freya Lust and dropped her mother's name 'Quinn'. Roman had a million emotions rolling through his heart and mind. He was thrilled, delighted, and terrified that he had learned that Freya and his late wife were distant sisters. Freya was ten years younger than himself, but this wasn't anything that mattered as she was a mature and a very grown, beautiful woman.

It made sense that they were both women born into different times, Anna had been a teenage mother, she was only fifteen and Roman understood that she made the best possible choice for Faye. Roman had no negative grudges against Anna as he knew that Faye was in the best possible care after her birth.

Roman stood up and paced, as he tried to think of a way to break the news to Freya, but he knew that it wasn't his place. This was something that had to be done by her mother. Roman thought that perhaps he should speak to Anna but then he shook his head as he didn't want to be responsible for frightening her away from Freya. As he kept pacing, he decided that it would be best that he knew this for himself as he was trying to process the way it may change things between, he and Freya. Roman was afraid that perhaps Freya would be changed towards him and that she wouldn't want to be with him anymore but then he decided to look at the positive and understand that in the end they all were 'unknowingly' family to each other. As Roman put his hand on his heart he thought about the way this was all affecting him and he was surer than ever that Freya was always supposed to be in his life. Roman sat again and leaned with his elbows on his desk as he blankly looked at the computer screen in front of his face. An unexpected feeling crept up in his chest when he thought about everything and the way it had unfolded. He felt like he had been lost for so long and finally after realising that there was more to the story of meeting and being with Freya, he was sure that he was on his way to letting love overcome him once again. There was more between them from the moment he first laid eyes on her and he knew then already that his life would never been the same if Freya couldn't be with him. Roman felt the pull towards Freya long before they made any physical connection. If anything, Roman was a very experienced man in love and all things loyal, this between them both was something right from the start and he had suppressed it for so long. The same feelings and sensations Freya made him feel were the same as Faye and there had never been any success from anyone else.

Roman made sure to put the papers away where they couldn't be found, he put them in his safe and locked it. This information needed to be kept from sight until the time was right and Roman only hoped that Freya's mother would be the one to tell her daughter about her beautiful and fragile sister. It would be painful for Anna, this Roman understood fully but it was Anna's right and her right alone.

***

When Freya was typing away at her computer, she was herself once again. She had plenty of rest and loving company to help in making her well. As she was about to start typing away at the story she was working on, she thought about the way that Roman had cared for her and even though the story was for her sight only, she wasn't afraid to type in the way she felt. She made sure that she mentioned that she loved him and hoped that one day he would tell her that he felt the same. The feelings she had for Roman were one of a kind and she knew that they could never be matched. Never had she felt this way about a man before and she wasn't afraid to tell her computer. As she typed, she felt like it was her only secret friend that carried the weight of her world and she would never be judged by anything that she would type. Happiness, joy, sadness, grief, and everything in-between could be put on a page and she never felt like she would suffer the wrath of judgement. She felt relief as she finally put the words down and she knew that it was truth. Even though there hadn't been a declaration of love between them, she thought that not any man and woman would be spending time together like they had and it was only because they were 'friends.'

Freya smiled as she finished her sentence and then made sure to save it and print it out. She put it in a pile that she kept in a leather file and she made sure that it stayed in her room away from anyone's reach. As she went to return to her small desk there was a knock at her door and she could see that it was Lynne. Freya called out to her to come in and then Freya was a little taken back when she saw the distraught look on Lynne's face.

Chapter 14

"Lynne, are you alright?" Freya asked as she took Lynne's hand and helped her sit down in her small living are.

Lynne nodded as she was a little shocked. She felt incredibly brave in the morning and wanted to come clean about everything with her daughter, but she suddenly got cold feet and she was terrified.

"Yes, I'm alright, Freya." Lynne smiled nervously, as she held a small bundle of envelopes in her pocket, she wasn't sure if she should pull them out, so she took out her hands and folded them in her lap.

"Well, you don't look alright, you look a little more pale than usual, I hope I didn't make you sick." Freya smiled, as she went to turn on her kettle and make them a cup of tea.

"That's alright, Freya, I won't be staying long. I just wanted to come and see how you were feeling today." Lynne steadied herself again and smiled, as she began to feel at ease and her nerves were settling down.

"I'm back to my silly self again." Freya smiled, as she sat down next to Lynne with two cups of tea even though Lynne said that she wouldn't be staying long. Freya couldn't help to think Roman was rubbing off on her and she was starting to just go with favours even if they weren't wanted.

Lynne smiled and was glad that Freya was feeling better she took her cup in her hands and held tightly as she went to sip.

"Mm, this is lovely, thank you Freya." Lynne put the tea back down on the table and then she grew restless as she didn't want to put up the act any longer.

"Freya, there is something I need to tell you." Freya's smile wavered as she always knew that it would be shock that followed when there was news to be told.

"Tell me then, Lynne what's wrong?" Freya put her cup down and sat up straight.

Lynne thought there was enough beating around the bush so, she took off her sunglasses and put them on the table then she pulled off her wig and looked at Freya.

Freya was struck in awe momentarily as she saw her mother and she wasn't sure how to take it.

"Mother?" Freya announced, as she stood up scoffing and began to pace around the room.

"Freya, I need you to know a few things please let me speak-"

Freya put up her hand to stop her as she looked at her mother with rage and a million other emotions running through her blood. The biggest emotion of all was grief. Freya wanted to yell, scream and cry, but she didn't know how to express herself she just kept exchanging glances as she had her arms crossed and could feel the tears well up in her eyes.

"This isn't easy, and I know there are many things that we need to talk about." Anna tried to reason with her daughter, but she knew that Freya was handling this differently then she expected.

Anna was waiting for the assault of words and feelings, but Freya didn't say anything she only stopped in her kitchen and then leaned against her counter.

"Please go back to your cabin, I need a moment." Freya turned her back and started to wipe away her tears that fell without control.

"You know where I am if you need me." Anna said, as she started to feel guilty and only prayed that she would speak to her eventually.

As she tried to process the reaction from her daughter, she didn't want to upset her further, so she obeyed her wishes and before she walked out, she placed one of the envelopes on the small coffee table.

"I'm not going to lose you again my dear girl, no matter how much time has passed I have loved you and do love you always."

Freya's tears fell more and then as she heard her mother leave, she went to her room and started packing some of her things. She stopped momentarily and thought about Roman but knowing him he would want them to sort out their differences and help them in the process. Freya shook her head as she didn't want Roman to take part in what was happening, so she wrote a note for him and left it on the counter. She knew that he would be returning so she would leave Mary a message to say that she needed to be alone for a few days as she had some upsetting news she needed to deal with. Freya knew that Roman would only mean well, but this was something that Freya needed to digest on her own. This whole time her mother was right around her and she only made the effort to reach out to her now. Why did she wait so long? What was Freya supposed to take from all this? Freya called a taxi and grabbed her laptop and USB sticks with her private story. She didn't want anyone to find her private notes if she wasn't around and it was a very private matter of saying that she was in love with Roman. As the car pulled in, Freya walked out of her room and bumped her bag on the door on the way out, she didn't know that her USB stick fell out and onto the carpeted floor in her room.

Once she was seated, she told the driver to take her to a hotel that was a about half an hour away and she made sure that the phone Roman had bought her was turned off so he couldn't track her. Once she arrived at her destination, she unpacked her things and ordered herself a big bottle of wine, she knew that getting drunk wouldn't be a good idea, but she was beyond caring as this had turned out to be the day she had dreaded. There were times when she thought how it would pan out, but after all this time, Freya wasn't ready. She thought she would be able to comprehend seeing her mother in the flesh but so much time had passed between them that she wasn't able to process everything fast enough. She thought about what she would say to her when she would see her again there were so many questions that she had going through her head that she felt like her head was spinning and turning into mud. She threw the glass into the sink as she nearly finished the bottle and ordered herself some room service. Even though her stomach was in knots she got out a paper and a pen and started to write down everything she needed answers to and then she wrote down things she wanted to say, but then she stopped and remembered that she had forgotten the envelope on the small coffee table in her living area. It was probably best that she didn't look what was inside as it would no doubt confuse her discombobulated mind more. Freya started to feel guilty about leaving Roman without a word, but she knew that he would be finding out the news from Mary. Freya wasn't brave enough to tell him, she felt terrible for walking out and leaving everyone behind, but she hoped that Roman would understand that if there was anything that Freya needed time with it would be this. Freya didn't want anything to come in-between her and Roman, she was afraid it would cause fights about what she wanted and what he thought would be best, she didn't want that to happen so at the risk of hurting him she thought that silence would be best. Roman understood silence and hopefully he understood Freya's silence also.

How could everything turn into such a disaster? Freya was trying to reason with herself and couldn't find any answers. But then as she laid down to rest, she knew that there was a disaster in her head and not in the physical world. She expected Roman to come knocking on her door any moment, but she knew that wouldn't happen, by leaving the way she did she knew she would be hurting Roman, and he didn't deserve it. As she began to realise that she was possibly making a mistake she decided that she didn't want judgment or opinions, so she decided to stay where she was and let it all settle in her mind. Freya felt her eyes becoming heavy as she was crying so hard that her head was burning, but she let the blanket fall over her ears so that she could block out the world. Freya felt like she was her young teenage self again running away and hiding from everyone. She didn't want anyone to help her and being familiar with being alone she wanted to see if she could work this out for herself.

***

When Roman returned to the cabin park he was greeted by a very worried Mary at the office door. She seemed very upset and told Roman that Freya had left, she also told him that Lynne had spoken to Freya, but Mary wasn't brave enough to tell Roman what their conversation was about. Roman steadied Mary and placed his hands on her shoulders. Roman could see the distress and tears in her eyes and he already knew that there was a possibility that Anna had tried to come clean to Freya.

"Please don't worry, Mary, I'm sure that Freya will return, there are things that I need to discuss with her also and I could only imagine that there is very important reason why she has gone to stay somewhere else for the evening." Mary wiped away a tear that rolled down her cheek and Roman stayed calm as he was trying to fight his fear that Freya may have run away from him also.

Roman looked at Mary calmly and asked her where Anna's cabin was, Mary told him the cabin number and then Roman made his way over. As he arrived, he climbed the three stairs to the porch of Anna's place, he knocked on her door and waited, only there was no answer, so he went to Freya's cabin and the door was open. When he went inside, he saw a very upset Anna sitting on the sofa holding the small envelope that she had left for her daughter and this time she wasn't wearing a wig or sunglasses, she was sobbing quietly and Roman entered slowly and sat down next to her.

"Anna?" Roman addressed her, as he placed his arm around her shoulder and Anna only cried more and he pulled her into his arms. He waited for her tears to stop for a moment so she could speak.

"It's all my fault, I've lost her again." Anna wiped the tears from her eyes as she looked directly at Roman, and he could see Faye and Freya in her eyes.

Just as he imagined Anna had dark amber eyes with flecks of gold in them and yellow lemon amber tones. Anna was just as beautiful as her daughters and Roman was so relieved that he finally was able to speak to the woman who gave the two beautiful girls life.

"Anna, what happened?" Roman pulled out a handkerchief from his pocket and handed it to her.

Anna wiped away her tears and frowned as she had never told Roman what her name was.

"How do you know that name?" Anna asked, as she wiped her tears away and straightened herself.

"I have my ways," Roman answered, as he could see that she was trying to find the words.

"I came here to speak to Freya, and I told her that it's me, her mother, but she just stood silent she didn't yell or scream or show any anger. She was silent and then asked that I leave her alone, so I went home again. I heard from Mary that she got into a car with some bags packed but I feel like she has run away again, it's all my fault I should have stayed away. I just wanted to make it right, I wanted to be in her life again. Please, Roman forgive me for everything, I'm so sorry." Anna started crying again and Roman only held her in his arms as she needed comforting and he was more than willing to help his true mother-in-law.

"What do you mean when you say that Freya has run away again? what's going on Anna?"

Anna knew from that moment on that Freya had not told Roman everything about herself, so Anna was torn about whether she should tell the story or leave it for Freya, but she looked at Roman and how he was peering into her eyes. His beautiful emerald eyes were full of love for her daughter and this she could see as a mother. Roman didn't have to say anything but she already knew that Roman was deeply in love with Freya.

"It's a very long story, Roman, and I only wish that Freya could tell you, it's been such a long and hard journey for both of us, but there are many things I would like us to talk about all together the three of us. It feels like it would be better that way." Roman nodded but he needed to understand why Freya had gone to hide.

"Please, Anna, I need to understand where Freya might be emotionally, so that we can work this out together." Anna nodded, so she started to tell the story of how Freya had run away from the boarding school and along with that she shared the story of her young marriage, divorce and when she became pregnant with Faye.

There were many things that they discussed and there was no bad feelings between them only love filled the room. Roman made sure that Anna understood he was going to do everything in his power to make sure that Freya didn't disappear again and then he assured her that Freya would return. Roman understood that Freya was possibly in shock and very confused, but he also understood that Freya needed to be alone. Roman made sure to send Freya a text message letting her know that he understands if she needs time, and he will support her when she returns home. Roman wasn't expecting a reply but he needed to make sure that Freya understood that he wasn't going to be angry with her or blame her in any way. He was going to respect her privacy and her space because Roman understood what it was like to be in emotional turmoil and how difficult it was to overcome.

Anna was grateful that Roman understood her and she also made sure to tell Roman how grateful she was that he had taken such good care of Faye. Roman assured Anna that Faye had the best life, and she enjoyed all good things. When Anna returned home Roman stayed behind in Freya's cabin and he paced around trying to think of where she may have gone, he could have called all the hotels, but it would only be like trying to find a needle in a haystack as it had been hours

since Freya had gone, and she could have been anywhere.

Roman also knew that if Freya had wanted to hide, she

may have given a false name, so he didn't think it was a good

idea to try and make a hundred calls in the night.

When he went into her room he saw a small USB stick

on the carpet. He picked it up and went to Freya's computer

in her living area. He looked at the clock and it was becoming

very late in the evening. He didn't have anywhere to be and

he wasn't able to sleep with all the things that had unfolded,

so he plugged in the stick and opened the files. He saw the

title 'Roman and Freya,' he knew that he was going to go into

her privacy, he well was past keeping secrets, so he clicked

on it and as the words appeared on the screen, he made sure

to keep an ear perked for any sign of Freya's return.

He pushed the chair back, put his feet up on the desk

crossing them at the ankles and he grinned as he started to

read the story he had been waiting for. He was very pleased

to learn so many things about Freya that he had never known

before and as he kept reading, he realised that there was a

connection between them that he had felt the entire time. He

understood that they both felt the exact same about each other and Roman was happy to know that he wasn't alone in the devotion he had for Freya.

***

In the morning Freya opened her eyes and was feeling a little more settled about everything that happened. 'One more day' she thought, as she pushed the covers back and took a long hot bath. After collecting herself she went to her laptop bag and set herself up on the small table that overlooked the balcony and the beautiful ocean. She ordered herself some room service and turned on her phone. She smiled when she saw the text that Roman had sent her and she replied that she was alright and that he had no need to worry. As she unzipped her bag, she reached in to look for her USB stick that had her story on it and she wanted to type all the things that had occurred in the last day but when she couldn't find it, she panicked and thought that she had dropped it in the cab. She quickly jumped to her feet and prayed that the USB was still at her cabin, as it had everything about her and Roman on it, she needed to find it. Calling another ride, she ran down the hotel stairs and climbed into the cab that was waiting.

Chapter 15

When she arrived at the park, she asked the driver to drop her off around the corner she didn't want Mary to see her, so she climbed the small fence that went through a nature reserve alley way and snuck around behind her cabin to enter. As she peeped around the corner, she could see that it was clear, so she climbed the stairs and saw that her door was unlocked she opened it only a little, she was hesitant but then she was relieved when she saw that her computer and everything was still in her living area. She then went into her cabin and closed the door behind her. When she retraced her steps, she looked on the ground and moved her head up to see that the small light was blinking on her computer. She went to check and see what was on the screen, thankfully it was a blank document, but then she heard a familiar deep voice behind her.

"Frey-Anna Lust Quinn." Freya turned around and saw Roman looking at her.

He seemed like he had been waiting very patiently and she also noticed a small tinge of fury in his emerald eyes. He stepped forward and reached out his long hand as he was holding the USB stick in his long fingers.

"You don't want to forget your auto biographical fictional." He placed the USB stick down on the table with a small thud.

Freya was speechless as she was aware that Roman knew absolutely, everything about her. She felt humiliation as he would no doubt know that she loved him and there were intimate details about her that she never told anyone else. Freya stayed calm and moved forwards slowly reaching out she took the stick in her hand. She couldn't look at Roman as she just needed to get away from everything all over again. Just when she was going to turn away Roman caught her wrist.

"Where do you think you are going?" Roman asked her, as he pulled her closer to him.

"I'm going home." She said, with her emotions crashing her heart and soul.

"You are home!" Roman said, as he could see she was in complete and utter turmoil.

She could feel the tears stinging her eyes and let them fall as fighting it was futile.

"This place, it's not mine, I didn't pay for it." Freya whispered, trying to move away from him.

Roman held her face in his hands and he crushed his mouth onto hers and he wrapped his arm around her tightly. Freya didn't fight the kiss she was happy that he still wanted to share this with her, so she just let her defences down and went along with what was becoming of them.

"Freya, you are home." He whispered to her, as he held her never wanting to let go.

"Roman-" She moved away from him, and he only held her by the top of her arms, he was tempted to shake her, as his patience were running thin.

"There is something I need to tell you." Roman had to fight his anger and tears but even he wasn't strong enough, so he let them build in his eyes as it has been so long since he had cried.

Freya softened as she saw his beautiful green eyes were beginning to shine with grief and what she hoped was his love for her.

"You had a sister, her name was, Faye-Lynne Mira Quinn." Roman choked out the last words as Freya was looking at him in shock.

Freya was told that her half-sister had died in hospital after birth. Roman swallowed hard and Freya touched his face as he held her close.

"Faye, was my wife."

Freya felt like her knees were buckling and she was completely overcome. Roman lowered them both to the floor and still held her as she dropped her head on his shoulder and wept.

"My mother told me that her first child died, I never knew- she never told me about-"

Freya couldn't finish as she held on to Roman and her tears fell like waterfalls. Roman gripped her tighter and let his tears fall also. Once he was able to speak, he held her face in his hands again.

"Freya, please understand when I tell you, you are home."

She only nodded and he kissed her softly as he looked into her beautiful gold eyes.

"Freya, I never want to be apart from you ever." Roman told her, as he felt the last stone around his heart fall away and he was free.

"I love you, Freya." He kissed her deeply and didn't care that he cried, he had her in his arms and that's all he needed.

Freya tried to happily weep, as he said the words, but her emotions were a whirlwind and hard to contain.

"I love you, Freya." Roman repeated, as he kissed her face and her eyes and nose, his heart was finally and completely at peace.

Freya looked into his eyes, and he wiped her tears away.

"Roman, I love you, so very much, you make me so happy. I finally feel like I belong to a part of something, a family, I need you with me always."

Roman kissed her more and they both rolled around on the floor as they were finally declaring their love for each other. Joy, happiness, and peace was in the atmosphere between them and in their hearts.

Roman picked her up and carried her to her bedroom. He lowered her and then began to smother her in kisses. They were both calming down from the emotion that was overtaking them earlier. They were only concentrating on each other, and this was a feeling that was like no other. They were open and honest and there was nothing more to hide. Roman was so glad that Freya didn't resent him, and Freya was also feeling the same about Roman. There was fear that they would both be thinking that somehow, they would be causing each other pain and grief, but that was not the case as they deepened their kisses and connected on a level that was new to both of them.

"Please don't run away ever again." Roman said, as he held Freya in his arms and was making sure that he would make her understand that he meant it.

"I'm sorry, Roman, I was just confused, everything was just too much for me. I was shocked more than anything when I saw my mother sitting in front of me, it had been so long since I saw her last as she was, when I was a little girl."

Roman nodded as he could see that Freya was telling the truth.

"I missed you, I was worried about you, Freya, make sure it doesn't happen again please, whatever the case may be, you and I can work things out together, just know that you can come to me for anything you need. Tell me you understand?" Roman looked deep into her eyes and made sure that she was able to understand that he was very serious and that she needed to know it couldn't happen again.

"Yes, Roman, I understand." Freya kissed Roman, as she was glad that he forgave her silly mistake, and she was also pleased that Roman wanted to help her and be there for her always.

"We will put it behind us." Roman said, as he stood from the bed and picked her up and threw her over his shoulder.

"Oh, Roman, what are we? Ouch!" Roman smacked her backside and he grinned satisfied that she he fully deserved her punishment. He kept making his way down her hall and towards the front door.

"We are going to see your mother!" Roman said, as he went to open the front door.

"Oh no." Freya said, as she knew that there was no way out of it, just then there was another small smack on her backside.

"Hey?" Freya said, as she looked around Roman's legs and he stood her on her feet.

"That's for running away you naughty girl!" Anna reached forward and embraced her daughter, squeezing her tightly in her arms.

"Oh, mother." Freya just gave in and hugged her mother back and Roman stepped back to give them both some space.

Anna released her daughter and pointed out a very motherly finger at her when she spoke.

"Don't ever do that again young lady!"

Freya tried to speak but she just stood there and understood that she was cared for and she wouldn't be able to turn back to her old ways.

"Yes, I'm sorry." Freya said, as she looked at both Roman and her mother.

Would you like to come in Anna?" Roman asked, as he stepped back and let the ladies make their way inside.

"We were just about to come and see you, mother." Freya said, as she sat next to her mother on the small sofa.

Roman sat on the desk chair and made sure to block the doorway so that Freya couldn't run away again. Freya looked at him and smiled as she knew what he was doing.

"Don't worry I won't be running away again. But I do have to go back to the hotel and collect my things." Freya said, as she folded her hands in her lap.

"Now, with all of this out of the way, there are things I need to discuss with my daughter, Roman, would you mind returning to the collect Freya's things? I need to have a moment with her."

Roman only nodded and stood, as he was happy to oblige.

"Very well, you both take your time, I will be back shortly. Freya where were you staying?"

"At 'The Cosy Beach Inn' about half an hour away from here. Take the key and the card I'm sure you will be able to sort it out."

Freya smiled as Roman kissed her and put the two items in his pocket he leaned in and kissed Anna on the cheek and made his way out.

"So, I have the envelope, that you didn't take with you I would like it if you saw the pictures that were in there." Freya held it in her hands, but she didn't want to open it.

"No, I think this is all best if it stays closed. Roman has told me about Faye and I don't want us to be babbling and a mess when he gets back There is time for everything and I think we should pace ourselves. There is a big part for Roman in all this and its some parts about Faye that I would prefer to hear from him if you don't mind?" Anna smiled and nodded as she never thought about putting it that way before, but she wholeheartedly agreed with her daughter.

"You make perfect sense. I only want you to know that I'm here and willing to answer anything that might be on your mind."

Freya nodded and hugged her mother as she was so glad that they were able to find a truce.

"Mum, I have one thing I would like of you if you don't mind?"

"Anything." Anna told her waiting for her daughter's request.

"Can you bake some cookies for me here? I miss the smell and hearing you in the kitchen, it would make me so happy to have you here with me for a little while today."

"Of course." Anna smiled and stood holding onto to her daughter's arm as they made their way to collect some ingredients from Anna's cabin.

"Your, holding my arm a little tight mother."

Anna laughed as she looked at her Freya and winked as she made sure that she wasn't going to let her go unless Freya wanted to suffer the wrath of a grumpy Roman.

"Be glad that I am my darling girl, Roman wouldn't have it any other way."

"I'm starting to think there are things you know about him that I don't." Freya said, as she was hoping her mother should share.

"Well, let's just say that your sister was very sure that Roman was her man, and she was his lady once upon a time. I'm sure you will learn that along the way. He makes sure that his woman is very well taken care of."

Freya rolled her eyes as her mother didn't give much away but she just shrugged her shoulders as they entered her cabin and started to fill a basket for the cookies.

As the afternoon progressed Roman returned with Freya's belongings. He made sure to unpack her things and then keep himself busy with work that he was able to catch up on from Freya's home. He enjoyed hearing the two ladies in his life talk amongst themselves and share small stories about each other. Roman was happy to sit quietly as he went about making phone calls and organising things that he needed to catch do as he hadn't had much time for work due to his private affairs that had been taking place. When Roman hung up his phone and the workday was over, Anna and Freya cooked a comfort meal for them all and they all gathered around the small table and ate happily. Freya couldn't help herself as she noticed that Roman had not yet shared a story about himself yet, so she mentioned the funny story of the rat which was her sisters first pet.

"Of course I will tell your mother, the story it is quite funny when I think about it, although at the time it wasn't quite so entertaining as a young boy." Roman said, as he finished his food and stood to start cleaning the dishes with Anna. Freya had some chores she needed to catch up on, so she worked around them and listened while laughing as Roman told the story again.

Throughout the evening many other stories were shared, tears were cried, but laughter prevailed in the end. All three of them found comfort in the way that they could share things together, and there was nothing more than joy between them all. Freya was so glad that her mother was here, and she was so close. She never wanted to be separated from her again. She understood that there were things her mother couldn't control when she was younger. She was too young, too naive, and too blinded by love to decide what was best for everybody. There's a lot of things that come with being in love, and Anna was also one of the people who experienced it at a very young age and Freya wouldn't keep this against her mother. She would never hold it against her that she left her at the boarding school. She understood that lots of things were out of her hands, and she was swayed with lots of promises and lies in the end. As the night was amongst them, they all spoke about the charity ball that was coming up and Roman invited Anna to come along. She was very nervous and thought that perhaps it wouldn't be her place to fit in, but Roman and Freya assured her that she needed to come along as this was a family event, and very important and in honour of Faye.

Anna accepted the invitation, and she was looking forward to getting ready with her daughter, even though Anna didn't have anything to wear, Freya simply tapped her mother on the hand.

"Don't worry mother, we will take care of that. We can get you a gown hair make up and anything else that you need, all you need to bring is yourself, I promise you, we will take care of you and make you look like a Queen."

Anna beamed as she too felt like she was getting spoilt. When Roman and Freya walked Anna back to her cabin, they all hugged and kissed each other with the enjoyment of the reunion. Roman and Freya made their way back home and then they too had much more 'physical' catching up they needed to do amongst themselves.

Chapter 16

As the evening of the charity ball came, they all made their way to the office where there would be a make-up artist and hair stylist for the ladies. Roman could hear the ladies fussing over each other and he was glad he had the easy part of dressing himself and getting ready alone. When the dressing room door opened Roman was standing in the waiting area and straightened his bow tie as he caught a breath when he saw the two most beautiful women in the world. He placed a hand on his heart and made his way over to them.

"My word and all things great, you both look absolutely breath-taking."

Roman kissed Freya's mother on both cheeks and then reached out for his love and held her in his arms.

"My God, Freya, you are a stunning beauty!" Roman kissed her and then held her hand as she twirled her around.

Roman was glad that Verika's design was kept a secret, and he noticed the yellow diamond around Freya's neck. He grinned to himself as he thought it was all going perfectly to what he secretly had planned for the evening.

"The driver is here." Anna announced, as she looked out the window and saw that it was a limo and Romans private chauffer.

"Ladies, shall we?" Roman asked, as they both took an arm and made their way out to the ride.

When they entered the hall heads turned and smiles beamed on every persons face so many people came to greet Roman and Freya. It felt almost like Roman was a celebrity amongst the people in the room. They all expressed their joy at seeing him and how much they had missed him being at the charity events. Freya was safe to assume that every person in the room knew of Romans wife and her passing. Hands were shaken, and kisses were exchanged as drinks were passed around and everyone welcomed him to the event. As they all were introduced to Freya and Anna they too were taken in with love and open arms by people from all walks of life, When the welcoming of the long anticipated Roman and Freya along with her mother had been done, they all sat to share a meal with many people who shared stories with one another, and laughter spread across the room.

The small auction had taken place and bids were made, charities were announced, and certificates and cheques were made out to those who were in great need of support. As Anna scanned the room, she saw Mary and her husband and was surprised that they walked through the doors of the great hall. Anna made her way over to them and showed them where they were sitting. Mary and Roger were also invited from a business they worked alongside for the council and working with the youth and homeless. As Mary and Roger were seated beside Anna, Freya and Roman, they felt like their tiny circle had grown and they were all glad to be in each other's company. As the evening progressed Roger asked Freya for a turn on the dance floor and she happily took his hand and shared a dance, Mary had a turn on the dance floor with Roman and she too was interrogated kindly by Roman as to why she never said anything to Freya, but Mary told him she was sworn to secrecy by Anna and Roman only understood her faithfulness to her friend. Once they had a break and the main course was served, then it was time for another dance, only this time Roman asked Anna if she would like to have a turn. Anna couldn't help but blush as he led her tall and proud to the centre of the floor and they began to dance slowly. Freya watched her mother with a tear in her eye as she thought her mother looked like the most beautiful woman in the room dancing with a man such as Roman.

"So, Roman, what are your intentions with my beautiful daughter." They both chuckled as they understood each other in their own secret language.

"As a matter of fact, there is something I need to discuss with you, Anna and I'm afraid it can't wait."

Roman turned her and then she went back to him waiting for him to continue.

"I'm all ears Roman."

"I would like to ask for your blessing, and that I may have your daughter's hand in marriage?"

Anna only welled up with tears and placed her head on his shoulder as she was already expecting Roman to ask her the question only, she wasn't expecting it on this night.

"Roman there is something I need you to know. You are the most wonderful man I could ever ask for to be with my daughter and I'm always going to be grateful and blessed that you are and have been in both of my daughter's lives, I couldn't ask for a better pairing then the two of you and also when you were with Faye. She will always be a part of you, and you will always be a part of her. So, yes, my blessing is given and make sure you keep her in check." Anna winked at Roman, as she could have guessed that her daughter may be a handful from time to time.

"Thank you, Anna." Roman raised her hand and kissed the top of her fingers as the music came to an end and they made their way back to their table.

The couple's dance was announced and Roman and Freya made their way to the dance floor. When Roman looked at her, he felt like he was holding a Queen in his arms and as the music began to play, they slowly waltzed along to the beautiful sounds. All the couples were captivated by the chemistry they could feel and see in Roman and Freya when they danced. Freya noticed that a couple bowed out and made their way to the side then as they kept dancing another and then another did the same. When she danced some more concentrating on Roman, and the way he was leading her, she felt like they were back at the studio, and she closed her eyes as she was whirled around the floor. She wasn't afraid of falling, she wasn't afraid of losing her balance or grip. She had complete faith in the strong man that she could feel in front of her. As the music began to get faster, she opened her eyes and saw that for the first time Roman was smiling at her and she was amazed at how beautiful he looked. His eyes sparkled and his features on his face looked even more handsome than ever. Once he finished the spin with Freya, he lifted her and then dipped her as the music ended and a loud sound of cheering and clapping was all they could hear as they looked into each other's eyes.

"I love you, Freya." Roman said, as he kissed her on the lips and then a sound of whistling came from the crowd as Roman stood her back onto her feet.

When they looked around them, they noticed that they were the only ones on the dance floor and all the other couples were standing around the outside of the floor clapping their hands and smiling at them. Some had tears in their eyes as they were all so glad to see Roman happy and smiling, after ten long years of being alone. Freya looked at Roman and she threw her arms around his neck as she was trying to hide from all the eyes that were staring at them.

"Roman, I love you, but why does this always happen when we dance?"

Roman only looked at her when she released him and told her the same words he had said once before.

"It seems they have been captivated by your beauty my love."

"After they were handed their reward, they made the cheque out to the Faye Mason foundation, and it was welcomed by every person in the room. They knew that it would be going to research so that perhaps someday there could be a cure for rare the illness that claimed Faye's young life.

Anna hugged and kissed them both as they returned to the table.

"I think you have some fans." Anna said, as she pinched Roman's cheek.

Roman only nodded as he knew that Anna wouldn't be swayed otherwise, and they all sat as desert was handed around the table along with coffee and warm refreshments.

Once the totals of all the charities were announced they all started to make their way home. Only Roman wasn't going to return home with Freya he had booked a hotel room in the city, and it was a very flashy and pricey place. Anna was also given a room for the evening where she could spoil herself and do as she pleased, as well as take a private chauffeur home after.

"Roman, I know that you had a lovely evening planned for us here, but I would really love to go back to the lake on your farm and I thought it would be nice to spend time together."

"Of course, Freya."

Roman reached into his pocket and handed Roger the key and card for his room.

"Spoil Mary." Roman said, as he shook Roger's hand and gave him the small items.

"Wow, are you sure?"

"Absolutely!" Roman said, as he took Freya under his arm and kissed her head.

"We have somewhere else we would like to be."

"Well thank you, Sir." Roger said, as he looked at his wife and dangled the card from the key chain.

"Shall we my dear?"

"Oh, yes!" Mary said, as she climbed in the car next to Anna.

Freya winked at her mother and Anna blew her a kiss she then winked at Roman and then they watched them drive away.

"Thank you, Roman, that was sweet of you to spoil Mary and Roger for the evening, not to mention my mother. You are a wonderful man, I'm the luckiest person to have you in my life."

"Oh no, Freya, I am the luckiest man alive."

Roman kissed her deeply and then they climbed into their car and Roman told the driver to take them home.

When they arrived, they walked the small distance to the lake from Roman's house. The night was clear and beautiful, Freya noticed that tiny wooden cabin had been placed next to the water.

"Oh my, this is beautiful."

"I had it built last week, I remembered you said it would be a beautiful place to sit and write."

Freya sat on the sunbed under the small porch and watched Roman as he made the fire come to life. Roman opened the door of the cabin and Freya could hear him open and close a refrigerator. Roman came out holding two champagne glasses and a chilled bottle of champagne.

Roman popped the cork and filled the two glasses handing one to Freya and sat next to her.

"Here is to us, to new beginnings, and to living and loving each other as long as we are able."

"Amen!" Freya replied, as they clinked their glasses together and sipped at the cold beverage.

"I remember the first time you and I made love here." Freya said, as she started to remove her shoes and make herself more comfortable.

"I've never experienced anybody making love to me the way you did."

Roman looked at her as he could see her eyes glittering as she said the words.

"I couldn't control myself." Roman said, as he smiled and finished his drink.

"And I have a very important question for you."

Roman stood up and got down on one knee he reached into his jacket pocket and pulled out a small black leather box. Freya was frozen but she sat up straight and tried hard to understand that this was all really happening.

Roman opened it and it was a thick gold band, at the top was a gold book, and a three-pronged claw, holding a huge yellow diamond. When Freya saw the stone, she knew it was the same yellow diamond he had unearthed with Verika, and it was the twin stone of the necklace she was still wearing.

Roman took Freya's hand and looked at her when he finally asked her his burning question.

"Freya, since the day I met you, I knew that you and I were always destined to be in each other's lives, I didn't believe that such miracles could happen, of two people coming together by fate and time, but as I knew more about you, I realised that you were always meant to come into my world."

Freya held her hand to her mouth as tears filled her eyes.

"I love you Freya, and I always will. I want nothing more than to be with you forever, I want us to build our lives together, experience joy, happiness and if we are so blessed created new life together. I want us to give our future the best possible head start and leave a legacy for all time to come. So, having said that, now I must ask you, Freya-Anna Lust Quinn, would you marry me? Please do the me the honour of becoming my wife?"

Freya was speechless as she looked at Roman and the ring, she had been finally experiencing the most cherished moment of her life, a man asking her to be his forever love.

Freya managed to whisper as she nodded her head and wiped away tears.

"My God, I love you Roman, and yes, I will marry you."

Roman kissed Freya as she was stunned and overjoyed. They both smiled and chuckled as Roman took the ring out of the box and placed it on her finger.

"Oh my, it's beautiful, Roman."

Freya smothered him in kisses as she was being held by him tightly. She looked at the ring and then closed her eyes as she silently thanked the universe for bringing them together. This man was her forever love and nothing would ever come between their happiness together.

When Roman released her, he held her face in his hands and wiped her happy tears away. Roman was so happy that they were finally settled in their rightful place. Roman laid her down cradling her in his arms as he was growing the heat and need for her. He could never quench his thirst for this beautiful woman. He began removing his clothes and nudged her dress down her shoulders as he kissed her neck.

"My God, you are so beautiful Freya." Roman mumbled as he was grasping at her dress and unlooping various ties.

Freya only started to fumble around with her zips and fasteners of her dress but Roman was quick to pull it loose and over her head.

"Oh my, you are so quick." Freya giggled, as she was in her stockings and corset Roman only grew hungrier as she was irresistible, and she looked like a delicious meal. His arousal started to bite, and he lowered himself on top of her devouring her flesh. As they rolled around on the sunbed, Roman removed her panties leaving her corset and stockings on, his appetite for this woman was going to be fulfilled as he pulled off his pants and threw them to the side. Roman spread her legs wide and lowered his hips down thrusting himself inside her and enjoyed her cheeks glow as she took him.

"My beautiful, Freya." He whispered over and over, as he pumped his hips and watched her move under him.

Roman gripped her corset and held her as he rode her more, Freya was gasping and moaned as she was desperately trying to hold on.

"That's it beautiful, I want to watch you come for me."

Roman licked his lips as he thrust more, and Freya gripped onto the sunbed and arched her back as Roman thought she looked beautiful wearing nothing more than a small piece of material and gold around her neck and on her finger.

"You are my Queen." Roman said, as he moved lower to kiss her deeply and Freya started to pant with need of release.

"Who is your King my love? Roman asked her, as he knew she was going to call out his name.

"Come baby, tell me."

"Yes, oh my, yes!" Freya said, as she was feeling Roman growing harder to fill her.

"Who is your King Freya?" Roman asked again, as he ran his teeth over her throat.

"You are, Roman." Freya gripped his hair hard and closed her eyes as she let the fall take her over.

"Come, my love." Roman ordered her, as he was letting himself take the fall with her.

Together they let the explosion of passion fill the night air, they gripped each other hard and like two hurricanes colliding they were completely taken over. Their worlds were overcome with bliss and the feeling of their hearts synchronizing and souls merging, it brought them together, to move, breath and live as one. Roman groaned out loud as he was overcome with the force of their spiritual union. Freya wrapped her legs around his waist as Roman released himself inside of her. The feeling of contentment and all things right and true was in the night all around them. Everything that they had feared and doubted was all taken away by the tidal wave of love that cleansed their unity with one another. As they looked into each other's eyes and caressed each other's skin they knew that they were both at peace and had finally found their forever home in each other.

***

Three Months Later

It was 'All Souls Day' the sun was shining, and sky was blue and clear. Roman, Freya and Anna went to the beautiful cemetery to visit Faye's grave. Anna pulled out the forget me nots from her bag and Roman noticed the flowers he had seen frequently when he visited his late wife's plot.

"Ah, so you are the one who always left them at the stone." Roman said, as they approached the clean and beautifully landscaped lane.

Anna smiled, as she did secretly visit her daughter every two weeks and left her flowers.

"Yes, I usually came here on a Sunday when it was early. I spent some time making sure that it was always clean, and the surrounding bushes were tended to. It was a way for me to connect with Faye again, I felt like I could talk to her and listened for her replies in my heart. Others may find that silly, but I found peace in spending time with her that way and after a while my healing process also made the pain lessen with time. I found that by tending to the gardens and making it look beautiful, it was a way for me to redeem myself, but I guess it was all about coming to terms with everything. It was hard at first but then I looked forward to coming here and it turned into a regular outing for me."

Roman nodded and smiled as they all gathered around the beautiful headstone. Roman bent down on one knee and opened the tiny jar containing the ashes of Faye's beloved pet, Fatty Rat. Freya giggled as Roman sprinkled the dust on the soft grass around Faye's headstone and Anna smiled as she was happy, they would be reunited once again.

"I have no doubt that you will keep Faye safe old friend, rest well and enjoy your time together." Roman said, as he tapped the empty jar and placed it back in his pocket.

Freya laid down her dried flowers and then opened the picnic blanket. Anna sat beside her placing out the food from the large basket they would share.

"Roman, I'm sure they are already planning a joke or two for you." Freya laughed softly, as she opened the jar of pickles and started to eat happily.

"I never pictured my daughter with a pet rat of all things, although after all I have discovered it wouldn't surprise me." Anna said, as she made a sandwich and handed it to Roman. Roman only grinned as he ate and poured them all a drink.

"Faye's adoptive parents were very open towards anything that made her happy, even if it seemed unethical or strange." Roman chuckled, as he took a big bite of his food and wrapped his arm around Freya when she leaned against him.

Anna couldn't help but laugh as she imagined that Roman had also needed to make strange things possible to please her first and very spoiled daughter.

"So do you still speak to Faye's legal parents Roman?" Anna asked, as she was curious about the wonderful couple who took in her baby.

Roman nodded his head as he cleaned his beard from the crumbs before he spoke.

"They moved to Canada a few years ago, as they had relatives they wanted to see after Faye passed. They decided that being around their own family helped them with the healing process, so they made peace with staying there. I don't blame them at all, it must have been hard for them to be so far away from loved ones for so long. We email each-other and occasionally speak on the phone, but they have nieces and nephews that keep them busy with children of their own. It's good for them and I wish them only the best in all things, keeping in mind Faye was the third of children they adopted, their son and daughter were older than Faye and they too had families of their own over time."

Anna smiled as she was glad they were happy, and Freya sighed as she looked up at the trees swaying softly in the breeze. She only wondered what her sister would have to say if she was still here, but as there was only positive energy in the atmosphere, she smiled at the thought of her spirit around them. Reaching into the jar, Freya ate another pickle and gently patted her small bump that was showing under her dress.

"It all seems so right and peaceful now." Freya said, as Roman kissed her on the forehead.

"Indeed." Roman agreed, as he bit into the pickle Freya was holding.

Anna laughed as Freya frowned at the empty jar and she pushed what was left of Roman's big bite into her mouth.

Once they had reunited with Faye and shared more stories, they began packing up their things and stood to make their way home but then two small butterflies floated down and landed on Faye's headstone. All three of them looked at each-other and smiled staying silent, as they knew they were in spiritual company. After a few moments, very slowly the two beautiful creatures flitted past them and made their way back to the flowers in the distance.

"Be free and may you both, rest in peace." Roman said, as he took Freya's hand and held out his other arm for Anna.

Coming full circle, the three of them walked slowly and happily. Hand in hand and arm in arm, they all agreed that it was all peaceful, complete, and very right.

Epilogue

As Freya was trying to hold still, her mother was adjusting the dress over her very heavy and pregnant belly, she was getting nervous as she could see that everyone was gathering in the park outside.

"Oh my, mother, I hope this baby stays inside until I say, I do."

She put a hand to her belly as she could feel a slight cramp.

"Well, we better get you married then, chop chop." Anna clapped her hands as they heard the music start to play and they made their way outside and down the stairs. Anna turned to Freya and kissed her just before she was about to walk her down the aisle.

"I'm so proud of you my girl, I love you."

Anna hugged Freya and tried not to squeeze her belly.

"I love you too." Freya replied, as she looked ahead and saw the one and only man, she truly desired.

Roman gave Freya a huge grin as he saw how beautiful she was, and then they walked slowly towards him. As they made their way Freya hissed as a cramp came upon her and the whole crowd gasped as they were suddenly worried, but then Freya smiled and straightened herself as Roman came to take her hand.

"Think we need the quick version." Finn said, as he laughed and looked at the celebrant.

"Very, very quick." Holt agreed quietly, as he was next to his brother in his chair.

"We are gathered here today- "

"Ow-ooo" Freya cried out, as she looked at Roman and then the celebrant knew he would have to be very fast.

The crowd giggled as the vows were read very quickly, and the couple was then asked the valuable questions.

"Roman do you take Freya, to be your wife?"

"I do!" Roman pushed the ring onto Freya's finger just as another cramp came on only this time Freya eyes widened as she froze, she could feel something warm running down her leg.

"Oh my God!" Freya said, as she moved her dress to see that her water had broken.

Roman looked down and his eyes widened when he saw that Freya was standing in a very large puddle.

"Very quick!" Roman said to the celebrant, as he picked up Freya and cradled her in his arms.

"Do you, Freya?"

"Oh, heaven's sake, yes, I do, quickly give me the ring." Freya was starting to get red cheeks as she was fighting another cramp.

Roman smiled as Finn handed her the ring, and she squeezed it on to Roman's finger.

"Blah blah, I now pronounce you husband and wife." The celebrant wiped sweat off his brow as he was glad it was done in time.

Before the celebrant could say 'Roman you may kiss your bride' Freya grabbed Roman's face and kissed him on the mouth.

"We need to go." She said, as she held her belly.

"Ouch." Freya said, as another big cramp came on and she kicked out her leg just as Roman turned and her wet end of the dress smacked Finn in his face and open mouth.

"Oh, ugh is that baby juice?" Finn said, as he wiped his wet face with his hand.

Holt looked at his brother as he lifted a glass of wine to his mouth, he couldn't help but gross him out more.

"Well, let's just say it wasn't always baby juice before."

"Oh, ugh, I'm going to be sick." Finn ran behind a bush and used a bottle of wine to try and gargle and wash out the taste.

Lady giggled as she looked at Holt and Holt only shrugged his shoulders.

"He will find out some day." Holt said, laughing as he drank his glass empty.

***

As Roman was waiting for Freya to come out of her shower he was laying on his bed and moved the soft pink blanket to see the beautiful tiny baby girl on his chest.

Roman smiled at the precious little angel and let her grip his pinkie with her delicately tiny hand. He kissed his beautiful daughter on the head and breathed in her scent. Freya peeked out of the bathroom door at her husband and baby. She giggled as she saw Roman's side of the bed full of small chocolate wrappers, as he had been eating the gift from Lady.

"Are those my chocolates?" Freya asked, as she pulled on her dressing gown and braided her hair. Roman was only grinning ear to ear as he shoved another treat in his mouth.

"I'm working on my dad bod."

Freya laughed and then made her way over to them both.

"Oh, look at you two all snuggled, is there room for me?"

Freya climbed in next to Roman and lay down on the large hospital bed in their private room.

"Come here, my love." Roman held out his arm and held Freya tightly as he kissed her on her forehead.

"I better get some sleep; she will be awake in a couple of hours."

"Yes, don't worry about anything Freya, I am very capable of making a bottle and changing her, you get some rest." Roman felt so complete with the two most beautiful women in his arms and he was switching the tv with the remote until he found an evening movie.

"Freya, there is something I need to ask you about your story that the wind blew away, how did it end?"

"I didn't write the ending, the last two pages that were missing were numbered but they were blank. I will however make sure the King makes her his Queen and they have a baby girl."

Roman smiled at Freya and gave her a chocolate that she gladly ate with joy.

"Sounds like a very fitting ending." Roman said, as he noticed the movie was about to begin.

"Have you ever seen anything so precious?" Freya asked as she played with her daughter's fingers.

"I have the two most precious creations in the world right here with me." Roman said, as she held them both close and stroked Freya's hair.

"I would like us to name her, Quinn Freya-Lee Mason." Freya said, as she stroked her baby daughters face.

Roman nodded as he heard Freya say the words and he felt like it was all so perfect.

"Absolutely, my love." He said, as he kissed Freya on the mouth and then his daughter on her tiny head.

"Both of you, can and will have, anything your heart's desire."

END

<u>TITLE COMING SOON</u>

FINN'S GRACE

BOOK 3 OF THE

EMERALD EYES TRILOGY

9 781763 530713